WELCOME TO

". . . Toogwik Tuk said with a respectful bow. "The presence of Clan Karuck and its worthy leader makes us greater."

Grguch let his gaze drift slowly across the three visitors then around the gathering to Hakuun. "You will learn the truth of your hopeful claim," he said, his eyes turning back to Toogwik Tuk, "when I have the bones of dwarves and elves and ugly humans to crush beneath my boot."

Dnark couldn't suppress a grin as he looked to Ung-thol, who seemed similarly pleased. Despite their squeamishness at being so badly outnumbered among the fierce and unpredictable tribe, things were going quite well.

A KINGDOM OF ORCS THAT WILL CHANGE

THE MAP OF FAERÛN FOREVER!

R.A. SALVATORE

R.A. SALVATORE

FORGOTTEN REALMS

THE ORC KING

I

TRANSITIONS

THE ORC KING
Transitions, Book I

©2008 Wizards of the Coast, Inc.

Cover art by Todd Lockwood
Map by Todd Gamble
Original Hardcover Edition First Printing: October 2007
First Paperback Printing: July 2008

9 8 7 6 5 4 3 2 1

ISBN: 978-0-7869-5046-1
620-21959740-001-EN

U.S., CANADA,	EUROPEAN HEADQUARTERS
ASIA, PACIFIC, & LATIN AMERICA	Hasbro UK Ltd
Wizards of the Coast, Inc.	Caswell Way
P.O. Box 707	Newport, Gwent NP9 0YH
Renton, WA 98057-0707	GREAT BRITAIN
+1-800-324-6496	Save this address for your records.

Visit our web site at www.wizards.com

PRELUDE

Drizzt Do'Urden crouched in a crevice between a pair of boulders on the side of a mountain, looking down at a curious gathering. A human, an elf, and a trio of dwarves—at least a trio—stood and sat around three flat-bedded wagons that were parked in a triangle around a small campfire. Sacks and kegs dotted the perimeter of the camp, along with a cluster of tents, reminding Drizzt that there was more to the company than the five in his view. He looked past the wagons to a small, grassy meadow, where several draft horses grazed. Just to the side of them, he saw again that which had brought him to the edge of the camp: a pair of stakes capped with the severed heads of orcs.

The band and their missing fellows, then, were indeed members of *Casin Cu Calas*, the "Triple C," an organization of vigilantes who took their name from the Elvish saying that meant "honor in battle."

Given the reputation of *Casin Cu Calas,* whose favorite tactic was to storm orc homesteads in the dark of night and decapitate any males found inside, Drizzt found the name more than a little ironic, and more than a little distasteful.

"Cowards, one and all," he whispered as he watched one man hold up a full-length black and red robe. The man flapped it clean of the night's dirt and reverently folded it, bringing it to his lips to kiss it before he replaced it in the back of one wagon. He reached down and picked up the second tell-tale garment, a black hood. He moved to

1

put that, too, in the wagon but hesitated, then slipped the hood over his head, adjusting it so that he could see through the two eye-holes. That drew the attention of the other four.

The other *five*, Drizzt noted as the fourth dwarf walked back around a corner of the wagon to regard the hooded man.

"Casin Cu Calas!" the man proclaimed, and held up both his arms, fists clenched, in an exaggerated victory pose. "Suffer no orc to live!"

"Death to the orcs!" the others cried in reply.

The hooded fool issued a barrage of insults and threats against the porcine-featured humanoids. Up on the side of the hill, Drizzt Do'Urden shook his head and deliberately slid his bow, Taulmaril, off his shoulder. He put it up, notched an arrow, and drew back in one fluid motion.

"Suffer no orc to live," the hooded man said again—or started to, until a flash of lightning shot through the camp and drove into a keg of warm ale beside him. As the keg exploded, liquid flying, a sheet of dissipating electricity momentarily stole the darkness from the growing twilight.

All six of the companions fell back, shielding their eyes. When they regained their sight, one and all saw the lone figure of a lean dark elf standing atop one of their wagons.

"Drizzt Do'Urden," gasped one of the dwarves, a fat fellow with an orange beard and an enormous temple-to-temple eyebrow.

A couple of the others nodded and mouthed their agreement, for there was no mistaking the dark elf standing before them, with his two scimitars belted at his hips and Taulmaril, the Heartseeker, again slung over one shoulder. The drow's long, thick white hair blew in the late afternoon breeze, his cloak flapped out behind him, and even the dull light remaining could do little to diminish the shine of his silvery-white mithral-lined shirt.

Slowly pulling off his hood, the human glanced at the elf then back at Drizzt. "Your reputation precedes you, Master Do'Urden," he said. "To what do we owe the honor of your presence?"

" 'Honor' is a strange word," Drizzt replied. "Stranger still coming from the lips of one who would wear the black hood."

A dwarf to the side of the wagon bristled and even stepped forward, but was blocked by the arm of the orange-bearded fellow.

The human cleared his throat uncomfortably and tossed the hood into the wagon behind him. "That thing?" he asked. "Found along the road, of course. Do you assign it any significance?"

"No more so than the significance I assign the robe you so reverently folded and kissed."

That brought another glance at the elf, who, Drizzt noticed, was sliding a bit more to the side—notably behind a line etched in the dirt, one glittering with shiny dust. When Drizzt brought his attention more fully back to the human, he noted the change in the man's demeanor, a clear scowl replacing the feigned innocence.

"A robe you yourself should wear," the man said boldly. "To honor King Bruenor Battlehammer, whose deeds—"

"Speak not his name," Drizzt interrupted. "You know nothing of Bruenor, of his exploits and his judgments."

"I know that he was no friend of—"

"You know nothing," Drizzt said again, more forcefully.

"The tale of Shallows!" one of the dwarves roared.

"I was there," Drizzt reminded him, silencing the fool.

The human spat upon the ground. "Once a hero, now gone soft," he muttered. "On orcs, no less."

"Perhaps," Drizzt replied, and in the blink of an astonished eye, he brought his scimitars out in his black-skinned hands. "But I've not gone soft on highwaymen and murderers."

"Murderers?" the human retorted incredulously. "Murderers of orcs?"

Even as he finished speaking, the dwarf at the side of the wagon pushed through his orange-bearded companion's arm and thrust his hand forward, sending a hand-axe spinning at the drow.

Drizzt easily side-stepped the unsurprising move, but not content to let the missile harmlessly fly past, and seeing a second dwarf charging from over to the left, he snapped out his scimitar Icingdeath into the path of the axe. He drew the blade back as it contacted the missile, absorbing the impact. A twist of his wrist had the scimitar's blade firmly up under the axe's head. In a single fluid movement, Drizzt pivoted back the other way and whipped Icingdeath around, launching the axe at the charging dwarf.

The rumbling warrior brought his shield up high to block the awkwardly spinning axe, which clunked against the wooden buckler and bounced aside. But so too fell away that dwarf's determined growl when he again lowered the shield, to find his intended target nowhere in sight.

For Drizzt, his speed enhanced by a pair of magical anklets, had timed his break perfectly with the rise of the dwarf's shield. He had taken only a few steps, but enough, he knew, to confuse the determined dwarf. At the last moment, the dwarf noticed him and skidded to a stop, throwing out a weak, backhanded swipe with his warhammer.

But Drizzt was inside the arch of the hammer, and he smacked its handle with one blade, stealing the minimal momentum of the swing. He struck harder with his second blade, finding the crease between the dwarf's heavy gauntlet and his metal-banded bracer. The hammer went flying, and the dwarf howled and grabbed at his bleeding, broken wrist.

Drizzt leaped atop his shoulder, kicked him in the face for good measure, and sprang away, charging at the orange-bearded dwarf and the axe thrower, both of whom were coming on fast.

Behind them, the human urged them in their charge, but did not follow, reaffirming Drizzt's suspicions regarding his courage, or lack thereof.

Drizzt's sudden reversal and rush had the two dwarves on their heels, and the drow came in furiously, his scimitars rolling over each other and striking from many different angles. The axe-thrower, a second small axe in hand, also held a shield, and so fared better in blocking the blades, but the poor orange-bearded fellow could only bring his great mace out diagonally before him, altering its angle furiously to keep up with the stream of strikes. He got nicked and clipped half a dozen times, drawing howls and grunts, and only the presence of his companion, and those others all around demanding the attention of the drow, prevented him from being seriously wounded, or even slain on the spot. For Drizzt could not finish his attacks without opening himself up to counters from the dwarf's companions.

After the initial momentum played out, the drow fell back. With typical stubbornness, the two dwarves advanced. The one with the orange beard, his hands bleeding and one finger hanging by a thread of skin, attempted a straightforward overhead chop. His companion half turned to lead with his shield then pivoted to launch a horizontal swing meant to come within a hair's breadth of his companion and swipe across from Drizzt's left to right.

The impressive coordination of the attack demanded either a straight and swift retreat or a complex two-angled parry, and normally, Drizzt would have just used his superior speed to skip back out of range.

But he recognized the orange-bearded dwarf's tenuous grip, and he was a drow, after all, whose entire youth was spent in learning how to execute exactly those sorts of multi-angled defenses. He thrust his left scimitar out before him, rode his hand up high and turned the blade down to intercept the sidelong swing, and brought his right hand across up high over his left, blade horizontal, to block the downward strike.

As the hammer coming across connected with his blade, Drizzt punched his hand forward and turned his scimitar to divert the dwarf's weapon low, and in doing so, the drow was able to take half a step to his left, lining himself up more fully with the other's overhead strike. When he made contact with that weapon, he had his full balance, his feet squarely set beneath his shoulders.

He dropped into a crouch as the weapon came down, then pushed up hard with all his strength. The dwarf's badly-injured top hand could not hold, and the drow's move forced the diminutive warrior to go right up to his tip-toes to keep any grasp on his weapon at all.

Drizzt turned back to the right as he rose, and with a sudden and powerful move, he angled and drove the dwarf's weapon across to his right, putting it in the path of the other dwarf's returning backhand. As the pair tangled, Drizzt disengaged and executed a reverse spin on the ball of his left foot, coming all the way around to launch a circle kick into the back of the orange-bearded dwarf that shoved him into his companion. The great mace went flying, and so did the dwarf with the orange beard, as the other dwarf ducked a shoulder and angled his shield to guide him aside.

"Clear for a shot!" came a cry from the side, demanding Drizzt's attention, and the drow abruptly halted and turned to see the elf, who held a heavy crossbow leveled Drizzt's way.

Drizzt yelled and charged at the elf, diving into a forward roll and turning as he went so that he came up into a sidelong step. He closed rapidly.

Then he rammed into an invisible wall, as expected, for he understood that the crossbow had been only a ruse, and no missile could have crossed through to strike at him through the unseen magical barrier.

Drizzt rebounded back and fell to one knee, moving shakily. He started up, but seemed to stumble again, apparently dazed.

He heard the dwarves charging in at his back, and they believed beyond any doubt that there was no way he could recover in time to prevent their killing blows.

"And all for the sake of orcs, Drizzt Do'Urden," he heard the elf, a wizard by trade, remark, and he saw the lithe creature shaking his head in dismay as he dropped the crossbow aside. "Not so honorable an end for one of your reputation."

* * * * *

Taugmaelle lowered her gaze, stunned and fearful. Never could she have anticipated a visit from King Obould VI, Lord of Many-Arrows, particularly on this, the eve of her departure for the Glimmerwood, where she was to be wed.

"You are a beautiful bride," the young orc king remarked, and Taugmaelle dared glance up to see Obould nodding appreciatively. "This human—what is his name?"

"Handel Aviv," she said.

"Does he understand the good fortune that has shone upon him?"

As that question digested, Taugmaelle found courage. She looked up again at her king and did not avert her eyes, but rather met his gaze.

"I am the fortunate one," she said, but her smile went away almost immediately as Obould responded with a scowl.

"Because he is human?" Obould blustered, and the other orcs in the small house all stepped away from him fearfully. "A higher being? Because you, a mere orc, are being accepted by this Handel Aviv and his kin? Have you elevated yourself above your race with this joining, Taugmaelle of Clan Bignance?"

"No, my king!" Taugmaelle blurted, tears rushing from her eyes. "No. Of course, nothing of the sort . . ."

"Handel Aviv is the fortunate one!" Obould declared.

"I . . . I only meant that I love him, my king," Taugmaelle said, her voice barely above a whisper.

The sincerity of that statement was obvious, though, and had Taugmaelle not averted her gaze to the floor again, she would have seen the young orc king shift uncomfortably, his bluster melting away.

"Of course," he replied after a while. "You are both fortunate, then."

"Yes, my king."

"But do not ever view yourself as his lesser," Obould warned. "You are proud. You are orc. You are Many-Arrows orc. It is Handel Aviv who is marrying above his heritage. Do not ever forget that."

"Yes, my king."

Obould looked around the small room to the faces of his constituents, a couple standing slack-jawed as if they had no idea how to react to his unexpected appearance, and several others nodding dully.

"You are a beautiful bride," the king said again. "A sturdy representative of all that is good in the Kingdom of Many-Arrows. Go forth with my blessing."

"Thank you, my king," Taugmaelle replied, but Obould hardly heard her, for he had already turned on his heel and moved out the door. He felt a bit foolish for his overreaction, to be sure, but he reminded himself pointedly that his sentiments had not been without merit.

"This is good for our people," said Taska Toill, Obould's court advisor. "Each of these extra-racial joinings reinforces the message that is Obould. And that this union is to be sanctified in the former Moonwood is no small thing."

"The steps are slow," the king lamented.

"Not so many years ago, we were hunted and killed," Taska reminded. "Unending war. Conquest and defeat. It has been a century of progress."

Obould nodded, though he did remark, "We are still hunted," under his breath. Worse, he thought but did not say, were the quiet barbs, where even those who befriended the people of Many-Arrows did so with a sense of superiority, a deep-set inner voice that told them of their magnanimity in befriending, even championing the cause of such lesser creatures. The surrounding folk of the Silver Marches would often forgive an orc for behavior they would not accept among their own, and that wounded Obould as greatly as those elves, dwarves, and humans who outwardly and openly sneered at his people.

* * * * *

Drizzt looked up at the elf wizard's superior smile, but when the drow, too, grinned, and even offered a wink, the elf's face went blank.

A split second later, the elf shrieked and flew away, as Guenhwyvar, six hundred pounds of feline power, leaped against him, taking him far, and taking him down.

One of the dwarves charging at Drizzt let out a little cry in surprise, but despite the revelation of a panther companion, neither of the charging dwarves were remotely prepared when the supposedly stunned Drizzt spun up and around at them, fully aware and fully balanced. As he came around, a backhand from Twinkle, the scimitar in his left hand, took half the orange beard from one dwarf, who was charging with abandon, his heavy weapon up over his head. He still tried to strike at Drizzt, but swirled and staggered, lost within the burning pain and shock. He came forward with his strike, but the scimitar was already coming back the other way, catching him across the wrists.

His great mace went flying. The tough dwarf lowered his shoulder in an attempt to run over his enemy, but Drizzt was too agile, and he merely shifted to the side and trailed his left foot, over which the wounded dwarf tumbled, cracking his skull against the magical wall.

His companion fared no better. As Twinkle slashed across in the initial backhand, the dwarf shifted back on his heels, turning to bring his shield in line, and brought his weapon arm back to begin a heavy strike. Drizzt's second blade thrust in behind the backhand, however, the drow cleverly turning his wrist over so that the curving blade of the scimitar rolled over the edge of the shield and dived down to strike that retracted weapon arm right where the bicep met the shoulder. As the dwarf, too far into his move to halt it completely, came around and forward with the strike, his own momentum drove the scimitar deeper into his flesh.

He halted, he howled, he dropped his axe. He watched his companion go tumbling away. Then came a barrage as the deadly drow squared up against him. Left and right slashed the scimitars, always just ahead of the dwarf's pathetic attempts to get his shield in their way. He got nicked, he got slashed, he got shaved, as edges, points and flats of two blades made their way through his defenses. Every hit stung, but none of them were mortal.

But he couldn't regain his balance and any semblance of defense, nor did he hold anything with which to counter, except his shield. In desperation, the dwarf turned and lunged, butting his shield arm forward. The drow easily rolled around it, though, and as he pivoted to the dwarf's right he punched out behind him, driving the pommel of his right blade against the dwarf's temple. He followed with a heavy left hook as he completed his turn, and the dazed dwarf offered no defense at all as fist and hilt smashed him across the face.

He staggered two steps to the side, and crumbled into the dirt.

Drizzt didn't pause to confirm the effect, for back the other way, the first dwarf he had cut was back to his feet and staggering away. A few quick strides brought Drizzt up behind him, and the drow's scimitar slashed across the back of the dwarf's legs, drawing a howl and sending the battered creature whimpering to the ground.

Again, Drizzt looked past him even as he fell, for the remaining two members of the outlaw band were fast retreating. The drow put up Taulmaril and set an arrow retrieved from the enchanted quiver he wore on his back. He aimed center mass on the dwarf, but perhaps in deference to King Bruenor—or Thibbledorf, or Dagnabbit, or any of the other noble and fierce dwarves he had known those decades before, he lowered his angle and let fly. Like a bolt of lightning, the magical arrow slashed the air and drove through the fleshy part of the dwarf's thigh. The poor dwarf screamed and veered then fell down.

Drizzt notched another arrow and turned the bow until he had the human, whose longer legs had taken him even farther away, in his sight. He took aim and drew back steadily, but held his shot as he saw the man jerk suddenly then stagger.

He stood there for just a moment before falling over, and Drizzt knew by the way he tumbled that he was dead before he ever hit the ground.

The drow glanced back over his shoulder, to see the three wounded dwarves struggling, but defeated, and the elf wizard still pinned by the ferocious Guenhwyvar. Every time the poor elf moved, Guenhwyvar smothered his face under a huge paw.

By the time Drizzt looked back, the killers of the human were in view. A pair of elves moved to gather the arrow-shot dwarf, while another went to the dead man, and another pair approached Drizzt, one riding on a white-winged steed, the pegasus named Sunrise. Bells adorned the mount's harness, bridle, and saddle, tinkling sweetly—ironically so—as the riders trotted up to the drow.

"Lord Hralien," Drizzt greeted with a bow.

"Well met and well done, my friend," said the elf who ruled the ancient expanse of the Glimmerwood that the elves still called the Moonwood. He looked around, nodding with approval. "The Night Riders have been dealt yet one more serious blow," he said, using another of the names for the orc-killing vigilantes, as did all the elves, refusing to assign a title as honorable as *Casin Cu Calas* to a band they so abhorred.

"One of many we'll need, I fear, for their numbers do not seem diminished," said Drizzt.

"They are more visible of late," Hralien agreed, and dismounted to stand before his old friend. "The Night Riders are trying to take advantage of the unrest in Many-Arrows. They know that King Obould VI is in a tenuous position." The elf gave a sigh. "As he always seems to be, as his predecessors always seemed to be."

"He has allies as well as enemies," said Drizzt. "More allies than did the first of his line, surely."

"And more enemies, perhaps," Hralien replied.

Drizzt could not disagree. Many times over the last century, the Kingdom of Many-Arrows had known inner turmoil, most often, as was still the case, brewing from a rival group of orcs. The old cults of Gruumsh One-eye had not flourished under the rule of the Oboulds, but neither had they been fully eradicated. The rumors said that yet another group of shamans, following the old warlike ways of goblinkind, were creating unrest and plotting against the king who dared diplomacy and trade with the surrounding kingdoms of humans, elves, and even dwarves, the most ancient and hated enemy of the orcs.

"You killed not one of them," Hralien remarked, glancing around at his warriors who gathered up the five wounded Night Riders. "Is this not in your heart, Drizzt Do'Urden? Do you not strike with surety when you strike to defend the orcs?"

"They are caught, to be justly tried."

"By others."

"That is not my province."

"You would not allow it to be," Hralien said with a wry grin that was not accusatory. "A drow's memories are long, perhaps."

"No longer than a moon elf's."

"My arrow struck the human first, and mortally, I assure you."

"Because you fiercely battle those memories, while I try to mitigate them," Drizzt replied without hesitation, setting Hralien back on his heels. If the elf, startled though he was, took any real offense, he didn't show it.

"Some wounds are not so healed by the passage of a hundred years," Drizzt went on, looking from Hralien to the captured Night Riders. "Wounds felt keenly by some of our captives here, perhaps, or by the grandfather's grandfather of the man who lies dead in the field beyond."

"What of the wounds felt by Drizzt Do'Urden, who did battle with King Obould in the orc's initial sweep of the Spine of the World?" Hralien asked. "Before the settlement of his kingdom and the treaty of Garumn's Gorge? Or who fought again against Obould II in the great war in the Year of the Solitary Cloister?"

Drizzt nodded with every word, unable to deny the truth of it all. He had made his peace with the orcs of Many-Arrows, to a great extent. But still, he would be a liar to himself if he failed to admit a twinge of guilt in battling those who had refused to end the ancient wars and ancient ways, and had continued the fight against the orcs—a war that Drizzt, too, had once waged, and waged viciously.

"A Mithral Hall trade caravan was turned back from Five Tusks," Hralien said, changing his tone as he shifted the subject. "A similar report comes to us from Silverymoon, where one of their caravans was refused entry to Many-Arrows at Ungoor's Gate north of Nesmé. It is a clear violation of the treaty."

"King Obould's response?"

"We are not certain that he even knows of the incidents. But whether he does or not, it is apparent that his shaman rivals have spread their message of the old ways far beyond Dark Arrows Keep."

Drizzt nodded.

"King Obould is in need of your help, Drizzt," Hralien said. "We have walked this road before."

Drizzt nodded in resignation at the unavoidable truth of that statement. There were times when he felt as if the road he walked was not a straight line toward progress, but a circling track, a futile loop. He let that negative notion pass, and reminded himself of how far the region had come—and that in a world gone mad from the Spellplague. Few places in all of Faerûn could claim to be *more* civilized than they had been those hundred years before, but the region known as the Silver Marches, in no small part because of the courage of a succession of orc kings named Obould, had much to be proud of.

His perspective and memories of that time a hundred years gone, before the rise of the Empire of Netheril, the coming of the aboleths, and the discordant and disastrous joining of two worlds, brought to Drizzt thoughts of another predicament so much like the one playing out before him. He remembered the look on Bruenor's face, as incredulous as any expression he had ever seen before or since, when he had presented the dwarf with his surprising assessment and astounding recommendations.

He could almost hear the roar of protest: "Ye lost yer wits, ye durned orc-brained, pointy-eared elf!"

On the other side of the magical barrier, the elf shrieked and Guenhwyvar growled, and Drizzt looked up to see the wizard stubbornly trying to crawl away. Guenhwyvar's great paw thumped against his back, and the panther flexed, causing the elf to drop back to the ground, squirming to avoid the extending claws.

Hralien started to call to his comrades, but Drizzt held his hand up to halt them. He could have walked around the invisible wall, but instead he sprang into the air beside it, reaching his hand as high as he could. His fingers slid over the top and caught a hold, and the drow rolled his back against the invisible surface and reached up with his other hand. A tuck and roll vaulted him feet-over-head over the wall, and he landed nimbly on the far side.

He bade Guenhwyvar to move aside then reached down and pulled the elf wizard to his feet. He was young, as Drizzt had expected—while some older elves and dwarves were inciting the *Casin Cu Calas*, the younger members, full of fire and hatred, were the ones executing the unrest in brutal fashion.

The elf, uncompromising, stared at him hatefully. "You would betray your own kind," he spat.

Drizzt cocked his eyebrows curiously, and tightened his grip on the elf's shirt, holding him firmly. "My own kind?"

"Worse then," the elf spar. "You would betray those who gave shelter and friendship to the rogue Drizzt Do'Urden."

"No," he said.

"You would strike at elves and dwarves for the sake of orcs!"

"I would uphold the law and the peace."

The elf mocked him with a laugh. "To see the once-great ranger siding with orcs," he muttered, shaking his head.

Drizzt yanked him around, stealing his mirth, and tripped him, shoving him backward into the magical wall.

"Are you so eager for war?" the drow asked, his face barely an inch from the elf's. "Do you long to hear the screams of the dying, lying helplessly in fields amidst rows and rows of corpses? Have you ever borne witness to that?"

"Orcs!" the elf protested.

Drizzt grabbed him in both hands, pulled him forward, and slammed him back against the wall. Hralien called to Drizzt, but the dark elf hardly heard it.

"I have ventured outside of the Silver Marches," Drizzt said, "have you? I have witnessed the death of once-proud Luskan, and with it, the death of a dear, dear friend, whose dreams lay shattered and broken beside the bodies of five thousand victims. I have watched the greatest cathedral in the world burn and collapse. I witnessed the hope of the goodly drow, the rise of the followers of Eilistraee. But where are they now?"

"You speak in ridd—" the elf started, but Drizzt slammed him again.

"Gone!" Drizzt shouted. "Gone, and gone with them the hopes of a tamed and gentle world. I have watched once safe trails revert to wilderness, and have walked a dozen-dozen communities that you will never know. They are gone now, lost to the Spellplague or worse! Where are the benevolent gods? Where is the refuge from the tumult of a world gone mad? Where are the candles to chase away the darkness?"

Hralien had quietly moved around the wall and walked up beside Drizzt. He put a hand on the drow's shoulder, but that brought no more than a brief pause in the tirade. Drizzt glanced at him before turning back to the captured elf.

"They are here, those lights of hope," Drizzt said, to both elves. "In the Silver Marches. Or they are nowhere. Do we choose peace or do we choose war? If it is battle you seek, fool elf, then get you gone from this land. You will find death aplenty, I assure you. You will find ruins where once proud cities stood. You will find fields of wind-washed bones, or perhaps the remains of a single hearth, where once an entire village thrived.

"And in that hundred years of chaos, amidst the coming of darkness, few have escaped the swirl of destruction, but we have flourished. Can you say the same for Thay? Mulhorand? Sembia? You say I betray those who befriended me, yet it was the vision of one exceptional dwarf and one exceptional orc that built this island against the roiling sea."

The elf, his expression more cowed, nonetheless began to speak out again, but Drizzt pulled him forward from the wall and slammed him back even harder.

"You fall to your hatred and you seek excitement and glory," the drow said. "Because you do not know. Or is it because you do not care that your pursuits will bring utter misery to thousands in your wake?"

Drizzt shook his head, and threw the elf aside, where he was caught by two of Hralien's warriors and escorted away.

"I hate this," Drizzt admitted to Hralien, quietly so that no one else could hear. "All of it. It is a noble experiment a hundred years long, and still we have no answers."

"And no options," Hralien replied. "Save those you yourself just described. The chaos encroaches, Drizzt Do'Urden, from within and without."

Drizzt turned his lavender eyes to watch the departure of the elf and the captured dwarves.

"We must stand strong, my friend," Hralien offered, and he patted Drizzt on the shoulder and walked away.

"I'm not sure that I know what that means anymore," Drizzt admitted under his breath, too softly for anyone else to hear.

PART 1

THE PURSUIT OF
HIGHER TRUTH

THE PURSUIT OF
HIGHER TRUTH

One of the consequences of living an existence that spans centuries instead of decades is the inescapable curse of continually viewing the world through the focusing prism employed by an historian.

I say "curse"—when in truth I believe it to be a blessing—because any hope of prescience requires a constant questioning of what is, and a deep-seated belief in the possibility of what can be. Viewing events as might the historian requires an acceptance that my own initial, visceral reactions to seemingly momentous events may be errant, that my "gut instinct" and own emotional needs may not stand the light of reason in the wider view, or even that these events, so momentous in my personal experience, might not be so in the wider world and the long, slow passage of time.

How often have I seen that my first reaction is based on half-truths and biased perceptions! How often have I found expectations completely inverted or tossed aside as events played out to their fullest!

Because emotion clouds the rational, and many perspectives guide the full reality. To view current events as an historian is to account for all perspectives, even those of your enemy. It is to know the past and to use such relevant history as a template for expectations. It is, most of all, to force reason ahead of instinct, to refuse to demonize that which you hate, and to, most of all, accept your own fallibility.

And so I live on shifting sands, where absolutes melt away with the passage of decades. It is a natural extension, I expect, of an existence in which I have shattered the preconceptions of so many people. With every stranger who comes to accept me for who I am instead of who he or she expected me to be, I roil the sands beneath that person's feet. It is a growth experience for them, no doubt, but we are all creatures of ritual and habit and accepted notions of what is and what is not. When true reality cuts against that internalized expectation—when you meet a goodly drow!—there is created an internal dissonance, as uncomfortable as a springtime rash.

There is freedom in seeing the world as a painting in progress, instead of a place already painted, but there are times, my friend . . .

There are times.

And such is one before me now, with Obould and his thousands camped upon the very door of Mithral Hall. In my heart I want nothing more than another try at the orc king, another opportunity to put my scimitar through his yellow-gray skin. I long to wipe the superior grin from his ugly face, to bury it beneath a spray of his own blood. I want him to hurt—to hurt for Shallows and all the other towns flattened beneath the stamp of orc feet. I want him to feel the pain he brought to Shoudra Stargleam, to Dagna and Dagnabbit, and to all the dwarves and others who lay dead on the battlefield that he created.

Will Catti-brie ever walk well again? That, too, is the fault of Obould.

And so I curse his name, and remember with joy those moments of retribution that Innovindil, Tarathiel, and I exacted upon the minions of the foul orc king. To strike back against an invading foe is indeed cathartic.

That, I cannot deny.

And yet, in moments of reason, in times when I sit back against a stony mountainside and overlook that which Obould has facilitated, I am simply not certain.

Of anything, I fear.

He came at the front of an army, one that brought pain and suffering to many people across this land I name as my home. But his army has stopped its march, for now at least, and the signs are visible that Obould seeks something more than plunder and victory.

Does he seek civilization?

Is it possible that we bear witness now to a monumental change in the nature of orc culture? Is it possible that Obould has established a situation, whether he intended this at first or not, where the interests of the orcs and the interests of all the other races of the region coalesce into a relationship of mutual benefit?

Is that possible? Is that even thinkable?

Do I betray the dead by considering such a thing?

Or does it serve the dead if I, if we all, rise above a cycle of revenge and war and find within us—orc and dwarf, human and elf alike—a common ground upon which to build an era of greater peace?

For time beyond the memory of the oldest elves, the orcs have warred with the "goodly" races. For all the victories—and they are countless!—and for all the sacrifices, are the orcs any less populous now than they were millennia ago?

I think not, and that raises the specter of unwinnable conflict. Are we doomed to repeat these wars, generation after generation, unendingly? Are we—elf and dwarf, human and orc alike—condemning our descendants to this same misery, to the pain of steel invading flesh?

I do not know.

And yet I want nothing more than to slide my blade between the ribs of King Obould Many-Arrows, to relish in the grimace of agony on his tusk-torn lips, to see the light dim in his yellow, bloodshot eyes.

But what will the historians say of Obould? Will he be the orc who breaks, at long, long last, this cycle of perpetual war? Will he, inadvertently or not, present the orcs with a path to a better life, a road they will walk—reluctantly at first, no doubt—in pursuit of bounties greater than those they might find at the end of a crude spear?

I do not know.

And therein lies my anguish.

I hope that we are on the threshold of a great era, and that within the orc character, there is the same spark, the same hopes and dreams, that guide the elves, dwarves, humans, halflings, and all the rest. I have heard it said that the universal hope of the world is that our children will find a better life than we.

Is that guiding principle of civilization itself within the emotional make-up of goblinkind? Or was Nojheim, that most unusual goblin slave I once knew, simply an anomaly?

Is Obould a visionary or an opportunist?

Is this the beginning of true progress for the orc race, or a fool's errand for any, myself included, who would suffer the beasts to live?

Because I admit that I do not know, it must give me pause. If I am to give in to the wants of my vengeful heart, then how might the historians view Drizzt Do'Urden?

Will I be seen in the company of those heroes before me who helped vanquish the charge of the orcs, whose names are held in noble esteem? If Obould is to lead the orcs forward, not in conquest, but in civilization, and I am the hand who lays him low, then misguided indeed will be those historians, who might never see the possibilities that I view coalescing before me.

Perhaps it is an experiment. Perhaps it is a grand step along a road worth walking.

Or perhaps I am wrong, and Obould seeks dominion and blood, and the orcs have no sense of commonality, have no aspirations for a better way, unless that way tramples the lands of their mortal, eternal enemies.

But I am given pause.

And so I wait, and so I watch, but my hands are near to my blades.

—Drizzt Do'Urden

CHAPTER

On the same day that Drizzt and Innovindil had set off for the east to find the body of Ellifain, Catti-brie and Wulfgar had crossed the Surbrin in search of Wulfgar's missing daughter. Their journey had lasted only a couple of days, however, before they had been turned back by the cold winds and darkening skies of a tremendous winter storm. With Catti-brie's injured leg, the pair simply could not hope to move fast enough to out-distance the coming front, and so Wulfgar had refused to continue. Colson was safe, by all accounts, and Wulfgar was confident that the trail would not grow cold during the delay, as all travel in the Silver Marches would come to a near stop through the frozen months. Over Catti-brie's objections, the pair had re-crossed the Surbrin and returned to Mithral Hall.

That same weather front destroyed the ferry soon after, and it remained out of commission though tendays passed. The winter was deep about them, closer to spring than to fall. The Year of Wild Magic had arrived.

For Catti-brie, the permeating cold seemed to forever settle on her injured hip and leg, and she hadn't seen much improvement in her mobility. She could walk with a crutch, but even then every stride made her wince. Still she wouldn't accept a chair with wheels, such as the one the dwarves had fashioned for the crippled Banak Brawnanvil, and she certainly wanted nothing to do with the contraption

Nanfoodle had designed for her: a comfortable palanquin meant to be borne by four willing dwarves. Stubbornness aside, her injured hip would not support her weight very well, or for any length of time, and so Catti-brie had settled on the crutch.

For the last few days, she had loitered around the eastern edges of Mithral Hall, across Garumn's Gorge from the main chambers, always asking for word of the orcs who had dug in just outside of Keeper's Dale, or of Drizzt, who had at last been seen over the eastern fortifications, flying on a pegasus across the Surbrin beside Innovindil of the Moonwood.

Drizzt had left Mithral Hall with Catti-brie's blessing those tendays before, but she missed him dearly on the long, dark nights of winter. It had surprised her when he hadn't come directly back into the halls upon his return from the west, but she trusted his judgment. If something had compelled him to go on to the Moonwood, then it must have been a good reason.

"I got a hunnerd boys beggin' me to let 'em carry ye," Bruenor scolded her one day, when the pain in her hip was obviously flaring. She was back in the western chambers, in Bruenor's private den, but had already informed her father that she would go back to the east, across the gorge. "Take the gnome's chair, ye stubborn girl!"

"I have my own legs," she insisted.

"Legs that ain't healing, from what me eyes're telling me." He glanced across the hearth to Wulfgar, who reclined in a comfortable chair, staring into the orange flames. "What say ye, boy?"

Wulfgar looked at him blankly, obviously having no comprehension of the conversation between the dwarf and the woman.

"Ye heading out soon to find yer little one?" Bruenor asked. "With the melt?"

"Before the melt," Wulfgar corrected. "Before the river swells."

"A month, perhaps," said Bruenor, and Wulfgar nodded.

"Before Tarsakh," he said, referring to the fourth month of the year.

Catti-brie chewed her lip, understanding that Bruenor had initiated the discussion with Wulfgar for her benefit.

"Ye ain't going with him with that leg, girl," Bruenor stated. "Ye're limpin' about here and never giving the durned thing a chance at mending. Now take the gnome's chair and let me boys carry ye about, and it might be—it just might be—that ye'll be able to go with Wulf-gar to find Colson, as ye planned and as ye started afore."

Catti-brie looked from Bruenor to Wulfgar, and saw only the twisting orange flames reflected in the big man's eyes. He seemed lost to them all, she noted, wound up too tightly in inner turmoil. His shoulders were bowed by the weight of guilt, to be sure, and the burden of grief, for he had lost his wife, Delly Curtie, who still lay dead under a blanket of snow on a northern field, as far as they knew.

Catti-brie was no less consumed by guilt over that loss, for it had been her sword, the evil and sentient Khazid'hea, that had over-whelmed Delly Curtie and sent her running out from the safety of Mithral Hall. Thankfully—they all believed—Delly hadn't taken her and Wulfgar's adopted child, the toddler girl, Colson, with her, but had instead deposited Colson with one of the other refugees from the northland, who had crossed the River Surbrin on one of the last ferries to leave before the onslaught of winter. Colson might be in the enchanted city of Silverymoon, or in Sundabar, or in any of a host of other communities, but they had no reason to believe that she had been harmed, or would be.

And Wulfgar meant to find her—it was one of the few declarations that held any fire of conviction that Catti-brie had heard the barbar-ian make in tendays. He would go to find Colson, and Catti-brie felt it was her duty as his friend to go with him. After they had been turned back by the storm, in no small part because of her infirmity, Catti-brie was even more determined to see the journey through.

Truly Catti-brie hoped that Drizzt would return before that departure day arrived, however. For the spring would surely bring tumult across the land, with a vast orc army entrenched all over the lands surrounding Mithral Hall, from the Spine of the World mountains to the north, to the banks of the Surbrin to the east, and to the passes just north of the Trollmoors in the south. The clouds of war roiled, and only winter had held back the swarms.

When that storm finally broke, Drizzt Do'Urden would be in the middle of it, and Catti-brie did not intend to be riding through the streets of some distant city on that dark day.

"Take the chair," Bruenor said—or said again, it seemed, from his impatient tone.

Catti-brie blinked and looked back at him.

"I'll be needin' both o' ye at me side, and soon enough," Bruenor said. "If ye're to be slowing Wulfgar down in this trip he's needing to make, then ye're not to be going."

"The indignity. . . ." Catti-brie said with a shake of her head.

But as she did that, she overbalanced just a bit on her crutch and lurched to the side. Her face twisted in a pained grimace as shooting pains like little fires rolled through her from her hip.

"Ye catched a giant-thrown boulder on yer leg," Bruenor retorted. "Ain't no indignity in that! Ye helped us hold the hall, and not a one o' Clan Battlehammer's thinking ye anything but a hero. Take the durned chair!"

"You really should," came a voice from the door, and Catti-brie and Bruenor turned to see Regis the halfling enter the room.

His belly was round once again, his cheeks full and rosy. He wore suspenders, as he had of late, and hooked his thumbs under them as he walked, eliciting an air of importance. And truly, as absurd as Regis sometimes seemed, no one in the hall would deny that pride to the halfling who had served so well as Steward of Mithral Hall in the days of constant battle, when Bruenor had lain near death.

"A conspiracy, then?" Catti-brie remarked with a grin, trying to lighten the mood.

They needed to smile more, all of them, and particularly the man seated across from where she stood. She watched Wulfgar as she spoke, and knew that her words had not even registered with him. He just stared into the flames, truly looking inward. The expression on Wulfgar's face, so utterly hopeless and lost, spoke truth to Catti-brie. She began to nod, and accepted her father's offer. Friendship demanded of her that she do whatever she could to ensure that she would be well enough to accompany Wulfgar on his most important journey.

So it was a few days later, that when Drizzt Do'Urden entered Mithral Hall through the eastern door, open to the Surbrin, that Catti-brie spotted him and called to him from on high. "Your step is lighter," she observed, and when Drizzt finally recognized her in her palanquin, carried on the shoulders of four strong dwarves, he offered her a laugh and a wide, wide smile.

"The Princess of Clan Battlehammer," the drow said with a polite and mocking bow.

On Catti-brie's orders, the dwarves placed her down and moved aside, and she had just managed to pull herself out of her chair and collect her crutch, when Drizzt crushed her in a tight and warm embrace.

"Tell me that you're home for a long while," she said after a lingering kiss. "The winter has been cold and lonely."

"I have duties in the field," Drizzt replied. He added, "Of course I do," when Catti-brie smirked helplessly at him. "But yes, I am returned, to Bruenor's side as I promised, before the snows retreat and the gathered armies move. We will know the designs of Obould before long."

"Obould?" Catti-brie asked, for she thought the orc king long dead.

"He lives," Drizzt replied. "Somehow he escaped the catastrophe of the landslide, and the gathered orcs are bound still by the will of that most powerful orc."

"Curse his name."

Drizzt smiled at her, but didn't quite agree.

"I am surprised that you and Wulfgar have already returned," Drizzt said. "What news of Colson?"

Catti-brie shook her head. "We do not know. We did cross the Surbrin on the same morning you flew off with Innovindil for the Sword Coast, but winter was too close on our heels, and brought us back. We did learn that the refugee groups had marched for Silverymoon, at least, and so Wulfgar intends to be off for Lady Alustriel's fair city as soon as the ferry is prepared to run once more."

Drizzt pulled her back to arms' length and looked down at her wounded hip. She wore a dress, as she had been every day, for the tight fit of breeches was too uncomfortable. The drow looked at the crutch the dwarves had fashioned for her, but she caught his gaze with her own and held it.

"I am not healed," she admitted, "but I have rested enough to make the journey with Wulfgar." She paused and reached up with her free hand to gently stroke Drizzt's chin and cheek. "I have to."

"I am no less compelled," Drizzt assured her. "Only my responsibility to Bruenor keeps me here instead."

"Wulfgar will not be alone on this road," she assured him.

Drizzt nodded, and his smile showed that he did indeed take comfort in that. "We should go to Bruenor," he said and started away.

Catti-brie grabbed him by the shoulder. "With good news?"

Drizzt looked at her curiously.

"Your stride is lighter," she remarked. "You walk as if unburdened. What did you see out there? Are the orc armies set to collapse? Are the folk of the Silver Marches ready to rise as one to repel—"

"Nothing like that," Drizzt said. "All is as it was when I departed, except that Obould's forces dig in deeper, as if they mean to stay."

"Your smile does not deceive me," Catti-brie said.

"Because you know me too well," said Drizzt.

"The grim tides of war do not diminish your smile?"

"I have spoken with Ellifain."

Catti-brie gasped. "She lives?" Drizzt's expression showed her the absurdity of that conclusion. Hadn't Catti-brie been there when Ellifain had died, to Drizzt's own blade? "Resurrection?" the woman breathed. "Did the elves employ a powerful cleric to wrest the soul—"

"Nothing like that," Drizzt assured her. "But they did provide Ellifain a conduit to relate to me . . . an apology. And she accepted my own apology."

"You had no reason to apologize," Catti-brie insisted. "You did nothing wrong, nor could you have known."

"I know," Drizzt replied, and the serenity in his voice warmed Catti-brie. "Much has been put right. Ellifain is at peace."

"Drizzt Do'Urden is at peace, you mean."

Drizzt only smiled. "I cannot be," he said. "We approach an uncertain future, with tens of thousands of orcs on our doorstep. So many have died, friends included, and it seems likely that many more will fall."

Catti-brie hardly seemed convinced that his mood was dour.

"Drizzt Do'Urden is at peace," the drow agreed against her unrelenting grin.

He moved as if to lead the woman back to the carriage, but Catti-brie shook her head and motioned instead for him to lead her, crutching, along the corridor that would take them to the bridge across Garumn's Gorge, and to the western reaches of Mithral Hall where Brucnor sat in audience.

"It is a long walk," Drizzt warned her, eyeing her wounded leg.

"I have you to support me," Catti-brie replied, and Drizzt could hardly disagree.

With a grateful nod and a wave to the four dwarf bearers, the couple started away.

* * * * *

So real was his dream that he could feel the warm sun and the cold wind upon his cheeks. So vivid was the sensation that he could smell the cold saltiness of the air blowing down from the Sea of Moving Ice.

So real was it all that Wulfgar was truly surprised when he awoke from his nap to find himself in his small room in Mithral Hall. He closed his eyes again and tried to recapture the dream, tried to step again into the freedom of Icewind Dale.

But it was not possible, and the big man opened his eyes and pulled himself out of his chair. He looked across the room to the bed. He hardly slept there of late, for that had been the bed he'd shared with Delly, his dead wife. On the few occasions he had dared to recline upon it, he had found himself reaching for her, rolling to where she should have been.

The feeling of emptiness as reality invaded his slumber had left Wulfgar cold every time.

At the foot of the bed sat Colson's crib, and looking at it proved even more distressing.

Wulfgar dropped his head in his hands, the soft feel of hair reminding him of his new-grown beard. He smoothed both beard and mustache, and rubbed the blurriness from his eyes. He tried not to think of Delly, then, or even of Colson, needing to be free of his regrets and fears for just a brief moment. He envisioned Icewind Dale in his younger days. He had known loss then, too, and had keenly felt the stings of battle. There were no delusions invading his dreams or his memories that presented a softer image of that harsh land. Icewind Dale remained uncompromising, its winter wind more deadly than refreshing.

But there was something simpler about that place, Wulfgar knew. Something purer. Death was a common visitor to the tundra, and monsters roamed freely. It was a land of constant trial, and with no room for error, and even in the absence of error, the result of any decision often proved disastrous.

Wulfgar nodded, understanding the emotional refuge offered by such uncompromising conditions. For Icewind Dale was a land without regret. It simply was the way of things.

Wulfgar pulled himself from his chair and stretched the weariness from his long arms and legs. He felt constricted, trapped, and as the walls seemed to close in on him, he recalled Delly's pleas to him regarding that very feeling.

"Perhaps you were right," Wulfgar said to the empty room.

He laughed then, at himself, as he considered the steps that had brought him back to that place. He had been turned around by a storm.

He, Wulfgar, son of Beornegar, who had grown tall and strong in the brutal winters of frozen Icewind Dale, had been chased back into the dwarven complex by the threat of winter snows!

Then it hit him. All of it. His meandering, empty road for the last eight years of his life, since his return from the Abyss and the torments of the demon, Errtu. Even after he had gathered up Colson from Meralda in Auckney, had retrieved Aegis-fang and his sense of who he was, and had rejoined his friends for the journey back to Mithral Hall, Wulfgar's steps had not been purposeful, had not been driven by a clear sense of where he wanted to go. He had taken Delly as his wife, but had never stopped loving Catti-brie.

Yes, it was true, he admitted. He could lie about it to others, but not to himself.

Many things came clear at last to Wulfgar that morning in his room in Mithral Hall, most of all the fact that he had allowed himself to live a lie. He knew that he couldn't have Catti-brie—her heart was for Drizzt—but how unfair had he been to Delly and to Colson? He had created a facade, an illusion of family and of stability for the benefit of everyone involved, himself included.

Wulfgar had walked his road of redemption, since Auckney, with manipulation and falsity. He understood that finally. He had been so determined to put everything into a neat and trim little box, a perfectly controlled scene, that he had denied the very essence of who he was, the very fires that had forged Wulfgar son of Beornegar.

He looked at Aegis-fang leaning against the wall then hefted the mighty warhammer in his hand, bringing its crafted head up before his icy-blue eyes. The battles he had waged recently, on the cliff above

Keeper's Dale, in the western chamber, and to the east in the breakout to the Surbrin, had been his moments of true freedom, of emotional clarity and inner calm. He had reveled in that physical turmoil, he realized, because it had calmed the emotional confusion.

That was why he had neglected Delly and Colson, throwing himself with abandon into the defenses of Mithral Hall. He had been a lousy husband to her, and a lousy father to Colson.

Only in battle had he found escape.

And he was still engaged in the self-deception, Wulfgar knew as he stared at the etched head of Aegis-fang. Why else had he allowed the trail to Colson to grow stale? Why else had he been turned back by a mere winter storm? Why else . . . ?

Wulfgar's jaw dropped open, and he thought himself a fool indeed. He dropped the hammer to the floor and swept on his trademark gray wolf cloak. He pulled his backpack out from under the bed and stuffed it with his blankets, then slung it over one arm and gathered up Aegis-fang with the other.

He strode out of his room with fierce determination, heading east past Bruenor's audience chamber.

"Where are you going?" he heard, and paused to see Regis standing before a door in the hallway.

"Out to check on the weather and the ferry."

"Drizzt is back."

Wulfgar nodded, and his smile was genuine. "I hope his journey went well."

"He'll be in with Bruenor in a short while."

"I haven't time. Not now."

"The ferry isn't running yet," Regis said.

But Wulfgar only nodded, as if it didn't matter, and strode off down the corridor, turning through the doors that led to the main avenue that would take him over Garumn's Gorge.

Thumbs hooked in his suspenders, Regis watched his large friend go. He stood there for a long while, considering the encounter, then turned for Bruenor's audience chamber.

He paused after only a few steps, though, and looked back again to the corridor down which Wulfgar had so urgently departed.

The ferry wasn't running.

CHAPTER

Grguch blinked repeatedly as he moved from the recesses of the cave toward the pre-dawn light. Broad-shouldered and more than seven feet in height, the powerful half-orc, half-ogre stepped tentatively with his thick legs, and raised one hand to shield his eyes. The chieftain of Clan Karuck, like all of his people other than a couple of forward scouts, had not seen the light of day in nearly a decade. They lived in the tunnels, in the vast labyrinth of lightless caverns known as the Underdark, and Grguch had not undertaken his journey to the surface lightly.

Scores of Karuck warriors, all huge by the standards of the orc race—approaching if not exceeding seven feet and weighing in at nearly four hundred pounds of honed muscle and thick bone—lined the cave walls. They averted their yellow eyes in respect as the great warlord Grguch passed. Behind Grguch came the merciless war priest Hakuun, and behind him the elite guard, a quintet of mighty ogres fully armed and armored for battle. More ogres followed the procession, bearing the fifteen-foot *Kokto Gung Karuck*, the Horn of Karuck, a great instrument with a conical bore and a wide, upturned bell. It was fashioned of *shroomwood*, what the orcs named the hard skin of certain species of gigantic Underdark mushrooms. To the orc warriors looking on, the horn was deserving of, and receiving of, the same respect as the chieftain who preceded it.

Grguch and Hakuun, like their respective predecessors, would have had it no other way.

Grguch moved to the mouth of the cave, and out onto the mountainside ledge. Only Hakuun came up beside him, the war priest signaling the ogres to wait behind.

Grguch gave a rumbling laugh as his eyes adjusted and he noted the more typical orcs scrambling among the mountainside's lower stones. For more than two days, the second orc clan had been frantically keeping ahead of Clan Karuck's march. The moment they'd at last broken free of the confines of the Underdark, their desire to stay far, far away from Clan Karuck grew only more apparent.

"They flee like children," Grguch said to his war priest.

"They *are* children in the presence of Karuck," Hakuun replied. "Less than that when great Grguch stands among them."

The chieftain took the expected compliment in stride and lifted his eyes to survey the wider view around them. The air was cold, winter still gripped the land, but Grguch and his people were not caught unprepared. Layers of fur made the huge orc chieftain appear even larger and more imposing.

"The word will spread that Clan Karuck has come forth," Hakuun assured his chieftain.

Grguch considered the fleeing tribe again and scanned the horizon. "It will be known faster than the words of running children," he replied, and turned back to motion to the ogres.

The guard quintet parted to grant passage to *Kokto Gung Karuck*. In moments, the skilled team had the horn set up, and Hakuun properly blessed it as Grguch moved into place.

When the war priest's incantation was complete, Grguch, the only Karuck permitted to play the horn, wiped the shroomwood mouthpiece and took a deep, deep breath.

A great bass rumbling erupted from the horn, as if the largest bellows in all the world had been pumped by the immortal titans. The low-pitched roar echoed for miles and miles around the stones and mountainsides of the lower southern foothills of the Spine of the World. Smaller stones vibrated under the power of that sound, and one field of snow broke free, creating a small avalanche on a nearby mountain.

Behind Grguch, many of Clan Karuck fell to their knees and began swaying as if in religious frenzy. They prayed to the great

One-eye, their warlike god, for they held great faith that when *Kokto Gung Karuck* was sounded, the blood of Clan Karuck's enemies would stain the ground.

And for Clan Karuck, particularly under the stewardship of mighty Grguch, it had never been hard to find enemies.

* * * * *

In a sheltered vale a few miles to the south, a trio of orcs lifted their eyes to the north.

"Karuck?" asked Ung-thol, a shaman of high standing.

"Could it be any other?" replied Dnark, chieftain of the tribe of the Wolf Jaw. Both turned to regard the smugly smiling shaman Toogwik Tuk as Dnark remarked, "Your call was heard. And answered."

Toogwik Tuk chuckled.

"Are you so sure that the ogre-spawn can be bent to your will?" Dnark added, stealing the smile from Toogwik Tuk's ugly orc face.

His reference to Clan Karuck as "ogre-spawn" rang as a clear reminder to the shaman that they were not ordinary orcs he had summoned from the lowest bowels of the mountain range. Karuck was famous among the many tribes of the Spine of the World—or infamous, actually—for keeping a full breeding stock of ogres among their ranks. For generations untold, Karuck had interbred, creating larger and larger orc warriors. Shunned by the other tribes, Karuck had delved deeper and deeper into the Underdark. They were little known in recent times, and considered no more than a legend among many orc tribes.

But the Wolf Jaw orcs and their allies of tribe Yellow Fang, Toogwik Tuk's kin, knew better.

"They are only three hundred strong," Toogwik Tuk reminded the doubters.

A second rumbling from *Kokto Gung Karuck* shook the stones.

"Indeed," said Dnark, and he shook his head.

"We must go and find Chieftain Grguch quickly," Toogwik Tuk said. "The eagerness of Karuck's warriors must be properly steered. If they come upon other tribes and do battle and plunder . . ."

"Then Obould will use that as more proof that his way is better," Dnark finished.

"Let us go," said Toogwik Tuk, and he took a step forward. Dnark moved to follow, but Ung-thol hesitated. The other two paused and regarded the older shaman.

"We do not know Obould's plan," Ung-thol reminded.

"He has stopped," said Toogwik Tuk.

"To strengthen? To consider the best road?" asked Ung-thol.

"To build and to hold his meager gains!" the other shaman argued.

"Obould's consort has told us as much," Dnark added, and a knowing grin crossed his tusky face, his lips, all twisted from teeth that jutted in a myriad of random directions, turning up with understanding. "You have known Obould for many years."

"And his father before him," Ung-thol conceded. "And I have followed him here to glory." He paused and looked around for effect. "We have not known victory such as this—" he paused again and lifted his arms high—"in living memory. It is Obould who has done this."

"It is the start, and not the end," Dnark replied.

"Many great warriors fall along the road of conquest," added Toogwik Tuk. "That is the will of Gruumsh. That is the glory of Gruumsh."

All three started in surprise as the great bass note of *Kokto Gung Karuck* again resonated across the stones.

Toogwik Tuk and Dnark stood quiet then, staring at Ung-thol, awaiting his decision.

The older orc shaman gave a wistful look back to the southwest, the area where they knew Obould to be, then nodded at his two companions and bade them to lead on.

* * * * *

The young priestess Kna curled around him seductively. Her lithe body slowly slid around the powerful orc, her breath hot on the side of his neck, then the back of his neck, then the other side. But while Kna stared intensely at the great orc as she moved, her performance was not for Obould's benefit.

King Obould knew that, of course, so his smile was double-edged as he stood there before the gathering of shamans and chieftains. He had chosen wisely in making the young, self-absorbed Kna his consort replacement for Tsinka Shinriil. Kna held no reservations. She welcomed the stares of all around as she writhed over King Obould. More than welcomed, Obould knew. She craved them. It was her moment of glory, and she knew that her peers across the kingdom clenched their fists in jealousy. That was her paramount pleasure.

Young and quite attractive by the standards of her race, Kna had entered the priesthood of Gruumsh, but was not nearly as devout or fanatical as Tsinka had been. Kna's god—goddess—was Kna, a purely self-centered view of the world that was so common among the young.

And just what King Obould needed. Tsinka had served him well in her tenure, in bed and out, for she had always spoken in the interests of Gruumsh. Feverishly so. Tsinka had arranged the magical ceremony that had imbued in Obould great prowess both physical and mental, but her devotion was absolute and her vision narrow. She had outlived her usefulness to the orc king before she had been thrown from the lip of the ravine, to fall to her death among the stones.

Obould missed Tsinka. For all of her physical beauty, practiced movements and enthusiasm for the position, Kna was no Tsinka in lovemaking. Nor was Kna possessed of Tsinka's intellect and cunning, not by any means. She could whisper nothing into Obould's ear worth listening to, regarding anything other than coupling. And so she was perfect.

King Obould was clear in his vision, and it was one shared by a collection of steady shamans, most notably a small, young orc named Nukkels. Beyond that group, Obould needed no advice and desired no nay-saying. And most of all, he needed a consort he could trust. Kna was too enamored of Kna to worry about politics, plots and varying interpretations of Gruumsh's desires.

He let her continue her display for a short while longer then gently but solidly pried her from his side and put her back to arms' length. He motioned for her to go to a chair, to which she returned an exaggerated pout. He gave her a resigned shrug to placate her and worked hard to keep his utter contempt for her well suppressed. The orc king motioned again to the chair, and when she hesitated, he forcefully guided her to it.

She started to protest, but Obould held up his huge fist, reminding her in no uncertain terms that she was nearing the limits of his

R. A. SALVATORE

patience. As she settled into a quiet pout, the orc king turned back to his audience, and motioned to Tornfang Brakk, a courier from General Dukka, who oversaw the most important military region.

"The valley known as Keeper's Dale is well secured, God-king," Tornfang reported. "The ground has been broken to prevent easy passage and the structures topping the northern wall of the valley are nearly complete. The dwarves cannot come out."

"Even now?" Obould asked. "Not in the spring, but even now?"

"Even now, Greatness," Tornfang answered with confidence, and Obould wondered just how many titles his people would bestow upon him.

"If the dwarves came forth from Mithral Hall's western doors, we would slaughter them in the valley from on high," Tornfang assured the gathering. "Even if some of the ugly dwarves managed to cross the ground to the west, they would find no escape. The walls are in place, and the army of General Dukka is properly entrenched."

"But can we go in?" asked Chieftain Grimsmal of Clan Grimm, a populous and important tribe.

Obould flashed the impertinent orc a less-than-appreciative glare, for that was the most loaded and dangerous question of all. That was the point of contention, the source of all the whispers and all the arguing between the various factions. Behind Obould they had trampled the ground flat and had marched to glory not known in decades, perhaps centuries. But many were openly asking, to what end? To further conquest and plunder? To the caves of a dwarf clan or to the avenues of a great human or elven city?

As he considered things, however, particularly the whispers among the various shamans and chieftains, Obould came to realize that Grimsmal might have just done him a favor, though inadvertently.

"No," Obould declared solidly, before the bristling could really begin. "The dwarves have their hole. They keep their hole."

"For now," the obstinate Grimsmal dared utter.

Obould didn't answer, other than to grin—though whether it was one of simple amusement or agreement, none could tell.

"The dwarves are out of their hole in the east," reminded another of the gathering, a slight creature in a shaman's garb. "They build through the winter along the ridgeline. They now seek to connect and strengthen walls and towers, from their gates to the great river."

38

"And foundations along the bank," another added.

"They will construct a bridge," Obould reasoned.

"The foolish dwarves do our work for us!" Grimsmal roared. "They will grant us easier passage to wider lands."

The others all nodded and grinned, and a couple slapped each other on the back.

Obould, too, grinned. The bridge would indeed serve the Kingdom of Many-Arrows. He glanced over at Nukkels, who returned his contented look and offered a slight nod in reply.

Indeed, the bridge would serve, Obould knew, but hardly in the manner that Grimsmal and many of the others, so eager for war, now envisioned.

While the chatter continued around him, King Obould quietly imagined an orc city just to the north of the defenses the dwarves were constructing along the mountain ridge. It would be a large settlement, with wide streets to accommodate caravans, and strong buildings suitable for the storage of many goods. Obould would need to wall it in to protect from bandits, or overeager warrior orcs, so that the merchants who arrived from across King Bruenor's bridge would rest easy and with confidence before beginning their return journey.

The sound of his name drew the orc king from his contemplations, and he looked up to see many curious stares aimed at him. Obviously he had missed a question.

It did not matter.

He offered a calm and disarming smile in response and used the hunger for battle permeating the air around him to remind himself that they were a long, long way from constructing such a city.

But what a magnificent achievement it would be.

* * * * *

"The yellow banner of Karuck," Toogwik Tuk informed his two companions as the trio made their way along a winding, snow-filled valley below the cave that served as the primary exit point for orcs leaving the Underdark.

Dnark and Ung-thol squinted in the midday glare, and both nodded as they sorted out the two yellow pennants shot with red that flew in the stiff, wintry wind. They had known they were getting close, for they had crossed through a pair of hastily abandoned campsites in the sheltered valley. Clan Karuck's march had apparently sent other orcs running fast and far.

Toogwik Tuk led the way up the rocky incline that ramped up between those banners. Hulking orc guards stood to block the way, holding pole arms of various elaborate designs, with side blades and angled spear tips. Half axe and half spear, the weight of the weapons was intimidating enough, but just to enhance their trepidation, the approaching trio couldn't miss the ease with which the Karuck guards handled the heavy implements.

"They are as large as Obould," Ung-thol quietly remarked. "And they are just common guards."

"The orcs of Karuck who do not achieve such size and strength are slave fodder, so it is said," Dnark said.

"And so it is true," Toogwik Tuk said, turning back to the pair. "Nor are any of the runts allowed to breed. They are castrated at an early age, if they are fortunate."

"And my eagerness grows," said Ung-thol, who was the smallest of the trio. In his younger years, he had been a fine warrior, but a wound had left him somewhat infirm, and the shaman had lost quite a bit of weight and muscle over the intervening two decades.

"Rest easy, for you are too old to be worth castrating," Dnark chided, and he motioned for Toogwik Tuk to go and announce them to the guards.

Apparently the younger priest had laid the groundwork well, for the trio was ushered along the trail to the main encampment. Soon after, they stood before the imposing Grguch and his war priest advisor, Hakuun. Grguch sat on a chair of boulders, his fearsome double-bladed battle-axe in hand. The weapon, Rampant by name, was obviously quite heavy, but Grguch easily lifted it before him with one hand. He turned it slowly, so that his guests would get a good view, and a good understanding of the many ways Rampant could kill them. The black metal handle of the axe, which protruded up past the opposing "wing" blades, was shaped in the form of a stretching and turning dragon, its small forelegs pulled in close and the widespread horns on its head presenting a formidable spear tip. At the base, the dragon's long tail curved up and over the grip, forming a guard. Spines extended all along the length so that a punch from Grguch would hit like the stab of several daggers. Most impressive were the blades, the symmetrical wings of the beast. Of shining silver mithral, they fanned out top and bottom, reinforced every finger's-breadth or so by a thin bar of dark adamantine, which created spines top and bottom along each blade. The convex edges were as long as the distance from Dnark's elbow to the tips of his extended fingers, and none of the three visitors had any trouble imagining being cut cleanly in half by a single swipe of Rampant.

"Welcome to Many-Arrows, great Grguch," Toogwik Tuk said with a respectful bow. "The presence of Clan Karuck and its worthy leader makes us greater."

Grguch led his gaze drift slowly across the three visitors then around the gathering to Hakuun. "You will learn the truth of your hopeful claim," he said, his eyes turning back to Toogwik Tuk, "when I have the bones of dwarves and elves and ugly humans to crush beneath my boot."

Dnark couldn't suppress a grin as he looked to Ung-thol, who seemed similarly pleased. Despite their squeamishness at being so badly outnumbered among the fierce and unpredictable tribe, things were going quite well.

* * * * *

Out of the same cavern from which Grguch and Clan Karuck had emerged came a figure much less imposing, save to those folk who held a particular phobia of snakes. Fluttering on wings that seemed more suited to a large butterfly, the reptilian creature wove a swaying, zig-zagging course through the chamber, toward the waning daylight.

The twilight was brighter than anything the creature had seen in a century, and it had to set down inside the cave and spend a long, long while letting its eyes properly adjust.

"Ah, Hakuun, why have you done this?" asked the wizard, who was not really a snake, let alone a flying one. Anyone nearby might have thought it a curious thing to hear a winged snake sigh.

He slithered into a darker corner, and peeked out only occasion-ally to let his eyes adjust.

He knew the answer to his own question. The only reason the brutes of Clan Karuck would come forth would be for plunder and war. And while war could be an interesting spectacle, the wizard Jack, or Jack the Gnome as he had once been commonly called, really didn't have time for it just then. His studies had taken him deep into the bowels of the Spine of the World, and his easy manipulation of Clan Karuck, from Hakuun's father's father's father's father, had provided him with most excellent cover for his endeavors, to say nothing of the glory it had rained upon Hakuun's miserable little family.

Quite a while later, and only with the last hints of daylight left in the air, Jack slipped up to the cavern exit and peered out over the vast landscape. A couple of spells would allow him to locate Hakuun and the others, of course, but the perceptive fellow didn't need any magic to sense that something was ... different. Something barely distinguishable in the air—a scent or distant sounds, perhaps—pricked at Jack's sensibilities. He had lived on the surface once, far back beyond his memories, before he had fallen in with the illithids and demons in his quest to learn magic more powerful and devious than the typical evocations of mundane spellcasters. He had lived on the surface when he truly was a gnome, something he could hardly claim anymore. He only rarely wore that guise, and had come to understand that physical form really wasn't all that important or defining anyway. He was a blessed thing, he knew, mostly thanks to the illithids, because he had learned to escape the bounds of the corporeal and of the mortal.

A sense of pity came over him as he looked out over the wide lands, populated by creatures so inferior, creatures who didn't understand the truth of the multiverse, or the real power of magic.

That was Jack's armor as he looked out over the land, for he needed such pride to suppress the other, inevitable feelings that whirled in his thoughts and in his heart. For all of his superiority, Jack had spent the last century or more almost completely alone, and while he had found wondrous revelations and new spells in his amazing workshop, with its alchemical equipment and reams of parchments and endless ink and spellbooks he could stack to several times his gnomish height, only by lying to himself could Jack even begin to accept the paradoxical twist of fate afforded him by practical immortality. For while—and perhaps because—he wouldn't die anytime soon of natural causes, Jack was acutely aware that the world was full of mortal danger. Long life had come to mean "more to lose," and Jack had been walled into his secure laboratory as much by fear as by the thick stones of the Underdark.

That laboratory, hidden and magically warded, remained secure even though his unwitting protectors, Clan Karuck, had traveled out of the Underdark. And still, Jack had followed them. He had followed Hakuun, though the pathetic Hakuun was hardly worth following, because, he knew deep inside but wasn't quite ready to admit, he had wanted to come back, to remember the last time he was Jack the Gnome.

He found himself pleasantly surprised by the view. Something tingled in the air around him, something exciting and teeming with possibility.

Perhaps he didn't know the extent of Hakuun's reasoning in allowing Grguch to come forth, Jack thought, and he was intrigued.

CHAPTER

THE SIMPLE QUALITY OF TIMES GONE BY

Wulfgar's long, powerful legs drove through the knee-deep—often hip-deep—snow, plowing a path north from the mountain ridge. Rather than perceive the snow as a hindrance, though, Wulfgar considered it a freeing experience. That kind of trailblazing reminded him of the crisp air of home, and in a more practical sense, the snow slowed to a grumbling halt the pair of dwarven sentries who stubbornly pursued him.

More snow fell, and the wind blew cold from the north, promising yet another storm. But Wulfgar did not fear, and his smile was genuine as he drove forward. He kept the river on his immediate right and scrolled through his thoughts all of the landmarks Ivan Boulder-shoulder had told him regarding the trail leading to the body of Delly Curtic. Wulfgar had grilled Ivan and Pikel on the details before they had departed Mithral Hall.

The cold wind, the stinging snow, the pressure on his legs from winter's deep . . . it all felt right to Wulfgar, familiar and comforting, and he knew in his heart that his course was the right one. He drove on all the harder, his stride purposeful and powerful, and no snow drift could slow him.

The calls of protest from Bruenor's kin dissipated into nothingness behind him, defeated by the wall of wind, and very soon the fortifications and towers, and the mountain ridge itself became indistinct black splotches in the distant background.

He was alone and he was free. He had no one on whom he could rely, but no one for whom he was responsible. It was just Wulfgar, son of Beornegar, ranging through the deep winter snow, against the wind of the newest storm. He was just a lone adventurer, whose path was his own to choose, and who had found, to his thrill, a road worth walking.

Despite the cold, despite the danger, despite the missing Colson, despite Delly's death and Catti-brie's relationship with Drizzt, Wulfgar knew only simple joy.

He traveled on long after the dim light had waned to darkness, until the cold night air became too intense for even a proud son of the frozen tundra to bear. He set up camp under the lowest boughs of thick pines, behind insulating walls of snow, where the wind could not find him. He passed the night in dreams of the caribou, and the wandering tribes that followed the herd. He envisioned his friends, all of them, beside him in the shadow of Kelvin's Cairn.

He slept well, and went out early the next day, under the gray sky.

The land was not unfamiliar to Wulfgar, who had spent years in Mithral Hall, and even as he had exited the eastern door of the dwarven complex, he had a good idea of where Ivan and Pikel had found the body of poor Delly. He would get there that day, he knew, but reminded himself repeatedly of the need for caution. He had left friendly lands, and from the moment he had crossed the dwarven battlements on the mountain spur, he was outside the realm of civilization. Wulfgar passed several encampments, the dark smoke of campfires curling lazily into the air, and he didn't need to get close enough to see the campers to know their orc heritage and their malicious intent.

He was glad that the daylight was dim.

The snow began again soon after midday, but it was not the driving stuff of the previous night. Puffy flakes danced lightly on the air, trailing a meandering course to the ground, for there was no wind other than the occasional small whisper of a breeze. Despite having to continually watch for signs of orcs and other monsters, Wulfgar made great progress, and the afternoon was still young when he breached one small rocky rise to look down upon a bowl-shaped dell.

Wulfgar held his breath as he scanned the region. Across the way, beyond the opposite rise, rose the smoke of several campfires, and in the small vale itself Wulfgar saw the remains of an older, deserted encampment. For though the dell was sheltered, the wind had found its way in on the previous day, and had driven the snow to the southeastern reaches, leaving a large portion of the bowl practically uncovered. Wulfgar could clearly see a half-covered ring of small stones, the remains of a cooking pit.

Exactly as Ivan Bouldershoulder had described it.

With a great sigh, the barbarian pulled himself over the ridge and began a slow and deliberate trudge into the dell. He slid his feet along slowly rather than lift them, aware that he might trip over a body buried beneath the foot or so of snow that blanketed the ground. He set a path that took him straight to the cooking pit, then lined himself up as Ivan had described and slowly made his way back out. It took him a long while, but sure enough, he noticed a bluish hand protruding from the edge of the snow.

Wulfgar knelt beside it and reverently brushed back the white powder. It was Delly, unmistakably so, for the deep freeze of winter had only intensified after her fall those months before, and little decomposition had set in. Her face was bloated, but not greatly, and her features were not too badly distorted.

She looked as if she were asleep and at peace, and it occurred to Wulfgar that the poor woman had never known such serenity in all of her life.

A pang of guilt stung him at that realization, for in the end, that truth had been no small part his own fault. He recalled their last conversations, when Delly had subtly and quietly begged him to get her out of Mithral Hall, when she had pleaded with him to free her from the confines of the dwarf-hewn tunnels.

"But I am a stupid one," he whispered to her, gently stroking her face. "Would that you had said it more directly, and yet I fear that still I would not have heard you."

She had given up everything to follow him to Mithral Hall. Truly her impoverished life in Luskan had not been an enviable existence. But still, in Luskan Delly Curtie had friends who were as her family, had a warm bed and food to eat. She had abandoned that much at least for Wulfgar and Colson, and had held up her end of that bargain all the way to Mithral Hall and beyond.

In the end, she had failed. Because of Catti-brie's evil and sentient sword, to be sure, but also because the man she had trusted to stand beside her had not been able to hear and recognize her quiet desperation.

"Forgive me," Wulfgar said, and he bent low to kiss her cold cheek. He rose back to his knees and blinked, for suddenly the dim daylight stung his eyes.

Wulfgar stood.

"Ma la, bo gor du wanak," he said, an ancient barbarian way of accepting resignation, a remark without direct translation to the common tongue.

It was a lament that the world "is as it would be," as the gods would have it, and it was the place of men to accept and discover their best path from what was presented them. Hearing the somewhat stilted and less-flowing tongue of the Icewind Dale barbarians rolling so easily from his lips gave Wulfgar pause. He never used that language anymore, and yet it had come back to him so easily just then.

With the winter thick about him, in the crisp and chill air, and with tragedy lying at his feet, the words had come to him, unbidden and irresistible.

"Ma la, bo gor du wanak," he repeated in a whisper as he looked down at Delly Curtie.

His gaze slid across the bowl to the rising lines of campfire smoke. His expression shifted from grimace to wicked grin as he lifted Aegis-fang into his hands, his current "best path" crystallizing in his thoughts.

Beyond the northern rim of the dell, the ground dropped away sharply for more than a dozen feet, but not far from the ridge sat a small plateau, a single flat-topped jut of stone, like the trunk of a gigantic, ancient tree. The main orc encampment encircled the base of that plinth, but the first thing Wulfgar saw when he charged over the rim of the dell was the single tent and the trio of orc sentries stationed there.

Aegis-fang led the way, trailing the leaping barbarian's cry to the war god Tempus. The spinning warhammer took the closest orc sentry in the chest and blew him across the breadth of the ten-foot diameter pillar, spreading the snow cover like the prow of a speeding ship before dropping him off the back side.

Encumbered by layers of heavy clothing and with only slippery footing beneath, Wulfgar didn't quite clear the fifteen-foot distance, and slammed his shins against the ledge of the pillar, which sent him sprawling into the snow. Roaring with battle-frenzy, thrashing about so that he would present no clear target to the remaining two orcs, the barbarian quickly got his hands under him and heaved himself to his feet. His shins were bleeding but he felt no pain, and he barreled forward at the nearest orc, who lifted a spear to block.

Wulfgar slapped the feeble weapon aside and bore in, grasping the front of the orc's heavy fur wrap. As he simply ran the creature over, Wulfgar caught a second grip down by the orc's groin, and he hoisted his enemy up over his head. He spun toward the remaining orc and let fly, but that last orc dropped low beneath the living missile, who went flailing into the small tent and took it with him in his continuing flight over the far side of the pillar.

The remaining orc took up its sword in both hands, lifting the heavy blade over its head, and charged at Wulfgar with abandon.

He had seen such eagerness many times before in his enemies, for, as was often the case, Wulfgar appeared unarmed. But as the orc came in, Aegis-fang magically reappeared in Wulfgar's waiting grasp, and he jabbed it ahead with one hand. The heavy hammerhead connected solidly on the chest of the charging orc.

The creature stopped as though it had rammed into a stone wall.

Wulfgar drew back Aegis-fang and took it up in both hands to strike again, but the orc made no move at all, just stood there staring at him blankly. He watched as the sword slipped from the creature's grasp, to fall to the ground behind it. Then, before he could strike, the orc simply fell over.

Wulfgar sprinted past it to the edge of the pillar. Below him, orcs scrambled, trying to discern the threat that had come so unexpectedly. One orc lifted a bow Wulfgar's way, but too slowly, for Aegis-fang was already spinning its way. The warhammer crashed through the orc's knuckles and laid the archer low.

Wulfgar leaped from the pillar, right over the nearest duo, who had set spears pointed his way. He crashed among a second group, far less prepared, and drove one down below his descending knee, and knocked two others aside with his falling bulk. He managed to keep his footing somehow, and staggered forward, beyond the reach of the spear-wielders. He used that momentum to flatten the next orc in line with a heavy punch, then grabbed the next and lifted it before him in his run, using its body as a shield as he charged into the raised swords of a pair of confused sentries.

Aegis-fang returned to him, and a mighty strike sent all of that trio flying to the ground. Purely on instinct, Wulfgar halted his momentum and pivoted, Aegis-fang swiping across to shatter the spears and arms of creatures coming in at his back. The overwhelmed orcs fell away in a jumble and Wulfgar, not daring to pause, ran off.

He crashed through the side of a tent, his hammer tearing the deerskin from the wooden supports. He dragged his feet and kicked powerfully, scattering bedrolls and supplies, and a pair of young orcs who crawled off yelping.

That pair was no threat to him, Wulfgar realized, so he didn't pursue, veering instead for the next that raised weapons against him. He came in swinging, rolling his arms in circles above his head. Aegis-fang hummed as it cut through the air. The three orcs fell back, but one tripped and went to the ground. It dropped its weapon and tried to scramble away, but Wulfgar kicked it hard on the hip, sending it sprawling. Stubbornly the orc rolled to its belly and hopped up to all fours, trying to get its feet under it for a dash.

His great muscled arms straining and bulging, Wulfgar halted the spin of Aegis-fang, slid his lead hand up the handle, and jabbed at the orc. The warhammer smacked off the orc's shoulder and cracked into the side of its head, and the creature fell flat to the ground and lay very still.

Wulfgar stomped on it for good measure as he ran past in pursuit of its two companions, who had halted their retreat and stood ready.

Wulfgar roared and lifted Aegis-fang above his head, eagerly accepting the challenge. On he charged . . . but he noted something out of the corner of his eye. He dug in his lead foot, stopped abruptly, and tried to turn. Then he threw himself around, a spear grazing his side painfully. The missile caught in his flying wolf cloak and held fast, hanging awkwardly, its handle dragging on the ground and tangling with Wulfgar's legs as he continued his turn. He could only give it a fraction of his attention, though, for a second spear flew his way. Wulfgar brought Aegis-fang in close to his chest and turned it down at the last moment to crack the spearhead out of line. Still, the missile flipped over the parry and slapped against Wulfgar's shoulder.

As it went over, the back point of the weapon's triangular head cut the barbarian chin to cheek.

And as he lurched away, his leg caught the spear shaft hanging from his cloak.

To his credit, Wulfgar managed to not fall over, but he was off balance, his posture and the positioning of his weapon all wrong, as the two nearer orcs howled and leaped at him.

He drove Aegis-fang across his body, left to right, blocking a sword cut, but more with his arm than with the warhammer. He lifted his lower hand up desperately, turning the warhammer horizontal to parry a spear thrust from the other orc.

But the thrust was a feint, and Wulfgar missed cleanly. As the orc retracted, its smile was all the barbarian needed to see to know that he had no way to stop the second thrust from driving the spear deep into his belly.

He thought of Delly, lying cold in the snow.

* * * * *

Bruenor stood with Catti-brie outside the eastern door of Mithral Hall. North of them, construction was on in full, strengthening the wall that ran from the steep mountainside along the spur all the way to the river. As long as that wall could hold back the orcs, Clan Battlehammer remained connected above ground to the rest of the Silver Marches. The ferry across the River Surbrin, barely a hundred feet from where Bruenor and Catti-brie stood, would be running soon, and it would only be needed for a short while anyway. The abutments of a strong bridge were already in place on both banks.

The orcs could not get at them from the south without many days of forewarning, and such a journey through that broken ground would leave an army vulnerable at many junctures. With the line of catapults, archer posts, and other defensive assault points already set on the banks, particularly across the river, any orc assault using the river for passage would result in utter ruin for the attackers, much as it had for the dwarves of Citadel Felbarr when they had come to join the Battlehammer dwarves in their attempt to secure that most vital piece of ground.

Neither Bruenor nor Catti-brie were looking at the dwarven handiwork at that point, however. Both had their eyes and thoughts turned farther north, to where Wulfgar had unexpectedly gone.

"Ye ready to walk with him to Silverymoon?" Bruenor asked his adopted daughter after a long and uncomfortable silence, for the dwarf knew that Catti-brie harbored the very same feelings of dread as he.

"My leg hurts with every step," the woman admitted. "The boulder hit me good, and I don't know that I'll ever walk easy again."

Bruenor turned to her, his eyes moist. For she spoke the truth, he knew, and the clerics had told him in no uncertain terms. Catti-brie's injuries would never fully heal. The fight in the western entry hall had left her with a limp that she would carry for the rest of her days, and possibly with more damage still. Priest Cordio had confided to Bruenor his fears that Catti-brie would never bear children, particularly given that the woman was nearing the end of her childbearing years anyway.

"But I'm ready for the walk today," Catti-brie said with determination, and without the slightest hesitance. "If Wulfgar crossed over that wall right as we're speaking, I'd turn him to the river that we could be on our way. It is past time that Colson was returned to her father."

Bruenor managed a wide smile. "Ye be quick to get the girl and get ye back," he ordered. "The snows're letting go early this year, I'm thinking, and Gauntlgrym's waiting!"

"You believe that it really was Gauntlgrym?" Catti-brie dared to ask, and it was the first time anyone had actually put the most important question directly to the driven dwarf king. For on their journey back to Mithral Hall, before the coming of Obould, one of the caravan wagons had been swallowed up by a strange sinkhole, one that led, apparently, to an underground labyrinth. Bruenor had immediately proclaimed the place Gauntlgrym, an ancient and long-lost dwarven city, the pinnacle of power for the clan called Delzoun, a common heritage for all the dwarves of the North, Battlehammer, Mirabarran, Felbarran, and Adbarran alike.

"Gauntlgrym," Bruenor said with certainty, a claim he had been making in that tone since his return from the dead. "Moradin put me back here for a reason, girl, and that reason'll be shown to me when

I get meself to Gauntlgrym. There we'll be findin' the weapons we're needing to drive the ugly orcs back to their holes, don't ye doubt."

Catti-brie wasn't about to argue with him, because she knew that Bruenor was in no mood for any debate. She and Drizzt had spoken at length about the dwarf's plan, and about the possibility that the sinkhole had indeed been an entry point to the lost avenues of Gauntlgrym, and she had discussed it at length with Regis, as well, who had been poring over ancient maps and texts. The truth of it was that none of them had any idea whether or not the place was what Bruenor had decided it to be.

And Bruenor wasn't about to argue the point. His litany against the darkness that had settled on the land was a simple one, a single word: Gauntlgrym.

"Durn stubborn fool of a boy," Bruenor muttered, looking back to the north, his mind's eye well beyond the wall that blocked his view. "He's to slow it all down."

Catti-brie started to respond, but found that she could not speak past the lump that welled in her throat. Bruenor was complaining, of course, but in truth, his anger that Wulfgar's rash decision to run off alone into orc-held lands would slow the dwarves' plans was the most optimistic assessment of all.

The woman gave in to her sense of dread for just a moment, and wondered if her duty to her friend would send her off alone across the Surbrin in search of Colson. And in that case, once the toddler had been retrieved, what then?

CHAPTER

BUILDING HIS KINGDOM

4

The beams creaked for a moment, then a great rush of air swept across the onlookers as the counterweights sent the massive neck of the catapult swinging past. The basket released its contents, tri-pointed caltrops, in a line from the highest peak of the arc to the point of maximum momentum and distance.

The rain of black metal plummeted from sight, and King Obould moved quickly to the lip of the cliff to watch them drop to the floor of Keeper's Dale.

Nukkels, Kna, and some of the others shifted uneasily, not pleased to see their god-king standing so near to a two-hundred-foot drop. Any of General Dukka's soldiers, or more likely, proud Chieftain Grimsmal and his guards, could have rushed over and ended the rule of Obould with a simple shove.

But Grimsmal, despite his earlier rumblings of discontent, nodded appreciatively at the defenses that had been set up on the northern ridge overlooking Mithral Hall's sealed western door.

"We have filled the valley floor with caltrops," General Dukka assured Obould. He motioned to the many baskets set beside the line of catapults, all filled with stones ranging in size from a large fist to twice an orc's head. "If the ugly dwarves come forth, we'll shower them with death."

Obould looked down to the southwest, about two-thirds of the way across the broken valley from the dwarven complex, where a line of orcs chopped at the stone, digging a wide, deep trench. Directly to the king's left, atop the cliff at the end of the trench, sat a trio of catapults, all sighted to rake the length of the ravine should the dwarves try to use it for cover against the orcs positioned in the west.

Dukka's plan was easy enough to understand: he would slow any dwarven advance across Keeper's Dale as much as possible, so that his artillery and archers on high could inflict massive damage on the break-out army.

"They came out of the eastern wall with great speed and cunning," Obould warned the beaming general. "Encased in metal carts. A collapsed mountain wall did not slow them."

"From their door to the Surbrin was not far, my king," Dukka dared reply. "Keeper's Dale offers no such sanctuary."

"Do not underestimate them," Obould warned. He stepped closer to General Dukka as he spoke, and the other orc seemed to shrink in stature before him. His voice ominous and loud, so that all could hear, Obould roared out, "They will come out with *fury*. They will have brooms before them to sweep aside your caltrops, and shielding above to block your arrows and stones. They will have folding bridges, no doubt, and your trench will slow them not at all. King Bruenor is no fool, and does not charge into battle unprepared. The dwarves will know exactly where they need to go, and they will get there with all speed."

A long and uncomfortable silence followed, with many of the orcs looking at each other nervously.

"Do you expect them to come forth, my king?" Grimsmal asked.

"All that I expect from King Bruenor is that whatever he chooses to do, he will do it well, and with cunning," Obould replied, and more than one orc jaw fell open to hear such compliments for a dwarf coming forth from an orc king.

Obould considered those looks carefully in light of his disastrous attempt to break into Mithral Hall. He could not let any of them believe that he was speaking from weakness, from memories of his own bad judgment.

"Witness the devastation of the ridge where you now place your catapults," he said, waving his arm out to the west. Where once had stood a ridge line—one atop which Obould had placed allied frost giants and their huge war engines—loomed a torn and jagged crevice of shattered stones. "The dwarves are on their home ground. They know every stone, every rise, and every tunnel. They know how to fight. But *we* . . ." he roared, striding about for maximum effect, and lifting his clawing hands to the sky. He let the words hang in the air for many heartbeats before continuing, "We do not deny them the credit they deserve. We accept that they are formidable and worthy foes, and in that knowledge, we prepare."

He turned directly to General Dukka and Chieftain Grimsmal, who had edged closer together. "We know them, but even against what we have shown to them in conquering this land, they still do not know us. This"—he swept his arm out to encompass the catapults, archers, and all the rest—"they know, and expect. Your preparations are half done, General Dukka, and half done well. Now envision how King Bruenor will try to counter everything you have done, and complete your preparations to defeat that counter."

"B-but . . . my king?" General Dukka stammered.

"I have all confidence in you," Obould said. "Begin by trapping your own entrenchments on the western side of Keeper's Dale, so that if the dwarves reach that goal, your warriors can quickly retreat and leave them exposed on another battlefield of your choosing."

Dukka began to nod, his eyes shining, and his lips curled into a wicked grin.

"Tell me," Obould bade him.

"I can set a second force in the south to get to the doors behind them," the orc replied. "To cut off any dwarf army that charges across the valley."

"Or a second force that appears to do so," said Obould, and he paused and let all around him digest that strange response.

"So they will turn and run back," Dukka answered at length. "And then have to cross yet again to gain the ground they covet."

"I have never wavered in my faith in you, General Dukka," said Obould, and he nodded and even patted the beaming orc on the shoulder as he walked past.

His smile was twofold, and genuine. He had just strengthened the loyalty of an important general, and had impressed the potentially troublesome Grimsmal in the process. Obould knew what played in Grimsmal's mind as he swept up behind the departing entourage. If Obould, and apparently his commanders, could think so far ahead of

King Bruenor, then what might befall any orc chieftain who plotted against the King of Many-Arrows?

Those doubts were the real purpose of his visit to Keeper's Dale, after all, and not any concerns about General Dukka's readiness. For it was all moot, Obould understood. King Bruenor would never come forth from those western doors. As the dwarf had learned in his breakout to the east—and as Obould had learned in trying to flood into Mithral Hall—any such advance would demand too high a cost in blood.

* * * * *

Wulfgar screamed at the top of his lungs, as if his voice alone might somehow, impossibly, halt the thrust of the spear.

A blue-white flash stung the barbarian's eyes, and for a moment he thought it was the burning pain of the spear entering his belly. But when he came out of his blink, he saw the spear-wielding orc flipping awkwardly in front of him. The creature hit the ground limp, already dead, and by the time Wulfgar turned to face its companion that orc had dropped its sword and grasped and clawed at its chest. Blood poured from a wound, both front and back.

Wulfgar didn't understand. He jabbed his warhammer at the wounded orc and missed—another streaking arrow, a bolt of lightning, soared past Wulfgar and hit the orc in the shoulder, throwing it to the ground near its fallen comrade. Wulfgar knew that tell-tale missile, and he roared again and turned to face his rescuer.

He was surprised to see Drizzt, not Catti-brie, holding Taulmaril the Heartseeker.

The drow sprinted toward him, his light steps barely ruffling the blanket of deep snow. He started to nock another arrow, but tossed the bow aside instead and drew forth his two scimitars. He tossed a salute at Wulfgar then darted to the side as he neared, turning into a handful of battle-ready orcs.

"Biggrin!" Drizzt shouted as Wulfgar charged in his wake.

"Tempus!" the barbarian responded.

He put Aegis-fang up behind his head, and let it fly from both hands, the warhammer spinning end-over-end for the back of Drizzt's head.

Drizzt ducked and dropped to his knees at the last moment. The five orcs, following the drow's movements, had no time to react to the spinning surprise. At the last moment, the orcs threw up their arms defensively and tangled each other in their desperation to get out of the way. Aegis-fang took one squarely, and that flying orc clipped another enough to send both tumbling back.

The remaining three hadn't even begun to re-orient themselves to their opponents when the fury of Drizzt fell over them. He skidded on his knees as the hammer flew past, but leaped right back up to his feet and charged forward with abandon, his deadly blades crossing before him, going out wide, then coming back in another fast cross on the backhand. He counted on confusion, and confusion he found. The three orcs fell away in moments, slashed and stabbed.

Wulfgar, still chasing, summoned Aegis-fang back to his waiting hands, then veered inside the drow's turn so that his long legs brought him up beside Drizzt as they approached the encampment's main area of tents, where many orcs had gathered.

But those orcs would not stand against them, and any indecision the porcine humanoids might have had about running away was snapped away a moment later when a giant panther roared from the side.

Weapons went flying, and orcs went running, scattering to the winter's winds.

Wulfgar heaved Aegis-fang after the nearest, dropping it dead in its tracks. He put his head down and plowed on even faster—or started to, until Drizzt grabbed him by the arm and tugged him around.

"Let them go," the drow said. "There are many more about, and we will lose our advantage in the chase."

Wulfgar skidded to a stop and again called his magical war hammer back to his grasp. He took a moment to survey the dead, the wounded, and the fleeing orcs then met Drizzt's gaze and nodded, his bloodlust sated.

And he laughed. He couldn't help it. It came from somewhere deep inside, a desperate release, a burst of protest against the absurdity of his own actions. It came from those distant memories again, of running free in Icewind Dale. He had caught the "Biggrin" reference so easily, understanding in that single name that Drizzt wanted him to throw the warhammer at the back of the drow's head.

How was that even possible?

"Wulfgar has a desire to die?" Drizzt asked, and he, too, chuckled.

"I knew you would arrive. It is what you do."

* * * * *

Kna curled around his arm, rubbing his shoulder, purring and growling as always. Seated at the table in the tent, King Obould seemed not even to notice her, which of course only made her twist, curl, and growl even more intensely.

Across the table, General Dukka and Chieftain Grimsmal understood all too clearly that Kna was their reminder that Obould was above them, in ways they simply could never hope to attain.

"Five blocks free," General Dukka explained, "block" being the orc military term coined by Obould to indicate a column of one thousand warriors, marching ten abreast and one hundred deep. "Before the turn of Tarsakh."

"You can march them to the Surbrin, north of Mithral Hall, in five days," Chieftain Grimsmal remarked. "Four days if you drive them hard."

"I would drive them through the stones for the glory of King Obould!" Dukka replied.

Obould did not appear impressed.

"There is no need of such haste," he said at length, after sitting with a contemplative stare that had the other two chewing their lips in anticipation.

"The onset of Tarsakh will likely bring a clear path to the dwarven battlements," Chieftain Grimsmal dared to reply.

"A place we will not go."

The blunt response had Grimsmal sliding back in his chair, and brought a stupefied blink from Dukka.

"Perhaps I can free six blocks," the general said.

"Five or fifty changes nothing," Obould declared. "The ascent is not our wisest course."

"You know another route to strike at them?" Dukka asked.

"No," said Grimsmal, shaking his head as he looked knowingly at Obould. "The whispers are true, then. King Obould's war is over."

The chieftain wisely kept his tone flat and non-judgmental, but Dukka's wide eyes betrayed the general's shock, albeit briefly.

"We pause to see how many roads are open to us," Obould explained.

"Roads to victory?" asked General Dukka.

"Victory in ways you cannot yet imagine," said Obould, and he wagged his large head and showed a confident and toothy grin. For greater effect, he brought one of his huge fists up on the table before him, and clenched it tightly so that the muscles of his bare forearm bulged and twisted to proportions that pointedly reminded the other orcs of the superiority of this creature. Grimsmal was large by orc standards, and a mighty warrior, which was how he had attained the leadership of his warrior tribe, of course. But even he blanched before the spectacle of Obould's sheer power. Truly it seemed that if the orc king had been holding a block of granite in that hand, he would have easily ground it to dust.

No less overpowering was Obould's expression of supreme confidence and power, heightened by his disciplined detachment to Kna's writhing and purring at his side.

Grimsmal and General Dukka left that meeting having no idea what Obould was planning, but having no doubt of Obould's certainty in that plan. Obould watched them go with a knowing smile that the two would not plot against him. The orc king grabbed Kna and yanked her around before him, deciding that it was time to celebrate.

* * * * *

The body was frozen solid, and Wulfgar and Drizzt could not bend Delly's arms back down against her. Tenderly, Wulfgar took the blankets from his pack and wrapped them around her, keeping her face exposed to the last, as if he wanted her to see his sincere remorse and sorrow.

"She did not deserve this," Wulfgar said, standing straight and staring down at the poor woman. He looked at Drizzt, who stood with Guenhwyvar at his side, one hand on the tuft at the back of the panther's neck. "She had her life in Luskan before I arrived to steal her from it."

"She chose the road with you."

"Foolishly," Wulfgar replied with a self-deprecating laugh and sigh.

Drizzt shrugged as if the point was moot, which of course it was. "Many roads end suddenly, in the wilds and also in the alleyways of Luskan. There is no way of truly knowing where a road will lead until it is walked."

"Her trust in me was misplaced, I fear."

"You did not bring her out here to die," said Drizzt. "Nor did you drive her from the safety of Mithral Hall."

"I did not hear her calls for help. She told me that she could not suffer the dwarven tunnels, but I would not hear."

"And her way was clear across the Surbrin, had that been the route she truly wanted. You are no more to blame for this than is Catti-brie, who did not anticipate the reach of that wicked sword."

The mention of Catti-brie jolted Wulfgar a bit, for he knew that she felt the weight of guilt indeed about Khazid'hea's apparent role in Delly Curtie's tragic death.

"Sometimes what is, just is," said Drizzt. "An accident, a cruel twist of fate, a conjunction of forces that could not have been anticipated."

Wulfgar nodded, and it seemed as if a great weight had been lifted from his broad shoulders. "She did not deserve this," he said again.

"Nor did Dagnabbit, nor did Dagna, nor did Tarathiel, and so many others, like those who took Colson across the Surbrin," said Drizzt. "It is the tragedy of war, the inevitability of armies crashing together, the legacy of orcs and dwarves and elves and humans alike. Many roads end suddenly—it is a reality of which we should all be aware—and Delly could just as easily have fallen to a thief in the dark of Luskan's night, or have been caught in the middle of a brawl in the Cutlass. We know for certain only one thing, my friend, that we will one day share in Delly's fate. If we walk our roads solely to avoid such an inevitability, if we step with too much caution and concern . . ."

"Then we should just as well lie under the snow and let the cold find our bones," Wulfgar finished. He nodded with every word, assuring Drizzt that he needn't worry about the weight of harsh reality bending Wulfgar low.

"You will go for Colson?" Drizzt asked.

"How could I not? You speak of our responsibility to ourselves in choosing our roads with courage and acceptance, yet there remains our responsibility to others. Mine is to Colson. It is the pact I willingly accepted when I took her from Meralda of Auckney. Even if I were assured that she was safe with the goodly refugees who crossed the Surbrin, I could not abandon my promise to Colson's mother, nor to the girl."

"For yourself there is Gauntlgrym?" Wulfgar asked. "Beside Bruenor?"

"That is his expectation, and my duty to him, yes."

Wulfgar gave a nod and scanned the horizon.

"Perhaps Bruenor is right, and Gauntlgrym will show us an end to this war," said Drizzt.

"There will be another war close behind," Wulfgar said with a helpless shrug and chuckle. "It is the way of things."

"Biggrin," Drizzt said, drawing a smile from his large friend.

"Indeed," said Wulfgar. "If we cannot change the way of things, then we are wise to enjoy the journey."

"You knew that I would duck, yes?"

Wulfgar shrugged. "I figured that if you did not, it was   "

"—the way of things," Drizzt finished with him.

They shared a laugh and Wulfgar looked down at Delly once more, his face somber. "I will miss her. She was so much more than she appeared. A fine companion and mother. Her road was difficult for all her days, but she oft found within herself a sense of hope and even joy. My life is lessened with her passing. There is a hole within me that will not be easily filled."

"Which cannot be filled," Drizzt corrected. "That is the thing of loss. And so you will go on, and you will take solace in your memories of Delly, in the good things you shared. You will see her in Colson, though the girl was not of her womb. You will feel her beside you on occasion, and though the sadness will ever remain, it will settle behind treasured memories."

Wulfgar bent down and gently slid his arms beneath Delly and lifted her. It didn't appear as if he was holding a body, for the frozen form did not bend at all. But he hugged her close to his chest and moisture filled his bright blue eyes.

"Do you now hate Obould as much as I do?" Drizzt asked.

Wulfgar didn't reply, but the answer that came fast into his thoughts surprised him. Obould was just a name to him, not even a symbol on which he could focus his inner turmoil. Somehow he had moved past rage and into acceptance.

It is what it is, he thought, echoing Drizzt's earlier sentiments, and Obould diminished to become a circumstance, one of many. An orc, a thief, a dragon, a demon, an assassin from Calimport—it did not matter.

"It was good to fight beside you again," Wulfgar said, and in such a tone as to give Drizzt pause, for the words sounded more like a farewell than anything else.

Drizzt sent Guenhwyvar out to the point, and side-by-side, he and Wulfgar began their trek back to Mithral Hall, with Wulfgar holding Delly close all the way.

CHAPTER

TAKING ADVANTAGE

"Clan Grimm has turned north," Toogwik Tuk told his two com-panions on a clear, calm morning in the middle of Ches, the third month of the year. "King Obould has granted Chieftain Grimsmal a favorable region, a sheltered and wide plateau."

"To prepare?" asked Ung-thol.

"To build," Toogwik Tuk corrected. "To raise the banner of Clan Grimm beside the flag of Many-Arrows above their new village."

"Village?" Dnark asked, spitting the word with surprise.

"King Obould will claim that this is a needed pause to strengthen the lines of supply," Toogwik Tuk said.

"A reasonable claim," said Dnark.

"But one we know is only half true," Toogwik Tuk said.

"What of General Dukka?" asked an obviously agitated Ung-thol. "Has he secured Keeper's Dale?"

"Yes," the other shaman answered.

"And so he marches to the Surbrin?"

"No," said Toogwik Tuk. "General Dukka and his thousands have not moved, though there are rumors that he will assemble several blocks . . . eventually."

Dnark and Ung-thol exchanged concerned glances.

"King Obould would not allow that collection of warriors to filter back to their tribes," Dnark said. "He would not dare."

"But will he send them around to strike at the dwarves at the

Surbrin?" asked Ung-thol. "The dwarf battlements grow higher with each passing day."

"We expected Obould would not proceed," Toogwik Tuk reminded. "Is that not why we coaxed Grguch to the surface?"

Looking at his co-conspirators, Toogwik Tuk recognized that typical doubt right before the moment of truth. The three had long shared their concerns that Obould was veering from the path of conquest, and that was something they, as followers of Gruumsh One-eye, could not suffer. Their shared expectations, however, were that the war was not quite over, and that Obould would strike hard one more time at least, to gain a more advantageous position before his halt.

Leaving the dwarves open to the Surbrin had seemed a more distinct possibility over the past few months, and particularly the past few tendays. The weather was soon to turn, and the appropriate forces were not being moved into a strike position.

Still, in the face of it, the other two couldn't help but be surprised—and concerned, as the weight of their conspiracy settled more heavily on their shoulders.

"Turn them against the elf raiders in the east," Toogwik Tuk said suddenly, jolting his two companions, both of whom looked at him curiously, almost plaintively.

"We had hoped to use Grguch to force the charge to the Surbrin," Toogwik Tuk explained. "But with Obould's waiting to position the warriors, that is not presently an option. But we must offer Grguch some blood."

"Or he will take ours," Ung-thol muttered.

"There have been reports of elf skirmishers along the Surbrin, north of the dwarves," Dnark said, aiming his comment mostly at Ung-thol.

"Grguch and Clan Karuck will build a reputation that will serve them—and us—well when at last it comes to dealing with King Bruenor's troublesome beasts," Toogwik Tuk nudged. "Let us go and bring the Kingdom of Many-Arrows its newest hero."

* * * * *

Like a leaf fluttering silently on a midnight breeze, the dark elf slipped quietly to the side of the darkened stone and mud structure.

The orc guards hadn't noted his quiet passing, nor was he leaving any obvious tracks on the frozen snow.

No corporeal creature could move more stealthily than a trained drow, and Tos'un Armgo was proficient even by the lofty standards of his race.

He paused at the wall and glanced around at the cluster of structures—the village of Tungrush, he knew through the conversations he had overheard from various "villagers." He noted the foundation, even a growing base in several places, of a wall that would eventually ring the compound.

Too late, the drow thought with an evil grin.

He inched toward an opening in the house's back wall, though whether it was an actual window or just a gap that had not yet been properly fitted, he could not tell. Nor did it matter, for the missing stone provided ample egress for the lithe creature. Tos'un slithered in like a snake, walking his hands down the inside of the wall until they braced him against the floor. His roll, like all of his other movements, was executed without a whisper of sound.

The room was nearly pitch black, the meager starlight barely filtering through the many breaks in the stone. A surface dweller would have had little chance of quietly navigating the cluttered place. But to Tos'un, who had lived almost all of his life in the lightless corridors of the Underdark, the place verily glowed with brightness. He stood in the main room, twice the size of the smaller chamber sectioned by an interior wall that extended from the front wall to within three feet of the back. From beyond that partition, he heard snoring.

His two swords, one drow made and the other, the sentient and fabulous Khazid'hea, came out in his hands as he silently approached. At the wall, he peeked in to see a large orc sleeping comfortably, face down on a cot against the house's outer side wall. In the corner near the front of the house rested a large pile of rags.

He meant to quietly slide his sword into the orc's lungs, defeating its shout and finishing it quickly and silently. Khazid'hea, though, had other ideas, and as Tos'un neared and readied the strike, the sword overwhelmed him with a sudden and unexpected burst of sheer outrage.

Down came the blade, through the back of the orc's neck, severing its head and cutting through the wooden frame of the cot with ease, sparking off the floor and drawing a deep line in the hard ground. The cot dropped at the break, clunking down.

Behind Tos'un the rags rose fast, for under them was another orc, a female. Purely on reflex, the drow drove his other arm around, his fine Menzoberranyr sword coming in hard against the female's neck and pinning her up against the wall. That blade could have easily opened her throat, of course, but as he struck, Tos'un, for some reason that had not consciously registered, turned to the flat edge. He had the orc's voice choked off, and a line of blood appeared above the blade, but the creature was not finished.

For Khazid'hea would not suffer that inferior sword to score a kill.

Tos'un shushed the orc, who trembled but did not, could not, resist.

Khazid'hea plunged through her chest, right out her back and into, and through, the stones of the house's front wall.

Surprised by his own movement, Tos'un fast retracted the blade.

The orc stared at him with disbelief. She slipped down to the floor and died with that same expression.

Are you always so hungry? the drow's thoughts asked the sentient sword.

He sensed that Khazid'hea was laughing in response.

It didn't matter anyway, of course. It was just an orc, and even if it had been a superior being, Tos'un Armgo never shied from killing. With the witnesses dispatched, the alarms silenced, the drow went back into the main chamber and found the couple's store of food. He ate and drank, and replenished his pack and his waterskin. He took his time, perfectly at ease, and searched the house for anything that might be of service to him. He even went back into the bedroom, and on a whim, placed the male orc's severed head between its legs, its face pressed into its arse.

He considered his work with a resigned shrug. Like his food, the lonely drow had to take his amusement where he could find it.

He went out soon after, through the same window that had allowed him access. The night was dark—still the time of the drow. He found the orc guards no more alert than when he had come in, and he thought to kill them for their lack of discipline.

A movement in some distant trees caught his attention, however, and the drow was fast to the shadows. It took him some time to realize . . .

There were elves about.

Tos'un wasn't really surprised. Many Moonwood elves had been reconnoitering the various orc settlements and caravan routes. He had been captured by just such a band not so many tendays before, and had thought to join with them after deceiving them into believing that he was not their enemy.

Or was it really a deception? Tos'un hadn't yet decided. Surely a life among the elves would be better than what he had. He'd thought that then, and thought it again with wretched orc food still heavy in his belly.

But it was not an option, he reminded himself. Drizzt Do'Urden was with the elves, and Drizzt knew that he, Tos'un, had been part and party to King Obould's advance. Furthermore, Drizzt would take Khazid'hea from him, no doubt, and without the sword, Tos'un would be vulnerable to the spells of priests, detecting any lies he might need to weave.

Tos'un shook the futile debate from his thoughts before Khazid'hea could weigh in, and tried to get a better idea of how many elves might be watching Tungrush. He tried to pick out more movement, but found nothing substantial. The drow was wiser than to take any sense of relief from that, however, for he knew well that the elves could move with stealth akin to his own. They had, after all, surrounded him once without him ever knowing they were near.

He went out carefully, even calling upon his natural drow abilities and summoning a globe of darkness around him at one point, as he broke past the tree line. He continued his scan afterward, and even did a wide circuit of the village.

The perimeter was thick with elves, so Tos'un melted away into the winter night.

* * * * *

Albondiel's sword cut the air, and cut the throat of the orc. Gasping and clawing, the creature spun and stumbled. An arrow drove into its side, dropping it to the red-stained snow.

Another orc emerged from a house and shouted for the guards.

But the guards were all dead. All of them lay out on the perimeter, riddled with elven arrows. No alarms had sounded. The orcs of the village had not a whisper of warning.

The shouting, frantic orc tried to run, but an arrow drove her to her knees and an elf warrior was fast to her side, his sword silencing her forever.

After the initial assault, no orcs had come out in any semblance of defense. Almost all the remaining orcs were running, nothing more, to the edge of the village and beyond, willy-nilly into the snow. Most soon lay dead well within the village's perimeter, for the elves were ready, and fast and deadly with their bows.

"Enough," Albondiel called to his warriors and to the archers who moved to launch a barrage of death on the remaining fleeing orcs. "Let them run. Their terror works in our favor. Let them spread the word of doom, that more will flee beside them."

"You have little taste for this," noted another elf, a young warrior standing at Albondiel's side.

"I shy not at all from killing orcs," Albondiel answered, turning a stern gaze the upstart's way. "But this is less battle than slaughter."

"Because we were cunning in our approach."

Albondiel smirked and shrugged as if it did not matter. For indeed it did not, the wizened elf understood. The orcs had come, had swept down like a black plague, stomping underfoot all before them. They were to be repelled by any means. It was that simple.

Or was it, the elf wondered as he looked down at his latest kill, an unarmed creature, still gurgling as the last air escaped its lungs. It wore only its nightclothes.

Defenseless and dead.

Albondiel had spoken the truth in his response. He did not shy from battle, and had killed dozens of orcs in combat. Raiding villages, however, left a sour taste in his mouth.

A series of cries from across the way told him that some of the orcs had not fled or come out from their homes. He watched as one emerged from an open door, staggering, bleeding. It fell down dead.

A small one, a child.

With brutal efficiency, the elf raiding party collected the bodies in a large pile. Then they began emptying the houses of anything that would burn, tossing furniture, bedding, blankets, clothes, and all the rest on that same pile.

"Lord Albondiel," one called to him, motioning him to a small house on the village's northern perimeter.

As he approached the caller, Albondiel noted a stain of blood running down the stones at the front of the house, to the left side of the door. Following his summoner's movements, Albondiel saw the hole, a clean gash, through the stones—all the way through to the interior.

"Two were in there, dead before we arrived," the elf explained. "One was beheaded, and the other stabbed against this wall."

"*Inside* the wall," Albondiel remarked.

"Yes, and by a blade that came right through."

"Tos'un," Albondiel whispered, for he had been in Sinnafain's hunting party when she had captured the drow. The drow who carried Khazid'hea, the sword of Catti-brie. A sword that could cut through solid stone.

"When were they killed?" Albondiel asked.

"Before the dawn. No longer."

Albondiel shifted his gaze outward, beyond the limits of the village. "So he is still out there. Perhaps even watching us now."

"I can send scouts . . ."

"No," Albondiel answered. "There is no need, and I would have none of our people confront the rogue. Be on with our business here, and let us be gone."

Soon after, the pile of rags, wood, and bodies was set ablaze, and from that fire, the elves gathered brands with which to light the thatched roofs. Using fallen trees from the nearby woods, the elves battered down the sides of the burning structures, and any stones that could be pried from the smoking piles were quickly carried to the western side of the village, which was bordered by a long, steep slope, and were thrown down.

What the orcs had created on that windswept hilltop, the elves fast destroyed. To the ground. As if the ugly creatures had never been there.

When they left later that same morning, dark smoke still lifting into the air behind them, Albondiel swept his gaze long and wide across the rugged landscape, wondering if Tos'un might be looking back at him.

* * * * *

He was.

Tos'un Armgo let his gaze linger on the thickest line of black smoke drifting skyward and dissipating into the smothering gray of the continuing overcast. Though he didn't know the specific players in that scene—whether or not Albondiel or Sinnafain, or any of the others he had met, even traveled with, might be up there—they were Moonwood elves. Of that he had no doubt.

They were growing bolder, and more aggressive, and Tos'un knew why. The clouds would soon break, and the wind would shift southward, ferrying the milder breezes of spring. The elves sought to create chaos among the orc ranks. They wanted to inspire terror, confusion, and cowardice, to erode King Obould's foundations before the turn of the season allowed for the orc army to march against the dwarves in the south.

Or even across the river to the east, to the Moonwood, their precious home.

A pang of loneliness stabbed at Tos'un's thoughts and heart as he looked back at the burned village. He would have liked to join in that battle. More than that, the drow admitted, he would have liked departing with the victorious elves.

CHAPTER

FAREWELL

A thousand candles flickered on the northern side of the twenty-five foot square chamber, set in rows on a series of steps carved into the wall for just that purpose. A slab of gray stone leaned against the eastern wall, beside the closed wooden door. It had been expertly cut from the center of the floor, and on it, engraved in the Dethek runes of the dwarves:

DELENIA CURTIE OF LUSKAN AND MITHRAL HALL
WIFE OF WULFGAR, SON OF KING BRUENOR
MOTHER OF COLSON
WHO FELL TO THE DARKNESS OF OBOULD
IN THE YEAR OF THE UNSTRUNG HARP
1371 DALERECKONING
TO THIS HUMAN
MORADIN OFFERS HIS CUP
AND DUMATHOIN WHISPERS HIS SECRETS
BLESSED IS SHE

Over the hole that had been made when the slab was removed, a stone sarcophagus rested on two heavy wooden beams. A pair of ropes ran out to either side from under it. The box was closed and sealed after Wulfgar paid his final respects.

Wulfgar, Bruenor, Drizzt, Catti-brie, and Regis stood solemnly in a line before the sarcophagus and opposite the candles, while the

73

other guests attending the small ceremony fanned out in a semi-circle behind them. Across from them, the cleric Cordio Muffinhead read prayers to the dead. Wulfgar paid no heed to those words, but used the rhythms of Cordio's resonant voice to find a state of deep contemplation. He recalled the long and arduous road that had brought him there, from his fall in the grasp of the yochlol in the battle for Mithral Hall, to his years of torment at the hands of Errtu. He looked at Catti-brie only once, and regretted what might have been.

What might have been but could not be reclaimed, he knew. There was an old Dwarvish saying: *k'niko burger braz-pex strame*— "too much rubble over the vein"—to describe the point at which a mine simply wasn't worth the effort anymore. So it was with him and Catti-brie. Neither of them could go back. Wulfgar had known that when he had taken Delly as his wife, and he had been sincere in their relationship. That gave him comfort, but it only somewhat mitigated the pain and guilt. For though he had been sincere with Delly, he had not been much of a husband, had not heard her quiet pleas, had not placed her above all else.

Or could he even do that? Were his loyalties to Delly or to Mithral Hall?

He shook his head and pushed that justification away before it could find root. His responsibility was to bring both of those responsibilities to a place of agreement. Whatever his duties to Bruenor and Mithral Hall, he had failed Delly. To hide from that would be a lie, and a lie to himself would destroy him.

Cordio's chanting anesthetized him. He looked at the casket, and he remembered Delly Curtie, the good woman who had been his wife, and who had done so well by Colson. He accepted his own failure and he moved past it. To honor Delly would be to serve Colson, and to make of himself a better man.

Delly forgave him, he knew in his heart, as he would forgive her if the situation had been reversed. That was all they could do in the end, really. Do their best, accept their mistakes, and go on to a better way.

He felt her spirit all around him, and in him. His mind scrolled through images of the woman, flashes of Delly's smile, the tenderness on her face when they finished making love—a look, he knew without asking, that was reserved for him alone.

He recalled a moment when he had observed Delly dancing with Colson, unaware of his presence. In all the time he had known her, never had Wulfgar seen her so animated, so free, so full of life. It was as if, through Colson, and for just that moment, she had found a bit of her own childhood—or the childhood that harsh circumstances had never allowed her to truly experience. That had been Wulfgar's rawest glance into the soul of Delly Curtie, more so even than in their lovemaking.

That was the image that lingered, the image he burned into his consciousness. Forever after, he decided, when he thought of Delly Curtie, he would first envision her dancing with Colson.

A wistful smile creased his face by the time Cordio stopped his chanting. It took Wulfgar a few moments to realize that everyone was looking at him.

"He asked if you wished to say a few words," Drizzt quietly explained to Wulfgar.

Wulfgar nodded and looked around at the dwarves, and at Regis and Catti-brie.

"This is not where Delly Curtie would have chosen to be buried," he said bluntly. "For all of her love for Clan Battlehammer, she was not fond of the tunnels. But she would be . . . she is honored that so fine a folk have done this for her."

He looked at the casket and smiled again. "You deserved so much more than life ever offered to you. I am a better man for having known you, and I will carry you with me forever. Farewell, my wife and my love."

He felt a hand clasp his own, and turned to see Catti-brie beside him. Drizzt put his hand over both of theirs, and Regis and Bruenor moved to join in.

Delly deserved better, Wulfgar thought, and I am not deserving of such friends as these.

* * * * *

The sun climbed into the bright blue sky across the Surbrin before them. To the north along the battlements, the hammers rang out, along with a chorus of dwarf voices, singing and whistling as they went about their important work. Across the Surbrin, too, many dwarves and humans were hard at work, strengthening the bridge abutments and pillars and bringing up many of the materials they'd need to properly construct the bridge that summer. For a strong hint of spring was surely in the air that fifth day of Ches, and behind the five friends, rivulets of water danced down the stony mountainside.

"It will be a short window, I am told," Drizzt said to the others. "The river is not yet swollen with the spring melt, and so the ferry can cross. But once the melt is on in full, the pilots do not expect to execute many crossings. If you cross, you may not be able to get back until after the onset of Tarsakh, at least."

"There is no choice in the matter," said Wulfgar.

"It will take you tendays to get to Silverymoon and Sundabar and back anyway," said Regis.

"Especially since my legs aren't ready for running," said Catti-brie. She smiled as she spoke to let the others know that there was no regret or bitterness in her off-handed comment.

"Well, we ain't waitin' for Ches to become an old man," Bruenor grumbled. "If the weather's holding, then we're out for Gauntlgrym in days. I'm not for knowin' how long that's to take, but it'll be tendays, I'm guessing. Might be the whole durned summer."

Drizzt watched Wulfgar in particular, and noted the distance in the man's blue eyes. Bruenor might as well have been talking about Menzoberranzan or Calimport for all Wulfgar seemed to note or to care. He looked outward—to Colson.

And farther, Drizzt knew. It didn't matter to Wulfgar whether or not the Surbrin could be crossed again.

A few moments of silence slipped past, the five friends standing there in the morning sun. Drizzt knew that he should savor that moment, should burn it into his memory. Across from Bruenor, Regis shifted uneasily, and when Drizzt looked that way, he saw the halfling looking back at him, as if at a loss. Drizzt nodded at him and offered an accepting smile.

"The ferry docks," said Catti-brie, turning their attention to the river, where the boat was being quickly off-loaded. "Our road awaits."

Wulfgar nodded for her to lead on and make the arrangements, and with a curious glance at him, she did so, limping slightly and using Taulmaril as a crutch. As she went, Catti-brie kept glancing back, trying to decipher the curious scene. Wulfgar wore a serious expression as he spoke to the three, then he hugged each of them in turn. He ended with his hand firmly grasping Drizzt's wrist, the drow similarly holding him, and the two staring long at each other, with respect and what seemed to Catti-brie to be solemn agreement.

She suspected what that might foretell, but she turned her attention back to the river and the ferry, and cast those suspicions aside.

* * * * *

"Come on, elf," Bruenor said before Wulfgar had even caught up to Catti-brie at the ferry. "I'm wanting to get our maps in order for the trip. No time for wasting!"

Muttering to himself and rubbing his hands together, the dwarf moved back into the complex. Regis and Drizzt waited just a bit longer then turned and followed. They slowed in unison as they neared the open doors and the darkness of the corridor, and turned to look back to the river, and to the sun climbing into the sky beyond.

"Summer cannot come quickly enough for me," said Regis.

Drizzt didn't answer, but his expression wasn't one of disagreement.

"Though I almost fear it," Regis added, more quietly.

"Because the orcs will come?" asked Drizzt.

"Because others may not," said Regis, and he tossed a glance at the departing duo, who had boarded the ferry and were looking to the east, and not back.

Again, Drizzt didn't disagree. Bruenor was too preoccupied to see it, perhaps, but Regis's fears had confirmed Drizzt's suspicions about Wulfgar.

* * * * *

"Pwent's going with us," Bruenor announced to Drizzt and Regis when they caught up to him in his audience chamber later that day. As he spoke, he reached down to the side of his stone throne, lifted a pack, and tossed it to Drizzt.

"Just you three?" Regis asked, but he bit off the question as Bruenor reached down again and brought up a second pack, and tossed it the halfling's way.

Regis gave a little squeak and managed to get out of the way. The pack didn't hit the floor, though, for Drizzt snapped out his hand and plucked it from the air. The drow kept his arm extended, holding the pack out to the startled halfling.

"I'm needin' a sneak. Yerself's a sneak," Bruenor explained. "Besides, ye're the only one who's been into the place."

"Into the place?"

"Ye fell in the hole."

"I was only in there for a few moments!" Regis protested. "I didn't see anything other than the wag—"

"That makes yerself the expert," stated Bruenor.

Regis looked to Drizzt for help, but the drow just stood there holding out the satchel. With a look back to Bruenor and his unrelenting grin, the halfling gave a resigned sigh and took the pack.

"Torgar's coming, too," said Bruenor. "I'm wantin' them Mirabar boys in this from the beginning. Gauntlgrym's a Delzoun place, and Delzoun's including Torgar and his boys."

"Five, then?" asked Drizzt.

"And Cordio's making it six," Bruenor replied.

"In the morning?" asked Drizzt.

"The spring, the first of Tarsakh," Regis argued—rather helplessly, since he was holding a full pack, and since, as he spoke, he noted that Pwent, Torgar, and Cordio all entered the room from a side door, all with heavy packs slung over their shoulders, and Pwent in his full suit of ridged and spiked armor.

"No time better'n this time," said Bruenor. He stood up and gave a whistle, and a door opposite from the one the three dwarves had just used pushed open and Banak Brawnanvil rolled himself out. Behind him came a pair of younger dwarves, carrying Bruenor's mithral armor, his one-horned helmet, and his old and battle-worn axe.

"Seems our friend has been plotting without us," Drizzt remarked to Regis, who didn't seem amused.

"Yerself's got the throne and the hall," Bruenor said to Banak, and he moved down from the dais and tightly clasped his old friend's offered hand. "Ye don't be too good a steward, so that me folk won't want me back."

"Not possible, me king," said Banak. "I'd make 'em take ye back, even if it's just to guard me throne."

Bruenor answered that with a wide, toothy smile, his white teeth shining through his bushy orange-red beard. Few dwarves of Clan Battlehammer, or elsewhere for that matter, would speak to him with such irreverence, but Banak had more than earned the right.

"I'm goin' in peace because I'm knowing that I'm leaving yerself in charge behind me," Bruenor said in all seriousness.

Banak's smile disappeared and he gave his king a grateful nod.

"Come on, then, elf, and yerself, Rumblebelly," Bruenor called, slipping his mithral mail over his head and dropping his battered old one-horned helm on his head. "Me boys've dug us a hole out in the west so that we're not needing to cross all the way back over Garumn's Gorge, then back around the mountain. No time for wasting!"

"Yeah, but I'm not thinking that stoppin' to wipe out a fort o' them orcs is wastin' time," Thibbledorf Pwent remarked as he eagerly led the other two across in front of Drizzt and Regis and over to Bruenor. "Might that we'll find the dog Obould himself and be rid o' the beast all at once."

"Simply wonderful," Regis muttered, taking the pack and slinging it over his shoulder. He gave another sigh, one full of annoyance, when he saw that his small mace was strapped to the flap of the pack. Bruenor had taken care of every little detail, it seemed.

"The road to adventure, my friend," said Drizzt.

Regis smirked at him, but Drizzt only laughed. How many times had he seen that same look from the halfling over the years? Always the reluctant adventurer. But Drizzt knew, and so did everyone else in the room, that Regis was always there when needed. The sighs were just a game, a ritual that somehow allowed Regis to muster his heart and his resolve.

"I am pleased that we have an expert to lead us down this hole," Drizzt remarked quietly as they fell into line behind the trio of dwarves.

Regis sighed.

It occurred to Drizzt as they passed the room where Delly had just been interred that some were leaving who wanted to stay, and some were staying who wanted to leave. He thought of Wulfgar and wondered if that pattern would hold.

CHAPTER

7

It looked like a simple bear den, a small hole covered by a crisscross of broken branches blanketed by snow. Tos'un Armgo knew better, for he had built that facade. The bear den was at the end of a long but shallow tunnel, chosen because it allowed Tos'un to watch a small work detail composed mostly of goblins, constructing a bridge over a trench they apparently hoped would serve as an irrigation canal through the melt.

Northeast of that, sheltered in a ravine, the elves of the Moonwood plotted. If they decided on an attack, it would come soon, that night or the next day, for it was obvious that they were running short on supplies, and shorter on arrows. Tos'un, following them south to north then northeast, realized that they were heading for their preferred ford across the Surbrin and back to the sheltering boughs of the Moonwood. The drow suspected that they wouldn't ignore a last chance at a fight.

The sun climbed in the sky behind him, and Tos'un had to squint against the painful glare off the wet snow. He noted movement in the sky to the north, and caught a glimpse of a flying horse before it swerved out of sight behind a rocky mountain jag.

The elves favored midday assaults against the usually nocturnal goblins.

Tos'un didn't have to go far to find a fine vantage point for the coming festivities. He slipped into a recess between a pair of high stones, settling back just in time to see the first volley of elven arrows lead the way into the goblin camp. The creatures began howling, hooting, and running around.

So predictable, Tos'un's fingers signaled in the intricate, silent drow code.

Of course, he had seen many goblins in his decades in the Underdark, in Menzoberranzan, where the ugly things were more numerous among the slaves than any other race—other than the kobolds who lived in the channels along the great chasm known as the Clawrift. Goblins could be molded into fierce fighting groups, but the amount of work that required made it hardly worth the effort. Their natural "fight or flight" balance leaned very heavily in the direction of the latter.

And so it was in the valley below him. Goblins rushed every which way, and on came the skilled and disciplined elf warriors, their fine blades gleaming in the sun. It looked to be a fast and uneventful rout.

But then a yellow banner, shot with red so that it looked like the bloodshot eye of an orc, appeared in the west, moving quickly through a pass between a pair of small, round-topped hills. Tos'un peered hard, and harder still as the standard-bearer and its cohorts came into view. He could almost smell them from his perch. They were orcs, but huge by orc standards, even more broad-shouldered than Obould's elite guards, some even bigger than Obould himself.

So caught up in the spectacle, Tos'un stood up and leaned forward, out of the shelter of the stones. He looked back to the rout, and saw that there, too, things had changed, for other groups of those hulking orcs had appeared, some coming up from under the snow near the center of the battle.

"A trap for the elves," the drow whispered in disbelief. A myriad of thoughts flitted through his mind at that realization. Did he want the elves destroyed? Did he care?

He didn't allow himself time to sort through those emotions, though, for the drow realized that he, too, might get swept up in the tumult—and that was something he most certainly did not want.

He looked back to the approaching banner, then to the fight, then back again, measuring the time. With a quick glance all around to ensure his own safety, he rushed out from his perch and back to the hidden tunnel entrance. When he got there, he saw that the battle had been fully joined, and fully reversed.

The elves, badly outnumbered, were on the run. They didn't flee like the goblins, though, and kept their defenses in place against incursions from the brutish orcs. They even managed a couple of stop-and-pivot maneuvers that allowed them to send a volley of arrows at the orc mass.

But that dark wall rolled on after them.

The winged horse appeared again, flying low over the battlefield then climbing gradually as it passed over the orcs, who of course threw a few spears in its direction. The rider and pegasus went up even higher as they glided over the elves.

The rider meant to direct the retreat, obviously, and good fortune sent the winged horse in Tos'un's general direction. As it neared, the drow's eyes widened, for though looking up at the midday sky surely stung his sensitive eyes, he recognized that elf rider, Sinnafain.

For a moment, the drow held his position just inside the tunnel, not sure whether to retreat through the passage or go back out into Sinnafain's view.

Hardly aware of his movements, he came out of that hole and waved at Sinnafain, and when she didn't look his way, he called out to her.

What are you doing? Khazid'hea imparted to him.

The sudden jerk of the reins had the pegasus banking sharply and told Tos'un that Sinnafain had spotted him. He took some comfort in the fact that her next movement was not to draw out her bow.

You would go back to them? Khazid'hea asked and the telepathic communication was edged with no small amount of anger.

Sinnafain brought the winged horse in a slow turn, her eyes locked on the drow the entire time. She was too far away for Tos'un to see her face or fathom what she might be thinking, but still she did not draw her bow. Nor had she signaled to her retreating friends to veer away.

Drizzt will kill you! Khazid'hea warned. *When he takes me from you, you will find yourself defenseless against the truth-finding spells of elf clerics!*

Tos'un lifted the twig barrier that covered his hole, and began motioning to the entrance.

Sinnafain continued to guide the pegasus in a slow circle. When she at last turned back to her companions, Tos'un sprinted off to the side, disappearing into the shadows of the foothills, much to the relief of his demanding sword.

The drow glanced back only one time, to see the elves filtering into the tunnel. He looked up for the pegasus, but it had flown over the ridge and out of sight at that moment.

But Sinnafain had trusted him.

Unbelievably, Sinnafain had trusted him.

Tos'un wasn't sure whether he should take pride in that, or whether his respect for the elves had just diminished.

Perhaps a bit of both.

* * * * *

Sinnafain couldn't track their progress, nor could she join her comrades in the tunnel, obviously, while riding Sunrise. She came back over the high ridge and flew near the entrance of the small cave. She drew out her bow and began peppering the leading edge of the orc advance.

She kept up her barrage even after all the elves had disappeared underground. But the huge orcs carried heavy shields to frustrate such attacks, and Sinnafain could only hope that she had held them back long enough for her friends to escape. She put Sunrise up higher then, and angled back the other way, over the rise once more. She looked for Tos'un as much as for her friends, but there was no sign of the drow.

A long while later, with Sunrise tiring beneath her, the elf was finally able to breathe a sigh of relief, as a flash of white from a copse of trees some distance to the east signaled to her that Albondiel and the other elves had gotten through the tunnel.

Sinnafain took a roundabout route to get to them, not wanting to tip off any orc spotters who might watch her descending from on high, and by the time she got down to the ground, much activity was already underway. Deep in the woods, in a small clearing, the wounded had been laid out side by side, with priests tending them. Another group carried heavy logs and stones to seal the tunnel exit, and the rest had taken to the trees on the perimeter of the copse, setting up a defensive line that allowed them many overlapping angles of fire on approaching enemies.

As she walked Sunrise along a path through the trees, Sinnafain heard whispers of King Obould over and over again, many of the elves certain that he had come. She found Albondiel near the wounded, standing off to the side of the field and sorting the extra packs and weapons.

"You saved many," Albondiel greeted when she approached. "Had you not directed us to that tunnel, more of us would have fallen. Perhaps a complete rout."

Sinnafain thought to mention that it was not her doing, but that of a certain drow, but she kept the thought to herself. "How many were taken down?"

"Four casualties," Albondiel said grimly. He nodded toward the small field, where the quartet of wounded lay on blankets on the snow. "Two of them were wounded seriously, perhaps mortally."

"We . . . I, should have seen the trap from on high," Sinnafain said, turning back to the ridge in the east that blocked the view of the battlefield.

"The orc ambush was well set," Albondiel replied. "Those who prepared this battlefield understood our tactics well. They have studied us and learned to counter our methods. Perhaps it is time for us to head back across the Surbrin."

"We are low on supplies," Sinnafain reminded him.

"Perhaps it is time for us to *stay* across the Surbrin," Albondiel clarified.

Again, thoughts of a certain dark elf popped into Sinnafain's mind. Had Tos'un betrayed them? He had fought beside them for a short while, and he knew much of their tactics. Plus, he was a drow, and no race in all the world knew better how to lay an ambush than the treacherous dark elves. Though of course, he had shown the elves the way to escape. With any other race, that alone might serve to dispel Sinnafain's suspicions. But Sinnafain could not allow herself to forget that Tos'un was a dark elf, and no Drizzt Do'Urden, who had proven himself repeatedly over a matter of years. Perhaps Tos'un was playing the elves and orcs against each other for personal gain, or simply for his own amusement.

"Sinnafain?" Albondiel asked, drawing her from her contemplations. "The Surbrin? The Moonwood?"

"You believe that we are finished here?" Sinnafain asked.

"The weather warms, and the orcs will find it easier to move in the coming days. They will be less isolated from each other and so our work here will become more difficult."

"And they have taken note of us."

"It is time to leave," said Albondiel.

Sinnafain nodded and looked to the east. In the distance, the silvery line of the Surbrin could just be seen, flickering out on the horizon.

"Would that we could collect Tos'un on our way," said Sinnafain. "I have much to ask that one."

Albondiel looked at her with surprise for just a few moments then nodded his agreement. Though seemingly out of context, it sounded like a reasonable desire—of course they both knew that they weren't going to catch a drow in those wilds anytime soon.

* * * * *

I know them, Tos'un assured the doubting Khazid'hea. *Dnark is chieftain of an important tribe. I was the one who coaxed him into Obould's coalition before they ever marched from the Spine of the World.*

Much has happened, Khazid'hea reminded him, *between Tos'un and Obould. If these three know of your last encounter with the orc king, they will not welcome you.*

They were not there, Tos'un assured the sword.

They have not heard of the fall of Kaer'lic Suun Wett? Khazid'hea asked. *Can you be certain?*

Even if they have, they are well aware of Obould's temper, Tos'un imparted. *They will accept that he was outraged at Kaer'lic, and so he killed her. Do you believe that any of these orcs have not lost friends to the temper of Obould? And yet they remain loyal to him.*

You risk much.

I risk nothing, Tos'un argued. *If Dnark and his friends know that Obould hunts for me, or if they have concluded that I am in league with the elves, then I . . . then we, will have to kill them. I did not expect that such a result would displease Khazid'hea.*

There, he had communicated the magic words, he knew, for the sword fell silent in his thoughts, and he even sensed eagerness coming from it. He considered the exchange as he made his way down toward the trio of orcs, who had drifted off to the side of the construction area where the unusually large orcs had gathered. He came to the conclusion that he had been paid a compliment, that Khazid'hea did not want to be pried from his grasp.

He chose his path to the three orcs carefully, allowing himself a fast route of escape should the need arise—and he feared it would. Several times he paused to search the surrounding area for any guards he might have missed.

Still some distance from the three, he called out the expected, respectful refrain to the chieftain. "Hail Dnark, may the Wolf Jaw bite strong," he said in his best Orcish, but with no attempt to hide his Underdark drow accent. He watched carefully then to gauge their initial reaction, knowing that to be the bare truth.

All three turned his way, their expressions showing surprise, even shock. Tellingly, however, not one flinched toward a weapon.

"To the throat of your enemy," Tos'un finished the Wolf Jaw tribe's salute. He continued his approach, noting that Ung-thol, the older shaman, visibly relaxed, but that the younger Toogwik Tuk remained very much on edge.

"Well met, again," Tos'un offered, and he climbed the last small rise to gain the sheltered flat ground the trio had staked out. "We have come far from the holes in the Spine of the World, as I predicted to you those months ago."

"Greetings, Tos'un of Menzoberranzan," said Dnark.

The drow measured the chieftain's voice as cautious, and neither warm or cold.

"I am surprised to see you," Dnark finished.

"We have learned the fate of your companions," Ung-thol added.

Tos'un stiffened, and had to consciously remind himself not to grasp his sword hilts. "Yes, Donnia Soldou and Ad'non Kareese," he said. "I have heard their sad fate, and a curse upon the murderous Drizzt Do'Urden."

The three orcs exchanged smug grins. They knew of the murdered priestess, Tos'un realized.

"And pity to Kaer'lic," he said lightly, as if it didn't really matter. "Foolish was she who angered mighty Obould." He found a surprising response to that from Toogwik Tuk, for the young orc's smile disappeared, and his lips grew tight.

"She and you, so it is said," Ung-thol replied.

"I will prove my value again."

"To Obould?" asked Dnark.

The question caught the drow off-balance, for he had no idea of where the chieftain might be going with it.

"Is there another who would seek that value?" he asked, keeping enough sarcasm out of his tone so that Dnark might seize it as an honest question if he so chose.

"There are many above ground now, and scattered throughout the Kingdom of Many-Arrows," said Dnark. He glanced back at the hulking orcs milling around the construction area. "Grguch of Clan Karuck has come."

"I just witnessed his ferocity in routing the cursed surface elves."

"Strong allies," said Dnark.

"To Obould?" Tos'un asked without hesitation, turning the question back in similar measure.

"To Gruumsh," said Dnark with a toothy grin. "To the destruction of Clan Battlehammer and all the wretched dwarves and all the ugly elves."

"Strong allies," said Tos'un.

They are not pleased with King Obould, Khazid'hea said in the drow's mind. Tos'un didn't respond, other than to not disagree. *An interesting turn.*

Again the drow didn't disagree. A tingling feeling came over him, that exciting sensation that befell many of Lady Lolth's followers when they first discovered that an opportunity for mischief might soon present itself.

He thought of Sinnafain and her kin, but didn't dwell on them. The joy of chaos came precisely from the reality that it was often so very easy, and not requiring too much deep contemplation. Perhaps the coming mayhem would benefit the elves, perhaps the orcs, Dnark or Obould, one or both. That was not for Tos'un to determine. His duty was to ensure that no matter which way the tumult broke, he would be in the best position to survive and to profit.

For all of his time with the elves of late, for all of his fantasies of living among the surface folk, Tos'un Armgo remained, first and foremost, drow.

He sensed clearly that Khazid'hea very much approved.

* * * * *

Grguch was not pleased. He stomped across the hillside before the tunnel entrance and all of Clan Karuck fled before him. All except for Hakuun, of course. Hakuun could not flee before Grguch. It was not permitted. If Grguch decided that he wanted to kill Hakuun then Hakuun had to accept that as his fate. Being the shaman of Clan Karuck carried such a responsibility, and it was one that Hakuun's family had accepted throughout the generations—and was one that had cost more than a few of his family their lives.

He knew that Grguch would not cleave him in half, though. The chieftain was angry that the elves had escaped, but the battle could not be called anything but a victory for Clan Karuck. Not only had they stung a few of the elves, but they had sent them running, and had it not been for that troublesome tunnel, the raiding elf band never would have escaped complete and utter ruin.

The hulking brutes of Clan Karuck could not follow them through that tunnel, however, to Grguch's ultimate frustration.

"This will not end here," he said in Hakuun's face.

"Of course not."

"I desired a greater statement to be made in our first meeting with these ugly faeric folk."

"The fleeing elves wore expressions of terror," Hakuun replied. "That will spread back to their people."

"Right before we fall upon them more decisively."

Hakuun paused, expecting the order.

"Plan it," said Grguch. "To their very home."

Hakuun nodded, and Grguch seemed satisfied with that and turned away, barking orders at the others. Elves were just the sort of cowardly creatures to run away and sneak back for quiet murder, of course, and so the chieftain began setting his defenses and his scouts, leaving Hakuun alone with his thoughts.

Or so Hakuun believed.

He flinched then froze when the foot-long serpent landed on his shoulder, and he held his breath, as he always did on those thankfully rare occasions when he found himself in the company of Jaculi—for that was the name that Jack had given him, the name of the winged serpent that Jack wore as a disguise when venturing out of his private workshops.

"I wish that you had informed me of your departure," Jack said in Hakuun's ear.

"I did not want to disturb you," Hakuun meekly replied, for it was hard for him to hold his steadiness with Jack's tongue flicking in his ear, close enough to send one of his forked lightning bolts right through the other side of poor Hakuun's head.

"Clan Karuck disturbs me often," Jack reminded him. "Sometimes I believe that you have told the others of me."

"Never that, O Awful One!"

Jack's laughter came out as a hiss. When he had first begun his domination and deception of the orcs those decades before, pragmatism alone had ruled his actions. But through the years he had come to accept the truth of it: he liked scaring the wits out of those ugly creatures! Truly, that was one of the few pleasures remaining for Jack the Gnome, who lived a life of simplicity and . . . And what? Boredom, he knew, and it stung him to admit it to himself. In the secret corners of his heart, Jack understood precisely why he had followed Karuck out of the caves: because his fear of danger, even of death, could not surmount his fear of letting everything stay the same.

"Why have you ventured out of the Underdark?" he demanded.

Hakuun shook his head. "If the tidings are true then there is much to be gained here."

"For Clan Karuck?"

"Yes."

"For Jaculi?"

Hakuun gulped and swallowed hard, and Jack hiss-laughed again into his ear.

"For Gruumsh," Hakuun dared whisper.

As weakly as it was said, that still gave Jack pause. For all of his domination of Hakuun's family, their fanatical service to Gruumsh had never been in question. It had once taken Jack an afternoon of torture to make one of Hakuun's ancestors—his grandfather, Jack believed, though he couldn't really remember—utter a single word against Gruumsh, and even then, the priest had soon after passed his duties down to his chosen son and killed himself in Gruumsh's name.

As he had in the cave, the gnome wizard sighed. With Gruumsh invoked, he wasn't about to turn Clan Karuck around.

"We shall see," he whispered into Hakuun's ear, and said to himself as well, a resigned acceptance that sometimes the stubborn orcs had their own agenda.

Perhaps he could find some amusement and profit out of it, and really, what did he have to lose? He sniffed the air again, and again sensed that something was different.

"There are many orcs about," he said.

"Tens of thousands," Hakuun confirmed. "Come to the call of King Obould Many-Arrows."

Many-Arrows, Jack thought, a name that registered deep in his memories of long ago. He thought of Citadel Fel . . . Citadel Felb . . . Fel-something-or-other, a place of dwarves. Jack didn't much like dwarves. They annoyed him at least as much as did the orcs, with their hammering and stupid chanting that they somehow, beyond all reason, considered song.

"We shall see," he said again to Hakuun, and noting that the ugly Grguch was fast approaching, Jack slithered down under Hakuun's collar to nestle in the small of his back. Every now and then, he flicked his forked tongue against Hakuun's bare flesh just for the fun of hearing the shaman stutter in his discussion with the beastly Grguch.

PART 2

GAUNTLGRYM

GAUNTLGRYM

I came from the Underdark, the land of monsters. I lived in Ice-wind Dale, where the wind can freeze a man solid, or a bog can swallow a traveler so quickly that he'll not likely understand what is happening to him soon enough to let out a cry, unless it is one muffled by loose mud. Through Wulfgar I have glimpsed the horrors of the Abyss, the land of demons, and could there be any place more vile, hate-filled, and tormenting? It is indeed a dangerous existence.

I have surrounded myself with friends who will fearlessly face those monsters, the wind and the bog, and the demons, with a snarl and a growl, a jaw set and a weapon held high. None would face them more fearlessly than Bruenor, of course.

But there is something to shake even that one, to shake us all as surely as if the ground beneath our feet began to tremble and break away.

Change.

In any honest analysis, change is the basis of fear, the idea of something new, of some paradigm that is unfamiliar, that is beyond our experiences so completely that we cannot even truly predict where it will lead us. Change. Uncertainty.

It is the very root of our most primal fear—the fear of death—that one change, that one unknown against which we construct elaborate scenarios and "truisms" that may or may not be true at all. These constructions, I think, are an extension of the routines of our lives. We dig ruts with the sameness of our daily paths, and drone and rail against those routines while we, in fact, take comfort in them. We awake and construct our days of habit, and follow the norms we have built fast, solid, and bending only a bit in our daily existence. Change is the unrolled die, the unused *sava* piece. It is exciting and frightening only when we hold some power over it, only when there is a potential reversal of course, difficult though it may be, within our control.

Absent that safety line of real choice, absent that sense of some control, change is merely frightening. Terrifying, even.

An army of orcs does not scare Bruenor. Obould Many-Arrows does not scare Bruenor. But what Obould represents, particularly if the orc king halts his march and establishes a kingdom, and more especially if the other kingdoms of the Silver Marches accept this new paradigm, terrifies Bruenor Battlehammer to the heart of his being and to the core tenets of his faith. Obould threatens more than Bruenor's kin, kingdom, and life. The orc's designs shake the very belief system that binds Bruenor's kin, the very purpose of Mithral Hall, the understanding of what it is to be a dwarf, and the dwarven concept of where the orcs fit into that stable continuum. He would not say it openly, but I suspect that Bruenor hopes the orcs will attack, that they will, in the end, behave in accordance with his expectations of orcs and of all goblinkind. The other possibility is too dissonant, too upsetting, too contrary to Bruenor's very identity for him to entertain the plausibility, indeed the probability, that it would result in less suffering for all involved.

I see before me the battle for the heart of Bruenor Battlehammer, and for the hearts of all the dwarves of the Silver Marches.

Easier by far to lift a weapon and strike dead a known enemy, an orc.

In all the cultures I have known, with all the races I have walked beside, I have observed that when beset by such dissonance, by events that are beyond control and that plod along at their own pace, the frustrated onlookers often seek out a beacon, a focal point—a god, a person, a place, a magical item—which they believe will set all the world aright. Many are the whispers in Mithral Hall that King Bruenor will fix it, all of it, and make everything as it had been before the onslaught of Obould. Bruenor has earned their respect many times over, and wears the mantle of hero among his kin as comfortably and deservedly as has any dwarf in the history of the clan. For most of the dwarves here, then, King Bruenor has become the beacon and focal point of hope itself.

Which only adds to Bruenor's responsibility, because when a frightened people put their faith in an individual, the ramifications of incompetence, recklessness, or malfeasance are multiplied many times over. And so becoming the focus of hope only adds to Bruenor's tension. Because he knows that it is not true, and that their expectations may well be beyond him. He cannot convince Lady Alustriel of Silverymoon or any of the other leaders, not even King Emerus Warcrown of Citadel Felbarr, to march in force against Obould. And to go out alone with Mithral Hall's own forces would lead to the wholesale slaughter of Clan Battlehammer. Bruenor understands that he has to wear the mantle not only of hero, but of savior, and it is for him a terrible burden.

And so Bruenor, too, has engaged in deflection and wild expectation, has found a focal point on which to pin his hopes. The most common phrase he has spoken throughout this winter has been, "Gauntlgrym, elf."

Gauntlgrym. It is a legend among Clan Battlehammer and all the Delzoun dwarves. It is the name of their common heritage, an immense city of splendor, wealth, and strength that represents to every descendant of the Delzoun tribes the apex of dwarven civilization. It is, perhaps, history wound with myth, a likely unintentional lionizing of that which once was. As heroes of old take on more gigantic proportions with each passing generation, so too does this other focal point of hope and pride expand.

"Gauntlgrym, elf," Bruenor says with steady determination. All of his answers lie there, he is certain. In Gauntlgrym, Bruenor will find a path to unravel the doings of King Obould. In Gauntlgrym, he will discover how to put the orcs back in their holes, and more importantly, how to realign the races of the Silver Marches into proper position, into places that make sense to an old, immovable dwarf.

He believes that we found this magical kingdom on our journey here from the Sword Coast. He has to believe that this unremarkable sinkhole in a long-dead pass was really the entrance to a place where he can find his answers.

Otherwise he has to become the answer for his anxious people. And Bruenor knows that their faith is misplaced, for at present, he has no answer to the puzzle that is Obould.

Thus, he says, "Gauntlgrym, elf," with the same conviction that a devout believer will utter the name of his savior god.

We will go to this place, this hole in the ground in a barren pass in the west. We will go and find Gauntlgrym, whatever that may truly mean. Perhaps Bruenor's instincts are correct—could it be that Moradin told him of this in his days of near death? Perhaps we will find something entirely different, but that will still bring to us, to Bruenor, the clarity he needs to find the answers for Mithral Hall.

Fixated and desperate as he is, and as his people are, Bruenor doesn't yet understand that the name he has affixed to our savior is not the point. The point is the search itself, for solutions and for the truth, and not the place he has determined as our goal.

"Gauntlgrym, elf."

Indeed.

—Drizzt Do'Urden

CHAPTER

THE FIRST STRIDES HOME

8

The gates of Silverymoon, shining silver and with bars decorated like leafy vines, were closed, a clear signal that things were amiss in the Silver Marches. Stern-faced guards, elf and human, manned all posts along the city's wall and around a series of small stone houses that served as checkpoints for approaching visitors.

Catti-brie—limping more profoundly from her days on the road—and Wulfgar noted the tense looks coming their way. The woman merely smiled, though, understanding that her companion, nearly seven feet tall and with shoulders broad and strong, could elicit such trepidation even in normal times. Predictably, those nervous guards relaxed and even offered waves as the pair neared, as they came to recognize the barbarian in his trademark wolf-skin cloak and the woman who had often served as liaison between Mithral Hall and Silverymoon.

There was no call for the pair to stop or even slow as they passed the stone structures, and the gate parted before them without request. Several of the sentries near that gate and atop the wall even began clapping for Wulfgar and Catti-brie and more than a few "huzzahs" were shouted as they passed.

"With official word or for pleasure alone?" the commander of the guard asked the couple inside the city gates. He looked at Catti-brie with obvious concern. "Milady, are you injured?"

Catti-brie replied with a dismissive look, as if it did not matter, but the guard continued, "I will provide a coach for you at once!"

"I have walked from Mithral Hall through snow and mud," the woman replied. "I would not deny myself the joy of Silverymoon's meandering ways."

"But . . ."

"I will walk," Catti-brie said. "Do not deny me this pleasure."

The guard relented with a bow. "Lady Alustriel will be pleased by your arrival."

"And we will be pleased to see her," said Wulfgar.

"With official word from King Bruenor?" the commander asked again.

"With word more personal, but equally pressing," the barbarian answered. "You will announce us?"

"The courier is already on his way to the palace."

Wulfgar nodded his gratitude. "We will walk the ways of Silverymoon, a course not direct, and will arrive at Lady Alustriel's court before the sun has passed its zenith," he explained. "Pleased we are to be here—truly Silverymoon is a welcomed sight and a welcoming city for road-weary travelers. Our business here might well include you and your men as well, commander. . . ."

"Kenyon," said Catti-brie, for she had met the man on many occasions, though briefly at each.

"I am honored that you remember me, Lady Catti-brie," he said with another bow.

"We arrive in search of refugees who have come from Mithral Hall and may have crossed into your fairest of cities," said Wulfgar.

"Many have come," Kenyon admitted. "And many have left. But of course, we are at your disposal, son of Bruenor, on word of Lady Alustriel. Go and secure that word, I bid you."

Wulfgar nodded, and he and Catti-brie moved past the guard station.

With their road-weathered clothes, one with a magical bow as a crutch and the other a giant of a man with a magnificent warhammer strapped across his back, the pair stood out in the city of philosophers and poets, and many a curious look turned their way as they walked the winding, seemingly aimless avenues of the decorated city. As with every visitor to Silverymoon, no matter how many times one traversed the place, their eyes were continually drawn upward, studying the intricate designs and artwork that covered the walls of every building, and upward still, to the tapering spires that topped every structure. Most communities were an expression of utility, with structures built suitable to the elements of their environment and the threats of regional monsters. Cities of commerce were built with wide avenues, port cities with fortified harbors and breakwaters, and frontier towns with thick walls. Silverymoon stood above all of these, for it was an expression of utility, of course, but more than that, an expression of spirit. Security and commerce were facilitated, but they were not paramount to the needs of the soul, where the library was grander than the barracks and the avenues were designed to turn visitors and residents to the most spectacular of views, rather than as efficient straight lines to the marketplace or the rows of houses and mercantiles.

It was hard to arrive in Silverymoon with urgent business, for few could walk swiftly through those streets, and fewer still could focus the mind sufficiently to defeat the intrusions of beauty.

Contrary to Wulfgar's stated expectations, the sun had passed its zenith before Wulfgar and Catti-brie came in sight of Lady Alustriel's wondrous palace, but that was all right, for the experienced guards had informed the Lady of Silverymoon that such would be the case.

"The finest humans of Clan Battlehammer," said the tall woman, coming out from behind the curtains that separated this private section of her palatial audience chamber from the main, public promenade.

There was no overt malice in her humorous remark, though of course the couple standing before her, the adopted son and daughter of King Bruenor, were the only humans of Clan Battlehammer. Wulfgar smiled and chuckled, but Catti-brie didn't quite find that level of mirth within her.

She stared at the great woman, Lady Alustriel, one of the Seven Sisters and leader of magnificent Silverymoon. She only remembered to offer a bow when Wulfgar dipped beside her, and even then, Catti-brie did not lower her head as she bent, staring intently at Alustriel.

For despite herself, Catti-brie was intimidated. Alustriel was nearly six feet tall and undeniably beautiful, by human standards, by elven standards—by any standards. Even the creatures of the higher planes would be pleased by her presence, Catti-brie knew in her heart, for there was a luminescence and gravity about Alustriel that was somehow beyond mortal existence. Her hair was silver and lustrous, and hung thick to her shoulders, and her eyes could melt a man's heart or strip him of all courage at her will. Her gown was a simple affair, green with golden stitching, and just a few emeralds sewn for effect. Most kings and queens wore robes far more decorated and elaborate, of course, but Alustriel didn't need any ornamentation. Any room that she entered was her room to command.

She had never shown Catti-brie anything but kindness and friendship, and the two had been quite warm on occasion. But Catti-brie hadn't seen Alustriel much of late, and she could not help but feel somewhat smaller in the great woman's presence. Once she had been jealous of the Lady of Silverymoon, hearing rumors that Alustriel had been Drizzt's lover, and she had never discerned whether or not that had been the case.

Catti-brie smiled genuinely and laughed at herself, and pushed all of the negative thoughts aside. She couldn't be jealous where Drizzt was concerned anymore, nor could she feel diminished by anyone when she thought of her relationship with the drow.

What did it matter if the gods themselves bowed to Lady Alustriel? For Drizzt had chosen Catti-brie.

To Catti-brie's surprise, Alustriel walked right over and embraced her, and kissed her on the cheek.

"Too many months pass between our visits, milady," Alustriel said, moving Catti-brie back to arms' length. She reached up and pushed back a thick strand of Catti-brie's auburn hair. "How you manage to stay so beautiful, as if the dirt of the road cannot touch you, I will never know."

Catti-brie hardly knew how to reply.

"You could fight a battle with a thousand orcs," Alustriel went on, "slay them all—of course—and bloody your sword, your fist, and your boots. Not even that stain would diminish your glow."

Catti-brie gave a self-deprecating laugh. "Milady, you are too kind," she said. "Too kind for reason, I fear."

"Of course you do, daughter of Bruenor. You are a woman who grew up among dwarves, who hardly appreciated your charms and your beauty. You have no idea of how tall you would stand among those of your own race."

Catti-brie's face twisted a bit in confusion, not quite knowing how to take that.

"And that, too, is part of the charm of Catti-brie," said Alustriel. "Your humility is not calculated, it is intrinsic."

Catti-brie looked no less confused, and that drew a bit of laughter from Wulfgar. Catti-brie shot him a frown to silence him.

"The wind whispers that you have taken Drizzt as your husband," Alustriel said.

Still glancing Wulfgar's way as Alustriel spoke, Catti-brie noted a slight grimace on the barbarian's face—or maybe it was just her imagination.

"You are married?" Alustriel asked.

"Yes," Catti-brie replied. "But we have not celebrated in formal ceremony yet. We will wait for the darkness of Obould to recede."

Alustriel's face grew very serious. "That will be a long time, I fear."

"King Bruenor is determined that it will not."

"Indeed," said Alustriel, and she offered a hopeful little smile and a shrug. "I do hope you will celebrate your joining with Drizzt Do'Urden soon, both in Mithral Hall, and here in Silverymoon, as my honored guests. I will gladly open the palace to you, for many of my subjects would wish well the daughter of good King Bruenor and that most unusual dark elf."

"And many of your court would prefer that Drizzt remain in Mithral Hall," Catti-brie said, a bit more harshly than she had intended.

But Alustriel only laughed and nodded, for it was true enough, and undeniable. "Well, Fret likes him," she said, referring to her favored advisor, a most unusual and uniquely tidy dwarf. "And Fret likes you, and so do I—both of you. If I spent my time worrying over the pettiness and posturing of court lords and ladies, I would turn endless circles of appeasement and apology."

"When you doubt, then trust in Fret," Catti-brie said. She winked and Alustriel gave a hearty laugh and hugged her again.

As she did, she whispered into Catti-brie's ear, "Come here more often, I beg of you, with or without your stubborn dark elf companion."

She stepped up to Wulfgar then and wrapped him in a warm embrace. When she moved back to arms' length, a curious look came over her. "Son of Beornegar," she said quietly, respectfully.

Catti-brie's mouth dropped open in surprise at that, for only recently had Wulfgar been wearing that title more regularly, and it seemed to her as if Alustriel had somehow just discerned that.

"I see contentment in your blue eyes," Alustriel remarked. "You have not been at peace like this ever before—not even when I first met you, those many years ago."

"I was young then, and too strong of spirit," said Wulfgar.

"Can one ever be?"

Wulfgar shrugged. "Too anxious, then," he corrected.

"You hold your strength deeper now, because you are more secure in it, and in how you wish to use it."

Wulfgar's nod seemed to satisfy Alustriel, but Catti-brie just kept looking from the large man to the tall woman. She felt as if they were speaking in code, or half-saying secrets, the other half of which were known only to them.

"You are at peace," said Alustriel.

"And yet I am not," Wulfgar replied. "For my daugh—the girl, Colson, is lost to me."

"She was slain?"

Wulfgar shook his head immediately to calm the gentle woman. "Delly Curtie was lost to the hordes of Obould, but Colson lives. She was sent across the river in the company of refugees from the conquered northern lands."

"Here to Silverymoon?"

"That is what I would know," Wulfgar explained.

Alustriel nodded and stepped back, taking them both in with her protective stare.

"We could go from inn to inn," Catti-brie said. "But Silverymoon is no small city, nor is Sundabar, and there are many more villages about."

"You will remain right here as my guests," Alustriel insisted. "I will call out every soldier of Silverymoon's garrison, and will speak with the merchant guilds. You will have your answer in short time, I promise."

"You are too generous," Wulfgar said with a bow.

"Would King Bruenor, would Wulfgar or Catti-brie, offer any less to me or one of mine if we similarly came to Mithral Hall?"

That simple truth ended any forthcoming arguments from the two grateful travelers.

"We thought that we might travel to some of the common inns and ask around," Catti-brie said.

"And draw attention to your hunt?" Alustriel replied. "Would this person who has Colson wish to give the child back to you?"

Wulfgar shook his head, but Catti-brie said, "We don't know, but it is possible that she would not."

"Then better for you to remain here, as my guests. I have many contacts who frequent the taverns. It is important for a leader to hear the commoners' concerns. The answers you seek will be easily found—in Silverymoon, at least." She motioned to her attendants. "Take them and make them comfortable. I do believe that Fret wishes to see Catti-brie."

"He cannot suffer the dirt of the road upon me," Catti-brie remarked dryly.

"Only because he cares, of course."

"Or because he so despises dirt?"

"That too," Alustriel admitted.

Catti-brie looked to Wulfgar and offered a resigned shrug. She was pleasantly surprised to see him equally at ease with this arrangement. Apparently he understood that their work was better left to Alustriel, and that they could indeed relax and enjoy the respite at the luxurious palace of the Lady of Silverymoon.

"And she came without proper clothing, I'll wager!" came an obviously annoyed voice, a chant that sounded both melodic and sing-song like an elf, and resonant like the bellow of a dwarf—a most unusual dwarf.

Wulfgar and Catti-brie turned to see the fellow, dressed in a fine white gown with bright green trim, enter the room. He looked at Catti-brie and gave a disapproving sigh and a wag of his meticulously manicured stubby finger. Then he stopped and sighed again, and put his chin in one hand, his fingers stroking the thin line of his well-trimmed silver beard as he considered the task of transforming Catti-brie.

"Well met, Fret," Alustriel said. "It would seem that you have your work cut out for you. Do try not to break this one's spirit."

"You confuse spirit with odor, milady."

Catti-brie frowned, but it was hard for her to cover her inner smile.

"Fret would put perfume and bells on a tiger, I do believe," Alustriel said, and her nearby attendants shared a laugh at the dwarf's expense.

"And colored bows and paint for its nails," the tidy dwarf proudly replied. He walked up to Catti-brie, gave a "tsk tsk," and grabbed her by the elbow, pulling her along. "As we appreciate beauty, so it is our divine task to facilitate it. And so I shall. Now come along, child. You've a long bath to suffer."

Catti-brie flashed her smile back at Wulfgar. After their long and arduous journey, she planned to "suffer" it well.

Wulfgar's returned smile was equally genuine. He turned to Alustriel, saluted, and thanked her.

"What might we do for Wulfgar while my scouts seek word of Colson?" Alustriel asked him.

"A quiet room with a view of your fair city," he replied, and he added quietly, "One that faces to the west."

* * * * *

Catti-brie caught up to Wulfgar early that evening on a high balcony of the main turret—one of a dozen that adorned the palace.

"The dwarf has his talents," Wulfgar said.

Catti-brie's freshly washed hair smelled of lilac and springtime. She almost always kept it loose to bounce over her shoulders, but she had one side tied up and the other had a hint of a curl teased into it. She wore a light blue gown that enhanced and highlighted the hue of her eyes, its straps revealing the smooth skin of her delicate shoulders. A white and gold sash was tied around her waist at an angle and a place to accentuate her shapely body. The dress did not go all the way to the floor, and Wulfgar's surprise showed as a smile when he noted that she wasn't wearing her doeskin boots, but rather a pair of delicate slippers, all lace and fancy trim.

"I found meself a choice to let him do it to me or punch him in the nose," Catti-brie remarked, her self-deprecation exaggerated because she allowed just a hint of her Dwarvish accent to come through.

"There is not a part of you that enjoys it?"

Catti-brie scowled at him.

"You would not wish for Drizzt to see you like this?" the barbarian pressed. "You would take no pleasure in the look upon his face?"

"I'll take me pleasure in killing orcs."

"Stop it."

Catti-brie looked at him as if he had slapped her.

"Stop it," Wulfgar repeated. "You need not your boots or your weapons here in Silverymoon, or your dwarf-bred pragmatism and that long-lost accent. Have you looked in the mirror since Fret worked his magic on you?"

Catti-brie snorted and turned away, or started to, but Wulfgar held her with his gaze and his grin.

"You should," he said.

"You are talking foolishness," Catti-brie replied, and her accent was no more.

"Far from that. Is it foolish to enjoy the sights of Silverymoon?" He half-turned and swept his arm out to the deepening gloom in the west, to the twilit structures of the free-form city, with candles burning in many windows. Glowing flames of harmless faerie fire showed on a few of the spires, accenting their inviting forms.

"Did you not allow your mind to wander as we walked through the avenues to this palace?" Wulfgar asked. "Could you help but feel that way with beauty all around you? So why is it any different with your own appearance? Why are you so determined to hide behind mud and simple clothes?"

Catti-brie shook her head. Her lips moved a few times as if she wanted to reply but couldn't find the words.

"Drizzt would be pleased by the sight before him," Wulfgar stated. "I am pleased, as your friend. Quit hiding behind the gruff accent and the road-worn clothing. Quit being afraid of who you are, of who you might dare to be, deep inside. You do not care if someone sees you after a hard day of labor, sweating and dirty. You don't waste your time primping and prettying yourself, and all of that is to your credit. But in times like this, when the opportunity presents itself, do not shy from it, either."

"I feel . . . vain."

"You should simply feel pretty, and be happy with that. If you really are one who cares not what others may think or say, then why would you hide from pleasant thoughts?"

Catti-brie looked at him curiously for a moment, and a smile spread on her face. "Who are you, and what have you done with Wulfgar?"

"The doppelganger is long dead, I assure you," Wulfgar replied. "He was thrown out with the weight of Errtu."

"I have never seen you like this."

"I have never before felt like this. I am content and I know my road. I answer to no one but myself now, and never before have I known such freedom."

"And so you wish to share that with me?"

"With everyone," Wulfgar replied with a laugh.

"I did look in a mirror . . . or two," Catti-brie said, and Wulfgar laughed harder.

"And were you pleased by what you saw?"

"Yes," she admitted.

"And do you wish that Drizzt was here?"

"Enough," she bade him, which of course meant "yes."

Wulfgar took her by the arm and guided her to the railing of the balcony. "So many generations of men and elves have built this place. It is a refuge for Fret and those akin to him, and it is also a place where we all might come from time to time to simply stand and look, and enjoy. That, I think, is the most important time of all. To look inside ourselves honestly and without regret or fear. I could be battling orcs or dragons. I could be digging mithral from the deep mines. I could be leading the hunt in Icewind Dale. But there are times, too few I fear, when this, when standing and looking and just enjoying, is more important than all of that."

Catti-brie wrapped her arm around Wulfgar's waist and leaned her head against his strong shoulder, standing side-by-side, two friends enjoying a moment of life, of perception, of simple pleasure.

Wulfgar draped his arm across her shoulders, equally at peace, and both of them sensed, deep inside, that the moment would be one they would remember for all their days, a defining and lasting image of all they had been through since that fateful day in Icewind Dale when Wulfgar the young warrior had foolishly smacked a tough old dwarf named Bruenor on the head.

They lingered for some time, but the moment was lost as Lady Alustriel came out onto the balcony. The two turned at the sound of her voice, to see her standing with a middle-aged man dressed in the apron of a tavernkeeper.

Alustriel paused when she looked upon Catti-brie, her eyes roaming the woman's form.

"Fret is full of magic, I am told," Catti-brie said, glancing at Wulfgar.

Alustriel shook her head. "Fret finds the beauty, he does not create it."

"He finds it as well as Drizzt finds orcs to slay, or Bruenor finds metal to mine, to be sure," said Wulfgar.

"He has mentioned that he would like to search for the same in Wulfgar, as well."

Catti-brie laughed as Wulfgar chuckled and shook his head. "I've not the time."

"He will be so disappointed," said Alustriel.

"Next time we meet, perhaps," said Wulfgar, and his words elicited a doubting glance from Catti-brie.

She stared at him deeply for a long while, measuring his every expression and movement, and the inflections of his voice. His offer to Fret may or may not have been disingenuous, she knew, but it was moot in any case because Wulfgar had decided that he would never again visit Silverymoon. Catti-brie saw that clearly, and had been feeling it since before they had departed Mithral Hall.

A sense of dread welled up inside her, mingling with that last special moment she had shared with Wulfgar. There was a storm coming. Wulfgar knew it, and though he hadn't yet openly shared it, the signs were mounting.

"This is Master Tapwell of the Rearing Dragon, a fine establishment in the city's lower ward," Alustriel explained. The short, round-bellied man came forward a step, rather sheepishly. "A common respite for visitors to Silverymoon."

"Well met," Catti-brie greeted, and Wulfgar nodded his agreement.

"And to yerselves, Prince and Princess of Mithral Hall," Tapwell replied, dipping a few awkward bows in the process.

"The Rearing Dragon played host to many of the refugees that crossed the Surbrin from Mithral Hall," Alustriel explained. "Master Tapwell believes that a pair who passed through might be of interest to you."

Wulfgar was already leaning forward eagerly. Catti-brie put her hand on his forearm to help steady him.

"Yer girl, Colson," Tapwell said, rubbing his hands nervously over his beer-stained apron. "Skinny thing with straw hair to here?" He indicated a point just below his shoulder, a good approximation of the length of Colson's hair.

"Go on," Wulfgar bade, nodding.

"She came in with the last group, but with her mother."

"Her mother?" Wulfgar looked to Alustriel for an explanation, but the woman deferred to Tapwell.

"Well, she said she was her mother," the tavernkeeper explained.

"What was her name?" Catti-brie asked.

Tapwell fidgeted as if trying to fathom the answer. "I remember her calling the girl Colson clear enough. Her own name was like that. Same beginning, if ye get my meaning."

"Please remember," Wulfgar prompted.

"Cottie?" Catti-brie asked.

"Cottie, yeah. Cottie," said Tapwell.

"Cottie Cooperson," Catti-brie said to Wulfgar. "She was with the group Delly tended in the hall. She lost her family to Obould."

"And Delly gave her a new one," said Wulfgar, but his tone was not bitter.

"You agree with this assessment?" Alustriel asked.

"It does make sense," said Catti-brie.

"This was the last group that crossed the Surbrin before the ferry was closed down, and not just the last group to arrive in Silverymoon," Alustriel said. "I have confirmed that from the guards of Winter Edge themselves. They escorted the refugees in from the Surbrin—all of them—and they, the guards, remain, along with several of the refugees."

"And have you found those refugees to ask them of Cottie and Colson?" asked Catti-brie. "And are Cottie and Colson among those who remain?"

"Further inquiries are being made," Alustriel replied. "I am fairly certain that they will only confirm what we have already discovered. As for Cottie and the child, they left."

Wulfgar's shoulders slumped.

"For Nesmé," Alustriel explained. "Soon after those refugees arrived, a general call came out from Nesmé. They are rebuilding, and offering homes to any who would go and join with them. The place is secure once more—many of the Knights in Silver stand watch with the Riders of Nesmé to ensure that all of the trolls were destroyed or chased back into the Trollmoors. The city will thrive this coming season, well defended and well supplied."

"You are certain that Cottie and Colson are there?" Wulfgar asked.

"I am certain that they were on the caravan that left for Nesmé, only days after they arrived here in Silverymoon. That caravan arrived, though whether Cottie and the child remained with it through the entirety of the journey, I cannot promise. They stopped at several way stations and villages along the route. The woman could have left at any of those."

Wulfgar nodded and looked to Catti-brie, their road clear before them.

"I could fly you to Nesmé upon my chariot," Alustriel offered. "But there is another caravan leaving by midday tomorrow, one that will follow the exact route that Cottie rode, and one in need of more guards. The drivers would be thrilled to have Wulfgar and Catti-brie along for the journey, and Nesmé is only a tenday away."

"And there is nowhere for Cottie to have gone beyond Nesmé," Wulfgar reasoned, "That will do, and well."

"Very good," said Alustriel. "I will inform the lead driver." She and Tapwell took their leave.

"Our road is clear, then," said Wulfgar, and he seemed content with that.

Catti-brie, though, shook her head.

"The southern road is secured and Nesmé is not so far," Wulfgar said to her doubting expression.

"This is not good news, I fear."

"How so?"

"Cottie," Catti-brie explained. "I happened upon her a few times after my wound kept me in the lower tunnels. She was a broken thing, in spirit and in mind."

"You fear that she would harm Colson?" Wulfgar said, his eyes widening with alarm.

"Never that," said Catti-brie. "But I fear that she will clutch the girl too tightly, and will not welcome the reaching hands of Wulfgar."

"Colson is not her child."

"And for some, truth is no more than an inconvenience," Catti-brie replied.

"I will take the child," Wulfgar stated in a tone that left no room for debate.

Aside from that undeniable determination, it struck Catti-brie that Wulfgar had named Colson as "the child," and not as "my child." She studied her friend carefully for a few moments, seeking a deeper read.

But it was not to be found.

CHAPTER

AT DESTINY'S DOOR

9

I don't like this place."

A trick of the wind, blowing down a channel between a pair of towering snow dunes, amplified Regis's soft-spoken words so that they seemed to fill the space around his four dwarf companions. The words blended with the mourn of the cold breeze, a harmony of fear and lament that seemed so fitting in a place called Fell Pass.

Bruenor, who was too anxious to be anywhere but up front, turned, and appeared as if he was about to scold the halfling. But he didn't. He just shook his head and left it at that, for how could he deny the undeniable?

The region was haunted, palpably so. They had felt it on their journey through the pass the previous spring, moving west to east toward Mithral Hall. That same musty aura remained very much alive in Fell Pass, though the surroundings had been transformed by the season. When they'd first come through, the ground was flat and even, a wide and easily-traversed pass between a pair of distant mountain ranges. Perhaps the winds from both of those ranges continually met here in battle, flattening the ground. Deep snow had since fallen in the teeth of those competing winds, forming a series of drifts that resembled the dunes of the Calim Desert, like a series of gigantic, bright white scallop shells evenly spaced perpendicular to the east-west line that marked the bordering mountain ranges. With the melting and refreezing of the late winter, the top surface of the snow had been crusted with ice, but not enough to bear the weight of a dwarf. Thus they had to make their trudging way along the low points of the still-deep snow, through the channels between the dunes.

Drizzt served as their guide. Running lightly, every now and then chopping a ledge into the snow with one of his scimitars, the drow traversed the dunes as a salmon might skip the waves of a slow river. Up one side and down another he went, pausing at the high points to set his bearings.

It had taken the party of six—Bruenor, Regis, Drizzt, Thibbledorf Pwent, Cordio, and Torgar Hammerstriker—four days to get to the eastern entrance of Fell Pass. They'd kept up a fine pace considering the snow and the fact that they had to circumvent many of King Obould's guard posts and a pair of orc caravans. Once in the pass, even with the scallop drifts, they had continued to make solid progress, with Drizzt scaling the dunes and instructing Pwent where to punch through.

Seven days out, the pace had slowed to a crawl. They were certain they were near to where they'd found the hole that Bruenor believed was the entrance to the legendary dwarven city of Gauntlgrym.

They had mapped the place well on that journey from the west, and had taken note, as Bruenor had ordered, of all the landmarks—the angles to notable mountain peaks north and south, and such. But with the wintry blanket of snow, Fell Pass appeared so different that Drizzt simply could not be certain. The very real possibility that they might walk right past the hole that had swallowed one of their wagons weighed on all of them, particularly Bruenor.

And there was something else there, a feeling hanging in the air that had the hairs on the backs of all their necks tingling. The mournful groan of the wind was full of the laments of the dead. Of that, there was no doubt. The cleric, Cordio, had cast divination spells that told him there was indeed something supernatural about the place, some rift or outsider presence. On the journey to Mithral Hall, Bruenor's priests had urged Drizzt not to call upon Guenhwyvar, for fear of inciting unwanted attention from other extraplanar sources in the process, and once again Cordio had reiterated that point. The Fell

Pass, the dwarf priest had assured his companions, was not stable in a planar sense—though even Cordio admitted that he wasn't really sure what that meant.

"Ye got anything for us, elf?" Bruenor called up to Drizzt. His gruff voice, full of irritation, echoed off the frozen snow.

Drizzt came into view atop the drift to the party's left, the west. He shrugged at Bruenor then stepped forward and began a balanced slide down the glistening white dune. He kept his footing perfectly, and slipped right past the halfling and dwarves to the base of the drift on their other side, where he used its sharp incline to halt his momentum.

"I have snow," he replied. "As much snow as you could want, extending as far as I can see to the west."

"We're goin' to have to stay here until the melt, ain't we?" Bruenor grumbled. He put his hands on his hips and kicked his heavy boot through the icy wall of one mound.

"We will find it," Drizzt replied, but his words were buried by the sudden grumbling of Thibbledorf Pwent.

"Bah!" the battlerager snorted, and he banged his hands together and stomped about, crunching the icy snow beneath his heavy steps. While the others wore mostly furs and layers of various fabrics, Pwent was bedecked in his traditional Gutbuster battle mail, a neck-to-toe suit of overlapping ridged metal plates, spiked at all the appropriate strike zones: fists, elbows, shoulders, and knees. His helmet, too, carried a tall, barbed spike, one that had skewered many an orc in its day.

"Ye got no magic to help me?" Bruenor demanded of Cordio.

The cleric shrugged helplessly. "The riddles of this maze extend beyond the physical, me king," he tried to explain. "Questions asked in spells're getting me nothin' but more questions. I'm knowin' that we're close, but more because I'm feeling that rift with me every spellcasting."

"Bah!" Pwent roared. He lowered his head and rammed through the nearest snow drift, disappearing behind a veil of white that fell behind him as he plowed through to the channel on the other side.

"We'll find it, then," said Torgar Hammerstriker. "If it was here when ye came through, then here it is still. And if me king's thinking it's Gauntlgrym, then nothin's stopping meself from seein' that place."

"Aye and huzzah!" Cordio agreed.

They all jumped as the snow erupted from up ahead. Drizzt's scimitars appeared in his hands as if they had been there all along.

From that break in the dune emerged a snow-encrusted Thibble-dorf Pwent, roaring still. He didn't slow, but plowed through the dune across the way, crunching through the icy wall with ease and disappearing from sight.

"Will ye stop it, ye durned fool?" Bruenor chastised, but Pwent was already gone.

"I am certain that we're near the entrance," Drizzt assured Brue-nor, and the drow slid his blades away. "We are the right distance from the mountains north and south. Of that, I am sure."

"We are close," Regis confirmed, still glancing all around as if he expected a ghost to leap out and throttle him at any moment. In that regard, Regis knew more than the others, for he had been the one who had gone into the hole after the wagon those months before, and who had encountered, down in the dark, what he believed to be the ghost of a long-dead dwarf.

"Then we'll just keep looking," said Bruenor. "And if it stays in hiding under the snow, its secrets won't be holding, for the melt's coming soon."

"Bah!" they heard Pwent growl from behind the dune to the east and they all scrambled, expecting him to burst through in their midst, and likely with that lethal helmet spike lowered.

The dune shivered as he hit it across the way, and he roared again fiercely. But his pitch changed suddenly, his cry going from defiance to surprise. Then it faded rapidly, as if the dwarf had fallen away.

Bruenor looked at Drizzt. "Gauntlgrym!" the dwarf declared.

Torgar and Cordio dived for the point on the drift behind which they had heard Pwent's cry. They punched through and flung the snow out behind them, working like a pair of dogs digging for a bone. As they weakened the integrity of that section of the drift, it crumbled down before them, complicating their dig. Still, within moments, they came to the edge of a hole in the ground, and the remaining pile of snow slipped in, but seemed to fill the crevice.

"Pwent?" Torgar called into the snow, thinking his companion buried alive.

He leaned over the edge, Cordio stabilizing his feet, and plunged his hand down into the snow pile. That blockage, though, was neither solid nor thick, and had merely packed in to seal the shaft below. When Torgar's hand broke the integrity of the pack, the collected snow broke and fell away, leaving the dwarf staring down into a cold and empty shaft.

"Pwent?" he called more urgently, realizing that his companion had fallen quite far.

"That's it!" Bruenor yelled, rushing up between the kneeling pair. "The wagon went in right there!" As he made the claim, he fell to his knees and brushed aside some more of the snow, revealing a rut that had been made by the wagon wheel those months before. "Gauntlgrym!"

"And Pwent fell in," Drizzt reminded him.

The three dwarves turned to see the drow and Regis feeding out a line of rope that Drizzt had already tied around his waist.

"Get the line, boys!" Bruenor yelled, but Cordio and Torgar were already moving anyway, rushing to secure the rope and find a place to brace their heavy boots.

Drizzt dropped down beside the ledge and tried to pick a careful route, but a cry came up from far below, followed by a high-pitched, sizzling roar that sounded unlike anything any of them had ever heard, like a cross between the screech of an eagle and the hiss of a gigantic lizard.

Drizzt rolled over the lip, turning and setting his hands, and Bruenor dived to add his strength to the rope brace.

"Quickly!" Drizzt instructed as the dwarves began to let out the line. Trusting in them, the drow let go of the lip and dropped from sight.

"There's a ledge fifteen feet down," Regis called, scrambling past the dwarves to the hole. He moved as if he would go right over, but he stopped suddenly, just short of the lip. There he held as the seconds passed, his body frozen by memories of his first journey into the place that Bruenor called Gauntlgrym.

"I'm on the ledge," Drizzt called up, drawing him from his trance. "I can make my way, but keep ready on the rope."

Regis peered over and could just make out the form of the drow in the darkness below.

"Ye be guidin' us, Rumblebelly," Bruenor instructed, and Regis found the fortitude to nod.

A loud crash from far below startled him again, though, followed by a cry of pain and another otherworldly shriek. More noise arose, metal scraping on stone, hissing snakes and eagle screams, and Dwarvish roars of defiance.

Then a cry of absolute terror, Pwent's cry, shook them all to their spines, for when had Thibbledorf Pwent ever cried out in terror?

"What do ye see?" Bruenor called out to Regis.

The halfling peered in and squinted. He could just make out Drizzt, inching down the wall below the ledge. As his eyes adjusted to the gloom, Regis realized it wasn't really a ledge, or a wall, but rather a stalagmite mound that had grown up beside the side of the cave below. He looked back to Drizzt, and the drow dropped from sight. The dwarves behind him gave a yelp and fell over backward as the rope released.

"Set it!" Bruenor yelled at Torgar and Cordio, and the dwarf king charged for the hole, yelling, "What do ye see, Rumblebelly?"

Regis pulled back and turned, shaking his head, but Bruenor wasn't waiting for an explanation anyway. The dwarf dived to the ground and grabbed up the rope, and without hesitation, flung himself over the lip, rapidly descending into the gloom. Back from the hole, Torgar and Cordio grunted from the strain and tried hard to dig their boots in.

Regis swallowed. He heard a grunt and a shriek from far below. Images of a dwarf ghost haunted him and told him to run far away. But Drizzt was down there, Bruenor was down there, Pwent was down there.

The halfling swallowed again and rushed to the hole. He fell to the ground atop the rope and with a glance back at Torgar and Cordio, he disappeared from sight.

* * * * *

As soon as he hit the ledge, Drizzt recognized it for what it was. The tall stalagmite mound rose up at an angle, melding with the sheerer stone of the wall behind him.

Even though he was only fifteen feet down from the lip, Drizzt's sensibilities switched to those of the person he used to be, a creature of the Underdark. He started down tentatively, feeding out the rope behind him, for just a couple of steps.

His eyes focused in the gloom, and he saw the contours of the stalagmite and the floor some twenty feet below. On that floor rested the broken remains of the wagon that had been lost in the journey east those months before. Also on that floor, Drizzt saw a familiar boot, hard and wrapped in metal. Below and to the left, he heard a muffled cry, and the sound of metal scraping on stone, as if an armored dwarf was being dragged.

With a flick of his wrist, Drizzt disengaged himself from the rope, and so balanced was he as he ran down the side of the stalagmite that he not only did not bend low and use his hands, but he drew out both his blades as he descended. He hit the floor in a run, thinking to head off down the narrow tunnel he had spotted ahead and to the right. But his left-hand scimitar, Twinkle, glowed with a blue light, and the drow's keen eyes and ears picked out a whisper of movement and a whisper of sound over by the side wall.

Skidding to a stop, Drizzt whirled to meet the threat, and his eyes went wide indeed when he saw the creature, unlike anything he had ever known, coming out fast for him.

Half again Drizzt's height from head to tail, it charged on strong back legs, like a bipedal lizard, back hunched low and tail suspended behind it, counterbalancing its large head—if it could even be called a head. It seemed no more than a mouth with three equidistant mandibles stretched out wide. Black tusks as large as Drizzt's hands curled inward at the tips of those mandibles, and Drizzt could make out rows of long, sharp teeth running back down its throat, a trio of ridged lines.

Even stranger came the glow from the creature's eyes—three of them—each centered on the flap of mottled skin stretched wide between the respective mandibles. The creature bore down on the drow like some triangular-mouthed snake unhinging its jaw to swallow its prey.

Drizzt started out to the left then reversed fast as the creature swerved to follow. Even with his speed-enhancing anklets, though, the drow could not get far enough back to the right to avoid the turning creature.

The mandibles snapped powerfully, but hit only air as Drizzt leaped and tumbled forward, over the top mandible. He slashed down hard with both hands as he went over, and used the contact to push himself even higher as he executed a twist and brought his feet fast under him. The creature issued a strange roaring, hissing protest—a fitting, other-worldly sound for an otherworldly beast, Drizzt thought.

Tucking and turning, Drizzt planted his feet against the side of the creature's shoulder and kicked out, but the beast was more solid than he'd thought. His strike did no more than bend it away from him at the shoulder as he went out to the side. And that bend, of course, again turned the terrible jaws his way.

But Drizzt flew backward with perfect balance and awareness. As the beast swung around he cut his scimitars across, one-two, scoring hits on the thick muscle and skin of the jaws' connecting flap.

The creature howled again and bit down at the passing blades, its three mandible tips not quite aligning as they clicked together. It opened wide its maw again as it turned to face Drizzt.

His blades worked in a flash, the backhand of Icingdeath slic-ing the opposing skin flap, and a hard strike of Twinkle passing through the muscle and flesh, then turning straight down to slash the base flap that connected the lower two mandible tips. Drizzt turned the blade just a bit as it connected, and leaned forward hard, forcing the jaws to angle down.

The creature snapped its head back up, accepting the cut, and leaped straight up, turning its back end under so that it landed on its outstretched tail with its hind legs free to claw at its opponent. Formidable indeed were the three claws tipping the feet of those powerful legs, and Drizzt barely dodged back in time to avoid the vicious rake.

Somehow the creature hopped forward in pursuit, using just its tail for propulsion. Its tiny front legs waved frantically in the air as its long, powerful rear legs slashed wildly at the drow.

Drizzt worked his scimitars in a blur to defend, connecting repeatedly, but never too solidly for fear of having a blade torn from his grasp. He retracted a blade and the creature's hind leg flailed free, then he stabbed straight out, piercing its foot.

The creature threw back its head and howled again—from up above there came a crash as a form rolled over the ledge—and Drizzt didn't miss the opportunity offered by the distraction. Rolling around those flailing legs and slashing across with Icingdeath, then with Twinkle in close pursuit, he scored two hits on the creature's thin neck. There was a sucking of air and Drizzt saw the bubbling of blood as his blades passed through flesh.

Not even slowing in his turn as the creature fell silent, then just fell over, the drow sprinted down the tunnel. A roar from behind made him glance back, to see Bruenor flying down the last few feet beside the stalagmite, axe over his head. The dwarf timed his landing perfectly with his overhand chop, driving his axe through the already mortally wounded creature's backbone with a sickening sound.

"Wait here!" Drizzt called to him, and the drow was gone.

* * * * *

Bruenor held on as the creature thrashed in its death throes. It tried to turn around to snap at him, but Drizzt had completely disabled the once-formidable jaws' ability to inflict any real damage. The mandibles flopped awkwardly and without coordination, most of the supporting muscles severed. Similarly, the creature's tail and hind legs exhibited only the occasional spasmodic twitch, for Bruenor's axe had cleaved its spine.

So the dwarf stayed at arms' length, holding his axe out far from his torso to avoid any incidental contact.

"Hurry, elf!" Bruenor called after Drizzt when he glanced to the side and noted Thibbledorf's boot lying on the stone floor. No longer willing to wait out the dying beast, Bruenor leaped atop its back and ripped through tendon and bone as he tugged and yanked his axe free. He thought to run off after Drizzt, but before he even had the weapon set in his hands, a movement to the side caught his eye.

The dwarf watched curiously as a darker patch of shadow coalesced near the side wall and the broken wagon, gradually taking shape—the shape of another of the strange beasts.

It came out hard and fast at him, and Bruenor wisely dropped down behind the fallen creature. On came the second beast, jaws snapping furiously, and the dwarf fell to the stone floor and heaved the fallen creature up as a meaty shield. The dwarf finally saw the damage those strange triangular jaws could inflict, for the ravenous newcomer tore through great chunks of flesh and bone in seconds.

Movement behind Bruenor had him half turning to his right.

"Just me!" Regis called to him before he came around, and the dwarf refocused on the beast before him.

Then Bruenor glanced left, to see Drizzt backing frantically out of the tunnel, his scimitars working fast and independently, each slashing quick lines to hold the snapping mouths of two more creatures at bay.

"Rumblebelly, ye help the elf!" Bruenor called, but when he glanced back, Regis was gone.

Bruenor's foe plowed over its fallen comrade then, and the dwarf king had no time to look for his halfling companion.

* * * * *

Drizzt noticed Regis flattened against the wall as he, and the pair of monsters pursuing him, moved past the halfling.

Regis nodded and waited for a responding nod. As soon as Drizzt offered it, the halfling came out fast and slapped his small mace against the tail of the creature on the left. Predictably, the beast wheeled to snap at this newest foe, but anticipating that, Drizzt moved faster, bringing his right hand blade over and across, cutting a gash across the side of the turning beast's neck.

With a roar of protest, the creature spun back, and the other, seeing the opening, came on suddenly.

But Drizzt was the quicker, and he managed to backstep fast enough to buy the time to realign his blades. He gave an approving nod to Regis as the halfling slipped down the tunnel.

* * * * *

Regis moved deliberately, but nervously, into the darkness, expecting a monster to spring out at him from every patch of shadow. Soon he heard the scraping of metal, and an occasional grumble and Dwarvish curse, and he could tell from the lack of bluster that Thibbledorf Pwent was in serious trouble.

Propelled by that, Regis moved with more speed, coming up to the edge of a side chamber from which issued the terrible, gnashing, metallic sounds. Regis summoned his courage and peeked around the rim of the opening. There in the room, silhouetted by the glow of lichen along the far wall, stood another creature, one larger than the others and easily more than ten feet from maw to tail tip. It stood perfectly still, except that it thrashed its head back and forth. Looking at it from the back, but on a slight angle, Regis could see why it did so. For out of the side of that mouth hung an armored dwarf leg with a dirty bare foot dangling limply at its end. Regis winced, thinking that his friend was being torn apart by that triangular maw. He could picture the black teeth crunching through Pwent's armored shell, tearing his flesh with fangs and ripped metal.

And the dwarf wasn't moving, other than the flailing caused by the limp limbs protruding from the thing's mouth, and no further protests or groans came forth.

Trembling with anger and terror, Regis charged with abandon, leaping forward and lifting high his small mace. But where could he even hit the murderous beast to hurt it?

He got his answer as the creature noticed him, whipping its head around. It was then that the halfling first came to understand the strange head, with its three equidistant eyes set in the middle of each of the skin flaps that connected the mandibles. Purely on instinct, the halfling swung for the nearest eye, and the creature's short forelimbs could not reach forward far enough to block.

The mace hit true, and the flap, taut about the knee and upper leg of the trapped dwarf, had no give that it might absorb the blow. With a sickening *splat*, the eye popped, gushing liquid all over the horrified halfling.

The creature hissed and whipped its head furiously—an attempt to throw the dwarf free.

But Pwent wasn't dead. He had gone into a defensive curl, a "turtle" maneuver that tightened the set of his magnificent armor, strengthening its integrity and hiding its vulnerable seams. As the creature loosened its death grip on him, the dwarf came out of his curl with a defiant snarl. He had no room to punch, or to maneuver his head spike, so he simply thrashed, shaking like a wide-leafed bush in a gale.

The creature lost interest in Regis, and tried to clamp down on the dwarf instead. But too late, for Pwent was in a frenzy, insane with rage.

Finally the creature managed to open wide its maw and angle down, expelling the dwarf. When Pwent came free, Regis's eyes widened to see the amount of damage—torn skin, broken teeth, and blood—the dwarf had inflicted on the beast.

And Pwent was far from done. He hit the ground in a turn that put his feet under him, and his little legs bent, then propelled him right back at the creature, head—and helmet spike—leading. He drove into and through the apex of the jaws, and the dwarf bored on, bending the creature backward. The dwarf punched out, both hands at the same time, launching twin roundhouse hooks that pounded the beast on opposite sides of its neck, fist-spikes digging in. Again and again, the dwarf retracted and punched back hard, both hands together, mashing the flesh.

And the dwarf's legs ground on, pushing the beast backward, up against the side-chamber's wall, and by the time they got there, the creature was not resisting at all, was not pushing back, and without the barrage it would have likely fallen over.

But Pwent kept hitting it, muttering profanities all the while.

* * * * *

Bruenor thrust his axe out horizontally before him, defeating the first attack. He turned the weapon and used it to angle the charging creature aside as he, too, ran ahead, sprinting by the beast to the remains of the wagon. All of the supply crates and sacks had been destroyed, either from the fall or torn apart thereafter, but Bruenor found what he was looking for in an intact portion of the side of the wagon, angling up to about waist height. Knowing the creature to be in full pursuit, the dwarf dived right over that, falling to the floor at its base and rolling to his back, axe up above his head along the ground.

The creature leaped over the planks, not realizing that Bruenor was so close to them until the dwarf's axe hit it hard in the side, cutting a long gash just behind its small, twitching foreleg.

Bruenor fell back flat and continued the momentum to roll him right over, coming back up to his feet. He didn't pause to look over his handiwork, but propelled himself forward, lifting his axe high over one shoulder as he went.

The creature was ready, though, and as the dwarf bore in, it snapped its mouth out at him, and when it had to retract far short of the mark to avoid a swipe of that vicious axe, the creature just fell back on its tail, as the other one had done, and brought up its formidable rear legs.

One blocked Bruenor's next swing, kicking out and catching the axe below the head, while the other lashed out, scraping deep lines on the dwarf's armor. Following that, the creature snapped its upper body forward, the triangular maw biting hard at the dwarf, who only managed at the last instant to get back out of range.

And right back came Bruenor, with a yell and a spit and a downward chop.

The creature rocked back and the axe whipped past cleanly. The creature reversed, coming in behind.

Bruenor didn't stop the axe's momentum and reverse it to parry. Rather, he let it flow through, turning sidelong as the blade came low, then turning some more, daring to roll his back around before the beast in the belief that he would be the quicker.

And so he was.

Bruenor came around, the axe in both hands and at full extension in a great sidelong slash. The creature scrambled to block. Bruenor shortened his grip, bringing the axe head in closer. When the creature kicked out to block, the axe met it squarely, removing one of the three toes and cleaving the blocking foot in half.

The creature threw itself forward, screaming in pain and anger, coming at Bruenor with blind rage. And the dwarf king backed frantically, his axe working to-and-fro to fend off the snapping assaults.

"Elf! I'm needin' ye!" the desperate dwarf bellowed.

* * * * *

Drizzt was in no position to answer. The wound he had inflicted on one of the beasts wasn't quite as serious as he'd hoped, apparently, for that creature showed no signs of relenting. Worse for Drizzt, he had been backed into a wider area, giving the creatures more room to maneuver and spread out before him.

They went wide, left and right, amazingly well coordinated for unthinking beasts—if they were indeed unthinking beasts. Drizzt worked his blades as far to either side as he could, and when that became impractical and awkward, the drow rushed ahead suddenly, back toward the tunnel.

Both creatures turned to chase, but Drizzt reversed even faster, spinning to meet their pursuit with a barrage of blows. He scored a deep gash on the side of one's mouth, and poked the other in its bottom eye.

Up above he heard a crash, and from the side Bruenor called for him. All he could do was look for options.

His gaze followed the trail of falling rocks, to see Torgar Hammerstriker in a wild and overbalanced run down the side of the stalagmite. The dwarf held a heavy crossbow before him, and just before his stumbling sent him into a headlong slide, he let fly a bolt, somehow hitting the creature to Drizzt's right. The crossbow went flying and so did Torgar, crashing and bouncing the rest of the way down.

The creature he had hit stumbled then spun to meet the dwarf's charge. But its jaws couldn't catch up to the bouncing and flailing Torgar, and the dwarf slammed hard against the back and side of the beast, bringing it down in a heap. Dazed beyond sensibility, Torgar couldn't begin to defend himself in that tumble as the creature moved to strike.

But Drizzt moved around the remaining creature and struck hard at the fallen beast, his scimitars slicing at its flesh in rapid succession, tearing deep lines. Drizzt had to pause to fend off the other, but as soon as that attack was repelled, he went back to the first, ensuring that it was dead.

Then the drow smiled, seeing that the tide had turned, seeing the lowered head spike rushing in hard at the standing creature's backside.

Even as Pwent connected, skewering the beast from behind, Drizzt broke off and ran toward the wagon. By the time he got there, he found Bruenor and his opponent in a wild back and forth of snapping and slashing.

Drizzt leaped up to the lip of the wagon side, looking for an opening. Noting him, Bruenor rushed out the other way, and the creature turned with the dwarf.

Drizzt leaped astride its back, his scimitars going to quick and deadly work.

"What in the Nine Hells are them things?" Bruenor asked when the vicious thing at last lay still.

"What *from* the Nine Hells, perhaps," said Drizzt with a shrug.

The two moved back to the center of the room, where Pwent continued pummeling the already dead beast and Regis tended to the dazed and battered Torgar.

"I can't be getting down," came a call from above, and all eyes lifted to see Cordio peering over the entrance, far above. "Ain't no place to set the rope."

"I'll get him," Drizzt assured Bruenor.

With agility that continued to awe, the drow ran up the side of the stalagmite, sliding his scimitars away. At the top, he searched and found his handholds, and between those and the rope, which Cordio had braced once more, Drizzt soon disappeared back out of the hole.

A few moments later, Cordio came down on the rope, gaining to the top of the mound, then, with Drizzt's help, he worked his way gingerly down to the ground. Drizzt came back into the cavern soon after, hanging by his fingertips. He fell purposely, landing lightly atop the stalagmite mound. From there, the drow trotted down to join his friends.

"Stupid, smelly lizards," Pwent muttered as he tried to put his boot back on. The metal bands had been bent, though, crimping the opening in the shoe, and so it was no easy task.

"What were them things?" Bruenor asked any and all.

"Extraplanar creatures," said Cordio, who was inspecting one of the bodies—one of the bodies that was smoking and dissipating before his very eyes. "I'd be keeping yer cat in its statue, elf."

Drizzt's hand went reflexively to his pouch, where he kept the onyx figurine he used to summon Guenhwyvar to the Prime Material Plane. He nodded his agreement with Cordio. If ever he had needed the panther, it would have been in the last fight, and even then, he hadn't dared call upon her. He could sense it, too, a pervasive aura of strange otherworldliness. The place was either truly haunted or somehow dimensionally unstable.

He slipped his hand in the pouch and felt the contours of the panther replica. He hoped the situation wouldn't force him to chance a call to Guenhwyvar, but in glancing around at his already battered companions, he had little confidence that it could be avoided for long.

CHAPTER

The orcs of Clan Yellowtusk swept into the forest from the north, attacking trees as if avenging some heinous crime perpetrated upon them by the inanimate plants. Axes chopped and fires flared to life, and the group, as ordered, made as much noise as they could.

On a hillside to the east, Dnark, Toogwik Tuk, and Ung-thol crouched and waited nervously, while Clan Karuck crept along the low ground behind them and to the south.

"This is too brazen," Ung-thol warned. "The elves will come out in force."

Dnark knew that his shaman's words were not without merit, for they'd encroached on the Moonwood, the home of a deadly clan of elves.

"We will be gone across the river before the main groups arrive," Toogwik Tuk replied. "Grguch and Hakuun have planned this carefully."

"We are exposed!" Ung-thol protested. "If we are seen here on open ground . . ."

"Their eyes will be to the north, to the flames that eat their beloved god-trees," said Toogwik Tuk.

"It is a gamble," Dnark interjected, calming both shamans.

"It is the way of the warrior," said Toogwik Tuk. "The way of the orc. It is something Obould Many-Arrows would have once done, but no more."

Truth resonated in those words to both Dnark and Ung-thol. The chieftain glanced down at the creeping warriors of Clan Karuck, many shrouded by branches they had attached to their dark armor and clothing. Further to the side, tight around the trees of a small copse, a band of ogre javelin throwers held still and quiet, atlatl throwing sticks in hand.

The day could bring disaster, a ruination of all of their plans to force Obould forward, Dnark knew. Or it could bring glory, which would then only push their plans all the more. In any event, a blow struck here would sound like the shredding of a treaty, and that, the chieftain thought, could only be a good thing.

He crouched back low in the grass and watched the scene unfolding before him. He wouldn't likely see the approach of the cunning elves, of course, but he would know of their arrival by the screams of Clan Yellowtusk's sacrificed forward warriors.

A moment later, and not so far to the north, one such cry of orc agony rent the air.

Dnark glanced down at Clan Karuck, who continued their methodical encirclement.

* * * * *

Innovindil could only shake her head in dismay to see the dark lines of smoke rising from the northern end of the Moonwood yet again. The orcs were nothing if not stubborn.

Her bow across her saddle before her, the elf brought Sunset up above the treetops, but kept the pegasus low. The forward scouts would engage the orcs before her arrival, no doubt, but she still hoped to get some shots in from above with the element of surprise working for her.

She banked the pegasus left, toward the river, thinking to come around the back of the orc mob so that she could better direct the battle to her companions on the ground. She went even lower as she broke clear of the thick tree line and eased Sunset's reins, letting the pegasus fly full out. The wind whipped through the elf's blond locks, her hair and cape flapping out behind her, her eyes tearing from the refreshingly chilly breeze. Her rhythm held perfect, posting smoothly with the rise and fall of her steed's powerful shoulders, her balance so centered and complete that she seemed an extension of the pegasus rather than a separate being. She let the fingers of one hand feel the fine design of her bow, while her other hand slipped down to brush the feathered fletching of the arrows set in a quiver on the side of her saddle. She rolled an arrow with her fingers, anticipating when she could let it fly for the face of an orc marauder.

Keeping the river on her left and the trees on her right, Innovindil cruised along. She came up on one hillock and had nearly flown over it by the time she noticed carefully camouflaged forms creeping along.

Orcs. South of the fires and the noise. South of the forward scouts.

The veteran elf warrior recognized an ambush when she saw one. A second group of orcs were set to swing against the rear flank of the Moonwood elves, which meant that the noisemakers and fire-starters in the north were nothing more than a diversion.

Innovindil did a quick scan of the forest beyond and the movement before her, and understood the danger. She took up the reins and banked Sunset hard to the right, flying over a copse of trees that left only a short open expanse to the forest proper. She focused on the greater forest ahead, trying to gauge the fight, the location of the orcs and of her people.

Still, the perceptive elf caught the movements around the trees below her, for she could hardly have missed the brutish behemoths scrambling in the leafless copse. They stood twice her height, with shoulders more than thrice her girth.

She saw them, and they saw her, and they rushed around below her, lifting heavy javelins on notched atlatls.

"Fly on, Sunset!" Innovindil cried, recognizing the danger even before one of the missiles soared her way. She pulled back the reins hard, angling her mount higher, and Sunset, understanding the danger, beat his wings with all his strength and speed.

A javelin cracked the air as it flew past, narrowly missing her, and Innovindil couldn't believe the power behind that throw.

She banked the pegasus left and right, not wanting to present an easy target or a predictable path. She and Sunset had to be at their best in the next few moments, and Innovindil steeled her gaze, ready to meet that challenge.

She couldn't know that she had been expected, and she was too busy dodging huge javelins to take note of the small flying serpent soaring along the treetops parallel to her.

* * * * *

Chieftain Grguch watched the darting and swerving pegasus with amusement and grudging respect. It quickly became clear to him that the ogres would not take the flying pair down, as his closest advisor had predicted. He turned to the prescient Hakuun then, his smile wide.

"This is why I keep you beside me," he said, though he doubted that the shaman, deep in the throes of casting a spell he had prepared precisely for that eventuality, even heard him.

The sight of a ridden pegasus over the previous battle with the elves had greatly angered Grguch, for he had thought on that occasion that his ambush had the raiding group fooled. The flyer had precipitated the elves' escape, Grguch believed, and so he had feared it would happen again—and worse, feared that an elf on high might discover the vulnerable Clan Karuck as well.

Hakuun had given him his answer, and that answer played out in full as the shaman lifted his arms skyward and shouted the last few words of his spell. The air before Hakuun's lips shuddered, a wave of shocking energy blaring forth, distorting images like a rolling ball of water or extreme heat rising from hot stone.

Hakuun's spell exploded around the dodging elf and pegasus, the air itself trembling and quaking in shock waves that buffeted and battered both rider and mount.

Hakuun turned a superior expression his beloved chieftain's way, as if to report simply, "Problem solved."

* * * * *

Innovindil didn't know what hit her, and perhaps more importantly, hit Sunset. They held motionless for a heartbeat, sudden, crackling gusts battering them from all sides. Then they were falling, dazed, but only for a short span before Sunset spread his wings and caught the updrafts.

But they were lower again, too near the ground, and with all momentum stolen. No skill, in rider or in mount, could counter that sudden reversal. Luck alone would get them through.

Sunset whinnied in pain and Innovindil felt a jolt behind her leg.

She looked down to see a javelin buried deep in the pegasus's flank, bright blood dripping out on the great steed's white coat.

"Fly on!" Innovindil implored, for what choice did they have?

Another spear flew past, and another sent Sunset into a sudden turn as it shot up in front of them.

Innovindil hung on for all her life, knuckles whitening, legs clamping the flying horse's flanks. She wanted to reach back and pull out the javelin, which clearly dragged at the pegasus, but she couldn't risk it in that moment of frantic twisting and dodging.

The Moonwood rose up before her, dark and inviting, the place she had known as her home for centuries. If she could just get there, the clerics would tend to Sunset.

She got hit hard on the side and nearly thrown from her perch, unexpectedly buffeted by Sunset's right wing. It hit her again, and the horse dropped suddenly. A javelin had driven through the poor pegasus's wing, right at the joint.

Innovindil leaned forward, imploring the horse for his own sake and for hers, to fight through the pain.

She got hit again, harder.

Sunset managed to stop thrashing and extend his wings enough to catch the updraft and keep them moving along.

As they left the copse behind, Innovindil believed that they could make it, that her magnificent pegasus had enough determination and fortitude to get them through. She turned again to see to the javelin in Sunset's flank—or tried to.

For as Innovindil pivoted in her saddle, a fiery pain shot through her side, nearly taking her from consciousness. The elf somehow settled and turned just her head, and realized then that the last buffet she had taken hadn't been from Sunset's wing, for a dart of some unknown origin hung from her hip, and she could feel it pulsing with magical energy, beating like a heart and flushing painful acid into her side. The closer line of blood pouring down Sunset's flank was her own and not the pegasus's.

Her right leg had gone completely numb, and patches of blackness flitted about her field of vision.

"Fly on," she murmured to the pegasus, though she knew that every stroke of wings brought agony to her beloved equine friend. But they had to get over the forward elf line. Nothing else mattered.

Valiant Sunset rose up over the nearest trees of the Moonwood, and brave Innovindil called down to her people, who she knew to be moving through the trees. "Flee to the south and west," she begged in a voice growing weaker by the syllable. "Ambush! Trap!"

Sunset beat his wings again then whinnied in pain and jerked to the left. They couldn't hold. Somewhere in the back of her mind, in a place caught between consciousness and blackness, Innovindil knew the pegasus could not go on.

She thought that the way before them was clear, but suddenly a large tree loomed where before there had been only empty space. It made no sense to her. She didn't even begin to think that a wizard might be nearby, casting illusions to deceive her. She was only dimly aware as she and Sunset plowed into the tangle of the large tree, and she felt no real pain as she and the horse crashed in headlong, tumbling and twisting in a bone-crunching descent through the branches and to the ground. At one point she caught a curious sight indeed, though it hardly registered: a little, aged gnome with only slight tufts of white hair above his considerable ears and dressed in beautiful shimmering robes of purple and red sat on a branch, legs crossed at the ankles and rocking childlike back and forth, staring at her with an amused expression.

Delirium, the presage to death, she briefly thought. It had to be.

Sunset hit the ground first, in a twisted and broken heap, and Innovindil fell atop him, her face close to his.

She heard his last breath.

She died atop him.

* * * * *

Back on the hillside, the three orcs lost sight of the elf and her flying horse long before the crash, but they had witnessed the javelin strikes, and had cheered each.

"Clan Karuck!" Dnark said, punching his fist into the air, and daring to believe in that moment of elation and victory that the arrival of the half-ogres and their behemoth kin would indeed deliver all the promises of optimistic Toogwik Tuk. The elves and their flying horses had been a bane to the orcs since they had come south, but would any more dare glide over the fields of the Kingdom of Many-Arrows?

"Karuck," Toogwik Tuk agreed, clapping the chieftain on the shoulder, and pointing below.

There, Grguch stood tall, arms upraised. "Take them!" the half-ogre cried to his people. "To the forest!"

With a howl and hoot that brought goosebumps to the chieftain and shamans, the warriors of Clan Karuck leaped up from their concealment and ran howling toward the forest. From the small copse to the south came the lumbering ogres, each with a throw-stick resting on one shoulder, a javelin set in its Y, angled forward and up, ready to launch.

The ground shook beneath their charge, and the wind itself retreated before the force of their vicious howls.

"Clan Karuck!" Ung-thol agreed with his two companions. "And may all the world tremble."

* * * * *

Innovindil's warning cry had been heard, and her people trusted her judgment enough not to question the command. As word filtered through the trees, the Moonwood elves let fly one last arrow and turned to the southwest, sprinting along from cover to cover. Whatever their anger, whatever the temptation of turning back to strike at the orcs in the north, they would not ignore Innovindil.

And true to their beliefs, within a matter of moments, they heard the roars from the east, and realized the trap that their companion had spied. With expert coordination, they tightened their ranks and moved toward the most defensible ground they could find.

Those farthest to the east, a group of a dozen forest folk, were the first to see the charge of Clan Karuck. The enormous half-breeds ran through the trees with wild abandon and frightening speed.

"Hold them," the leader of that patrol told her fellow elves.

Several others looked at her incredulously, but from the majority came nothing but determination. The charge was too ferocious. The other elves moving tree to tree would be overrun.

The group settled behind an ancient, broken, weatherworn wall of piled stones. Exchanging grim nods, they set their arrows and crouched low.

The first huge orcs came into sight, but the elves held their shots. More and more appeared behind the lead runners, but the elves did not break, and did not let fly. The battle wasn't about them, they understood, but about their kin fleeing behind them.

The nearest Clan Karuck warriors were barely five strides from the rock wall when the elves popped up as one, lowered their bows in unison and launched a volley of death.

Orcs shrieked and fell, and the snow before the wall was splattered with red. More arrows went out, but more and more orcs came on. And leaping out before those orcs came a small flaming sphere, and the elves knew what it portended. As one, they crouched and covered against the fireball—one that, in truth, did more damage to the front rank of the charging orcs than to the covering elves, except that it interrupted the stream of the elves' defense.

Clan Karuck fed on the cries of its dying members. Fear was not known among the warriors, who wanted only to die in the service of Gruumsh and Grguch. In a frenzy they defied the rain of arrows and the burning branches falling from the continuing conflagration on high. Some even grabbed their skewered companions and tugged them along as shields.

Behind the wall, the elves abandoned their bows and drew out long, slender swords. In shining mail and with windblown cloaks, most still trailing wisps of smoke and a couple still burning, they met the charge with splendor, strength, and courage.

But Grguch and his minions overran them and slaughtered them, and their weapons gleamed red, not silver, and their cloaks, weighted with blood, would not flap in the breeze.

Grguch led the warriors through the forest a short distance farther, but he knew that he was traveling on elven ground, where defensive lines of archers would sting his warriors from the tops of hills and the boughs of trees, and where powerful spells would explode without warning. He pulled up and raised his open hand, a signal to halt the charge, then he motioned to the south, sending a trio of ogres forward.

"Take their heads," he ordered to his orcs, and nodded back to the stone wall. "We'll pike them along the western bank of the river to remind the faerie folk of their mistake."

Up ahead, some distance already, an ogre cried out in pain. Grguch nodded his understanding, knowing that the elves would regroup quickly—that they probably already had. He looked around at his charges and grinned.

"To the river," he ordered, confident that his point had been made, to Clan Karuck and to the three emissaries who had brought them forth from their tunnels under the Spine of the World.

He didn't know about the fourth non-Karuck onlooker, of course, who had played a role in it all. Jack was back in his Jaculi form, wrapped around the limb of a tree, watching it all unfold around him with mounting curiosity. He would have to have a long talk with Hakuun, and soon, he realized, and he felt a bit of joy then that he had followed Clan Karuck out of the Underdark.

He had long forgotten about the wide world and the fun of mischief.

Besides, he'd never liked elves.

* * * * *

Toogwik Tuk, Ung-thol, and Dnark beamed with toothy grins as they made their way back to orc-held lands.

"We have brought forth the fury of Gruumsh," Dnark said when the trio stood on the western bank of the Surbrin, looking back east at the Moonwood. The sun was low behind them, dusk falling, and the forest took on a singular appearance, as if its tree line was the defensive wall of an immense castle.

"It will remind King Obould of our true purpose," Ung-thol posited.

"Or he will be replaced," said Toogwik Tuk.

The other two didn't even wince at those words, spoken openly. Not after seeing the cunning, the ferocity, and the power of Giguch and Clan Karuck. Barely twenty feet north of their position, an elf head staked upon a tall pike swayed in the wind.

* * * * *

Albondiel's heart sank when he spotted the flash of white against the forest ground. At first he thought it just another patch of snow, but as he came around one thick tree and gained a better vantage point, he realized the truth.

Snow didn't have feathers.

"Hralien," he called in a voice breaking on every syllable. Time seemed to freeze for the shocked elf, as if half the day slid by, but in only a few moments, Hralien was at Albondiel's side.

"Sunset," Hralien whispered and moved forward.

Albondiel summoned his courage and followed. He knew what they would find.

Innovindil still lay atop the pegasus, her arms wrapped around Sunset's neck, her face pressed close to his. From Albondiel's first vantage point when he came around the tree that had abruptly ended Innovindil and Sunset's flight, the scene was peaceful and serene, almost as if his friend had fallen asleep atop her beloved equine friend. Scanning farther down, though, revealed the truth, revealed the blood and the gigantic javelins, the shattered wings and the magical wound of dissolved flesh behind Innovindil's hip.

Hralien bent over the dead elf and gently stroked her thick hair, and ran his other hand over the soft and muscled neck of Sunset.

"They were ready for us," he said.

"Ready?" said Albondiel, shaking his head and wiping the tears from his cheeks. "More than that. They lured us. They anticipated our counterstrike."

"They are orcs!" Hralien protested, rising fast and turning away.

He brought his arms straight out before him, then slowly moved them out wide to either side then behind him, arching his back and lifting his face to the sky as he went. It was a ritual movement, often used in times of great stress and anguish, and Hralien ended by issuing a high-pitched keen toward the sky, a protest to the gods for the pain visited upon his people that dark day.

He collected himself quickly, his grief thrown out for the moment, and spun back at Albondiel, who still kneeled, stroking Innovindil's head.

"Orcs," Hralien said again. "Have they become so sophisticated in their methods?"

"They have always been cunning," Albondiel replied.

"They know too much of us," Hralien protested.

"Then we must change our tactics."

But Hralien was shaking his head. "It is more, I fear. Could it be that they are guided by a dark elf who knows how we fight?"

"We do not know that," Albondiel cautioned. "This was a simple ambush, perhaps."

"One ready for Innovindil and Sunset!"

"By design or by coincidence? You assume much."

Hralien knelt beside his friends, living and dead. "Can we afford not to?"

Albondiel pondered that for a few moments. "We should find Tos'un."

"We should get word to Mithral Hall," said Hralien. "To Drizzt Do'Urden, who will grieve for Innovindil and Sunset. He will understand better the methods of Tos'un, and has already vowed to find the drow."

A shadow passed over them, drawing their attention skyward.

Sunrise circled above them, tossing his head and crying out pitifully for the lost pegasus.

Albondiel looked at Hralien and saw tears streaking his friend's face. He looked back up at the pegasus, but could hardly make out the flying horse through the glare of his own tears in the morning sunlight.

"Get Drizzt," he heard himself whisper.

CHAPTER
MISDIRECTING CLUES

11

"Pack it up and move it out," Bruenor grumbled, slinging his backpack over his shoulder. He snatched up his axe, wrapping his hand around the handle just under the well-worn head. He prodded the hard ground with it as if it were a walking stick as he moved away from the group.

Thibbledorf Pwent, wearing much of his lunch in his beard and on his armor, hopped up right behind, eager to be on his way, and Cordio and Torgar similarly rose to Bruenor's call, though with less enthusiasm, even with a wary glance to each other.

Regis just gave a sigh and looked down at the remainder of his meal, a slab of cold beef wrapped with flattened bread, and with a bowl of thick gravy and a biscuit on the side.

"Always in a hurry," the halfling said to Drizzt, who helped him rewrap the remaining food.

"Bruenor is nervous," said Drizzt, "and anxious."

"Because he fears more monsters?"

"Because these tunnels are not to his expectations or to his liking," the drow explained, and Regis nodded at the revelation.

They had come into the hole expecting to find a tunnel to the dwarven city of Gauntlgrym, and at first, after their encounter with the strange beasts, things had seemed pretty much as they had anticipated, including a sloping tunnel with a worked wall. The other side seemed more natural stone and dirt, as were the ceiling and floor, but that one wall had left no doubt that it was more than a natural cave, and the craftsmanship evident in the fitted stones made Bruenor and the other dwarves believe that it was indeed the work of their ancestors.

But that tunnel hadn't held its promise or its course, and though they were deeper underground, and though they still found fragments of old construction, the trail seemed to be growing cold.

Drizzt and Regis moved quickly to close the distance to the others. With the monsters about, appearing suddenly from the shadows as if from nowhere, the group didn't dare separate. That presented a dilemma a hundred feet along, when Bruenor led them all into a small chamber they quickly recognized to be a hub, with no fewer than six tunnels branching out from it.

"Well, there ye be!" Bruenor cried, hefting his axe and punching it into the air triumphantly. "Ain't no river or burrowing beast made this plaza."

Looking around, it was hard for Drizzt to disagree, for other than one side, where dirt had collapsed into the place, the chamber seemed perfectly circular, and the tunnels too equidistant for it to be a random design.

Torgar fell to his knees and began digging at the hard-packed dirt, and his progress multiplied many times over when Pwent dropped down beside him and put his spiked gauntlets to work. In a few moments, the battlerager scraped stone, and as he worked his way out to the sides, it became apparent that the stone was flat.

"A paver!" Torgar announced.

"Gauntlgrym," Bruenor said to Drizzt and Regis with an exaggerated wink. "Never doubt an old dwarf."

"Another one!" Pwent announced.

"Sure'n the whole place is full o' them," said Bruenor. "It's a trading hub for caravans, or I'm a bearded gnome. Yerself's knowing that," he said to Torgar, and the Mirabarran dwarf nodded.

Drizzt looked past the three dwarves to the fourth, Cordio, who had moved to the wall between a pair of the tunnels and was scraping at the wall. The dwarf nodded as his knife sank in deeper along a crease in the stone behind the accumulated dirt and mud, revealing a vertical line.

"What do ye know?" Bruenor asked, leading Torgar and Thibbledorf over to the cleric.

A moment later, as Cordio broke away a larger piece of the covering grime, it became apparent to all that the cleric had found a door. After a few moments, they managed to clear it completely, and to their delight they were able to pry it open, revealing a single-roomed structure behind it. Part of the back left corner had collapsed, taking a series of shelves down with it, but other than that, the place seemed frozen in time.

"Dwarven," Bruenor was saying as Drizzt moved to the threshold.

The dwarf stood off to the side of the small door, examining a rack holding a few ancient metal artifacts. They were tools or weapons, obviously, and Bruenor upended one to examine its head, which could have been the remnants of a pole arm, or even a hoe, perhaps.

"Might be dwarven," Torgar agreed, examining the shorter-handled item beside the one Bruenor had lifted, one showing the clear remains of a spade. "Too old to know for sure."

"Dwarven," Bruenor insisted. He turned and let his gaze encompass the whole of the small house. "All the place is dwarven."

The others nodded, more because they couldn't disprove the theory than because they had reached the same conclusions. The remnants of a table and a pair of chairs might well have been dwarf-made, and seemed about the right size for the bearded folk. Cordio moved around those items to a hearth, and as he began clearing the debris from it and scraping at the stone, that, too, seemed to bolster Bruenor's argument. For there was no mistaking the craftsmanship evident in the ancient fireplace. The bricks had been so tightly set that the passage of time had done little to diminish the integrity of the structure, and indeed it seemed as if, with a bit of cleaning, the companions could safely light a fire.

Drizzt, too, noted that hearth, and paid particular heed to the shallowness of the fireplace, and the funnel shape of the side walls, widening greatly into the room.

"The plaza's a forward post for the city," Bruenor announced as they began moving back out. "So I'm guessing that the city's opposite the tunnel we just came down."

"In the lead!" said Pwent, heading that way at once.

"Good guess on the door," Bruenor said to Cordio, and he patted the cleric on the shoulder before he and Torgar started off after the battlerager.

"It wasn't a guess," Drizzt said under his breath, so that only Regis could hear. And Cordio, for the dwarf glanced back at Drizzt—his expression seeming rather sour, Regis thought—then moved off after his king, muttering, "Wouldn't need pavers this far down."

Regis looked from him to Drizzt, his expression begging answers.

"It was a free-standing house, and not a reinforced cave dwelling," Drizzt explained.

Regis glanced around. "You think there are others, separating the exit tunnels?"

"Probably."

"And what does that mean? There were many free-standing houses in the bowels of Mirabar. Not so uncommon a thing in underground cities."

"True enough," Drizzt agreed. "Menzoberranzan is comprised of many similar structures."

"Cordio's expression spoke of some significance," the halfling remarked. "If this type of structure is to be expected, then why did he wear a frown?"

"Did you note the fireplace?" Drizzt asked.

"Dwarven," Regis replied.

"Perhaps."

"What's wrong?"

"The fireplace was not a cooking pit, primarily," Drizzt explained. "It was designed to throw heat into the room."

Regis shrugged, not understanding.

"We are far enough underground so that the temperature hardly varies," Drizzt informed him, and started off after the others.

Regis paused for just a moment, and glanced back at the revealed structure.

"Should we search this area more completely?" the halfling asked.

"Follow Bruenor," Drizzt replied. "We will have our answers soon enough."

They kept their questions unspoken as they hurried to join up with the four dwarves, which took some time, for the excited Bruenor led them down the tunnel at a hurried pace.

The tunnel widened considerably soon after, breaking into what seemed to be a series of parallel tracks of varying widths continuing in the same general direction. Bruenor moved without hesitation down the centermost of them, but they found it to be a moot choice anyway, since the tunnels interconnected at many junctures. What they soon discerned was that this wasn't so much a series of tunnels as a singular pathway, broken up by pillars, columns, and other structures.

At one such interval, they came upon a low entrance, capped diagonally by a structure that had obviously been made by skilled masons, for the bricks could still be seen, and they held fast despite the passage of centuries and the apparent collapse of the building, which had sent it crashing to the side into another wall.

"Could be a shaft, pitched for a fast descent," Bruenor remarked.

"It's a building that tipped," Cordio argued, and Bruenor snorted and waved his hand dismissively.

But Torgar, who had moved closer, said, "Aye, it is." He paused and looked up. "And one that fell a long way. Or slid."

"And how're ye knowin' that?" Bruenor asked, and there was no mistaking the hint of defiance. He was catching on, obviously, that things weren't unfolding the way he'd anticipated.

Torgar was already motioning them over, and began pointing out the closest corner of the structure, where the edge of the bricks had been rounded, but not by tools.

"We see this in Mirabar all the time," Torgar explained, running a fat thumb over the corner. "Wind wore it round. This place was under the sky, not under the rock."

"There's wind in some tunnels," said Bruenor. "Currents and such blowin' down strong from above."

Torgar remained unconvinced. "This building was up above," he said, shaking his head, "for years and years afore it fell under."

"Bah!" Bruenor snorted. "Ye're guessin'."

"Might be that Gauntlgrym had an aboveground market," Cordio interjected.

Drizzt looked at Regis and rolled his eyes, and as the dwarves moved off, the halfling grabbed Drizzt by the sleeve and held him back.

"You don't believe that Gauntlgrym had an aboveground market?" he asked.

"Gauntlgrym?" Drizzt echoed skeptically.

"You don't believe?"

"More than the market of this place was above ground, I fear," said Drizzt. "Much more. And Cordio and Torgar see it, too."

"But not Bruenor," said Regis.

"It will be a blow to him. One he is not ready to accept."

"You think this whole place was a city above ground?" Regis stated. "A city that sank into the tundra?"

"Let us follow the dwarves. We will learn what we will learn."

The tunnels continued on for a few hundred more feet, but the group came to a solid blockage, one that sealed off all of the nearby corridors. Torgar tapped on that wall repeatedly with a small hammer, listening for echoes, and after inspecting it at several points in all the tunnels, announced to the troop, "There's a big open area behind it. I'm knowin' it."

"Forges?" Bruenor asked hopefully.

Torgar could only shrug. "Only one way we're goin' to find out, me king."

So they set their camp right there, down the main tunnel at the base of the wall, and while Drizzt and Regis went back up the tunnel some distance to keep watch back near the wider areas, the four dwarves devised their plans for safely excavating. Soon after they had shared their next meal, the sound of hammers rang out against the stone, none more urgent than Bruenor's own.

CHAPTER

I had hoped to find the woman before we crossed the last expanse to Nesmé," Wulfgar remarked to Catti-brie. Their caravan had stopped to re-supply at a nondescript, unnamed cluster of houses still a couple of days' travel from their destination, and the last such scheduled stop on their journey.

"There are still more settlements, Catti-brie reminded him, for indeed, the drivers had told them that they would pass more secluded lodges in the next two days.

"The houses of hunters and loners," Wulfgar replied. "No places appropriate for Cottie to remain with Colson."

"Unless all the refugees remained together and decided to begin their own community."

Wulfgar replied with a knowing smile, a reflection of Catti-brie's own feelings on the subject, to be sure. She knew as Wulfgar knew that they would find Cottie Cooperson and Colson in Nesmé.

"Two days," Catti-brie said. "In two days, you will have Colson in your arms once more. Where she belongs."

Wulfgar's grim expression, even a little wince, caught her by surprise.

"We have heard of no tragedies along the road," Catti-brie added. "If the caravan bearing Cottie and the others had been attacked, word would have already spread through these outposts. Since we are so close, we can say with confidence that Cottie and Colson reached Nesmé safely."

"Still, I have no love of the place," he said, "and no desire to see the likes of Galen Firth or his prideful companions ever again."

Catti-brie moved closer and put her hand on Wulfgar's shoulder. "We will collect the child and be gone," she said. "Quickly and with few words. We come with the backing of Mithral Hall, and to Mithral Hall we will return with your child."

Wulfgar's face was unreadable, though that, of course, only reaffirmed Catti-brie's suspicions that something was amiss.

The caravan rolled out of the village before the next dawn, wheels creaking against the uneven strain of the perpetually muddy ground. As they continued west, the Trollmoors, the fetid swamp of so many unpleasant beasts, seemed to creep up toward them from the south. But the drivers and those more familiar with the region appeared unconcerned, and were happy to explain, often, that things had quieted since the rout of the trolls by Alustriel's Knights in Silver and the brave Riders of Nesmé.

"The road's safer than it's been in more than a decade," the lead driver insisted.

"More's the pity," one of the regulars from the second wagon answered loudly. "I been hoping a few trolls or bog blokes might show their ugly faces, just so I can watch the work of King Bruenor's kids!"

That brought a cheer from all around, and a smile did widen on Catti-brie's face. She looked to Wulfgar. If he had even heard the remarks, he didn't show it.

Wulfgar and Catti-brie weren't really sure what they might find when their caravan finally came into view of Nesmé, but they knew at once that it was not the same town through which they had traveled on their long-ago journey to rediscover Mithral Hall. Anticipated images of ruined and burned-out homes and shoddy, temporary shelters did not prepare them for the truth of the place. For Nesmé had risen again already, even through the cold winds of winter.

Most of the debris from the troll rampage had been cleared, and newer buildings, stronger, taller, and with thicker walls, replaced the old structures. The double wall surrounding the whole of the place neared completion, and was particularly fortified along the southern borders, facing the Trollmoors.

Contingents of armed and armored riders patrolled the town, meeting the caravan far out from the new and larger gate.

Nesmé was alive again, a testament to the resiliency and determination, and sheer stubbornness that had marked the frontiers of human advancement throughout Faerûn. For all of their rightful negativity toward the place, given their reception those years before, neither Wulfgar nor Catti-brie could hide their respect.

"So much like Ten-Towns," Catti-brie quietly remarked as their wagon neared the gate. "They will not bend."

Wulfgar nodded his agreement, slightly, but he was clearly distracted as he continued to stare at the town.

"They've more people now than before the trolls," Catti-brie said, repeating something the caravan drivers had told the both of them earlier along the road. "Twice the number, say some."

Wulfgar didn't blink and didn't look her way. She sensed his inner turmoil, and knew that it wasn't about Colson. Not only, at least.

She tried one last time to engage him, saying, "Nesmé might inspire other towns to grow along the road to Silverymoon, and won't that be a fitting response to the march of the murderous trolls? It may well be that the northern border will grow strong enough to build a militia that can press into the swamp and be rid of the beasts once and for all."

"It might," said Wulfgar, in such a tone as to show Catti-brie that he hadn't even registered that to which he agreed.

The town gates, towering barriers thrice the height of a tall man and built of strong black-barked logs banded together with heavy straps of metal, groaned in protest as the sentries pulled them back to allow the caravan access to the town's open courtyard. Beyond that defensive wall, Wulfgar and Catti-brie could see that their initial views of Nesmé were no illusion, for indeed the town was larger and more impressive than it had been those years before. It had an official barracks to support the larger militia, a long, two-story building to their left along the defensive southern wall. Before them loomed the tallest structure in town, aside from a singular tower that was under work somewhere in the northwestern quadrant. Two dozen steps led off the main plaza where the wagons parked, directly west of the eastern-facing gates. At the top of those steps ran a pair of parallel, narrow bridges, just a short and defensible expanse, to the impressive front of the new Nesmian Town Hall. Like all the rest of the town, the building was under construction, but like most of the rest, it was ready to stand against any onslaught the Trollmoors in the south, or King Obould in the north, might throw against it.

Wulfgar hopped down from the back of the wagon, then helped Catti-brie to the ground so that she didn't have to pressure her injured hip. She spent a moment standing there, using his offered arm for support, as she stretched the tightness out of her pained leg.

"The folk ye seek could be anywhere in the town," their wagon driver said to them, walking over and speaking quietly.

He alone among the caravan had been in on the real reason Wulfgar and Catti-brie were journeying to Nesmé, for fear that someone else might gossip and send word to Cottie and her friends to flee ahead of their arrival. "They'll not be in any common rooms, as ye saw in Silverymoon, for Nesmé's being built right around the new arrivals. More than half the folk ye'll find here just came from other parts, mostly from lands Obould's darkened with his hordes. Them and some of the Knights in Silver, who remained with the Lady's blessing so that they could get closer to where the fighting's likely to be. . . ."

"Surely there are scribes making note of who's coming in and where they're settling," said Catti-brie.

"If so, ye'll find them in there," said the driver, motioning toward the impressive town hall. "If not, yer best chance is in frequenting the taverns after work's done. Most all the workers find their way to those places—and there're only a few such establishments, and they're all together on one avenue near the southwestern corner. If any're knowing of Cottie, there's the place to find them."

* * * * *

Word spread fast through Nesmé that the arriving caravan had carried with it a couple of extraordinary guards. When the whispers of Catti-brie and Wulfgar reached the ears of Cottie Cooperson's fellow refugees, they knew at once that their friend was in jeopardy.

So by the time Wulfgar and Catti-brie had made their way to the tavern avenue, a pair of concerned friends had whisked Cottie and Colson to the barracks area and the separate house of the town's current leader, Galen Firth.

"He's come to take the child," Teegorr Reth explained to Galen, while his friend Romduul kept Cottie and Colson out in the anteroom.

Galen Firth settled back in his chair behind his desk, digesting it all. It had come as a shock to him, and not a pleasant one, that the human prince and princess of Mithral Hall had arrived in his town. He had assumed it to be a diplomatic mission, and given the principals involved, he had suspected that it wouldn't be a friendly one. Mithral Hall had suffered losses for the sake of Nesmé in the recent battles. Could it be that King Bruenor sought some sort of recompense?

Galen had never been friendly with the dwarves of Mithral Hall or with these two.

"You cannot let him have her," Teegorr implored the Nesmian leader.

"What is his claim?" Galen asked.

"Begging your pardon, sir, but Cottie's been seeing to the girl since she left Mithral Hall. She's taken Colson as her own child, and she's been hurt."

"The child?"

"No, Cottie, sir," Teegorr explained. "She's lost her own—all her own."

"And the child is Wulfgar's?"

"No, not really. He brought the girl to Mithral Hall, with Delly, but then Delly gave her to Cottie."

"With or without Wulfgar's agreement?"

"Who's to say?"

"Wulfgar, I would assume."

"But . . ."

"You assume that Wulfgar has come here to take the child, but could it be that he is merely passing through to check up on her?" Galen asked. "Or might it be that he is here for different reasons—would he even know that your friend Cottie decided to settle in Nesmé?"

"I . . . I . . . I can't be saying for sure, sir."

"So you presume. Very well, then. Let Cottie stay here for now until we can determine why Wulfgar has come."

"Oh, and I thank you for that!"

"But make no mistake, good Teegorr, if Wulfgar's claim is true and he wants the child back, I am bound to honor his claim."

"Your pardon, sir, but Cottie's got twenty folk with her. Good strong hands, who know the frontier and who know how to fight."

"Are you threatening me?"

"No, sir!" Teegorr was quick to reply. "But if Nesmé's not to protect our own, then how are our own to stay in Nesmé?"

"What are you asking?" Galen replied, standing up forcefully. "Am I to condone kidnapping? Is Nesmé to become an outpost for criminals?"

"It's not so simple as that, is all," said Teegorr. "Delly Curtie gave the girl to Cottie, so she's no kidnapper, and not without claim."

That settled Galen Firth back a bit. He couldn't keep the disdain from his face, for it was not a fight he wanted to entertain just then. Clan Battlehammer and Nesmé were not on good terms, despite the fact that the dwarves had sent warriors down to help the Nesmians. In the subsequent sorting of events, the rebuilding of Nesmé had taken precedence over King Bruenor's desire to take the war back to Obould, something that had clearly simmered behind the angry eyes of the fiery dwarf.

And there remained that old issue of the treatment Bruenor and his friends, including Wulfgar and the drow elf Drizzt, had met with on their initial pass through Nesmé those years ago, an unpleasant confrontation that had set Galen Firth and the dwarf at odds.

Neither could Galen Firth keep the wry grin from breaking through his otherwise solemn expression on occasion as he pondered the possibilities. He couldn't deny that there would be a measure of satisfaction in causing grief to Wulfgar, if the opportunity presented itself.

"Who knows that you came here?" Galen asked.

Teegorr looked at him curiously. "To Nesmé?"

"Who knows that you and your friend brought Cottie and the child here to me?"

"Some of the others who crossed the Surbrin beside us."

"And they will not speak of it?"

"No," said Teegorr. "Not a one of us wants to see the child taken from Cottie Cooperson. She's suffered terribly, and now she's found peace—and one that's better for the girl than anything Wulfgar might be offering."

"Wulfgar is a prince of Mithral Hall," Galen reminded. "A man of great wealth, no doubt."

"And Mithral Hall is no place for a man, or a girl—particularly a girl!" Teegorr argued. "Good enough for them dwarves, and good for them. But it's no place for a human girl to grow."

Galen Firth rose up from his seat. "Keep her here," he instructed. "I will go and see my old friend Wulfgar. Perhaps he is here for reasons other than the girl."

"And if he is?"

"Then you and I never had this discussion," Galen explained.

He set a pair of guards outside the anteroom, with orders that no one should enter, and he gathered up a couple of others in his wake as he headed out across the darkening town to the taverns and the common rooms. As he expected, he found Wulfgar and Catti-brie in short order, sitting at a table near the bar of the largest of the taverns, and listening more than speaking.

"You have come to join our garrison!" Galen said with great exaggeration as he approached. "I always welcome strong arms and a deadly bow."

Wulfgar and Catti-brie turned to regard him, their faces, particularly the large barbarian's, hardening upon recognition.

"We have need for a garrison of our own in Mithral Hall," Catti-brie replied politely.

"The orcs have not been pushed back," Wulfgar added, his sharp tone reminding Galen Firth that Galen himself, and his insistence on Nesmé taking precedence, had played no minor role in the decision to not dislodge King Obould.

The other folk in the town knew that as well, and didn't miss the reference, and all in the tavern hushed as Galen stood before the two adopted children of King Bruenor Battlehammer.

"Everything in its time," Galen replied, after looking around to ensure his support. "The Silver Marches are stronger now that Nesmé has risen from the ruins." A cheer started around him, and he raised his voice in proclamation, "For never again will the trolls come forth from the mud to threaten the lands west of Silverymoon or the southern reaches of your own Mithral Hall."

Wulfgar's jaw tightened even more at the notion that Nesmé was serving as Mithral Hall's vanguard, particularly since Mithral Hall's efforts had preserved what little had remained of Nesmé's population.

Which was exactly the effect Galen Firth had been hoping for, and he grinned knowingly as Catti-brie put her hand on Wulfgar's enormous forearm in an effort to keep him calm.

"We had no word that we would be so graced," Galen said. "Is it customary among Clan Battlehammer for emissaries to arrive unannounced?"

"We are not here on the business of Bruenor," said Catti-brie, and she motioned for Galen Firth to sit down beside her, opposite Wulfgar.

The man did pull out the chair, but he merely turned it and put his foot up on it, which made him tower over the two even more. Until, that is, Wulfgar rose to his feet, his nearly seven foot frame, his giant shoulders, stealing that advantage.

But Galen didn't back down. He stared hard at Wulfgar, locking the man's gaze. "Then why?" he asked, his voice lower and more insistent.

"We came in as sentries for a caravan," Catti-brie said.

Galen glanced down at her. "The children of Bruenor hire out as mercenaries?"

"Volunteers doing our part in the collective effort," Catti-brie answered.

"It was a way to serve others as we served our own needs," Wulfgar said.

"To come to Nesmé?" asked Galen.

"Yes."

"Why, if not for Brue—"

"I have come to find a girl, Colson, who was taken from Mithral Hall," Wulfgar stated.

" 'Taken'? Wrongly?"

"Yes."

Behind Wulfgar, several people bustled about. Galen recognized them as friends of Teegorr and Cottie, and expected that there might soon be trouble—which he didn't think so dire a possibility. In truth, the man was interested in testing his strength against that of the legendary Wulfgar, and besides, he had enough guards nearby to ensure that there would be no real downside to any brawl.

"How is it that a child was abducted from Mithral Hall," he asked, "and ferried across the river by Bruenor's own? What dastardly plot turned that result?"

"The girl's name is Colson," Catti-brie intervened, as Wulfgar and Galen Firth leaned in closer toward each other. "We have reason to believe that she has come to Nesmé. In fact, that seems most assured."

"There are children here," Galen Firth admitted, "brought in with the various groups of displaced people, who have come to find community and shelter."

"No one can deny that Nesmé has opened her gates to those in need," Catti-brie replied, and Wulfgar shot a glare her way. "A mutually beneficial arrangement for a town that grows more grand by the day."

"But there is a child here that does not belong in Nesmé, nor to the woman who brought her here," Wulfgar insisted. "I have come to retrieve that girl."

Someone moved fast behind Wulfgar, and he spun, quick as an elf. He brought his right arm across, sweeping aside a two-handed grab by one of Cottie's friends, then turned the arm down, bringing the fool's arms with it. Wulfgar's left hand snapped out and grabbed the man by the front of his tunic. In the blink of an astonished eye, Wulfgar had the man up in the air, fully two feet off the ground, and shook him with just the one hand.

The barbarian turned back on Galen Firth, and with a flick of his arm sent the shaken fool tumbling aside.

"Colson is leaving with me. She was wrongly taken, and though I bear no ill will"—he paused and turned to let his penetrating gaze sweep the room—"to any of those who were with the woman to whom she was entrusted, and no ill will toward the woman herself—surely not!—I will leave with the girl rightfully returned."

"How did she get out of Mithral Hall, a fortress of dwarves?" an increasingly annoyed Galen Firth asked.

"Delly Curtie," said Wulfgar.

"Wife of Wulfgar," Catti-brie explained.

"Was she not then this child's mother?"

"Adopted mother, as Wulfgar is Colson's adopted father," said Catti-brie.

Galen Firth snorted, and many in the room muttered curses under their breath.

"Delly Curtie was under the spell of a powerful and evil weapon," Catti-brie explained. "She did not surrender the child of her own volition."

"Then she should be here to swear to that very thing."

"She is dead," said Wulfgar.

"Killed by Obould's orcs," Catti-brie added. "For after she handed the child to Cottie Cooperson, she ran off to the north, to the orc lines, where she was found, murdered and frozen in the snow."

Galen Firth did grimace a bit at that, and the look he gave to Wulfgar was almost one tinged with sympathy. Almost.

"The weapon controlled her," said Catti-brie. "Both in surrendering the child and in running to certain doom. It is a most foul blade. I know well, for I carried it for years."

That brought more murmurs from around the room and a look of astonishment from Galen. "And what horrors did Catti-brie perpetrate under the influence of such a sentient evil?"

"None, for I controlled the weapon. It did not control me."

"But Delly Curtie was made of stuff less stern," said Galen Firth. "She was no warrior. She was not raised by dwarves."

Galen Firth didn't miss the pointed reminder of both facts, of who these two were and what they had behind their claim.

He nodded and pondered the words for a bit, then replied, "It is an interesting tale."

"It is a demand that will be properly answered," said Wulfgar, narrowing his blue eyes and leaning even more imposingly toward the leader of Nesmé. "We do not ask you to adjudicate. We tell you the circumstance and expect you to give back the girl."

"You are not in Mithral Hall, son of Bruenor," Galen Firth replied through gritted teeth.

"You deny me?" Wulfgar asked, and it seemed to all that the barbarian was on the verge of a terrible explosion. His blue eyes were wide and wild.

Galen didn't back down, though he surely expected an attack.

And again Catti-brie intervened. "We came to Nesmé as sentries on a caravan from Silverymoon, as a favor to Lady Alustriel," she explained, turning her shoulder and putting her arm across the table to block Wulfgar, though of course she couldn't hope to slow his charge, should it come. "For it was Lady Alustriel, friend of King Bruenor Battlehammer, friend of Drizzt Do'Urden, friend of Wulfgar and of Catti-brie, who told us that Colson would be found in Nesmé."

Galen Firth tried to hold steady, but he knew he was giving ground.

"For she knows Colson well, and well she knows of Colson's rightful father, Wulfgar," Catti-brie went on. "When she heard our purpose in traveling to Silverymoon, she put all of her assets at our disposal, and it was she who told us that Cottie Cooperson and Colson had traveled to Nesmé. She wished us well on our travels, and even offered to fly us here on her fiery chariot, but we felt indebted and so we agreed to travel along with the caravan and serve as sentries."

"Would not a desperate father take the quicker route?" asked Galen Firth, and around him, heads bobbed in agreement.

"We did not know that the caravan bearing Colson made it to Nesmé, or whether perhaps the hearty and good folk accompanying the child decided to debark earlier along the road. And that is not for you to decide in any case, Galen Firth. Do you deny Wulfgar's rightful claim? Would you have us go back to Lady Alustriel and tell her that the proud folk of Nesmé would not accede to the proper claim of Colson's own father? Would you have us return at once to Silverymoon and to Mithral Hall with word that Galen Firth refused to give Wulfgar his child?"

"Adopted child," remarked one of the men across the way.

Galen Firth didn't register that argument. The man had thrown him some support, but only because he obviously needed it at that moment. That poignant reminder had him squaring his shoulders, but he knew that Catti-brie had delivered a death blow to his obstinacy. For he knew that she spoke the truth, and that he could ill afford to anger the Lady of Silverymoon. Whatever might happen between King Bruenor and Galen would not likely ill affect Nesmé, for the dwarves would not come south to do battle, but for Lady Alustriel to take King Bruenor's side was another matter entirely. Nesmé needed Silverymoon's support. No caravan would travel to Nesmé that did not originate in, or at least pass through, the city of Lady Alustriel.

Galen Firth was no fool. He did not doubt the story of Catti-brie and Wulfgar, and he had seen clearly the desperation on Cottie Cooperson's face when he had left her in the barracks. That type of desperation was borne of knowing that she had no real claim, that the child was not hers.

For of course, Colson was not.

Galen Firth looked over his shoulder to his guards. "Go and fetch Cottie Cooperson and the girl," he said.

Protests erupted around the room, with men shaking their fists in the air.

"The child is mine!" Wulfgar shouted at them, turning fiercely, and indeed, all of those in front stepped back. "Would any of you demand any less if she was yours?"

"Cottie is our friend," one man replied, rather meekly. "She means the girl no harm."

"Fetch your own child, then," said Wulfgar. "Relinquish her, or him, to me in trade!"

"What foolish words are those?"

"Words to show you your own folly," said the big man. "However good Cottie Cooperson's heart, and I do not doubt your claim that she is worthy both as a friend and a mother, I cannot surrender to her a girl that is my own. I have come for Colson, and I will leave with Colson, and any man who stands in my way would do well to have made his peace with his god."

He snapped his arm in the air before him and called to Aegis-fang, and the mighty warhammer appeared magically in his grasp. With a flick, Wulfgar rapped the hammer atop a nearby table, shattering all four legs and dropping the kindling to the floor.

Galen Firth gasped in protest, and the one guard behind him reached for his sword—and stared down the length of an arrow set on Catti-brie's Taulmaril.

"Which of you will come forward and deny my claim to Colson?" Wulfgar asked the group, and not surprisingly, his challenge was met with silence.

"You will leave my town," Galen Firth said.

"We will, on the same caravan that brought us in," Catti-brie replied, easing her bow back to a rest position as the guard relinquished his grip on the sword and raised his hands before him. "As soon as we have Colson."

"I intend to protest this to Lady Alustriel," Galen Firth warned.

"When you do," said Catti-brie, "be certain to explain to Lady Alustriel how you almost incited a riot and a tragedy by playing the drama out before the hot humors of men and women who came to your town seeking naught but refuge and a new home. Be certain to tell Lady Alustriel of Silverymoon of your discretion, Galen Firth, and we will do likewise with King Bruenor."

"I grow tired of your threats," Galen Firth said to her, but Catti-brie only smiled in reply.

"And I long ago tired of you," Wulfgar said to the man.

Behind Galen Firth, the tavern door opened, and in came Cottie Cooperson holding Colson and pulled along by a guard. Outside the door two men jostled with another pair of guards, who would not let them enter.

The question of Wulfgar's claim was answered the moment Colson came into the room. "Da!" the toddler cried, verily leaping out of Cottie's grasp to get to the man she had known as her father for all her life. She squealed and squirmed and reached with both her arms for Wulfgar, calling for her "Da!" over and over again.

He rushed to her, dropping Aegis-fang to the ground, and took her in his arms then gently, but forcefully, removed her from Cottie's desperate grasp. Colson made no movement back toward the woman at all, but crushed her da in a desperate hug.

Cottie began to tremble, to cry, and her desperation grew by the second. In a few moments, she went down to her knees, wailing.

And Wulfgar responded, dropping to one knee before her. With his free hand, he lifted her chin and brushed back her hair, then quieted her with soft words. "Colson has a mother who loves her as much as you loved your own children, dear woman," he said.

Behind him, Catti-brie's eyes widened with surprise.

"I can take care o' her," Cottie wailed.

Wulfgar smiled at her, brushed her hair back again, then rose. He called Aegis-fang to his free hand and stalked past Galen Firth, snickering in defiance of the man's glare. As he went through the door, Cottie's two companions, for all their verbal protests, parted before him, for few men in all the world would dare stand before Wulfgar, son of Beornegar, a warrior whose legend had been well earned.

"I will speak with our drivers," Catti-brie informed Wulfgar when they exited the inn, with a chorus of shouts and protests echoing behind them. "We should be on our way as soon as possible."

"Agreed," said Wulfgar. "I will wait for the wagons to depart."

Catti-brie nodded and started for the door of a different tavern, where she knew the lead driver to be. She stopped short, though, as she considered the curious answer, and turned back to regard Wulfgar.

"I will not be returning to Silverymoon," Wulfgar confirmed.

"You can't be thinking of going straight to Mithral Hall with the child. The terrain is too rough, and in the hands of orcs for much of the way. The safest road back to Mithral Hall is through Silverymoon."

"It is, and so you must go to Silverymoon."

Catti-brie stared at him hard. "Are you planning to stay here, that Cottie Cooperson can help with Colson?" she said with obvious and pointed sarcasm. To her ultimate frustration, she couldn't read Wulfgar's expression. "You've got family in the hall. I'll be there for you and for the girl. I'm knowing that it will be difficult for you without Delly, but I won't be on the road anytime soon, and be sure that the girl will be no burden to me."

"I will not return to Mithral Hall," Wulfgar stated bluntly, and a gust of wind would have likely knocked Catti-brie over at that moment. "Her place is with her mother," Wulfgar went on. "Her real mother. Never should I have taken her, but I will correct that error now, in returning her where she belongs."

"Auckney?"

Wulfgar nodded.

"That is halfway across the North."

"A journey I have oft traveled and one not fraught with peril."

"Colson has a home in Mithral Hall," Catti-brie argued, and Wulfgar was shaking his head even as the predictable words left her mouth.

"Not one suitable for her."

Catti-brie licked her lips and looked from the girl to Wulfgar, and she knew that he might as well have been speaking about himself at that moment.

"How long will you be gone from us?" the woman dared to ask.

Wulfgar's pause spoke volumes.

"Ye cannot," Catti-brie whispered, seeming very much like a little girl with a Dwarvish accent again.

"I have no choice before me," Wulfgar replied. "This is not my place. Not now. Look at me!" He paused and swept his free hand dramatically from his head to his feet, encompassing his gigantic frame. "I was not born to crawl through dwarven tunnels. My place is the tundra. Icewind Dale, where my people roam."

Catti-brie shook her head with every word, in helpless denial. "Bruenor is your father," she whispered.

"I will love him to the end of my days," Wulfgar admitted. "His place is there, but mine is not."

"Drizzt is your friend."

Wulfgar nodded. "As is Catti-brie," he said with a wistful smile. "Two dear friends who have found love, at long last."

Catti-brie mouthed, "I'm sorry," but she couldn't bring herself to actually speak the words aloud.

"I am happy for you both," said Wulfgar. "Truly I am. You complement each other's every movement, and I have never heard your laughter more full of contentment, nor Drizzt's. But this was not as I had wanted it. I am happy for you—both, and truly. But I cannot stand around and watch it."

The admission took the woman's breath away. "It doesn't have to be like this," she said.

"Do not be sad!" Wulfgar roared. "Not for me! I know now where my home is, and where my destiny lies. I long for the song of Icewind Dale's chill breeze, and for the freedom of my former life. I will hunt caribou along the shores of the Sea of Moving Ice. I will battle goblins and orcs without the restraints of political prudence. I am going home, to be among my own people, to pray at the graves of my ancestors, to find a wife and carry on the line of Beornegar."

"It is too sudden."

Again Wulfgar shook his head. "It is as deliberate as I have ever been."

"You have to go back and talk to Bruenor," Catti-brie said. "You owe him that."

Wulfgar reached under his tunic, produced a scroll, and handed it to her. "You will tell him for me. My road is easier west from here than from Mithral Hall."

"He will be outraged!"

"He will not even be in Mithral Hall," Wulfgar reminded. "He is out to the west with Drizzt in search of Gauntlgrym."

"Because he is in dire need of answers," Catti-brie protested. "Would you desert Bruenor in these desperate days?"

Wulfgar chuckled and shook his head. "He is a dwarf king in a land of orcs. Every day will qualify as you describe. There will be no end to this, and if there is an end to Obould, another threat will rise from the depths of the halls, perhaps, or from Obould's successor. This is the way of things, ever and always. I leave now or I wait until the situation is settled—and it will only be settled for me when I have crossed to Warrior's Rest. You know the truth of it," he said with a disarming grin, one that Catti-brie could not dismiss. "Obould today, the drow yesterday, and something—of course something—tomorrow. That is the way of it."

"Wulfgar . . ."

"Bruenor will forgive me," said the barbarian. "He is surrounded by fine warriors and friends, and the orcs will not likely try again to capture the hall. There is no good time for me to leave, and yet I know that I cannot stay. And every day that Colson is apart from her mother is a tragic day. I understand that now."

"Meralda gave the girl to you," Catti-brie reminded him. "She had no choice."

"She was wrong. I know that now."

"Because Delly is dead?"

"I am reminded that life is fragile, and often short."

"It is not as dark as you believe. You have many here who support . . ."

Wulfgar shook his head emphatically, silencing her. "I loved you," he said. "I loved you and lost you because I was a fool. It will always be the great regret of my life, the way I treated you before we were to be wed. I accept that we cannot go back, for even if you were able and willing, I know that I am not the same man. My time with Errtu left marks deep in my soul, scars I mean to erase in the winds of Icewind Dale, running beside my tribe, the Tribe of the Elk. I am content. I am at peace. And never have I been more certain of my road."

Catti-brie shook her head with every word, in helpless and futile denial, and her blue eyes grew wet with tears. This wasn't how it was supposed to be. The five Companions of the Hall were together again, and they were supposed to stay that way for all their days.

"You said that you support me, and so I ask you to now," said Wulfgar. "Trust in my judgment, in that I know what course I must follow. I take with me my love for you and for Drizzt and for Bruenor and for Regis. That is ever in the heart of Wulfgar. I will never let the image of you and the others fade from my thoughts, and never let the lessons I have learned from all of you escape me as I walk my road."

"Your road so far away."

Wulfgar nodded. "In the winds of Icewind Dale."

CHAPTER

A CITY UNDWARVEN

13

The six companions stood just inside the opening they had carved through the stone, their mouths uniformly agape. They had their backs to the wall of a gigantic cavern that held a magnificent and very ancient city. Huge structures rose up all around them: a trio of stepped pyramids to their right and a beautifully crafted series of towers to their left, all interconnected with flying walkways, and every edge adorned with smaller spires, gargoyles, and minarets. A collection of smaller buildings sat before them, around an ancient pond that still held brackish water and many plants creeping up around its stone perimeter wall. The plants near the pool and scattered throughout the cavern, the common Underdark luminous fungi, provided a minimal light beyond the torches held by Torgar and Thibbledorf, and of course Regis, who would not let his go. The pool and surrounding architecture hardly held their attention at that moment, though, for beyond the buildings loomed the grandest structure of all, a domed building—a castle, cathedral, or palace. Many stone stairs led up to the front of the place, where giant columns stood in a line, supporting a heavy stone porch. In the shadowy recesses, the six could make out gigantic doors.

"Gauntlgrym," Bruenor mouthed repeatedly, and his eyes were wet with tears.

Less willing to make such a pronouncement, Drizzt instead continued to survey the area. The ground was broken, but not excessively, and he could see that the entire area had been paved with flat stones, shaped and fitted to define specific avenues winding through the many buildings.

"The dwarves had different sensibilities then," Regis remarked, and fittingly, Drizzt thought.

Indeed, the place was unlike any dwarven city he had known. No construction under Kelvin's Cairn in Icewind Dale, or in Mirabar, Felbarr, or Mithral Hall, approached the height of even the smallest of the many grand structures around them, and the main building before them loomed larger even than the individual stalagmite-formed great houses of Menzoberranzan. That building was more suited to Waterdeep, he thought, or to Calimport and the marvelous palaces of the pashas.

As the overwhelming shock and awe faded a bit, the dwarves fanned out and moved away from the wall. Drizzt focused on Torgar, who went down to one knee and began scraping between the edges of two flagstones. He brought up a bit of dirt and tasted it then spat it aside, nodding his head and wearing an expression of concern.

Drizzt looked ahead to Bruenor, who seemed oblivious to his companions, walking zombielike toward the giant structure as if pulled by unseen forces.

And indeed the dwarf king was, Drizzt understood. He was tugged forward by pride and by hope, that it truly was Gauntlgrym, the fabulous city of his ancestors, glorious beyond his expectations, and that he would somehow find answers to the question of how to defeat Obould.

Thibbledorf Pwent walked behind Bruenor, while Cordio moved near to Torgar, the latter two striking up a quiet conversation.

One of doubt, Drizzt suspected.

"Is it Gauntlgrym?" Regis asked the drow.

"We will learn soon enough," Drizzt replied and started after Bruenor.

But Regis grabbed him by the arm, forcing him to turn back around.

"It doesn't sound like you believe it is," the halfling said quietly.

Drizzt scanned the cavern, inviting Regis to follow his gaze. "Have you ever seen such structures as these?"

"Of course not."

"No?" Drizzt asked. "Or is it that you have never seen such structures as these in such an environment as this?"

"What do you mean?" Regis asked, but his voice trailed away and his eyes widened as he finished, and Drizzt knew that he had caught on.

The pair scurried to catch up to Torgar and Cordio, who were fast gaining on the front two.

"Check the buildings as we pass," Bruenor instructed, motioning to Pwent and Torgar. "Elf, ye take the flank, and Rumblebelly come close up to me and Cordio."

As they moved by doorways, Pwent and Torgar alternately kicked them in, or rushed in through those that were already opened, as Bruenor continued his march, but more slowly, toward the huge structure, with Regis seemingly glued to his side. Cordio, though, kept hanging back, close enough to get to any of the other three dwarves in a hurry.

Drizzt, moving out into the shadows on the right flank, watched them all with quick glances while focusing his attention primarily on the deeper shadows. He wanted to unravel the mystery of the place, of course, but his main concern was ensuring that no current monstrous residents of the strange city made a sudden and unexpected appearance. Drizzt had been a creature of the Underdark long enough to know that few places so full of shelter would remain uninhabited for long.

"A forge!" Thibbledorf Pwent called from one building—one that had an open back, Drizzt noted, much like a smithy in the surface communities. "I got me a forge!"

Bruenor paused for just a moment before starting again for the huge building, his grin wide and his pace quicker. The other dwarves and Regis, even the stupidly grinning Pwent, hurried to catch up, and by the time Bruenor put his foot on the bottom step, all five were grouped together.

The stairs were wider than they were tall, and while they rose up a full thirty feet, they extended nearly twice that to Bruenor's left and right. Over at the very edge to the right, Drizzt moved fast to get up ahead of the others. Silent as a shadow and nearly invisible in the dim light, Drizzt rushed along, and Bruenor had barely taken his tenth step up when Drizzt crested the top, coming under the darker shadows of the pillared canopy.

And in there, the drow saw that they were not alone, and that danger was indeed waiting for his friends, for behind one of the centermost pillars loomed a behemoth unlike any Drizzt had even seen. Tall and sinewy, the hairless humanoid was blacker than a drow, if that was possible. It stood easily thrice Drizzt's height, perhaps four times, and exuded an aura of tremendous power, the strength of a mountain giant, monstrous and brutish despite its lean form.

And it moved with surprising speed.

* * * * *

Perched in the rafters of the canopy behind and above Drizzt, another beast of darkness studied the approaching group. Batlike in appearance, but huge and perfectly black, the nightwing took note of the movements, particularly those of the drow elf and the behemoth, a fellow denizen of the Plane of Shadow, a fearsome creature known as a nightwalker.

* * * * *

"Bruenor!" Drizzt cried as the giant started moving, and at the sound of his warning the dwarves reacted at once, particularly Thibbledorf Pwent, who leaped defensively before his king.

And when the giant, black-skinned nightwalker appeared, twenty feet of muscle and terror, Thibbledorf Pwent met its paralyzing gaze with a whoop of battlerager delight, and charged.

He got about three strides up the stairs before the nightwalker bent and reached forward, with long arms more akin in proportion to those of a great ape than to a human. Giant black hands clamped about the ferocious dwarf, long fingers fully engulfing him. Kicking and thrashing like a child in his father's arms, Pwent lifted off the ground.

Behind him, Bruenor could not move quickly enough to stop the hoist, and Cordio fell to spellcasting, and Regis and Torgar didn't move at all, both of them captured by the magical gaze of the powerful giant, both of them standing and trembling and gasping for breath.

That would have been the sudden end of Thibbledorf Pwent, surely, for the nightwalker could turn solid stone to dust in the crush of its tremendous grasp, but from the stairs above and to the right came Drizzt Do'Urden, leaping high, scimitars drawn. He executed a vicious double slash across the upper left arm of the nightwalker, his magical blades tearing through flesh and muscle.

In its lurch, the nightwalker dropped its left hand away, and so lost half the vice with which to crush the wildly flailing dwarf. So the behemoth took the second best option and instead of crushing Thibbledorf Pwent, it flung him high and far.

Pwent's cry changed pitch like the screech of a diving hawk, and he slammed hard against the front of the porch's canopy, some forty feet from the ground. He somehow kept the presence of mind to smash his spiked gauntlets against that facing, and luck was with him as one caught fast in a seam in the stone and left him hanging helplessly, but very much alive.

Down below, Drizzt landed on the stairs, more than a dozen feet below where he had begun his leap, and only his quickness and great agility kept him from serious harm, as he scrambled down the steps to absorb his momentum, even keeping the presence of mind to swat Torgar with the flat of one blade as he rushed past.

Torgar blinked and came back to his senses, just a bit, and turned to regard the running drow.

Drizzt finally stopped his run and swung around, to see Bruenor darting between the nightwalker's legs, his axe chopping hard against one. The behemoth roared—a strange and otherworldly howl that changed pitch multiple times, as if several different creatures had been given voice through the same horn. Again the nightwalker moved with deceiving speed, twisting and turning, lifting one foot and slamming it down at the dwarf.

But Bruenor saw it coming and threw himself back the other way, and even managed to whack at the other leg as he tumbled past. The nightwalker hit only stone with its stomp, but it cracked and crushed that stone.

Drizzt charged to join his friend, but noted a movement to his right that he could not dismiss. Looking past the thrashing, cursing, hanging Thibbledorf, he saw the gigantic, batlike creature drop from the canopy, spreading black wings fully forty feet across as it commenced its swoop. The air shimmered in front of it before it ever really began, though. It sent forth a wave of devastating magical energy that struck the drow with tremendous force.

Drizzt felt his heart stop as if it had been grabbed by a giant hand. Blood came from his eyes and blackness filled his vision. He staggered and stumbled, and as the nightwing came on, he knew he was helpless. He did see, but didn't consciously register, Thibbledorf Pwent curling up against the canopy, tucking his feet against the stone.

* * * * *

Torgar Hammerstriker, proud warrior from Mirabar, whose family had served the various Marchions of Mirabar for generations, and who had bravely marched from that city to Mithral Hall, pledging allegiance to King Bruenor, could not believe his fright. Torgar Hammerstriker, who had leaped headlong into an army of orcs, who had battled giants and giant mottled worms, who had once fought a dragon, cursed himself for being held in the paralysis of fear from the black-skinned behemoth.

He saw Drizzt stagger and stumble, and noted the swoop of the giant batlike creature. But he went for Bruenor, only for Bruenor, his king, his great-axe held high.

Beside him as he sped past, Cordio Muffinhead cast the first of his spells, throwing a wave of magic out at Bruenor that infused the dwarf king with added strength so that with his next swing, his many-notched axe bit in a little deeper. Cordio, too, turned to meet the rush of the nightwing, and deduced immediately that it had somehow rendered Drizzt helpless. The dwarf began another spell, but doubted he could cast it in time.

But Thibbledorf Pwent loosed his own type of spell, a battlerager dweomer, indeed. With a roar of defiance, the already battered dwarf shoved off with all his strength, his powerful legs tearing free his embedded hand spikes with a terrible screeching noise. Pwent flew out and up backward from the canopy and executed a half-twist, half-somersault as he went.

He came around as the nightwing glided under him, and he punched out, one fist after another, latching on with forged metal spikes.

The nightwing dipped under the dwarf's weight as he crashed down on its back, then it shrieked in protest. It finished with a great intake of breath, and Pwent felt it grow cold beneath him—not as if in death, but magically so, as if he had leaped not on a living, giant bat, but upon the Great Glacier itself.

The nightwing started to swing its head, but Pwent moved faster, tucking his chin and snapping every muscle in his body to propel himself forward and down, driving his head spike into the base of the nightwing's skull. The sheer power of the dwarf's movement straightened the creature's head back out and facing forward as the nightwing executed its magic, breathing a cone of freezing air before it.

Unfortunately for the humanoid giant, it stood right in the path of the devastating cone of cold.

The behemoth roared in protest and thrashed its arms to block the blinding and painful breath. White frost appeared all over the black skin of its head, arms, and chest, and strictly on reflex the giant punched out as the frantic nightwing fluttered past, scoring a solid slam against the base of its wing that sent both bat and dwarf into a fast-spinning plummet. They soared over the stairs and off toward the towers, skipped off the top of one building and barreled into another, crashing down in a tangled heap.

Thibbledorf Pwent never stopped shouting, cursing, or thrashing.

* * * * *

Drizzt fought through the pain and wiped the blurriness from his bloodied eyes. He had no time to go after Pwent and the giant shadowy bat. None of them did, for the black-skinned giant was far from defeated.

Bruenor and Torgar raced across the stairs, swatting at the tree-like legs with their masterwork weapons, and indeed several gashes showed on those legs, and from them issued grayish ooze that smoked as it dribbled to the ground. But they would have to hit the giant a hundred times to fell it, Drizzt realized, and if the behemoth connected solidly on either of them but once. . . .

Drizzt winced as the nightwalker kicked out, just clipping the dodging Torgar, but still hitting him hard enough to send him bouncing down the stone stairs, his axe flying from his grasp. Knowing that

Bruenor couldn't stand alone against the beast, Drizzt started for him, but stumbled, still weak and wounded, disoriented from the magical attack of the flying creature.

The drow felt another magical intrusion then, a wave of soothing, healing energy, and as he renewed his charge Bruenor's way, he managed a quick glance, a quick nod of appreciation, to Cordio.

As he did, he noted Regis simply walking away, muttering to himself, as if oblivious to the events unfolding around him.

As with Pwent, though, the drow had no time to concern himself with it, and when he refocused on his giant target, he winced in fear, for the behemoth chopped down its huge hand, leaving a trail of blackness hanging in the air, and more than opaque, that blackness had dimension.

A magical gate. And one with shapes already moving within its inviting swirls.

Drizzt took heart as Bruenor scored a solid hit, nearly tripping up the giant as it lifted a foot to stomp at him. The nightwalker howled and grabbed at its torn foot, giving Bruenor time to move safely aside, and more importantly, giving Torgar time to begin his charge back up the stairs, limping though he was.

Drizzt, though, had stopped his own advance. The warnings of the priests echoing in his thoughts, the drow pulled forth his onyx figurine. He could see the dangers clearly, the instability of the region, the appearance of a gate to the Plane of Shadow. But as the first wraith-like form began to slide through that smoky portal, Drizzt knew they could not win without help.

"Come to me, Guenhwyvar!" he yelled, and dropped the statue to the stone. "I need you."

"Drizzt, no!" Cordio cried, but it was too late, already the gray mist that would become the panther had begun to form.

Torgar sprinted by the drow, taking the stairs two at a time. He veered from his path to the behemoth to intercept the first floating, shadowy creature to emerge from the gate, which resembled an emaciated human dressed in tattered dark gray robes. Torgar leaped at it with a great two-handed swipe of his axe, and the creature, a dread wraith, met that with a sweep of its arm, trailing tendrils of smoke.

The axe struck home and the creature's hand slapped across the dwarf's shoulder, its permeating and numbing touch reaching into Torgar and leaching his life-force. Blanching, weaker, Torgar growled through the sudden weariness and pulled back his axe, spinning a complete circuit the other way and coming around with a second chop that bludgeoned the dread wraith straight back into the smoky portal.

But another was taking its place, and Torgar's legs shook beneath him. He hadn't the strength to charge, so he tried to firm himself up to meet the newest wraith's approach.

Leaving Drizzt with a dilemma, to be sure, for while Torgar obviously needed his help, so did Bruenor up above, where the giant was moving deliberately, cutting off the dwarf's avenues of escape.

But the choice didn't materialize, for there came a flash of blackness and time seemed to stand still for many long heartbeats.

Light turned to dark and dark to light, so that the giant seemed to become a brighter gray in hue, as did Drizzt, and the dwarves' faces darkened. Everything reversed, torches flaring black, and the hush of surprise engulfed the creatures of shadow and the companions alike.

Guenhwyvar's roar broke the spell.

When Drizzt turned to see his beloved companion, his hope turned to horror, for Guenhwyvar, whiter than Drizzt or the behemoth, seemed only half-formed, and she elongated as she leaped for the second emerging wraith, as if she were somehow dragging her magical gate with her very form. She hit the wraith and went back into the shadow portal with it, and as those two portals merged into a weird weave of conflicting energies, there came another blinding burst of black energy. The wraith hissed in protest, and Guenhwyvar's roar flooded with pain.

The behemoth howled, too, its agony obvious. The portal stretched, twisted, and reached out to grab at the gigantic creature of shadow, as if to bring it home.

No, Drizzt realized, his eyes straining to make sense through the myriad of free-flowing shapes, not to bring it home but as if to engulf the giant and swallow it, and the behemoth's howls only confirmed that the assault of the twisting portals was no pleasant embrace.

The giant proved the stronger, though, and the portals winked out, and the light returned to normal torch- and lichen light, and all was as it had been before the giant had enacted its gate and Drizzt had responded with one of his own.

Except that the behemoth was clearly wounded, clearly off-balance and staggering. And not everyone had been frozen by the stunning events of the merging gates and the dizzying reversals of light and dark.

Far up the stairs, King Bruenor Battlehammer seized the moment of opportunity. He came down like a rolling boulder, skipped out to the edge of a stair, and leaped as high and as far as his short legs would carry him.

Drizzt charged at the behemoth, demanding its attention with a wild flurry of his blades and a piercing battle cry, and so the giant was fully focused on him when Bruenor's axe, clutched in both his hands, cracked into its spine.

The behemoth threw its shoulders back in pain and surprise, its elbows tucked against its ribs, its forearms and long fingers flailing and grabbing at the empty air.

Drizzt's charge became real, focused, and he went right for the giant's most obviously injured leg, his scimitars digging many lines as he quick-stepped past.

The behemoth whirled to follow the movements of the drow, and Bruenor could not hold on. His axe remained deep into the giant's back as the dwarf flew off down the stairs. He crashed in a twisted mess, but Cordio was there at once, infusing him with waves of magical healing.

The giant grimaced and staggered, and Drizzt easily got out of reach. He turned fast, thinking to charge right back in.

But he paused when he saw a tell-tale mist reappearing by the small figurine lying on the stairs.

The giant set itself again. It tried to reach back to extract the dwarf's axe, but the placement prevented it from getting any grip. Down below, Torgar tried to join in, but his legs gave out and he slumped to the stone. No help would come soon from Bruenor, either, Drizzt could see, nor from Cordio, who attended the dwarf king. And Regis was nowhere to be seen.

Giving up on the axe, the behemoth turned its hateful glare at Drizzt. The drow felt a wave of energy flow forth, and for just an instant, he forgot where he was or what was happening. In that split second, he even thought about leaping down at the dwarves, somehow envisioning them as mortal enemies.

But the spell, a dizzying enchantment of confusion, could not take hold on the veteran dark elf the way it had so debilitated Regis, and Drizzt leaped down to the side, coming to the same level as the giant, surrendering the higher ground to limit the giant's attack options. Better to force it to reach for him, he thought, and better still for it to try to stomp or kick at him.

The giant did just that, lifting its leg, and Guenhwyvar did just as Drizzt wanted and sprang upon the one planted leg, raking at the back of the behemoth's knee.

In charged Drizzt, forcing the giant to twist, or try to twist, to keep pace. The drow's magical anklets allowed him to accelerate suddenly past the stomping foot, and he reversed immediately, spinning and slashing at the back of the leading leg. The giant twisted and tried to kick, but Guenhwyvar clamped powerful jaws on the back of its knee, feline fangs tearing deep into dark muscle.

That leg buckled. Arms flailing, the giant fell over backward down the stairs, landing with a tremendous, stone-crunching crash, and just missing crushing poor unconscious Torgar.

Drizzt sprinted and leaped atop it, running down its length to reach its neck before it could bring its arms in to fend him off. Drizzt found less resistance than he expected, for the giant's fall had driven Bruenor's axe in all the deeper, severing its spine.

The behemoth was helpless, and Drizzt showed it no mercy. He crossed its massive chest. Its head was back due to the angle of the stairs, leaving its neck fully exposed.

He leaped from the gurgling, dying behemoth a moment later, landing gracefully on the stairs in full run, angling toward where the batlike creature and Pwent had tumbled. It was quiet there, the fight apparently ended, and Drizzt winced when he saw a leathery wing flop, thinking the monster still alive.

But it was just Pwent, he saw, grumbling as he extracted himself from the broken body.

Drizzt veered back the way they'd come, thinking to go after Regis, but before he could even begin, Regis appeared between the buildings, walking back swiftly toward the group, his mace in hand, his chubby cheeks flushed with embarrassment.

"It took me strength, me king," Torgar Hammerstriker was saying when Drizzt, Guenhwyvar in tow, moved back to the three dwarves.

"Like it pulled me spine right out."

"A wraith," explained Cordio, who was still working on the battered Bruenor, bandaging a cut along the dwarf king's scalp. "Their chilling touch steals yer inner strength—and it can suren kill ye to death if it gets enough o' the stuff from ye! Take heart, for ye'll be fine in a short bit."

"As will me king?" Torgar asked.

"Bah!" Bruenor snorted. "Got me a bigger bounce fallin' off me throne after a proper blessing to Moradin. A night o' the holy mead's hurtin' me more than that thing e'er could!"

Torgar moved over to the dead giant and tried to lift its shoulder. He looked back at the others, shaking his head. "Gonna be a chore for ten in gettin' back yer axe," he said.

"Then take yer own and cut yer way through the durned thing," Bruenor ordered.

Torgar considered the giant, then looked to his great-axe. He gave a "hmm" and a shrug, spat in both his hands, and hoisted the weapon. "Won't take long," he promised. "But take care with yer axe when I get it for ye, for the handle's sure to be slick."

"Nah, it crusts when it dries," came a voice from the side, and the group turned to regard Thibbledorf Pwent, who certainly knew of what he spoke. For Pwent was covered in blood and gore from the thrashing he had given the batlike monster, and a piece of the creature's skull was still stuck to his great head spike, with gobs of bloody brain sliding slowly down the spike's stem. To emphasize his point, Pwent held up his hand and clenched and unclenched his fist, making sounds both sloppy wet and crunchy.

"And what happened to yerself?" Pwent demanded of Regis as the halfling approached. "Ye find something to hit back there, did ye?"

"I don't know," the halfling honestly answered.

"Bah, let off the little one," Bruenor told Pwent, and he included all the others as he swept his gaze around. "Ain't nothing chasing Rumblebelly off."

"I don't know what happened," Regis said to Bruenor, and he looked at the dead giant and shrugged. "For any of it."

"Magic," said Drizzt. "The creatures were possessed of more than physical prowess, as is typical of extraplanar beings. One of those spells attacked the mind. A disorienting dweomer."

"True enough, elf," Cordio agreed. "It delayed me spellcasting."

"Bah, but I didn't feel nothing," said Pwent.

"Attacked the *mind*," Bruenor remarked. "Yerself was well defended."

Pwent paused and pondered that for a few moments before bursting into laughter.

"What is this place?" Torgar asked at length, finding the strength to rise and walk, taking in the sights, the sculpture, the strange designs.

"Gauntlgrym," Bruenor declared, his dark eyes gleaming with intensity.

"Then yer Gauntlgrym was a town above the ground," said Torgar, and Bruenor glared at him.

"This place was above ground, me king," Torgar answered that look. "All of it. This building and those, too. This plaza, set with stones to protect from the mud o' the spring melt. . . ." He looked at Cordio, then Drizzt, who nodded his agreement. "Something must've melted the tundra beneath the whole of it. Turned it all to mud and sank this place from sight."

"And the melts bring water, every year," Cordio added, pointing to the north. "Washing away the mud, bucket by bucket, but leaving the stones behind."

"Yer answer's in the ceiling," Torgar explained, pointing up. "Can ye get a light up there, priest?"

Cordio nodded and moved away from Bruenor. He began casting again, gently waving his arms, creating a globe of light up at the cavern's ceiling, right at the point where it joined in with the top of the great building before them. Some tell tale signs were revealed with that light, confirming Torgar's suspicions.

"Roots," the Mirabarran dwarf explained. "Can't be more than a few feet o' ground between that roof and the surface. And these taller buildings're acting like supports to keep that ceiling up. The tangle o' roots and the frozen ground're doin' the rest. Whole place sank, I tell ye, for these buildings weren't built for the Underdark."

Bruenor looked at the ceiling, then at Drizzt, but the drow could only nod his agreement.

"Bah!" Bruenor snorted. "Gauntlgrym was akin to Mirabar, then, and ye're for knowin' that. So this must be the top o' the place, with more below. All we need be looking for is a shaft to take us to the lower levels, akin to that rope and come-along dumbwaiter ye got in Mirabar. Now let's see what this big place is all about—important building, I'm thinking. Might be a throne room."

Torgar nodded and Pwent ran up in front of Bruenor to lead the way up the stairs, with Cordio close on his heels. Torgar, though, lagged behind, something Drizzt didn't miss.

"Not akin to Mirabar," the dwarf whispered to Drizzt and Regis.

"A dwarf city above ground?" Regis asked.

Torgar shrugged. "I'm not for knowing." He reached to his side and pulled an item from his belt, one he had taken from the smithy he had found back across the plaza. "Lots of these and little of anything else," he said.

Regis sucked in his breath, and Drizzt nodded his agreement with the dwarf's assessment of the muddy catastrophe that had hit the place. For in his hand, Torgar held an item all too common on the surface and all too rare in the Underdark: a horseshoe.

At Drizzt's insistence, he, and not the noisy Thibbledorf, led the way into the building with Guenhwyvar beside him. The drow and panther filtered out to either side of the massive, decorated doors— doors filled with color and gleaming metal much more indicative of a construction built under the sun. The drow and his cat melted into the shadows of the great hall that awaited them, moving with practiced coordination. They sensed no danger. The place seemed still and long dead.

It was no audience chamber, though, no palace for a dwarf king. When the others came in and they filled the room with torchlight, it became apparent that the place had been a library and gallery, a place of art and learning.

Rotted scrolls filled ancient wooden shelves all around the room and along the walls, interspersed with tapestries whose images had long ago faded, and with sculptures grand and small alike.

Those sculptures set off the first waves of alarm in the companions, particularly in Bruenor, for while some depicted dwarves in their typically heroic battle poses and regalia, others showed orc warriors standing proud. And more than one depicted orcs in other dress, in flowing robes or with pen in hand.

The most prominent of all stood upon a dais at the far end of the room, directly across from the doors. The image of Moradin, stocky and strong, was quite recognizable to the dwarves.

So was the image of Gruumsh One-eye, god of the orcs, standing across from him, and while the two were shown eyeing each other with expressions that could be considered suspicious, the simple fact that they were not shown with Moradin standing atop the vanquished Gruumsh's chest elicited stares of disbelief on the faces of all four dwarves. Thibbledorf Pwent even babbled something undecipherable.

"What place was this?" Cordio asked, giving sound to the question that was on all their minds. "What hall? What city?"

"Delzoun," muttered Bruenor. "Gauntlgrym."

"Then she's no place akin to the tales," said Cordio, and Bruenor shot a glare his way.

"Grander, I'm saying," the priest quickly added.

"Whatever it was, it was grand indeed," said Drizzt. "And beyond my expectations when we set out from Mithral Hall. I had thought we would find a hole in the ground, Bruenor, or perhaps a small, ancient settlement."

"I telled ye it was Gauntlgrym," Bruenor replied.

"If it is, then it is a place to do your Delzoun heritage proud," said the drow. "If it is not, then let us discover other accomplishments of which you can be rightly proud."

Bruenor's stubborn expression softened a bit at those words, and he offered Drizzt a nod and moved off deeper into the room, Thibble dorf at his heel. Drizzt looked to Cordio and Torgar, both of whom nodded their appreciation of his handling of the volatile king.

It was not Gauntlgrym, all three of them knew—at least, it was not the Gauntlgrym of dwarven legend. But what then?

There wasn't much to salvage in the library, but they did find a few scrolls that hadn't fully succumbed to the passage of time. None of them could read the writing on the ancient paper, but there were a few items that could give hints about the craftsmanship of the former residents, and even one tapestry that Regis believed could be cleaned enough to reveal some hints of its former depictions. They gathered their hoard together with great care, rolling and tying the tapestry and softly packing the other items in bags that had held the food they had thus far consumed.

They were done scouring the hall in less than an afternoon's time, and finished with a cursory and rather unremarkable examination of the rest of the cavern for just as long after that. Abruptly, and at Bruenor's insistence, so ended their expedition. Soon after, they climbed back up through the hole that had brought them underground and were greeted by a late winter's quiet night. At the next break of dawn they began their journey home, where they hoped to find some answers.

CHAPTER

POSSIBILITIES

14

King Obould normally liked the cheering of the many orcs that surrounded his temporary palace, a heavy tent set within a larger tent, set within a larger tent. All three were reinforced with metal and wood, and their entrances opened at different points for further security. Obould's most trusted guards, heavily armored and with great gleaming weapons, patrolled the two outer corridors.

The security measures were relatively new, as the orc king cemented his grip and began to unfold his strategy—a plan, the cheering that day only reminded him, that might not sit well with the warlike instincts of some of his subjects. He had already waged the first rounds of what he knew would be his long struggle among the stones of Keeper's Dale. His decision to stand down the attack on Mithral Hall had been met with more than a few mutterings of discontent.

And that had only been the beginning, of course.

He moved along the outer ring of his tent palace to the opened flap and looked out on the gathering on the plaza of the nomadic orc village. At least two hundred of his minions were out there, cheering wildly, thrusting weapons into the air, and clapping each other on the back. Word had come in of a great orc victory in the Moonwood, tales of elf heads spiked on the riverbank.

"We should go there and see the heads," Kna said to Obould as she curled at his side. "It is a sight that would fill me with lust."

179

Obould swiveled his head to regard her, and he offered a smile, knowing that stupid Kna would never understand it to be one of pity.

Out in the plaza, the cheering grew a backbone chant: "Karuck! Karuck! Karuck!"

It was not unexpected. Obould, who had received word of the fight in the east the previous night, before the public courier had arrived, motioned to the many loyalists he had set in place, and on his nod, they filtered into the crowd.

A second chant bubbled up among the first, "Many-Arrows! Many-Arrows! Many-Arrows!" And gradually, the call for kingdom overcame the cheer for clan.

"Take me there and I will love you," Kna whispered in the orc king's ear, tightening her hold on his side.

Obould's bloodshot eyes narrowed as he turned to regard her again. He brought his hand up to grab the back of her hair and roughly bent her head back so that she could see the intensity on his face. He envisioned those elf heads he'd heard of, set on tall pikes. His smile widened as he considered putting Kna's head in that very line.

Misconstruing his intensity as interest, the consort grinned and writhed against him.

With almost godlike strength, Obould tugged her from his side and tossed her to the ground. He turned back to the plaza and wondered how many of his minions—those not in his immediate presence—would add the chant of Many-Arrows to the praises of Clan Karuck as word of the victory spread throughout the kingdom.

* * * * *

The night was dark, but not to the sensitive eyes of Tos'un Armgo, who had known the blackness of the Underdark. He crouched by a rocky jag, looking down at the silvery snake known as the Surbrin River, and more pointedly at the line of poles before it.

The perpetrators had moved to the south, along with the prodding trio of Dnark, Ung-thol, and the upstart young Toogwik Tuk. They had talked of attacking the Battlehammer dwarves at the Surbrin.

Obould would not be pleased to see such independence among his ranks. And strangely, the drow wasn't overly thrilled at the prospect himself. He'd personally led the first orc assault on that dwarven position, infiltrating and silencing the main watchtower before the orc tide swept Clan Battlehammer back into its hole.

It had been a good day.

So what had changed, wondered Tos'un. What had left him with such melancholy when battle was afoot, particularly a battle between orcs and dwarves, two of the ugliest and smelliest races he had ever had the displeasure of knowing?

As he looked down at the river, he came to understand. Tos'un was a drow, had been raised in Menzoberranzan, and held no love for his surface elf cousins. The war between the surface and Underdark elves was among the fiercest rivalries in the world, a long history of dastardly deeds and murderous raids that equaled anything the continually warring demons of the Abyss and devils of the Nine Hells could imagine. Cutting out the throat of a surface elf had never presented Tos'un with a moral dilemma, surely, but there was something about the current situation, about those heads, that unnerved him, that filled him with a sense of dread.

As much as he hated surface elves, Tos'un despised orcs even more. The idea that orcs could have scored such a victory over elves of any sort left the drow cold. He had grown up in a city of twenty thousand dark elves, and with probably thrice that number of orc, goblin, and kobold slaves. Was there, perhaps, a Clan Karuck in their midst, ready to spike the heads of the nobles of House Barrison Del'Armgo or even of House Baenre?

He scoffed at the absurd notion, and reminded himself that surface elves were weaker than their drow kin. This group fell to Clan Karuck because they deserved it, because they were weak or stupid, or both.

Or at least, that's what Tos'un told himself over and over again, hoping that repetition would provide comfort where reason could not. He looked to the south, where the receding pennants of Clan Karuck had long been lost to the uneven landscape and the darkness. Whatever he might tell himself about the slaughter in the Moonwood, deep inside the true echoes of his heart and soul, Tos'un hoped that Grguch and his minions would all die horribly.

* * * * *

The sound of dripping water accompanied the wagon rolling east from Nesmé, as the warm day nibbled at winter's icy grip. Several times the wagon driver grumbled about muddy ruts, even expressing his hope that the night would be cold.

"If the night's warm, we'll be walking!" he warned repeatedly.

Catti-brie hardly heard him, and hardly noticed the gentle symphony of the melt around her. She sat in the bed of the wagon, with her back up against the driver's seat, staring out to the west behind them.

Wulfgar was out there, moving away from her. Away forever, she feared.

She was full of anger, full of hurt. How could he leave them with an army of orcs encamped around Mithral Hall? Why would he ever want to leave the Companions of the Hall? And how could he go without saying farewell to Bruenor, Drizzt, and Regis?

Her mind whirled through those questions and more, trying to make sense of it all, trying to come to terms with something she could not control. It wasn't the way things were supposed to be! She had tried to say that to Wulfgar, but his smile, so sure and serene, had defeated her argument before it could be made.

She thought back to the day when she and Wulfgar had left Mithral Hall for Silverymoon. She remembered the reactions of Bruenor and Drizzt—too emotional for the former and too stoic for the latter, she realized.

Wulfgar had told them. He'd said his good-byes before they set out, whether in explicit terms or in hints they could not miss. It hadn't been an impulsive decision brought about by some epiphany that had come to him on the road.

Catti-brie grimaced through a sudden flash of anger, at Bruenor and especially at Drizzt. How could they have known and not have told her?

She suppressed that anger quickly, and realized that it had been Wulfgar's choice. He had waited to tell her until after they'd recovered Colson. Catti-brie nodded as she considered that. He'd waited because he knew that the sight of the girl, the girl who had been taken from her mother and was to be returned, would make things more clear for Catti-brie.

"My anger isn't for Wulfgar, or any of them," she whispered.

"Eh?" asked the driver, and Catti-brie turned her head and gave him a smile that settled him back to his own business.

She held that smile as she turned back to stare at the empty west, and squinted, putting on a mask that might counter the tears that welled within. Wulfgar was gone, and if she sat back and considered his reasons, she knew she couldn't fault him. He was not a young man any longer. His legacy was still to be made, and time was running short. It would not be made in Mithral Hall, and even in the cities surrounding the dwarven stronghold, the people, the humans, were not kin to Wulfgar in appearance or in sensibility. His home was Icewind Dale. His people were in Icewind Dale. In Icewind Dale alone could he truly hope to find a wife.

Because Catti-brie was lost to him. And though he bore her no ill will, she understood the pain he must have felt when he looked upon her and Drizzt.

She and Wulfgar had had their moment, but that moment had passed, had been stolen by demons, both within Wulfgar and in the form of the denizens of the Abyss. Their moment had passed, and there seemed no other moments for Wulfgar to find in the court of a dwarf king.

"Farewell," Catti-brie silently mouthed to the empty west, and never had she so meant that simple word.

* * * * *

He bent low to bring Colson close to the flowering snowdrops, their tiny white bells denying the snow along the trail. The first flowers, the sign of coming spring.

"For Ma, Dell-y," Colson chattered happily, holding the first syllable of Delly's name for a long heartbeat, which only tugged all the more at Wulfgar's heart. "Flowvers," she giggled, and she pulled one close to her nose.

Wulfgar didn't correct her lisp, for she beamed as brightly as any "flowvers" ever could.

"Ma for flowvers." Colson rambled, and she mumbled through a dozen further sounds that Wulfgar could not decipher, though it was apparent to him that the girl thought she was speaking in cogent sentences. Wulfgar was sure that Colson made perfect sense to Colson, at least!

There was a little person in there—Wulfgar only truly realized at that innocent moment. A thinking, rational individual. She wasn't a baby anymore, wasn't helpless and unwitting.

The joy and pride that brought to Wulfgar was tempered, to be sure, by his realization that he would soon turn Colson over to her mother, to a woman the girl had never known in a land she had never called home.

"So be it," he said, and Colson looked at him and giggled, and gradually Wulfgar's delight overcame his sense of impending dread. He felt the season in his heart, as if his own internal, icy pall had at last been lifted. Nothing could change that overriding sensation. He was free. He was content. He knew in his heart that what he was doing was good, and right.

As he bent lower to the flower, he noted something else: a fresh print in the mud, right on the edge of the hardened snow. It had come from a shoddily-wrapped foot, and since it was so far from any town, Wulfgar recognized it at once as the print of a goblinkin's foot. He stood back up and glanced all around.

He looked to Colson and smiled comfortingly, then hustled along down the broken trail, his direction, fortunately, opposite the one the creature had taken. He wanted no battle that day, or any other day Colson was in his arms.

All the more reason to get the child back where she belonged.

Wulfgar hoisted the girl onto his broad shoulder and whistled quietly for her as his long legs carried them swiftly down the road, to the west.

Home.

* * * * *

North of Wulfgar's position, four dwarves, a halfling, and a drow settled around a small fire in a snowy dell. They had stopped their march early, that they could better light a fire to warm some stones that would get them more comfortably through the cold night. After briskly rubbing their hands over the dancing orange flames, Torgar, Cordio, and Thibbledorf set off to find the stones.

Bruenor hardly noticed their departure, for his gaze had settled on the sack of scrolls and artifacts, and on a tied tapestry lying nearby.

While Regis began preparing their supper, Drizzt just sat and watched his dwarf friend, for he knew that Bruenor was churning inside, and that he would soon enough need to speak his mind.

As if on cue, Bruenor turned to the drow. "Thought I'd find Gauntlgrym and find me answers," he said.

"You don't know whether you've found them or not," Drizzt reminded.

Bruenor grunted. "Weren't Gauntlgrym, elf. Not by any o' the legends o' the place. Not by any stories I e'er heard."

"Likely not," the drow agreed.

"Weren't no place I ever heared of."

"Which might prove even more important," said Drizzt.

"Bah," Bruenor snorted half-heartedly. "A place of riddles, and none that I'm wanting answered."

"They are what they are."

"And that be?"

"Hopefully revealed in the writings we took."

"Bah!" Bruenor snorted more loudly, and he waved his hands at Drizzt and at the sack of scrolls. "Gonna get me a stone to warm me bed," he muttered, and started away. "And one I can bang me head against."

The last remark brought a grin to Drizzt's face, reminding him that Bruenor would follow the clues wherever they led, whatever the implications. He held great faith in his friend.

"He's afraid," Regis remarked as soon as the dwarf was out of sight.

"He should be," Drizzt replied. "At stake are the very foundations of his world."

"What do you think is on the scrolls?" Regis asked, and Drizzt shrugged.

"And those statues!" the halfling went on undeterred. "Orcs and dwarves, and not in battle. What does it mean? Answers for us? Or just more questions?"

Drizzt thought about it for just a moment, and was nodding as he replied, "Possibilities."

PART
3

A WAR WITHIN A WAR

A WAR WITHIN

A WAR

We construct our days, bit by bit, tenday by tenday, year by year. Our lives take on a routine, and then we bemoan that routine. Predictability, it seems, is a double-edged blade of comfort and boredom. We long for it, we build it, and when we find it, we reject it.

Because while change is not always growth, growth is always rooted in change. A finished person, like a finished house, is a static thing. Pleasant, perhaps, or beautiful or admirable, but not for long exciting.

King Bruenor has reached the epitome, the pinnacle, the realization of every dream a dwarf could fathom. And still King Bruenor desires change, though he would refuse to phrase it that way, admitting only his love of adventure. He has found his post, and now seeks reasons to abandon that post at every turn. He seeks, because inside of him he knows that he must seek to grow. Being a king will make Bruenor old before his time, as the old saying goes.

Not all people are possessed of such spirits. Some desire and cling to the comfort of the routine, to the surety that comes with the completion of the construction of life's details. On the smaller scale, they become wedded to their daily routines. They become enamored of the predictability. They calm their restless souls in the confidence that they have found their place in the multiverse, that things are the way they are supposed to be, that there are no roads left to explore and no reason to wander.

On the larger scale, such people become fearful and resentful—sometimes to extremes that defy logic—of anyone or anything that intrudes on that construct. A societal change, a king's edict, an attitude shift in the neighboring lands, even events that have nothing to do with them personally can set off a reaction of dissonance and fear. When Lady Alustriel initially allowed me to walk the streets of Silverymoon openly, she found great resistance. Her people, well protected by one of the finest armies in all the land and by a leader whose magical abilities are renowned throughout the world, did not fear Drizzt Do'Urden. Nay, they feared the change that I represented. My very presence in Silverymoon infringed upon the construct of their lives, threatened their understanding of the way things were, threatened the way things were supposed to be. Even though, of course, I posed no threat to them whatsoever.

That is the line we all straddle, between comfort and adventure. There are those who find satisfaction, even fulfillment, in the former, and there are those who are forever seeking.

It is my guess, and can only be my guess, that the fears of the former are rooted in fear of the greatest mystery of all, death. It is no accident that those who construct the thickest walls are most often rooted firmly, immovably, in their faith. The here and now is as it is, and the better way will be found in the afterlife. That proposition is central to the core beliefs that guide the faithful, with, for many, the added caveat that the afterlife will only fulfill its promise if the here and now remains in strict accord with the guiding principles of the chosen deity.

I count myself among the other group, the seekers. Bruenor, too, obviously so, for he will ever be the discontented king. Cattibrie cannot be rooted. There is no sparkle in her eyes greater than the one when she looks upon a new road. And even Regis, for all his complaints regarding the trials of the road, wanders and seeks and fights. Wulfgar, too, will not be confined. He has seen his life in

Mithral Hall and has concluded, rightfully and painfully, that there is for him a better place and a better way. It saddens me to see him go. For more than a score of years he has been my friend and companion, a trusted arm in battle and in life. I miss him dearly, every day, and yet when I think of him, I smile for him. Wulfgar has left Mithral Hall because he has outgrown all that this place can offer, because he knows that in Icewind Dale he will find a home where he will do more good—for himself and for those around him.

I, too, hold little faith that I will live out my days in Bruenor's kingdom. It is not just boredom that propels my steps along paths unknown, but a firm belief that the guiding principle of life must be a search not for what is, but for what could be. To look at injustice or oppression, at poverty or slavery, and shrug helplessly, or worse to twist a god's "word" to justify such states, is anathema to the ideal, and to me, the ideal is achieved only when the ideal is sought. The ideal is not a gift from the gods, but a promise from them.

We are possessed of reason. We are possessed of generosity. We are possessed of sympathy and empathy. We have within us a better nature, and it is one that cannot be confined by the constructed walls of anything short of the concept of heaven itself. Within the very logic of that better nature, a perfect life cannot be found in a world that is imperfect.

So we dare to seek. So we dare to change. Even knowing that we will not get to "heaven" in this life is no excuse to hide within the comfort of routine. For it is in that seeking, in that continual desire to improve ourselves and to improve the world around us, that we walk the road of enlightenment, that we eventually can approach the gods with heads bowed in humility, but with confidence that we did their work, that we tried to lift ourselves and our world to their lofty standards, the image of the ideal.

—Drizzt Do'Urden

CHAPTER
CONVERGENCE OF CRISES

15

Magical horses striding long, the fiery chariot cut a line of orange across the pre-dawn sky. Flames whipped in the driving wind, but for the riders they did not burn. Standing beside Lady Alustriel, Catti-brie felt that wind indeed, her auburn hair flying wildly behind her, but the bite of the breeze was mitigated by the warmth of Alustriel's animated cart. She lost herself in that sensation, allowing the howl of the wind to deafen her thoughts as well. For a short time, she was free to just exist, under the last twinkling stars with all of her senses consumed by the extraordinary nature of the journey.

She didn't see the approaching silver line of the Surbrin, and was only vaguely aware of a dip in altitude as Alustriel brought the conjured chariot down low over the water, and to a running stop on the ground outside the eastern door of Mithral Hall.

Few dwarves were out at that early hour, but those who were, mostly those standing guard along the northern wall, came running and cheering for the Lady of Silverymoon. For of course they knew it was she, whose chariot had graced them several times over the past few months.

Their cheering grew all the louder when they noted Alustriel's passenger, the Princess of Mithral Hall.

"Well met," more than one of the bearded folk greeted.

"King Bruenor's not yet returned," said one, a grizzled old sort, with one eye lost and patched over, and half his great black beard torn away. Catti-brie smiled as she recognized the fierce and fiercely loyal Shingles McRuff, who had come to Mithral Hall beside Torgar Hammerstriker. "Should be along any day."

"And be knowin' that ye're all welcome, and that ye'll find all the hospitality o' Mithral Hall for yerself," another dwarf offered.

"That is most generous," said Alustriel. She turned and looked back to the east as she continued, "More of my people—wizards from Silverymoon—will be coming in throughout the morn, on all manner of flight, some self-propelled and some riding ebony flies, and two on broomsticks and another on a carpet. I pray your archers will not shoot them down."

"Ebony flies?" Shingles replied. "Flying on bugs, ye mean?"

"Big bugs," said Catti-brie.

"Would have to be."

"We come armed with spells of creation, for we wish to see the bridge across the Surbrin opened and secure as soon as possible," Alustriel explained. "For the sake of Mithral Hall and for all the goodly kingdoms of the Silver Marches."

"More well met, then!" bellowed Shingles, and he led yet another cheer.

Catti-brie moved toward the back edge of the chariot, but Alustriel took her by the shoulder. "We can fly out to the west and seek King Bruenor," she offered.

Catti-brie paused and looked that way, but shook her head and replied, "He will return presently, I'm sure."

Catti-brie accepted Shingles's offered hand, and let the dwarf ease her down to the ground. Shingles was quick to Alustriel, similarly helping her, and the Lady, though not injured as was Catti-brie, graciously accepted. She moved back from her cart and motioned for the others to follow.

Alustriel could have simply dismissed the flaming chariot and the horses made of magical fire. Dispelling her own magic was easy work, of course, and the fiery team and cart alike would have flared for an instant before they winked into blackness, a final puff of smoke drifting and dissipating into the air.

But Lady Alustriel had been using that particular spell for many years, and had put her own flavor into it, both in the construction of the cart and team and in the dismissal of the magic. Figuring that the dwarves could use a bit of spirit-lifting, the powerful wizardess performed her most impressive variation of the dispelling.

The horse team snorted and reared, flames shooting from swirling, fiery nostrils. As one, they leaped into the air, straight up, the cart lurching behind them. Some twenty feet off the ground, the many sinews of fire that held the form broke apart, orange tendrils soaring every which way, and as they reached their limits, exploded with deafening bangs, throwing showers of sparks far and wide.

The dwarves howled with glee, and Catti-brie, for all of her distress, couldn't contain a giggle.

When it ended a few heartbeats later, their ears ringing with the echoes of the retorts, their eyes blinking against the sting of the brilliant flashes, Catti-brie offered an appreciative smile to her friend and driver.

"It was just the enchantment they needed," she whispered, and Alustriel replied with a wink.

They went into Mithral Hall side-by-side.

* * * * *

Early the next morning, Shingles again found himself in the role of official greeter in the region east of the hall's eastern gate, for it was he who first caught up with the six adventurers returning from the place Bruenor had named Gauntlgrym. The old Mirabarran dwarf had directed the watch overnight, and was sorting out assignments for the workday, both along the fortifications on the northern mountain spur and at the bridge. No stranger to the work of wizards, Shingles repeatedly warned his boys to stay well back when Alustriel's gang came out to work their dweomers. When word came that King Bruenor and the others had returned, Shingles moved fast to the south to intercept them.

"Did ye find it, then, me king?" he asked excitedly, giving voice to the thoughts and whispers of all the others around him.

"Aye," Bruenor replied, but in a tone surprisingly unenthusiastic. "We found something, though we're not for knowing if it's Gauntlgrym just yet." He motioned to the large sack that Torgar carried, and the rolled tapestry slung over Cordio's shoulder. "We've some things for Nanfoodle and me scholars to look over. We'll get our answers."

"Yer girl's come home," Shingles explained. "Lady Alustriel flew her in on that chariot o' fire. And the Lady's here, too, along with ten Silverymoon wizards, all come to work on the bridge."

Bruenor, Drizzt, and Regis exchanged glances as Shingles finished.

"Me girl alone?" Bruenor asked.

"With the Lady."

Bruenor stared at Shingles.

"Wulfgar's not returned with 'em," the old Mirabarran dwarf said. "Catti-brie said nothing of it, and I didn't think it me place to ask."

Bruenor looked to Drizzt.

"He is far west," the drow said quietly, and Bruenor inadvertently glanced out that way then nodded.

"Get me to me girl," Bruenor instructed as he started off at a swift pace for Mithral Hall's eastern door.

They found Catti-brie, Lady Alustriel, and the Silverymoon wizards not far down the corridor inside, the lot of them having spent the night in the hall's easternmost quarters. After a quick and polite greeting, Bruenor begged the Lady's pardon, and Alustriel and her wizards quickly departed the hall, heading for the Surbrin bridge.

"Where's he at?" Bruenor asked Catti-brie when it was just the two of them, Drizzt, and Regis.

"You're knowing well enough."

"Ye found Colson, then?"

Catti-brie nodded.

"And he's taking her home," Bruenor stated.

Another nod. "I offered to journey with him," Catti-brie explained, and she glanced at Drizzt and was relieved to see him smile at that news. "But he would not have me along."

"Because the fool ain't for coming back," said Bruenor, and he spat and stalked off. "Durned fool son of an over-sized orc."

Drizzt motioned to Regis to go with Bruenor, and the halfling nodded and trotted away.

"I think Bruenor is right," Catti-brie said, and she shook her head in futile denial, then rushed over and wrapped Drizzt in a tight hug and kissed him deeply. She put her head on his shoulder, not relenting a bit in her embrace. She sniffed back tears.

"He knew that Wulfgar would not likely return," Drizzt whispered.

Catti-brie pushed him back to arms' length. "As did yourself, but you didn't tell me," she said.

"I honored Wulfgar's wishes. He was not sure of where his road would lead, but he did not wish discussion of it all the way to Silverymoon and beyond."

"If I had known along our road, I might've been able to change his mind," Catti-brie protested.

Drizzt gave her a helpless look. "More the reason to not tell you."

"You agree with Wulfgar's choice?"

"I think it is not my place to agree or to argue," Drizzt said with a shrug.

"You think it's his place to be deserting Bruenor at this time of—?"

"This time or any time."

"How can you say that? Wulfgar is family to us, and he just left . . ."

"As you and I did those years ago, after the drow war when Wulfgar fell to the yochlol," Drizzt reminded her. "We longed for the road and so we took to the road, and left Bruenor to his hall. For six years."

That reminder seemed to deflate Catti-brie's ire quite a bit. "But now Bruenor's got an army of orcs on his doorstep," she protested, but with far less enthusiasm.

"An army that will likely be there for years to come. Wulfgar told me that he could not see his future here. And truly, what is there for him here? No wife, no children."

"And it pained him to look upon us."

Drizzt nodded. "Likely."

"He told me as much."

"And so you wear a mantle of guilt?"

Catti-brie shrugged.

"It doesn't suit you," Drizzt said. He drew her in close once more, and gently pushed her head onto his shoulder. "Wulfgar's road is Wulfgar's own to choose. He has family in Icewind Dale, if that is where he decides to go. He has his people there. Would you deny him the chance to find love? Should he not sire children, who will follow his legacy of leadership among the tribes of Icewind Dale?"

Catti-brie didn't respond for a long while then merely said, "I miss him already," in a voice weak with sorrow.

"As do I. And so too for Bruenor and Regis, and all else who knew him. But he isn't dead. He did not fall in battle, as we feared those years ago. He will follow his road, to bring Colson home, as he sees fit, and then perhaps to Icewind Dale. Or perhaps not. It might be that when he is away, Wulfgar will come to realize that Mithral Hall truly is his home, and turn again for Bruenor's halls. Or perhaps he'll take another wife, and return to us with her, full of love and free of pain."

He pushed Catti-brie back again, his lavender eyes locking stares with her rich blue orbs. "You have to trust in Wulfgar. He has earned that from us all many times over. Allow him to walk whatever road he chooses, and hold confidence that you and I, and Bruenor and Regis, all go with him in his heart, as we carry him in ours. You carry with you guilt you do not deserve. Would you truly desire that Wulfgar not follow his road for the sake of mending your melancholy?"

Catti-brie considered the words for a few heartbeats, then managed a smile. "My heart is not empty," she said, and she came forward and kissed Drizzt again, with urgency and passion.

* * * * *

"Whate'er ye're needin', ye're gettin'," Bruenor assured Nanfoodle as the gnome gently slid one of the parchment scrolls out of the sack. "Rumblebelly here is yer slave, and he'll be running to meself and all me boys at the command o' Nanfoodle."

The gnome began to unroll the document, but winced and halted, hearing the fragile parchment crackle.

"I will have to brew oils of preservation," he explained to Bruenor. "I dare not put this under bright light until it's properly treated."

"Whate'er ye need," Bruenor assured him. "Ye just get it done, and get it done quick."

"How quick?" The gnome seemed a bit unnerved by that request.

"Alustriel's here now," said Bruenor. "She's to be working on the bridge for the next few days, and I'm thinkin' that if them scrolls're saying what I'm thinkin' they're saying, it might be good for Alustriel to go back to Silverymoon muttering and musing on the revelations."

But Nanfoodle shook his head. "It will take me more than a day to prepare the potions—and that's assuming that you have the ingredients I will require." He looked to Regis. "Bat guano forms the base."

"Wonderful," the halfling muttered.

"We'll have it or we'll get it," Bruenor promised him.

"It will take more than a day to brew anyway," said Nanfoodle. "Then three days for it to set on the parchment—at least three. I'd rather it be five."

"So four days total," said Bruenor, and the gnome nodded.

"Just to prepare the parchments for examination," Nanfoodle was quick to add. "It could take me tendays to decipher the ancient writing, even with my magic."

"Bah, ye'll be faster."

"I cannot promise."

"Ye'll be faster," Bruenor said again, in a tone less encouraging and more demanding. "Guano," he said to Regis, and he turned and walked from the room.

"Guano," Regis repeated, looking at Nanfoodle helplessly.

"And oil from the smiths," said the gnome. He drew another scroll from the sack and placed it beside the first, then put his hands on his hips and heaved a great sigh. "If they understood the delicacy of the task, they would not be so impatient," he said, more to himself than to the halfling.

"Bruenor is well past delicacy, I'm guessing," said Regis. "Too many orcs about for delicacy."

"Orcs and dwarves," muttered the gnome. "Orcs and dwarves. How is an artist to do his work?" He heaved another sigh, as if to say "if I must," and moved to the side of the room, to the cabinet where he kept his mortar and pestle, and assorted spoons and vials.

"Always rushing, always grumbling," he griped. "Orcs and dwarves, indeed!"

* * * * *

The companions had barely settled into their chambers in the dwarven hall west of Garumn's Gorge when word came that yet another unexpected visitor had arrived at the eastern gate. It wasn't often that elves walked through King Bruenor's door, but those gates were swung wide for Hralien of the Moonwood.

Drizzt, Catti-brie, and Bruenor waited impatiently in Bruenor's audience chamber for the elf.

"Alustriel and now Hralien," Bruenor said, nodding with every word. "It's all coming together. Once we get the words from them scrolls, we'll get both o' them to agree that the time's now for striking them smelly orcs."

Drizzt held his doubts private and Catti-brie merely smiled and nodded. There was no reason to derail Bruenor's optimism with an injection of sober reality.

"We know them Adbar and Felbarr boys'll fight with us," Bruenor went on, oblivious to the detachment of his audience. "If we're getting the Moonwood and Silverymoon to join in, we'll be puttin' them orcs back in their holes in short order, don't ye doubt!"

He rambled on sporadically for the next few moments, until at last Hralien was led into the chamber and formally introduced.

"Well met, King Bruenor," the elf said after the list of his accomplishments and titles was read in full. "I come with news from the Moonwood."

"Long ride if ye've come just to break bread," said Bruenor.

"We have suffered an incursion from the orcs," Hralien explained, talking right past Bruenor's little jest. "A coordinated and cunning attack."

"We know yer pain," Bruenor replied, and Hralien bowed in appreciation.

"Several of my people were lost," Hralien went on, "elves who should have known the birth and death of centuries to come." He looked squarely at Drizzt as he continued, "Innovindil among them."

Drizzt's eyes widened and he gasped and slumped back, and Catti-brie brought her arm across his back to support him.

"And Sunset beneath her," said Hralien, his voice less steady. "It would appear that the orcs had anticipated her arrival on the field, and were well prepared."

Drizzt's chest pumped with strong, gasping breaths. He looked as if he was about to say something, but no words came forth and he had the strength only to shake his head in denial. A great emptiness washed through him, a cold loss and callous reminder of the harsh immediacy of change, a sudden and irreversible reminder of mortality.

"I share your grief," Hralien said. "Innovindil was my friend, beloved by all who knew her. And Sunrise is bereaved, do not doubt, for the loss of Innovindil and of Sunset, his companion for all these years."

"Durned pig orcs," Bruenor growled. "Are ye all still thinkin' we should leave them to their gains? Are ye still o' the mind that Obould's kingdom should stand?"

"Orcs have attacked the Moonwood for years uncounted," Hralien replied. "They come for wood and for mischief, and we kill them and send them running. But their attack was better this time—too much so for the simplistic race, we believe." As he finished, he was again looking directly at Drizzt, so much so that he drew curious stares from Bruenor and Catti-brie in response.

"Tos'un Armgo," Drizzt reasoned.

"We know him to be in the region, and he learned much of our ways in his time with Albondiel and Sinnafain," Hralien explained.

Drizzt nodded, determination replacing his wounded expression. He had vowed to hunt down Tos'un when he and Innovindil had returned Ellifain's body to the Moonwood. Suddenly that promise seemed all the more critical.

"A journey full o' grief is a longer ride by ten, so the sayin' goes," said Bruenor. "Ye make yerself comfortable, Hralien o' the Moonwood. Me boys'll see to yer every need, and ye stay as long as ye're wantin'. Might be that I'll have a story for ye soon enough—one that'll put us all in better stead for ridding ourselves o' the curse of Obould. A few days at the most, me friends're tellin' me."

"I am a courier of news, and have come with a request, King Bruenor," the elf explained, and he gave another respectful and appreciative bow. "Others will journey here from the Moonwood to your call, of course, but my own road is back through your eastern door no later than dawn tomorrow." Again he looked Drizzt in the eye. "I hope I will not be alone."

Drizzt nodded his agreement to go out on the hunt before he even turned to Catti-brie. He knew that she would not deny him that.

* * * * *

The couple were alone in their room soon after, and Drizzt began to fill his backpack.

"You're going after Tos'un," Catti-brie remarked, but did not ask.

"Have I a choice?"

"No. I only wish that I were well enough to go with you."

Drizzt paused in his packing and turned to regard her. "In Menzoberranzan, they say, *Aspis tu drow bed n'tuth drow.* 'Only a drow can hunt a drow.'"

"Then hunt well," said Catti-brie, and she moved to the side wardrobe to aid Drizzt in his preparations. She seemed not upset with him in the least, which was why she caught Drizzt completely off his guard when she quietly asked, "Would you have married Innovindil when I am gone?"

Drizzt froze, and slowly mustered the courage to turn and look at Catti-brie. She wore a slight smile and seemed quite at ease and comfortable. She moved to their bed and sat on the edge, and motioned for Drizzt to join her.

"Would you have?" she asked again as he approached. "Innovindil was very beautiful, in body and in mind."

"It is not something I think about," said Drizzt.

Catti-brie's smile grew wider. "I know," she assured him. "But I am asking you to consider it now. Could you have loved her?"

Drizzt thought about it for a few moments then admitted, "I do not know."

"And you never wondered about it at all?"

Drizzt's thoughts went back to a moment he had shared with Innovindil when the two of them were out alone among the orc lines. Innovindil had nearly seduced him, though only to let him see more clearly his feelings for Catti-brie, whom he had thought dead at the time.

"You could have loved her, I think," Catti-brie said.

"You may well be right," he said.

"Do you think she thought of you in her last moments?"

Drizzt's eyes widened in shock at the blunt question, but Catti-brie didn't back down.

"She thought of Tarathiel, likely, and what was," he answered.

"Or of Drizzt and what might have been."

Drizzt shook his head. "She would not have looked there. Not then. Likely her every thought was for Sunset. To be an elf is to find the moment, the here and now. To revel in what is with knowledge and acceptance that what will be, will be, no matter the hopes and plans of any."

"Innovindil would have had a fleeting moment of regret for Drizzt, and potential love lost," Catti-brie said.

Drizzt didn't disagree, and couldn't, given the woman's generous tone and expression. Catti-brie wasn't judging him, wasn't looking for reasons to doubt him. She confirmed that a moment later, when she laughed and put her hand up to stroke his cheek.

"You will outlive me by centuries, in all likelihood," she explained. "I understand the implications of that, my love, and what a selfish fool I would be if I expected you to remain faithful to a memory. Nor would I want—nor do I want—that for you."

"It doesn't mean that we have to speak of it," Drizzt retorted. "We know not where our roads will lead, nor which of us will outlive the other. These are dangerous times in a dangerous world."

"I know."

"Then is this something we should bother to discuss?"

Catti-brie shrugged, but gradually her smile dissipated and a cloud crossed her fair features.

"What is it?" Drizzt asked, and lifted his hand to turn her to face him directly.

"If the dangers do not end our time together, how will Drizzt feel, I wonder, in twenty years? Or thirty?"

The drow wore a puzzled expression.

"You will still be young and handsome, and full of life and love to give," Catti-brie explained. "But I will be old and bent and ugly. You will stay by my side, I am sure, but what life will that be? What lust?"

It was Drizzt's turn to laugh.

"Can you look at a human woman who has seen the turn of seventy years and think her attractive?"

"Are there not couples of humans still in love after so many years together?" Drizzt asked. "Are there not human husbands who love their wives still when seventy is a birthday passed?"

"But the husbands are not usually in the springtime of their lives."

"You err because you pretend that it will happen overnight, in the snap of fingers," Drizzt said. "That is far from the case, even for an elf looking upon the human lifespan. Every wrinkle is earned, my love. Day by day, we spend our time together, and the changes that come will be well earned. In your heart you know that I love you, and I have no doubt but that my love will grow with the passage of years. I know your heart, Catti-brie. You are blissfully predictable to me in some ways, never so in others. I know where your choices will be, time and again, and ever are they on the right side of justice and integrity."

Catti-brie smiled and kissed him, but Drizzt broke it off fast and pushed her back.

"If a dragon's fiery breath were to catch up with me, and scar my skin hideously, blind me, and keep about me a stench of burnt flesh, would Catti-brie still love me?"

"Wonderful thought," the woman said dryly.

"Would she? Would you stand beside me?"

"Of course."

"And if I thought otherwise, at all, then never would I have desired to be your husband. Do you not similarly trust in me?"

Catti-brie grinned and kissed him again, then pushed him on his back on the bed.

The packing could wait.

* * * * *

Early the next morning, Drizzt leaned over the sleeping Catti-brie and gently brushed her lips with his own. He stared at her for a long while, even while he walked from the bed to the door. He at last turned and nearly jumped back in surprise, for set against the door was Taulmaril, the Heartseeker, Catti-brie's bow, and lying below it was her magical quiver, one that never ran out of arrows. For a moment, Drizzt stood confused, until he noticed a small note on the floor by the quiver. From a puncture in its side, he deduced that it had been pressed onto the top of the bow but had not held its perch.

He knew what it said before he ever brought it close enough to read the scribbling.

He looked back at Catti-brie once more. She couldn't be with him in body, perhaps, but with Taulmaril in his hand, she'd be there in spirit.

Drizzt slung the bow over his shoulder then retrieved the quiver and did likewise. He looked back once more to his love then left the room without a sound.

CHAPTER

16

The warriors of Clan Karuck paraded onto the muddy plaza center-ing a small orc village one rainy morning, the dreary overcast and pounding rain doing nothing to diminish the glory of their thunder-ous march.

"Stand and stomp!" the warriors sang in voices that resonated deeply from their massive half-ogre chests. "Smash and crush! All for the glory of One-eye Gruumsh!"

Yellow pennants flapping in the wind, waves of mud splatter-ing with every coordinated step, the clan came on in tight and precise formation, their six flags moving, two-by-two, in near perfect synchronization. The curious onlookers couldn't help but notice the stark contrast between the huge half-ogre, half-orcs and the scores of orcs from other tribes that had been swept up into their wake from the first villages through which Chieftain Grguch had marched.

Only one full-blooded orc marched with Grguch, a young and fiery shaman. Toogwik Tuk wasted no time as the villagers gathered. He moved out in front as Grguch halted his march.

"We are fresh from victory in the Moonwood!" Toogwik Tuk proclaimed, and every orc along the eastern reaches of Obould's fledgling kingdom knew well that hated place. Thus, predictably, a great cheer greeted the news.

"All hail Chieftain Grguch of Clan Karuck!" Toogwik Tuk

proclaimed, and that was met with an uncomfortable pause until he added, "For the glory of King Obould!"

Toogwik Tuk glanced back to Grguch, who nodded his agreement, and the young shaman started the chant, "Grguch! Obould! Grguch! Obould! Grguch! Grguch! Grguch!"

All of Clan Karuck fell in quickly with the cadence, as did the orcs who had already joined in with the march, and the villagers' doubts were quickly overwhelmed.

"As Obould before him, Chieftain Grguch will bring the judgment of Gruumsh upon our enemies!" Toogwik Tuk cried, running through the mob and whipping them into frenzy. "The snow retreats, and we advance!" With every glorious proclamation, he took care to add, "For the glory of Obould! By the power of Grguch!"

Toogwik Tuk understood well the weight that had settled on his shoulders. Dnark and Ung-thol had departed for the west to meet with Obould regarding the new developments, and it fell squarely upon Toogwik Tuk to facilitate Grguch's determined march to the south. Clan Karuck alone would not stand against Obould and his thousands, obviously, but if Clan Karuck carried along with them the orc warriors from the dozen villages lining the Surbrin, their arrival on the field north of King Bruenor's fortifications would carry great import—enough, so the conspirators hoped, to coerce the involvement of the army Obould had likely already positioned there.

That sort of rabble rousing had been Toogwik Tuk's signature for years. His rise through the ranks to become the chief shaman of his tribe—almost all of whom were dead, crushed in the mysterious, devastating explosion of a mountain ridge north of Keeper's Dale—had been expedited by precisely that talent. He knew well how to manipulate the emotions of the peasant orcs, to conflate their present loyalties with what he wanted their loyalties to be. Every time he mentioned Obould, he was quick to add the name Grguch. Every time he spoke of Gruumsh, he was quick to add the name of Grguch. Mingle them, say them together enough times so that his audience would unwittingly add "Grguch" whenever they heard the names of the other two.

His energy again proved infectious, and he soon had all of the villagers hopping about and chanting with him, always for the glory of Obould, and always by the power of Grguch.

Those two names needed to be intimately linked, the three conspirators had decided before Dnark and Ung-thol had departed. To even hint against Obould after such dramatic and sweeping victories as the orc king had brought would have spelled a fast end to the coup. Even considering the disastrous attempt to enter Mithral Hall's western gate, or the loss of the eastern ground between the dwarven halls and the Surbrin, or the stall throughout winter and the whispers that it might be longer than that, the vast majority of orcs spoke of Obould in the hushed tones usually reserved for Gruumsh himself. But Toogwik Tuk and two companions planned to move the tribes to oppose their king, one baby-step at a time.

"By the power of Grguch!" Toogwik Tuk cried again, and before the cheer could erupt, he added, "Will the dwarven wall hold against a warrior who burned the Moonwood?"

Though he expected a cheer, Toogwik Tuk was answered with looks of suspicion and confusion.

"The dwarves will flee before us," the shaman promised. "Into their hole they will run, and we will control the Surbrin for King Obould! *For the glory of King Obould!*" he finished, screaming with all his power.

The orcs around him cheered wildly, insanely.

"By the power of Grguch!" the not-quite-so-out-of-control Toogwik Tuk cleverly added, and many of the villagers, so used to the chant by then, shouted the words right along beside him.

Toogwik Tuk glanced back at Chieftain Grguch, who wore a most satisfied grin.

Another step taken, Toogwik Tuk knew.

Taking many offered supplies, Clan Karuck soon resumed their march, and a new pennant flew among the many in the mob behind them, and another forty warriors eagerly melded into Chieftain Grguch's trailing ranks. With several larger villages before them, both the chieftain and his shaman spokesman expected that they would number in the thousands when they at last reached the dwarven wall.

Toogwik Tuk held faith that when they smashed that wall, the cries for Grguch would be louder than those for Obould. The next cheers he led would hold fewer references to the glory of Obould and more to the glory of Gruumsh. But he would not lessen the number of his claims that all of it was being wrought by the power of Grguch.

* * * * *

Jack could see that the sprout of hair on one side of Hakuun's mis-shapen, wart-covered nose tingled with nervous energy as he walked out from the main host, among dark pines and broken fir trees.

"By sprockets and elemental essences, that was exciting, wasn't it?"

The orc shaman froze in place at the all-too-familiar voice, composed himself with a deep breath that greatly flared his nostrils, and slowly turned to regard a curious little humanoid in brilliant purple robes sitting on a low branch, swinging his feet back and forth like a carefree child. The form was new to Hakuun. Oh, he knew what a gnome was, indeed, but he had never seen Jaculi in that state before.

"That young priest is so full of spirit," Jack said. "I almost walked out and joined in with Grguch myself! Oh, what a grand march they have planned!"

"I didn't ask you to come up here," Hakuun remarked.

"Did you not?" said Jack, and he hopped down from the tree and brushed the twigs from his fabulous robes. "Tell me, Shaman of Clan Karuck, what am I to think when I peer out from my work to find that the one to whom I have bestowed such great gifts has run off?"

"I did not run off," Hakuun insisted, trying to keep his voice steady, though he was visibly near panic. "Often does Clan Karuck go hunting."

Hakuun gave ground as the gnome walked up to him. Jack continued to advance as Hakuun retreated.

"But this was no ordinary excursion."

Hakuun looked at Jack with dull curiosity, obviously not understanding him.

"No ordinary *hunt,*" Jack explained.

"I have told you."

"Of Obould, yes, and of his thousands," said Jack. "A bit of mis-chief and a bit of loot to be found, so you said. But it is more than that, is it not?"

Again Hakuun wore a puzzled expression.

Jack snapped his stubby fingers in the air and whirled away. "Do you not feel it, shaman?" he asked, his voice full of excitement. "Do you not recognize that this is no ordinary hunt?"

Jack spun back on Hakuun to measure his response, and still he saw that the shaman wasn't quite catching on. For Jack, so perceptive and cunning, had deduced the subtext of Toogwik Tuk's speech, and the implications it offered.

"Perhaps it is just my own suspicion," the gnome said, "but you must tell me all that you know. Then we should speak with that spirited young priest."

"I have told you . . ." Hakuun protested. His voiced trailed off and he retreated a step, knowing what awful thing was about to befall him.

"No, I mean that you must tell me everything," Jack said, all humor gone from his voice and his expression as he took a step toward the shaman. Hakuun shrank back, but that only made Jack stride more purposefully.

"Ah, you do forget," the gnome said as he closed the gap. "All that I have done for you, and so little have I asked in return. With great power, Hakuun, comes great expectations."

"There is nothing more," the shaman started to plead, and he held up his hands.

Jack the Gnome wore a mask of evil. He said not a word, but pointed to the ground. Hakuun shook his head feebly and continued to wave, and Jack continued to point.

But it was no contest, the outcome never in doubt. With a slight whimper, Hakuun, the mighty shaman of Clan Karuck, the conduit between Giguel and Gruumsh, prostrated himself on the ground, face down.

Jack looked straight ahead and lowered his arms to his sides as he quietly mouthed the words to his spell. He thought of the mysterious illithids, the brilliant mind flayers, who had taught him so much of one particular school of magic.

His robes fluttered only briefly as he shrank, then they and all his other gear melded into his changing form. In an instant Jack the Gnome was gone and a sightless rodent padded across the ground on four tiny feet. He went up to Hakuun's ear and sniffed for a few moments, hesitating simply because he recognized how uncomfortable it was making the cowering creature.

Then Jack the Gnome-cum-brain mole crawled into Hakuun's ear and disappeared from sight.

Hakuun shuddered and jerked in agonized spasms as the creature burrowed deeper, through the walls of his inner ear and into the seat of his consciousness. The shaman forced himself up to all fours as he began to gag. He vomited and spat, though of course the feeble defenses of his physical body could not begin to dislodge his unwelcome guest.

A few moments later, Hakuun staggered to his feet.

There, said the voice of Jack in his head. *Now I better understand the purpose of this adventure, and together we will learn the extent of this spirited young shaman's plans.*

Hakuun didn't argue—there was no way he could, of course. And for all his revulsion and pain, Hakuun knew that with Jack inside him, he was much more perceptive, and many times more powerful.

A private conversation with Toogwik Tuk, Jack instructed, and Hakuun could not disagree.

* * * * *

Even with their sensitive elf ears, Drizzt and Hralien could only make out the loudest chants from the gathered orcs. Still, the purpose of the march became painfully obvious.

"They are the ones," Hralien remarked. "The yellow banner was seen in the Moonwood. It appears that their numbers have . . ."

He paused as he looked over at his companion, who didn't seem to be listening. Drizzt crouched, perfectly still, his head turned back to the south, toward Mithral Hall.

"We have already passed several orc settlements," the drow said a few heartbeats later. "No doubt this march will cross through each."

"Swelling their numbers," Hralien agreed, and Drizzt finally looked at him.

"And they'll continue southward," the drow reasoned.

Hralien said, "This may be renewed aggression brewing. And I fear that there is an instigator."

"Tos'un?" said Drizzt. "I see no dark elf among the gathering."

"He's likely not far afield."

"Look at them," Drizzt said, nodding his chin in the direction of the chanting, cheering orcs. "If Tos'un did instigate this madness, could he still be in control of it?"

It was Hralien's turn to shrug. "Do not underestimate his cunning," the elf warned. "The attack on the Moonwood was well-coordinated, and brutally efficient."

"Obould's orcs have surprised us at every turn."

"And they were not without drow advisors."

The two locked stares at that remark, a cloud briefly crossing Drizzt's face.

"I truly believe that Tos'un orchestrated the attack on the Moon-wood," Hralien said. "And that he is behind this march, wherever it may lead."

Drizzt glanced back to the south, toward Bruenor's kingdom.

"It may well be that their destination is Mithral Hall," Hralien conceded. "But I beg you to continue on the road that led you out of Bruenor's depths. For all our sakes, find Tos'un Armgo. I will shadow these orcs, and will give ample warning to King Bruenor should it become necessary—and I will err on the side of caution. Trust me in this, I beg, and free yourself for this most important task."

Drizzt looked from the gathered orcs back toward Mithral Hall yet again. He envisioned a battle fought along the Surbrin, fierce and vicious, and felt the pangs of guilt in considering that Bruenor and Regis, perhaps even Catti-brie and the rest of Clan Battlehammer, would yet again be fighting for their survival without him by their side. He winced as he saw again the fall of the tower at Shallows, with Dagnabbit, whom he had then thought to be Bruenor, tumbling down to his death atop it.

He took a deep breath and turned back to the orc frenzy, the chanting and dancing continuing unabated. If a dark elf from Barrison Del'Armgo, one of the most formidable Houses of Menzo-berranzan, was to blame then the orcs would no doubt prove many times more formidable than they appeared. Drizzt nodded grimly, his responsibility and thus his path clear before him.

"Follow their every move," he bade Hralien.

"On my word," the elf replied. "Your friends will not be caught unprepared."

The orcs moved along soon after, and Hralien shadowed their southwestern march, leaving Drizzt alone on the mountainside. He considered going down to the orc village and snooping around, but decided that Tos'un, if he was about, would likely be along the periphery, among the stones, as was Drizzt.

"Come to me, Guenhwyvar," the drow commanded, drawing forth the onyx figurine. When the gray mist coalesced into the panther, Drizzt sent her out hunting. Guenhwyvar could cover a tremendous amount of ground in short order, and not even a lone drow could escape her keen senses.

Drizzt, too, set off, moving deliberately but with great caution in the opposite direction from the panther, who was already cutting across the wake of the departing army. If Hralien's guess was correct and Tos'un Armgo was directing the orcs from nearby, Drizzt held all faith that he would soon confront the rogue.

His hands went to his scimitars as he considered Khazid'hea, Catti-brie's sword, the weapon that had fallen into the hands of Tos'un. Any drow warrior was formidable. A warrior of a noble House likely more so. Even thinking in those respectful terms, Drizzt consciously reminded himself that the drow noble was even more potent, for those who underestimated Khazid'hea usually wound up on the ground.

In two pieces.

* * * * *

Interesting, Jack said to Hakuun's mind when they walked away from their quiet little meeting with Toogwik Tuk, one in which Jack had used the power of magical suggestion to complement Hakuun's spells of lie detection, allowing the dual being to extract much more honest answers from Toogwik Tuk than the young shaman had ever meant to offer. *So the conspirators have not brought you here to enhance Obould's forces.*

"We must tell Grguch," Hakuun whispered.

Tell him what? That we have come to do battle?

"That our venture into the Moonwood and now against the dwarves will likely anger Obould."

Inside his head, Hakuun could feel Jack laughing. *Orcs plotting against orcs,* Jack silently related. *Orcs manipulating orcs to plot against orcs. All of this will be surprising news to old Chieftain Grguch, I am sure.*

Hakuun's determined stride slowed, his tailwind stolen by Jack's cynical sarcasm—sarcasm effective only because it held the ring of truth.

Let the play play, said Jack. *The plots of the conspirators will be bent to our favor when we need them to be. For now, all the risk is theirs, for Clan Karuck is unwitting. If they have played the part of fools to even consider such a plot, their fall will be enjoyable to witness. If they are not fools, then all to our gain.*

"Our gain?" said Hakuun, emphasizing Jack's inclusion into it all.

"For as long as I am interested," Hakuun's voice replied, though it was Jack who controlled it.

A not-so-subtle reminder, Hakuun understood, of who was leading whom.

CHAPTER

DEFINING GRUUMSH

17

Chieftain Dnark did not miss the simmer behind King Obould's yellow eyes whenever the orc king's glance happened his and Ungthol's way. Obould was continually repositioning his forces, which all of the chieftains understood was the king's way of keeping them in unfamiliar territory, and thus, keeping them dependent upon the larger kingdom for any real sense of security. Dnark and Ung-thol had rejoined their clan, the tribe of the Wolf Jaw, only to learn that Obould had summoned them to work on a defensive position north of Keeper's Dale, not far from where Obould had settled to ride out the fleeting days of winter.

As soon as Obould had met Wolf Jaw at the new site, the wise and perceptive Dnark understood that there had been more to that movement than simple tactical repositioning, and when he'd first met the orc king's gaze, he had known beyond doubt that he and Ung-thol had been the focus of Obould's decision.

The annoying Kna squirmed around his side, as always, and shaman Nukkels kept to a respectful two paces behind and to his god-figure's left. That meant that Nukkels's many shamans were filtered around the common warriors accompanying the king. Dnark presumed that all of the orcs setting up Obould's three-layered tent were fanatics in the service of Nukkels.

Obould launched into his expected tirade about the importance of the mountain ridge upon which the tent was being erected, and how the fate of the entire kingdom could well rest upon the efforts of Clan Wolf Jaw in properly securing and fortifying the ground, the tunnels, and the walls. They had heard it all before, of course, but Dnark couldn't help but marvel at the rapt expressions on the faces of his minions as the undeniably charismatic king wove his spell yet again. Predictability didn't diminish the effect, and that, the chieftain knew, was no small feat.

Dnark purposely focused on the reactions of the other orcs, in part to keep himself from listening too carefully to Obould, whose rhetoric was truly hard to resist—sometimes so much so that Dnark wondered if Nukkels and the other priests weren't weaving a bit of magic of their own behind the notes of Obould's resonating voice.

Wound in his contemplations, it took a nudge from Ung-thol to get Dnark to realize that Obould had addressed him directly. Panic washing through him, the chieftain turned to face the king squarely, and he fumbled for something to say that wouldn't give away his obliviousness.

Obould's knowing smile let him know that nothing would suffice.

"My pennant will be set upon the door of my tent when it is ready for private audience," the orc king said—said again, obviously. "When you see it, you will come for a private parlay."

"Private?" Dnark dared ask. "Or am I to bring my second?"

Obould, his smile smug indeed, looked past him to Ung-thol. "Please do," he said, and it seemed to Dnark the enticing purr of a cat looking to sharpen its claws.

Wearing a smug and superior smile, Obould walked past him, carrying Kna and with Nukkels scurrying in tow. Dnark scanned wider as the king and his entourage moved off to the tent, noting the glances from the king's warriors filtering across his clan, and identifying those likely serving the priests. If it came to blows, Dnark would have to direct his own warriors against the magic-wielding fanatics, first and foremost.

He winced as he considered that, seeing the futility laid bare before him. If it came to blows with King Obould and his guard, Dnark's clan would scatter and flee for their lives, and nothing he could say would alter that.

He looked to Ung-thol, who stared at Obould without blinking, watching the king's every receding step.

Ung-thol knew the truth of it as well, Dnark realized, and wondered—not for the first time—if Toogwik Tuk hadn't led them down a fool's path.

"The flag of Obould is on the door," Ung-thol said to his chieftain a short while later.

"Let us go, then," said Dnark. "It would not do to keep the king waiting."

Dnark started off, but Ung-thol grabbed him by the arm. "We must not underestimate King Obould's network of spies," the shaman said. "He has sorted the various tribes carefully throughout the region, where those more loyal to him remain watchful of others he suspects. He may know that you and I were in the east. And he knows of the attack on the Moonwood, for Grguch's name echoes through the valleys, a new hero in the Kingdom of Many-Arrows."

Dnark paused and considered the words, then began to nod.

"Does Obould consider Grguch a hero?" Ung-thol asked.

"Or a rival?" asked Dnark, and Ung-thol was glad that they were in agreement, and that Dnark apparently understood the danger to them. "Fortunately for King Obould, he has a loyal chieftain"— Dnark patted his hand against his own chest—"and wise shaman who can bear witness here that Chieftain Grguch and Clan Karuck are valuable allies."

With a nod at Ung-thol's agreeing grin, Dnark turned and started for the tent. The shaman's grin faded as soon as Dnark looked away. None of it, Ung-thol feared, was to be taken lightly. He had been at the ceremony wherein King Obould had been blessed with the gifts of Gruumsh. He had watched the orc king break a bull's neck with his bare hands. He had seen the remains of a powerful drow priestess, her throat bitten out by Obould after the king had been taken down the side of a ravine in a landslide brought about by a priestess's earth-shaking enchantment. Watching Grguch's work in the east had been heady, invigorating and inspiring, to be sure. Clan Karuck showed the fire and mettle of the very best orc warriors, and the priest of Gruumsh could not help but feel his heart swell with pride at their fast and devastating accomplishments.

But Ung-thol was old enough and wise enough to temper his elation and soaring hopes against the reality that was King Obould Many-Arrows.

As he and Dnark entered the third and final off-set entrance into Obould's inner chamber, Ung-thol was only reminded of that awful reality. King Obould, seeming very much the part, sat on his throne on a raised dais, so that even though he was seated, he towered over any who stood before him. He wore his trademark black armor, patched back together after his terrific battle with the drow, Drizzt Do'Urden. His greatsword, which could blaze with magical fire at Obould's will, rested against the arm of his throne, within easy reach.

Obould leaned forward at their approach, dropping one elbow on his knee and stroking his chin. He didn't blink as he measured the steps of the pair, his focus almost exclusively on Dnark. Ung-thol hoped that his wrath, if it came forth, would be equally selective.

"Wolf Jaw performs brilliantly," Obould greeted, somewhat dissipating the tension.

Dnark bowed low at the compliment. "We are an old and disciplined clan."

"I know that well," said the king. "And you are a respected and feared tribe. It is why I keep you close to Many-Arrows, so that the center of my line will never waver."

Dnark bowed again at the compliment, particularly the notion that Wolf Jaw was feared, which was about as high as orc praise ever climbed. Ung-thol considered his chieftain's expression when he came back up from that bow. When the smug Dnark glanced his way, Ung-thol shot him a stern but silent retort, reminding him of the truth of Obould's reasoning. He was keeping Wolf Jaw close, indeed, but Dnark had to understand that Obould's aim was more to keep an eye on the tribe than to shore up his center. After all, there was no line of battle, so there was no center to fortify.

"The winter was favorable to us all," said Dnark. "Many towers have been built, and miles of wall."

"Every hilltop, Chieftain Dnark," said Obould. "If the dwarves or their allies come against us, they will have to fight over walls and towers on every hilltop."

Dnark glanced at Ung-thol again, and the cleric nodded for him to let it go at that. There was no need to engage Obould in an argument of defensive versus offensive preparations, certainly. Not with their schemes unfolding in the east.

"You were gone from your tribe," Obould stated, and Ung-thol started and blinked, wondering if the perceptive Obould had just read his mind.

"My king?" Dnark asked.

"You have been away in the east," said Obould. "With your shaman."

Dnark had done a good job keeping his composure, Ung-thol believed, but then the shaman winced when Dnark swallowed hard.

"There are many rogue orcs left over from the fierce battles with the dwarves," Dnark said. "Some strong and seasoned warriors, even shamans, have lost all their kin and clan. They have no banner."

As soon as he spoke the words, Dnark shrank back a step, for a murderous scowl crossed Obould's powerful features. At either side of the tent chamber, guards bristled, a couple even growling.

"They have no banner?" Obould calmly—too calmly—asked.

"They have the flag of Many-Arrows, of course," Ung-thol dared to interject, and Obould's eyes widened then narrowed quickly as he regarded the shaman. "But your kingdom is arranged by tribe, my king. You send tribes to the hills and the vales to do the work, and those who have lost their tribes know not where to go. Dnark and other chieftains are trying to sweep up the rogues to better organize your kingdom, so that you, with great plans opening wide before your Gruumsh-inspired visions, are not cluttered by such minor details."

Obould eased back in his throne and the moment of distress seemed to slip back from the edge of disaster. Of course with Obould, whose temper had left uncounted dead in his murderous wake, none could be sure.

"You were in the east," Obould said after many heartbeats had passed. "Near the Moonwood."

"Not so near, but yes, my king," said Dnark.

"Tell me of Grguch."

The blunt demand rocked Dnark back on his heels and crippled his denial as he replied with incredulity, "Grguch?"

"His name echoes through the kingdom," said Obould. "You have heard it."

"Ah, you mean Chieftain Grguch," Dnark said, changing the inflection of the name to put emphasis on the "Gr," and acting as if Obould's further remarks had spurred recognition. "Yes, I have heard of him."

"You have met him," said Obould, his tone and the set of his face conveying that his assertion was not assumption, but known fact.

Dnark glanced at Ung-thol, and for a moment the shaman thought his chieftain might just turn on his heel and flee. And indeed, Ung-thol wanted to do the same. Not for the first time and not for the last time, he wondered how they could have been foolish enough to dare conspire against King Obould Many-Arrows.

A soft chuckle from Dnark settled Ung-thol, though, and reminded him that Dnark had risen through difficult trials to become the chieftain of an impressive tribe—a tribe that even then surrounded Obould's tent.

"Chieftain Grguch of Clan Karuck, yes," Dnark said, matching Obould's stare. "I witnessed his movement through Teg'ngun's Dale near the Surbrin. He was marching to the Moonwood, though we did not know that at the time. Would that I had, for I would have enjoyed witnessing his slaughter of the foolish elves."

"You approve of his attack?"

"The elves have been striking at your minions in the east day after day," said Dnark. "I think it good that the pain of battle was taken to their forest, and that the heads of several of the creatures were placed upon pikes at the river's edge. Chieftain Grguch did you a great service. I had thought his assault on the Moonwood to be at your command."

He ended with an inflection of confusion, even suspicion, craftily turning the event back upon the orc king.

"Our enemies do not avoid their deserved punishment," Obould said without hesitation.

At Dnark's side, Ung-thol realized that his companion's quick-thinking had likely just saved both their lives. For King Obould would not kill them and tacitly admit that Grguch had acted independent of the throne.

"Chieftain Grguch and Clan Karuck will serve the kingdom well," Dnark pressed. "They are as fierce as any tribe I have ever seen."

"They breed with ogres, I am told."

"And carry many of the brutes along to anchor their lines."

"Where are they now?"

"In the east, I expect," said Dnark.

"Near the Moonwood still?"

"Likely," said Dnark. "Likely awaiting the response of our ene-mies. If the ugly elves dare cross the Surbrin, Chieftain Grguch will pike more heads on the riverbank."

Ung-thol eyed Obould carefully through Dnark's lie, and he easily recognized that the king knew more than he was letting on. Word of Grguch's march to the south had reached Obould's ear. Obould knew that the chieftain of Clan Karuck was a dangerous rival.

Ung-thol studied Obould carefully, but the cunning warrior king gave little more away. He offered some instructions for shoring up the defense of the region, included a punishing deadline, then dismissed the pair with a wave of his hand as he turned his attention to the annoying Kna.

"Your hesitance in admitting your knowledge of Grguch warned him," Ung-thol whispered to Dnark as they left the tent and crossed the muddy ground to rejoin their clan.

"He pronounced it wrong."

"You did."

Dnark stopped and turned on the shaman. "Does it matter?"

CHAPTER

The wizard held his hand out, fingers locked as if it were the talon of a great hunting bird. Sweat streaked his forehead despite the cold wind, and he locked his face into a mask of intensity.

The stone was too heavy for him, but he kept up his telekinetic assault, willing it into the air. Down at the riverbank, dwarf masons on the far bank furiously cranked their come-alongs, while others rushed around the large stone, throwing an extra strap or chain where needed. Still, despite the muscle and ingenuity of the dwarf crafts-men, and magical aid from the Silverymoon wizard, the floating stone teetered on the brink of disaster.

"Joquim!" another citizen of Silverymoon called.

"I . . . can't . . . hold . . . it," the wizard Joquim grunted back, each word forced out through gritted teeth.

The second wizard shouted for help and rushed down to Joquim's side. He had little in the way of telekinetic prowess, but he had memorized a dweomer for just that eventuality. He launched into his spellcasting and threw his magical energies out toward the shaking stone. It stabilized, and when a third member of the Silverymoon contingent rushed over, the balance shifted in favor of the builders. It began to seem almost effortless as the combination of dwarf and wizard guided the stone out over the rushing waters of the River Surbrin.

With a dwarf on the end of a beam guiding the way, the team with the come-alongs positioned the block perfectly over the even larger stones that had already been set in place. The guide dwarf called for a hold, rechecked the alignment, then lifted a red flag.

The wizards eased up their magic gradually, slowly lowering the block.

"Go get the next one!" the dwarf yelled to his companions and the wizards on the near bank. "Seems the Lady's almost ready for this span!"

All eyes turned to the work at the near bank, the point closest to Mithral Hall, where Lady Alustriel stood on the first length of span over the river, her features serene as she whispered the words of a powerful spell of creation. Cold and strong she appeared, almost godlike above the rushing waters. Her white robes, highlighted in light green, blew about her tall and slender form. There was hardly a gasp of surprise when a second stone span appeared before her, reaching out to the next set of supports.

Alustriel's arms slipped down to her sides and she gave a deep exhale, her shoulders slumping as if her effort had thrown out more than magical strength.

"Amazing," Catti-brie said, coming up beside her and inspecting the newly conjured slab.

"The Art, Catti-brie," Alustriel replied. "Mystra's blessings are wondrous indeed." Alustriel turned a sly look her way. "Perhaps I can tutor you."

Catti-brie scoffed at the notion, but coincidentally, as she threw her head back, she twisted her leg at an angle that sent a wave of pain rolling through her damaged hip, and she was reminded that her days as a warrior might indeed be at their end—one way or another.

"Perhaps," she said.

Alustriel's smile beamed genuine and warm. The Lady of Silverymoon glanced back and motioned to the dwarf masons, who flooded forward with their tubs of mortar to seal and smooth the newest span.

"The conjured stone is permanent?" Catti-brie asked as she and Alustriel moved back down the ramp to the bank.

Alustriel looked at her as if the question was completely absurd. "Would you have it vanish beneath the wheels of a wagon?"

They both laughed at the flippant response.

"I mean, it is real stone," the younger woman clarified.

"Not an illusion, to be sure."

"But still the stuff of magic?"

Alustriel furrowed her brow as she considered the woman. "The stone is as real as anything the dwarves could drag in from a quarry, and the dweomer that created it is permanent."

"Unless it is dispelled," Catti-brie replied, and Alustriel said, "Ah," as she caught on to the woman's line of thought.

"It would take Elminster himself to even hope to dispel the work of Lady Alustriel," another nearby wizard interjected.

Catti-brie looked from the mage to Alustriel.

"A bit of an exaggeration, of course," Alustriel admitted. "But truly, any mage of sufficient power to dispel my creations would also have in his arsenal evocations that could easily destroy a bridge constructed without magic."

"But a conventional bridge can be warded against lightning bolts and other destructive evocations," Catti-brie reasoned.

"As this one shall be," promised Alustriel.

"And so it will be as safe as if the dwarves had . . ." Catti-brie started, and Alustriel finished the thought with her, "dragged the stones from a quarry."

They shared another laugh, until Catti-brie added, "Except from Alustriel."

The Lady of Silverymoon stopped cold and turned to stare directly at Catti-brie.

"It is an easy feat for a wizard to dispel her own magic, so I am told," Catti-brie remarked. "There will be no wards in place to prevent you from waving your hands and making expanse after expanse disappear."

A wry grin crossed Alustriel's beautiful face, and she cocked an eyebrow, an expression of congratulations for the woman's sound and cunning reasoning.

"An added benefit should the orcs overrun this position and try to use the bridge to spread their darkness to other lands," Catti-brie went on.

"Other lands like Silverymoon," Alustriel admitted.

"Do not be quick to sever the bridge to Mithral Hall, Lady," Catti-brie said.

"Mithral Hall is connected to the eastern bank through tunnels in any case," Alustriel replied. "We will not abandon your father, Catti-brie. We will never abandon King Bruenor and the valiant dwarves of Clan Battlehammer."

Catti-brie's responding smile came easy to her, for she didn't doubt a word of the pledge. She glanced back at the conjured slabs and nodded appreciatively, both for the power in creating them and the strategy of Alustriel in keeping the power to easily destroy them.

* * * * *

The late afternoon sun reflected moisture in Toogwik Tuk's jaundiced brown eyes, for he could hardly contain his tears of joy at the ferocious reminder of what it was to be an orc. Grguch's march through the three remaining villages had been predictably success-ful, and after Toogwik Tuk had delivered his perfected sermon, every able-bodied orc warrior of those villages had eagerly marched out in Grguch's wake. That alone would have garnered the fierce chieftain of Clan Karuck another two hundred soldiers.

But more impressively, they soon enough discovered, came the reinforcements from villages through which they had not passed. Word of Grguch's march had spread across the region directly north of Mithral Hall, and the war-thirsty orcs of many tribes, frustrated by the winter pause, had rushed to the call.

As he crossed the impromptu encampment, Toogwik Tuk sur-veyed the scores—no, hundreds—of new recruits. Grguch would hit the dwarven fortifications with closer to two thousand orcs than one thousand, by the shaman's estimation. Victory at the Surbrin was all but assured. Could King Obould hope to hold back the tide of war after that?

Toogwik Tuk shook his head with honest disappointment as he considered the once-great leader. Something had happened to Obould. The shaman wondered if it might have been the stinging defeat Bruenor's dwarves had handed him in his ill-fated attempt to breach Mithral Hall's western door. Or had it been the loss of the con-spiring dark elves and Gerti Orelsdottr and her frost giant minions? Or perhaps it had come about because of the loss of his son, Urlgen, in the fight on the cliff tops north of Keeper's Dale.

Whatever the cause, Obould hardly seemed the same fierce warrior who had led the charge into Citadel Adbar, or who had begun his great sweep south from the Spine of the World only a few months before. Obould had lost his understanding of the essence of the orc. He had lost the voice of Gruumsh within his heart.

"He demands that we wait," the shaman mused aloud, staring out at the teeming swarm, "and yet they come by the score to the promise of renewed battle with the cursed dwarves."

Never more certain of the righteousness of his conspiracy, the shaman moved quickly toward Grguch's tent. Obould no longer heard the call of Gruumsh, but Grguch surely did, and after the dwarves were smashed and chased back into their holes, how might King Obould claim dominion over the chieftain of Clan Karuck? And how might Obould secure fealty from the tens of thousands of orcs he had brought forth from their holes with promises of conquest?

Obould demanded they sit and wait, that they till the ground like peasant human farmers. Grguch demanded of them that they sharpen their spears and swords to better cut the flesh of dwarves.

Grguch heard the call of Gruumsh.

The shaman found the chieftain standing on the far side of a small table, surrounded by two of his Karuck warlords and with a much smaller orc standing across from them and manipulating a pile of dirt and stones that had been set upon the table. As he neared, Toogwik Tuk recognized the terrain being described by the smaller orc, for he had seen the mountain ridge that stretched from the eastern end of Mithral Hall down to the Surbrin.

"Welcome, Gruumsh-speaker," Grguch greeted him. "Join us."

Toogwik Tuk moved to an open side of the table and inspected the scout's work, which depicted a wall nearly completed to the Surbrin and a series of towers anchoring it.

"The dwarves have been industrious throughout the winter," said Grguch. "As you feared. King Obould's pause has given them strength."

"They will anticipate an attack like ours," the shaman remarked.

"They have witnessed no large movements of forces to indicate it," said Grguch.

"Other than our own," Toogwik Tuk had to remind him.

But Grguch laughed it off. "Possibly they have taken note of many orcs now moving nearer to their position," he agreed. "They may expect an attack in the coming tendays."

The two Karuck warlords beside the brutish chieftain chuckled at that.

"They will never expect one this very night," said Grguch.

Toogwik Tuk's face dropped into a sudden frown, and he looked down at the battlefield in near panic. "We have not even sorted out our forces . . ." he started to weakly protest.

"There is nothing to sort," Grguch replied. "Our tactic is swarm fodder and nothing more."

"Swarm fodder?" asked the shaman.

"A simple swarm to and through the wall," said Grguch. "Darkness is our ally. Speed and surprise are our allies. We will hit them as a wave flattens the ridge of a boot print on a beach."

"You know not the techniques of the many tribes who have come into the fold."

"I don't need to," Grguch declared. "I don't need to count my warriors. I don't need to place them in lines and squares, to form reserves and ensure that our flanks are protected back far enough to prevent an end run by our enemies. That is the way of the dwarf." He paused and looked around at the stupidly grinning warlords and the excited scout. "I see no dwarves in this room," he said, and the others laughed.

Grguch looked back at Toogwik Tuk. His eyes went wide, as if in alarm, and he sniffed at the air a couple of times. "No," he declared, looking again to his warlords. "I *smell* no dwarves in this room."

The laughter that followed was much more pronounced, and despite his reservations, Toogwik Tuk was wise enough to join in.

"Tactics are for dwarves," the chieftain explained. "Discipline is for elves. For orcs, there is only . . ." He looked directly at Toogwik Tuk.

"Swarm fodder?" the shaman asked, and a wry grin spread on Grguch's ugly face.

"Chaos," he confirmed. "Ferocity. Bloodlust and abandon. As soon as the sun has set, we begin our run. All the way to the wall. All the way to the Surbrin. All the way to the eastern doors of Mithral Hall. Half, perhaps more than half, of our warriors will find tonight the reward of glorious death."

Toogwik Tuk winced at that, and silently berated himself. Was he beginning to think more like Obould?

Grguch reminded him of the words of Gruumsh One-eye. "They will die with joy," the chieftain promised. "Their last cry will be of elation and not agony. And any who die otherwise, with regret or with sorrow or with fear, should have been slaughtered in sacrifice to Gruumsh before our attack commenced!"

The sudden volume and ferocity of his last proclamation set Toogwik Tuk back on his heels and had both the Clan Karuck warlords and guards at the perimeter of the room growling and gnashing their teeth. For a brief moment, Toogwik Tuk almost reconsidered his call to the deepest holes to rouse Chieftain Grguch.

Almost.

"There has been no sign from the dwarves that they know of our march," Grguch told a great gathering later that day, when the sunlight began to wane. Toogwik Tuk noted the dangerous priest Hakuun standing at his side, and that gave the younger shaman pause. He got the feeling that Hakuun had been watching him all along.

"They do not see the doom that has come against them," Grguch ordered. "Do not shout out, but run. Run fast to the wall, without delay, and whispering praise for Gruumsh with every stride."

There were no lines or coordinated movements, just a wild charge begun miles from the goal. There were no torches to light the way, no magical lights conjured by Toogwik Tuk or the other priests of Gruumsh. They were orcs, after all, raised in the upper tunnels of the lightless Underdark.

The night was their ally, the dark their comfort.

* * * * *

Once, when he was a child, Hralien had found a large pile of sand down by one of the Moonwood's two lakes. From a distance, that mound of light-colored sand had seemed discolored with streaks of red, and as he moved closer, young Hralien realized that the streaks weren't discolored sand, but were actually moving upon the surface of the mound. Being young and inexperienced, he had at first feared that he had happened upon a tiny volcano, perhaps.

On closer inspection, though, the truth had come clear to him, for the pile of sand had been an ant mound, and the red streaks were lines of the six-legged creatures marching to and fro.

Hralien thought of that long-ago experience as he witnessed the charge of the orcs, swarming the small, rocky hills north of King Bruenor's eastern defenses. Their movements seemed no less frenetic, and truly their march appeared no less determined. Given their speed and intensity, and the obstacle that awaited them barely two miles to the south, Hralien recognized their intent.

The elf bit his lip as he remembered his promise to Drizzt Do'Urden. He looked south, sorting out the landscape and recalling the trails that would most quickly return him to Mithral Hall.

Then he was running, and fearing that he could not keep his promise to his drow friend, for the orc line stretched ahead of him and the creatures had not far to travel. With great grace and agility, Hralien sprang from stone to stone. He leaped up and grabbed a low tree branch and swung out across a narrow chasm, landing lightly on the other side and in a full run. He moved with hardly a whisper of sound, unlike the orcs, whose heavy steps echoed in his keen elf's ears.

He knew that he should be cautious, for he could ill afford the delay if he happened into a fight. But neither could he slow his run and carefully pick his path, for some of the orcs were ahead of him, and the dwarves would need every heartbeat of warning he could give them. So he ran on, leaping and scrambling over bluffs and through low dales, where the melting snow had streamed down and pooled in clear, cold pockets. Hralien tried to avoid those pools as much as possible, for they often concealed slick ice. But even with his great dexterity and sharp vision, he occasionally splashed through, cringing at the unavoidable sound.

At one point, he heard an orc cry out, and feared that he had been spotted. Many strides later, he realized that the creature was just calling to a companion, a stark reminder that the lead runners and scouts of the brutish force were all around him.

Finally he left the sounds of orcs behind, for though the brutes could move with great speed, they could not match the pace of a dexterous elf, even across such broken ground.

Soon after, coming up over a rocky rise, Hralien caught sight of squat stone towers in the south, running down from tall mountains to the silvery, moonlit snake that was the River Surbrin.

"Too soon," the elf whispered in dismay, and he glanced back as if expecting Obould's entire army to roll over him. He shook his head and winced, then sprinted off for the south.

* * * * *

"We will have it completed within the tenday," Alustriel said to Catti-brie, the two sitting with some of the other Silverymoon wizards around a small campfire. One of the wizards, a robust human with thick salt and pepper hair and a tightly trimmed goatee, had conjured the flames and was playing with them, casting cantrips to change their color from orange to white to blue and red. A second wizard, a rather eccentric half-elf with shiny black hair magically streaked by a bloom of bright red locks, joined in and wove enchantments to make the red flames form into the shape of a small dragon. Seeing the challenge, the first wizard likewise formed blue flames, and the two spellcasters set their fiery pets into a proxy battle. Almost immediately, several other wizards began excitedly placing their bets.

Catti-brie watched with amusement and interest—more than she would have expected, and Alustriel's words to her about dabbling in the dark arts flitted unbidden through her thoughts. Her experience with wizards was very limited, and mostly involved the unpredictable and dangerously foolish Harpell family from Longsaddle.

"Asa Havel will win," Alustriel whispered to her, leaning in close and indicating the half-elf wizard who had manipulated the red flame. "Duzberyl is far more powerful at manipulating fire, but he has taxed his powers to their limit this day conjuring bright hot flames to seal the stone. And Asa Havel knows it."

"So he challenged," Catti-brie whispered back, "And his friends know, too, so they wager."

"They would wager anyway," Alustriel explained. "It is a matter of pride. Whatever is lost here will be reclaimed soon enough in another challenge."

Catti-brie nodded and watched the unfolding drama, the many faces, elf and human alike, glowing in varying shades and hues in the uneven light, turning blue as the blue dragon leaped atop the red, but then drifting back, green and yellow and toward a feverish red as Asa Havel's drake filtered up through Duzberyl's and gradually gained supremacy. It was all good-natured, of course, but Catti-brie didn't miss the intensity etched onto the faces of the combatants and onlookers alike. It occurred to her that she was looking into an entirely different world. She could relate it to the drinking games, and the arm-wrestling and sparring that so often took place in the taverns of Mithral Hall, for though the venue was different, the emotions were not. Still, there remained enough of a difference to intrigue her. It was a battle of strength, but of mental strength and concentration, and not of muscle and intestinal fortitude.

"Within a month, you could form flames into such shapes, yourself," Alustriel teased.

Catti-brie looked at her and laughed dismissively, but that hardly hid her interest.

She looked back to the fire just in time to see Duzberyl's blue roll over and consume Asa Havel's red, contrary to Alustriel's prediction. The backers of both wizards gasped in surprise and Duzberyl gave a yelp that was more shock than of victory. Catti-brie's gaze turned to Asa Havel, and her surprise turned to confusion.

The half-elf was not looking at the fight, and seemed oblivious to the fact that his dragon had been consumed by the human's blue. He stared out to the north, his sea-blue eyes scanning high above the flames. Catti-brie felt Alustriel turn beside her, then stand. The woman glanced over her shoulder, up at the dark wall, but shook her head slightly in confusion, seeing nothing out of the ordinary. Beside her, Alustriel cast a minor spell.

Other wizards rose and peered out to the north.

"An elf has come," Alustriel said to Catti-brie. "And the dwarves are scrambling."

"It's an attack," Asa Havel announced, rising and moving past the two women. He looked right at Alustriel and the princess of Mithral Hall and asked, "Orcs?"

"Prepare for battle," Alustriel said to her contingent. "Area spells to disrupt any charge."

"We have little left this day," Duzberyl reminded her.

In response, Alustriel reached inside one of the folds of her robes and drew forth a pair of slender wands. She half-turned and tossed one to Duzberyl. "Your necklace, too, if needed," she instructed, and the human nodded and brought a hand to a gaudy choker he wore, its golden links set with large stones like rubies of varying sizes, including one so large that Catti-brie couldn't have closed her fist around it.

"Talindra, to the gates of the dwarven halls," Alustriel said to a young elf female. "Warn the dwarves and help them sort the battle."

The elf nodded and took a few fast steps to the west, then disappeared with a flash of blue-white light. A second flash followed almost instantly, over near the hall's eastern gates, transporting Talindra to her assigned position, the surprised Catti-brie assumed, for she couldn't actually see the young elf.

She turned back to hear Alustriel positioning Asa Havel and another pair. "Secure fast passage to the far bank, should we need it. Prepare enough to carry any dwarves routed from the wall."

Catti-brie heard the first shouts from the wall, followed by the blare of horns, many horns, from beyond to the north. Then came the blare of one that overwhelmed all the others, a resonating, low-pitched grumble that shook the stones beneath Catti-brie's feet.

"Damn Obould to the Nine Hells," Catti-brie whispered, and she grimaced at the realization that she had loaned Taulmaril to Drizzt. She looked over at Alustriel. "I haven't my bow, or a sword. A weapon, please? Conjure one or produce one from a deep pocket."

To Catti-brie's surprise, the Lady of Silverymoon did just that, pulling yet another wand from inside her robes. Catti-brie took it, not knowing what to make of the thing, and when she looked back at Alustriel, the tall woman was tugging a ring from her finger.

"And this," she said, handing over the thin gold band set with a trio of sparkling diamonds. "I trust you are not already in the possession of two magical rings."

Catti-brie took it and held it pressed between her thumb and index finger, her expression dumbfounded.

"The command word for the wand is 'twell-in-sey,' " Alustriel explained. "Or 'twell-in-sey-sey' if you wish to loose two magical bolts."

"I don't know . . ."

"Anyone can use it," Alustriel assured her. "Point it at your target and speak the word. For the bigger orcs, choose two."

"But . . ."

"Put the ring on your finger and open your mind to it, for it will impart to you its dweomers. And know that they are powerful indeed." With that, Alustriel turned away, and Catti-brie understood that the lesson was at its end.

The Lady of Silverymoon and her wizards, except for those working near the river preparing a magical escape to the far bank, headed off for the wall, nearly all of them drawing forth wands or rods, or switching rings and other jewelry. Catti-brie watched it all with an undeniable sense of excitement, so much so that she was trembling so badly she could hardly line up the ring to slip it on her finger.

Finally she did, and she closed her eyes and took a deep breath. She felt as if she were looking up at the heavens, to see stars shooting across the darkened night sky, to see flashes of brilliance so magnificent that it seemed to her as if the gods must be throwing bolts at each other.

The first sounds of battle shook her from her contemplation. She opened her eyes and nearly fell over due to dizziness from the sudden change, as if she had just stepped back to solid ground from the Astral Plane.

She started after Alustriel, inspecting the wand, and garnered quickly which end to hold from a leather strap wrapped diagonally as a hand grip. At least she hoped it was the right end, and she winced at the thought of unloading enchanted bolts of magic into her own face. She dismissed the worry, noting that she wasn't gaining much on Alustriel, and noting more pointedly that the dwarves at the wall scrambled and yelled for support in many places already. She dropped her arms down beside her and ran as fast as her battered hip would allow.

"Twell-in-sey," she whispered, trying to get the inflection correct. She did.

The wand discharged and a red dart of energy burst forth, snapping into the ground with a hiss right before her running feet. Catti-brie yelped and stumbled, nearly falling over. She caught her balance and her composure, and was glad that no one seemed to notice.

On she ran, or tried to, but a wave of hot fire ran up her leg and nearly toppled her yet again. She looked down to her boot, smoking and charred on the side just back of her little toe. She paused again and composed herself, taking heart that the wound was not too severe, and thanking Moradin himself that Lady Alustriel hadn't given her a wand of lightning bolts.

* * * * *

The orc gained the wall in a wild rush, stabbing powerfully at the nearest dwarf, who seemed an easy kill as he was busy driving a second orc back over the wall and into the darkness.

But that dwarf, Charmorffe Dredgewelder of Fine Family Yellow-beard—so named because none of the Dredgewelders was ever known to have a yellow beard—was neither particularly surprised nor particularly impressed by the aggressive move. Trained under Thibbledorf Pwent himself, having served more than a score of years in the Gutbuster Brigade, Charmorffe had faced many a finer foe than that pathetic creature.

As Charmorffe had never gotten familiar with a formal buckler, his plate-shielded arm swooped down to intercept the spear, block-ing it solidly and sweeping it back behind him as he turned. That same movement brought his cudgel swinging around, and a quick three-step forward caught the overbalanced orc cleanly in range. The creature grunted, as did the dwarf, as the cudgel slammed it right behind the shoulder, launching it into a dive and spin forward, right off the ten-foot parapet.

As the path before him cleared, Charmorffe looked down the tip of an arrow set on a short bow. He yelped and fell over backward, buckling at both his knees, and as soon as he was clear, Hralien let fly. The missile hummed through the air right above the dwarf, and splattered into the chest of an orc that had been sneaking up on him from behind.

As soon as his back hit the stone, Charmorffe snapped all of his muscles forward, throwing his arms up high, and brought himself right back to his feet.

"That's twice I'm owin' ye, ye durned elf!" the dwarf protested. "First for savin' us all, and now for savin' meself!"

"I did neither, good dwarf," Hralien replied, running across the parapet to the waist-high wall, where he set his bow to work immediately. "I've faith that Clan Battlehammer is more than able to save itself."

He shot off an arrow as he spoke, but as soon as he finished, a large orc rose into the air right before him, sword ready to strike a killing blow. The orc landed lightly on the wall top and struck, but a spinning cudgel hit both the sword and the orc, turning its blow harmlessly short. And when the orc managed to hold its balance and throw itself forward at Hralien, it too was intercepted, by a flying Charmorffe Dredgewelder. The dwarf connected with a shoulder block, driving the orc tight against the wall. The orc began raining ineffective blows upon the dwarf's back for Charmorffe's powerful legs kept grinding, pressing in even tighter.

Hralien stabbed the orc in the eye with an arrow.

The elf jumped back fast, though, set the arrow and let fly, point blank into yet another orc flying up to the top of the wall. Hralien hit it squarely, and though its feet landed atop the narrow rail, the jolt of the hit dropped it right back off.

Charmorffe leaped up and clean-and-jerked the thrashing orc up high over his head. The dwarf threw himself into the wall, which hit him about mid chest, and snapped forward, tossing the orc over. As he went forward, Charmorffe solved the riddle, for just below him, and off to both sides as well, stood ogres, their backs tight against the wall. As each bent low and cupped its hands down near the ground, another orc ran up and stepped into that brace. A slight toss by the ogres had orcs sailing up over the wall.

"Pig-faced goblin kissers," Charmorffe growled. He turned and shouted, "Rocks over the wall, boys! We got ogres playing as ladders!"

Hralien rushed up beside Charmorffe, leaned far out and shot an arrow into the top of the nearest ogre's head. He marveled at his handiwork, then saw it all the more clearly as a fireball lit up the night, down to the east of his position, closer to the Surbrin where the wall was far from complete.

When Hralien looked that way, he thought their position surely lost, for though Alustriel and her wizards had entered the fray, a mass of huge orcs and larger foes swarmed across the defenses.

"Run for Mithral Hall, good dwarf," the elf said.

"That's what I be thinking," said Charmorffe.

* * * * *

Duzberyl ambled toward the wall, grumbling incessantly. "Two hundred pieces of gold for this one alone," he muttered, pulling another glittering red jewel from his enchanted necklace. He reached back and threw it at the nearest orcs, but his estimate of distance in the low light was off and the jewel landed short of the mark. Its fiery explosion still managed to engulf and destroy a couple of the creatures, and the others fell back in full flight, shrieking with every stride.

But Duzberyl griped all the more. "A hundred gold an orc," he grumbled, glancing back at Alustriel, who was far off to the side. "I could hire an army of rangers to kill ten times the number for one-tenth the cost!" he said, though he knew she was too far away to hear him.

And she wasn't listening anyway. She stood perfectly still, the wind whipping her robes. She lifted one arm before her, a jeweled ring on her clenched fist sparking with multicolored light.

Duzberyl had seen that effect before, but still he was startled when a bolt of bright white lightning burst forth from Alustriel's ring, splitting the night. The powerful wizard's aim was, as always, right on target, her bolt slamming an ogre in the face as it climbed over the wall. Hair dancing wildly, head smoking, the brute flew back into the darkness as Alustriel's bolt bounced away to hit another nearby attacker, an orc that seemed to simply melt into the stone. Again and again, Alustriel's chain lightning leaped away, striking orc or ogre or half-ogre, sending foes flying or spinning down with smoke rising from bubbling skin.

But every vacancy was fast-filled, ten attackers for every one that fell, it seemed.

The apparent futility brought a renewed growl to Duzberyl's chubby face, and he stomped along to a better vantage point.

* * * * *

Limping from foot and hip, Catti-brie watched it all with equal if not greater frustration, for at least Alustriel and her wizards were equipped to battle the monsters. The woman felt naked without her bow, and even with the gifts Alustriel had offered, she believed that she would prove more a burden than an asset.

She considered removing herself from the front lines, back to the bridge where she might prove of some use to Asa Havel in directing the retreat, should it come to that. That in mind, she glanced back—and noted a small group of orcs sprinting along the riverbank toward the distracted wizards.

Catti-brie thrust forth the wand, but brought it back and punched out with her other fist instead. The ring's teeming magical energies called out to her and she listened, and though she didn't know exactly the effects of her call, she followed the magical path toward the strongest sensation of stored energy.

The ring jolted once, twice, thrice, each burst sending forth a fiery ball at Catti-brie's targets. Like twinkling little stars, they seemed, as if the ring had reached up to the heavens and pulled celestial bodies down for its wielder to launch at her enemies. At great speed, they shot out across the night, leaving fiery trails, and when they reached the orc group, they exploded into larger blasts of consuming flames.

Orcs shrieked and scrambled frantically, and more than one leaped into the river to be washed away by cold, killing currents. Others rolled on the ground, trying to douse the biting flames, and when that failed, they ran off like living torches into the dark night, only to fall a few steps away, to crumble and burn on the frozen ground.

It lasted only a heartbeat, but seemed like much longer to Catti-brie, who stood transfixed, breathing hard, her eyes wide with shock. With a thought, she had blown apart nearly a score of orcs. As if they were nothing. As if she were a goddess, passing judgment on insignificant creatures. Never had she felt such power!

At that moment, if someone had asked Catti-brie the Elvish name of her treasured longbow, she would not have recalled it.

* * * * *

"It's not to hold!" Charmorffe cried to Hralien, and a swipe of the dwarf's heavy cudgel sent another orc flying aside.

Hralien wanted to shout back words of encouragement, but his view of the battlefield, since he wielded a weapon that made it incumbent upon him to seek a wider perspective, was more complete, and he understood that the situation was even worse than Charmorffe likely believed.

Few dwarves came forth from Mithral Hall and a host of orcs poured through the lower, uncompleted sections of the defensive wall. Huge orcs, some two feet taller and more than a hundred pounds heavier than the dwarves. Among them were true ogres, though it was hard for Hralien to distinguish where some of the orcs ended and the clusters of ogres began.

More orcs came up over the wall, launched by their ogre step-stools, putting pressure on the dwarves and preventing them from organizing a coordinated defense against the larger mass rolling in from the east.

"It's not to hold!" Charmorffe yelled again, and the words rang true. Hralien knew that the end was coming fast. The wizards intervened—one fireball then another, and a lightning chain that left many creatures smoking on the ground. But that wouldn't be enough, and Hralien understood that the wizards had been at their magical work all day long and had little power left to offer.

"Start the retreat," the elf said to Charmorffe. "To Mithral Hall!"

Even as he spoke, the orc mass surged forward, and Hralien feared that he and Charmorffe and the others had waited too long.

* * * * *

"By the gods, and the gemstone vendors!" Duzberyl roared, watching the sudden break in the dwarven line, the bearded folk sprinting back to the west along the wall, leaping down from the parapets and veering straight for Mithral Hall's eastern door. All semblance of a defensive posture had flown, creating a full and frantic retreat.

And it wouldn't be enough, the wizard calculated, for the orcs, hungry for dwarf blood, closed with every stride. Duzberyl grimaced as a dwarf was swallowed in the black cloud of the orc horde.

The portly wizard ran, and he reached up to his necklace, grasping the largest stone of all. He tore it free, cursed the gemstone merchant again for good measure, and heaved it with all his strength.

The magical grenade hit the base of the wall just behind the leading orcs, and exploded, filling the area, even up onto the parapet, with biting, killing fires. Those monsters immediately above and near the blast charred and died, while others scrambled in an agonized and horrified frenzy, flames consuming them as they ran. Panic hit the orc line, and the dwarves ran free.

* * * * *

"Mage," Grguch muttered as he alighted on the wall some distance back of the enormous fireball.

"Of considerable power," said Hakuun, who stood beside him, having blessed himself and Grguch with every conceivable ward and enhancement.

The chieftain turned back and fell prone on the parapet railing. "Hand it up," he called down to the ogre who had flipped him up, indicating a weapon. A moment later, Grguch stood again on the wall, hoisting on one shoulder a huge javelin at the end of an atlatl.

"Mage," Grguch grumbled again with obvious disgust.

Hakuun held up a hand, motioning for the chieftain to pause. Then, from inside the orc priest, Jack the Gnome cast a most devious enchantment on the head of the missile.

Grguch grinned and brought his shoulder back, shifting the angle of the ten-foot missile. As Hakuun cast a second, complimentary spell upon the intended victim, Grguch launched the spear with all his might.

* * * * *

The stubborn orc lurched toward her, one of its legs still showing flashes of biting flame.

Catti-brie didn't flinch, didn't even start as the orc awkwardly threw a spear her way. She kept her eyes locked on the creature, met its gaze and its hate, and slowly lifted her wand.

She wished at that moment that she had Khazid'hea at her side, that she could engage the vile creature in personal combat. The orc took another staggering step, and Catti-brie uttered the command word.

The red missile sizzled into the orc's chest, knocking it backward. Somehow it held its balance and even advanced another step. Catti-brie said the last word of the trigger twice, as she had been schooled, and the first red missile knocked the orc back yet again, and the second dropped it to the ground where it writhed for just a heartbeat before laying very still.

Catti-brie stood calm and motionless for a few moments, steadying herself. She turned back to the wall, and blinked against the bursts of fiery explosions and the sharp cuts of lightning bolts, a fury that truly left her breathless. In her temporary blindness, she almost expected that the battle had ended, that the wizardly barrage had utterly destroyed the attackers as she had laid low the small group by the river.

But there came the largest blast of all, a tremendous fireball some distance back along the wall to the west, toward Mithral Hall. Catti-brie saw the truth of it, saw the dwarves, and one elf, in desperate retreat, saw all semblance of defense stripped from the wall, buried under the trampling boots of a charging orc horde.

The wall was lost. All from Mithral Hall to the Surbrin was lost. Even Lady Alustriel was withdrawing, not quite in full flight, but in a determined retreat.

Looking past Alustriel, Catti-brie noted Duzberyl. For a moment, she wondered why he, too, was not in retreat, until she realized that he stood strangely, leaning too far back for his legs to support him, his arms lolling limply at his sides.

One of the other wizards threw a lightning bolt—a rather feeble one—and in the flash, Catti-brie saw the huge javelin that had been driven half of its ten-foot length through his chest, its tip buried into the ground, pinning the wizard in that curious, angular stance.

* * * * *

"We have them routed! Now is the moment of victory!" a frustrated Hakuun said as he stood alone behind the charging horde. He wanted to go with them, or to serve as Jaculi's conduit, as he often had, to launch a barrage of devastating magic.

But Jaculi would not begin that barrage, and worse, the uninvited parasite interrupted him every time he tried to use his more conventional shaman's magic.

A temporary moment, to be sure, Jack said in his thoughts.

"What foolishness . . . ?"

That is Lady Alustriel, Jack explained. *Alustriel of the Seven Sisters. Do not draw her attention!*

"She is running!" Hakuun protested.

She will know me. She will recognize me. She will turn loose her army and all of her wizards and all of her magic to destroy me, Jack explained. *It is an old grudge, but one that neither I nor she has forgotten! Do nothing to draw her attention.*

"She is running! We can kill her," said Hakuun.

Jack's incredulous laughter filled his head with dizzying volume, so much so that the shaman couldn't even start off after Grguch and the others. He just stood there, swaying, as the battle ended around him.

Inside Hakuun's head, Jack the brain mole breathed a lot easier. In truth, he had no idea if Alustriel remembered the slight he had given her more than a century earlier. But he surely remembered her wrath from that dangerous day, and it was nothing that Jack the Gnome ever wanted to see again.

* * * * *

One of Lady Alustriel's wizards ran past Catti-brie at that moment, shouting, "Be quick to the bridge!"

Catti-brie shook her head, but she knew it to be a futile denial. Mithral Hall hadn't expected an assault of such ferocity so soon. They had been lulled by a winter of inaction, by the many reports that the bulk of the orc army remained in the west, near to Keeper's Dale, and by the widespread rumors that King Obould had settled in place, satisfied with his gains.

"To the Nine Hells with you, Obould," she cursed under her breath. "I pray that Drizzt won't kill you, only that I may find the pleasure myself."

She turned and started for the bridge with as much speed as she could muster, stepping awkwardly, as each time she brought her right foot forward, she felt the pangs from her damaged hip, and each time she placed that foot onto the ground, she was reminded by a burning sting of her foolishness with the magical wand.

When another wizard running by skidded to a stop beside her and offered her shoulder, Catti-brie, for all her pride and all her determination to not be a burden, gratefully accepted. If she had refused a hand, she would have fallen to the back of the line and likely would have never made it to the bridge.

Asa Havel greeted the returning contingent, directing them to floating disks of glowing magic that hovered nearby. As each seat filled, the wizard who had created it climbed aboard, but for a few moments, none started out across the river, for none wanted to leave the fleeing dwarves.

"Be gone!" Alustriel ordered them, coming in at the end of the line and with orc pursuit not far behind. "Because of Duzberyl's sacrifice, the retreating dwarves will make the safety of the hall, and I have sent a whisper on the wind to Talindra to instruct them to hold fast their gates and wait for morning. Across the river for us, to the safety of the eastern bank. Let us prepare our spells for a morning reprisal that will leave our enemies melted between the river and King Bruenor's hall."

Many heads nodded in agreement, and as Alustriel's eyes flashed with the sheerest intensity, Catti-brie could only wonder what mighty dweomers the Lady of Silverymoon would cast upon the foolish orcs when dawn revealed them.

Seated on the edge of a disk, her feet dangling just inches above the cold and dark rushing waters of the Surbrin, Catti-brie stared back at Mithral Hall with a mixture of emotions, not least among them guilt, and fear for her beloved home and for her beloved husband. Drizzt had gone to the north, and the army had descended from that direction. Yet he had not returned in front of the marching force with a warning, she knew, for she had not seen the lightning arrows of Taulmaril streaking through the night sky.

Catti-brie looked down at the water and steeled her thoughts and her heart.

Asa Havel, sitting beside her, put a hand on her shoulder. When she looked at the half-elf, he offered a warm and comforting smile. That smile turned a bit mischievous, and he nodded down to her torn boot. Catti-brie followed his gaze then looked back up at him, her face flushed with embarrassment.

But the elf nodded and shrugged, and lifted his red and black hair by his left ear, turning his head to catch the moonlight so that she could take note of a white scar running up the side of his head. He took her wand and assumed a pensive pose, tapping it against the side of his face, in line with the scar.

"You won't err like that again," he assured her with a playful wink, handing the wand back. "And take heart, for your impressive meteor shower gave us the time to complete the floating disks."

"It wasn't mine. It came from the ring Lady Alustriel loaned to me."

"However you accomplished it, your timing and your calm action saved our efforts. You will find a role in the morning."

"When we avenge Duzberyl," Catti-brie said grimly.

Asa Havel nodded, and added, "And the dwarves who no doubt fell this dark night."

The shouting across the river ended soon after, silenced by a resounding *bang* as Mithral Hall slammed shut her eastern door. But as the wizards and Catti-brie set their camp for the evening, they heard more commotion across the dark water. The orcs scrambled around the towers and the wizards' previous encampment, tearing and smashing and looting, their grunts and assaults punctuated by the occasional *crack* of a thrown boulder hitting the bridge abutments, and bouncing into the water.

Others settled down to sleep, but Catti-brie remained sitting, staring back at the darkness, where an occasional fire sprang to life, consuming a tent or some other item.

"I had an extra spellbook over there," one wizard grumbled.

"Aye, and I, the first twenty pages of a spell I was penning," said another.

"And I, my finest robes," a third wailed. "Oh, but orcs will burn for this!"

A short while later, a rustle from the other direction, back to the east, turned Catti-brie and the few others who hadn't yet settled in for the night. The woman rose and limped across to stand beside Alustriel, who greeted the Felbarran contingent as they rushed in to investigate the night's tumult.

"We'd set off for Winter Edge to quarry more stones," explained the leader, a squat and tough old character with a white beard and eyebrows so bushy that they hid his eyes. "What in the grumble of a dragon's belly hit ye?"

"Obould," Catti-brie said before Alustriel could respond.

"So much then for the good intentions," said the Felbarran dwarf. "Never thought them dogs'd sit quiet on the ground they'd taken. Mithral Hall get breached?"

"Never," said Catti-brie.

"Good enough then," said the dwarf. "We'll push 'em back north o' the wall in short order."

"In the morning," said Alustriel. "My charges are preparing their spells. I have ears and a voice in Mithral Hall to coordinate the counterattack."

"Might be then that we'll kill 'em all and not let any be running," said the dwarf. "More's the fun!"

"Set your camp by the river, and order your forces into small and swift groups," Alustriel explained. "We will open magical gates of transport to the other bank and your speed and coordination in entering the battlefield will prove decisive."

"Pity them orcs, then," said the dwarf, and he nodded and bowed, then stormed off, barking orders at his grim-faced forces.

He had barely gone a few strides, though, when there came a tremendous crash from across the way, followed by wild orc cheering.

"A tower," Alustriel explained to the surprised stares of all around her.

Catti-brie cursed under her breath.

"We will extend our time at Mithral Hall," the Lady of Silverymoon promised her. "Our enemies have exploited a vulnerability that cannot be allowed to hold. We will sweep the orcs back to the north and chase them far from the doors."

"Then finish the bridge," another nearby wizard offered, but Alustriel was shaking her head.

"The wall first," she explained. "Our enemies did us a favor by revealing our weakness. Woe to all in the North if the orcs had taken this ground after the bridge's completion. So our first duty after they are expelled is to complete and fortify that wall. Any orc excursion back to Mithral Hall's eastern door must come at a great cost to them, and must provide the time for us to disassemble the bridge. We will finish the wall and then we will finish the bridge."

"And then?" Catti-brie asked, and Alustriel and the other wizards looked at her curiously.

"You will return to Silverymoon?" Catti-brie asked.

"My duties are there. What else would you suggest?"

"Obould has shown his hand," Catti-brie replied. "There is no peace to be found while he is camped north of Mithral Hall."

"You ask me to rally an army," said Alustriel.

"Have we a choice?"

Alustriel paused and considered the woman's words. "I know not," she admitted. "But let us first concentrate on the battle at hand." She turned to the nearby wizards. "Sleep well, and when you awaken, prepare your most devastating evocations. Join with each other when you open your spellbooks, and coordinate your efforts and comple-ment your spells. I want these orcs utterly destroyed. Let their folly serve as a warning that will keep their kin at bay long enough for us to strengthen the defenses."

Many nods came back at her, along with a sudden and unexpected shout, "For Duzberyl!"

"Duzberyl!" another cried, and another, and even those Silvery-moon wizards who had settled down for the night rose and joined in the chant. Soon enough, even the Felbarran dwarves joined in, though none of them knew what a "Duzberyl" might be.

It didn't matter.

More than once that night, Catti-brie awoke to the sound of a thunderous crash from across the river. That only steeled her deter-mination, though, and each time, she fell back asleep with Lady Alustriel's promise in her thoughts. They would pay the orcs back in full, and then some.

The preparations began before dawn, wizards ruffling the pages of their spellbooks, dwarves sharpening weapons. With a wave of yet another wand, Lady Alustriel turned herself into an owl, and flew off silently to scout out the coming battlefield.

She returned in mere moments, and reverted to her human form as the first rays of dawn crept across the Surbrin, revealing to all the others what Alustriel had returned to report.

Spellbooks snapped shut and the dwarves lowered their weapons and tools, moving to the riverbank and staring in disbelief.

Not an orc was to be seen.

Alustriel set them to motion, her minions opening dimensional doors that soon enough got all of them, dwarf, wizard, and Catti-brie alike, across the Surbrin, the last of them crossing even as Mithral

Hall's eastern door banged open and King Bruenor himself led the charge out from the stronghold.

But all they found were a dozen dead dwarves, stripped naked, and a dead wizard, still standing, held in place by a mighty javelin.

The wizards' encampment had been razed and looted, as had the small shacks the dwarf builders had used. An assortment of boulders lay around the base of the damaged bridge abutment, and all of the towers and a good portion of the northern wall had been toppled.

And not an orc, dead or alive, was anywhere to be found.

CHAPTER

AN ORC KING'S CONJECTURE

19

"By all the glories of Gruumsh!" Kna squealed happily when the reports of the victory at the Surbrin made their way like wildfire back to King Obould's entourage. "We have killed the dwarves!"

"We have stung them and left them vulnerable," said the messenger who had come from the battle, an orc named Oktule, who was a member of one of the many minor tribes that had been swept up in the march of Chieftain Grguch—a name Oktule used often, Obould had sourly noted. "Their walls are reduced and the winter is fast receding. They will have to work through the summer, building as they defend their position at the Surbrin."

The orcs all around began to cheer wildly.

"We have severed Mithral Hall from their allies!"

The cheering only increased.

Obould sat there, digesting it all. He knew that Grguch hadn't done any such thing, for the cunning dwarves had tunnels under the Surbrin, and many others that stretched far to the south. Still, it was hard to dismiss the victory, from both practical and symbolic terms. The bridge, had it been completed, would have provided a comfortable and easy approach to Mithral Hall from Silverymoon, Winter Edge, the Moonwood, and the other surrounding communities, and an easy way for King Bruenor to continue doing his profitable business.

Of course, one orc's victory was another orc's setback. Obould, too, had wanted to claim a piece of the Surbrin bridge, but not in

such a manner, not as an enemy. And certainly not at the cost of
assuring the mysterious Grguch all the glory. He fought hard to keep
the scowl from his face. To go against the tide of joy then was to invite
suspicion, perhaps even open revolt.

"Chieftain Grguch and Clan Karuck did not hold the ground?"
he asked, not so innocently, for he knew well the answer.

"Lady Alustriel and a gang of wizards were with the dwarves,"
Oktule explained. "Chieftain Grguch expected that the whole of the
dwarven hall would come forth with the morning light."

"No doubt with King Bruenor, Drizzt Do'Urden, and the rest of
that strange companionship at its head," Obould muttered.

"We did not have the numbers to hold against that," Oktule
admitted.

Obould glanced past the messenger to the gathered crowd. He
saw more trepidation on their faces than anything else, along with an
undercurrent of . . . what? Suspicion?

The orc king stood up and stretched to his full height, towering
over Oktule. He looked up and let his gaze sweep in the mob then
said with a wicked grin, "A great victory anyway!"

The cheering reached new heights, and Obould, his anger beginning to boil within him, used that opportunity to steal off into his tent,
the ever-present Kna and the priest Nukkels following close behind.

Inside the inner chamber, Obould dismissed all of his guards.

"You, too," Kna snapped at Nukkels, errantly presuming that the
glorious news had excited her partner as it had her.

Nukkels grinned at her and looked to Obould, who confirmed
his suspicions.

"You, too," Obould echoed, but aimed the comment at Kna and
not the priest. "Be gone until I summon you back to my side."

Kna's yellow eyes widened in shock, and she instinctively moved
to Obould's side and began to curl sensually around him. But with
one hand, with the strength of a giant, he yanked her away.

"Do not make me ask you again," he said slowly and deliberately,
as if he were a parent addressing a child. With a flick of his wrist he
sent Kna skipping and tumbling backward, and she kept scrambling
away, her eyes wide with shock as she locked her stare on Obould's
frightening expression.

"We must commune with Gruumsh to determine the next victory,"

Obould said to her, purposely softening his visage. "You will play with Obould later."

That seemed to calm the idiot Kna a bit, and she even managed a smile as she exited the chamber.

Nukkels started to talk then, but Obould stopped him with an upraised hand. "Give Kna time to be properly away," the king said loudly. "For if my dear consort inadvertently overhears the words of Gruumsh, the One-eye will demand her death."

As soon as he finished, a rustling just to the side of the exit confirmed his suspicions that his foolish Kna had been thinking to eavesdrop. Obould looked at Nukkels and sighed.

"An informative idiot, at least," the priest offered, and Obould could only shrug. Nukkels began spellcasting, waving his arms and releasing wards to silence the area around himself and Obould.

When he finished, Obould nodded his approval and said, "I have heard the name of Chieftain Grguch far too often of late. What do you know of Clan Karuck?"

It was Nukkels's turn to shrug. "Half-ogres, say the rumors, but I cannot confirm. They are not known to me."

"And yet they heard my call."

"Many tribes have come forth from the deep holes of the Spine of the World, seeking to join in the triumph of King Obould. Surely Clan Karuck's priests could have heard of our march through communion with Gruumsh."

"Or from mortal voices."

Nukkels mulled that over for a bit. "There has been a chain of whispers and shouts, no doubt," he replied cautiously, for Obould's tone hinted at something more nefarious.

"He comes forth and attacks the Moonwood then sweeps south and overruns the dwarves' wall. For a chieftain who lived deep in the holes of the distant mountains, Grguch seems to know well the enemies lurking on the borders of Many-Arrows."

Nukkels nodded and said, "You believe that Clan Karuck was called here with purpose."

"I believe I would be a fool not to find out if that was the case," Obould replied. "It is no secret that many have disagreed with my decision to pause in our campaign."

"Pause?"

"As far as they know."

"So they bring forth an instigator, to drive Obould forward?"

"An instigator, or a rival?"

"None would be so foolish!" the priest said with proper and prudent astonishment.

"Do not overestimate the intelligence of the masses," Obould said. "But whether as an instigator or a rival, Grguch has brought trouble to my designs. Perhaps irreparable damage. We can expect a counterattack from King Bruenor, I am sure, and from many of his allies if we are unlucky."

"Grguch stung them, but he left," Nukkels reminded the king. "If they see his strike as bait, Bruenor will not be so foolish as to come forth from his defended halls."

"Let us hope, and let us hope that we can quickly contain this eager chieftain. Send Oktule back to Grguch, with word that I would speak to him. Offer an invitation to Clan Karuck for a great feast in honor of their victories."

Nukkels nodded.

"And prepare yourself for a journey, my trusted friend," Obould went on, and that reference took Nukkels off-guard, for he had only known Obould for a short time, and had only spoken directly to the orc king since Obould had climbed back up from the landslide that had nearly killed him and the dark elf.

"I would go to Mithral Hall itself for King Obould Many-Arrows," Nukkels replied, standing straight and determined.

Obould grinned and nodded, and Nukkels knew that his guess had been correct. And his answer had been sincere and well-placed—and expected, since it had, after all, come from the king's "trusted friend."

"Shall I invite Kna and your private guard to return to you, Great One?" Nukkels asked, bowing low.

Obould paused for a moment then shook his head. "I will call for them when they are needed," he told the priest. "Go and speak with Oktule. Send him on his way, and return to me this night, with your own pack readied for a long and trying road."

Nukkels bowed again, turned, and swiftly departed.

* * * * *

"Ah, but it's good that ye're here, Lady," Bruenor said to Alustriel when they met out by the wall. Catti-brie stood beside the Lady of Silverymoon, with Regis and Thibbledorf Pwent close behind Bruenor.

Not far away, Cordio Muffinhead and another dwarf priest went to work immediately on the poor, impaled Duzberyl, extricating the dead wizard as gently as possible.

"Would that we could have done more," Alustriel replied solemnly. "Like your kin, we were lulled by the passing months of quiet, and so the orc assault caught us by surprise. We had not the proper spells prepared, for our studies have focused on working the Surbrin Bridge to completion."

"Ye did a bit o' damage to the pigs, and got most o' me boys back to the hall," said Bruenor. "Ye did good by us, and we're not for forgettin' that."

Alustriel responded with a bow. "And now that we know, we will not be caught unawares again," she promised. "Our efforts on the bridge will be slowed, of course, as half our magical repertoire each day will be focused on spells for defending the ground and repelling invaders. And indeed, we will have just a small crew at the bridge until the wall and towers are repaired and completed. The bridge will serve no useful purpose until—"

"Bah!" Bruenor snorted. "The point's all moot. We seen the truth o' Obould, suren as there is any. Put all yer spells for orc-killing—excepting them ye'll be needin' to get yer Knights in Silver across the Surbrin. When we're done with the damned orcs, we can worry about the bridge and the wall, though I'm thinkin' we won't be needing much of a wall!"

Behind him, Thibbledorf Pwent snorted, as did several others, but Alustriel just looked at him curiously, as if she didn't understand. As her expression registered to Bruenor, his own face became a scowl of abject disbelief. That look only intensified as he noted Catti-brie's wince at Alustriel's side, confirmation that he wasn't misreading the Lady of Silverymoon.

"Ye're thinkin' we're to dig in and let Obould play it as Obould wants?" the dwarf asked.

"I advise caution, good king," Alustriel said.

"Caution?"

"The orcs did not hold the ground," Alustriel noted. "They struck and then they ran—likely to evoke just such a response from you. They would have you roar out of Mithral Hall, all full of fight and rage. And out there"—she motioned to the wild north—"they would have their battle with you on the ground of their own choosing."

"Her words make sense," Catti-brie added, but Bruenor snorted again.

"And if they're thinking that Clan Battlehammer's to come out alone, then I'm thinkin' their plan to be a good one," Bruenor said. "But what a trap they'll find when the trap they spring closes on all the force o' the Silver Marches. On Alustriel's wizards and the Knights in Silver, on Felbarr's thousands and Adbar's tens o'! On Sundabar's army, guided in on Obould's flank by them Moonwood elves, who're not too fond o' the damned orcs, in case ye're missing the grumbles."

Alustriel drew her lips very tight, as clear a response as she could possibly give.

"What?" Bruenor roared. "Ye're not for calling them? Not now? Not when we seen what Obould's all about? Ye hoped for a truce, and now ye're seein' the truth o' that truce! What more're ye needing?"

"It is not a matter of evidence, good dwarf," Alustriel replied, calmly and evenly, though her voice rang much thinner than usual. "It is a matter of practicality."

"Practicality, or cowardice?" Bruenor demanded.

Alustriel accepted the barb with a light, resigned shrug.

"Ye said ye'd be standin' with me boys when we needed ye," Bruenor reminded.

"They will . . ." Catti-brie started to say, but she shut up fast when Bruenor snapped his scowl her way.

"Ye're friendship's all pretty when it's words and building, but when there's blood. . . ." Bruenor accused, and Alustriel swept her arm out toward Duzberyl, who lay on the ground with Cordio praying over him.

"Bah, so ye got caught in one fight, but I'm not talking about one!" Bruenor kept on. "Lost me a dozen good boys last night."

"All the Silver Marches weep for your dead, King Bruenor."

"I ain't askin' ye to weep!" Bruenor screamed at her, and all around, work stopped, and dwarf, human, and elf—including Hralien—stood and stared at the outraged king of Mithral Hall and the great Lady of Silverymoon, who not a one of them had ever imagined could be yelled at in such a manner. "I'm askin' ye to fight!" the unrelenting Bruenor fumed on. "I'm askin' ye to do what's right and send yer armies—*all* yer durned armies! Obould's belongin' in a hole, and ye're knowing that! So get yer armies, and get all the armies, and let's put him where he belongs, and let's put the Silver Marches back where the Silver Marches're belonging!"

"We will leave all the ground between Mithral Hall and the Spine of the World stained with the blood of dwarves and men and elves," Alustriel warned. "Obould's thousands are well en—"

"And well meaning to strike out until they're stopped!" Bruenor shouted over her. "Ye heared o' the Moonwood and their dead, and now ye're seein' this attack with yer own eyes. Ye can't be doubtin' what that foul orc's got in his head."

"But to go out from defensive positions against that force—"

"Is to be our only choice, now or tomorrow, or me and me boys'll forever be on yer point, fighting Obould one bridge, one door at a time," said Bruenor. "Ye think we're to take their hits? Ye think we can be keeping both our doors always sealed and secured, and our tunnels, too, lest the durned pigs tunnel in and pop up in our middle?"

Bruenor's eyes narrowed, his expression taking on a clear look of suspicion. "Or would that arrangement please Alustriel and all th' others about? Battlehammer dwarves'll die, and that's suitin' ye all, is it?"

"Of course not," Alustriel protested, but her words did little to soften the scowl of King Bruenor.

"Me girl beside ye just got back from Nesmé, and what a fine job yer knights've done pushing them trolls back into the swamp," Bruenor went on. "Seems Nesmé's grander than afore the attacks, mostly because o' yer own work—and don't that make Lady Alustriel proud?"

"Father," Catti-brie warned, shocked by the sarcasm.

"But then, them folk're more akin to yer own, in looks and thoughts."

"We should continue this discussion in private, King Bruenor," said Alustriel.

Bruenor snorted at her and waved his hand, turned on his heel, and stomped away, Thibbledorf Pwent in tow.

Regis remained, and he turned a concerned look at Alustriel then at Catti-brie.

"He will calm down," Regis said unconvincingly.

"Not so sure I'm wantin' him to," Catti-brie admitted, and she glanced at Alustriel.

The Lady of Silverymoon had nothing more than helplessly upraised hands in reply, and so Catti-brie limped off after her beloved father.

"It is a dark day, my friend Regis," Alustriel said when the woman had gone.

Regis's eyes popped open wide, surprised at being directly addressed by one of Alustriel's stature.

"This is how great wars begin," Alustriel explained. "And do not doubt that no matter the outcome, there will be no winners."

* * * * *

As soon as the priest had gone, Obould was glad of his decision not to call in his entourage. He needed to be alone, to vent, to rant, and to think things through. He knew in his heart that Grguch was no ally, and had not arrived by accident. Ever since the disaster in the western antechamber of Mithral Hall and the pushback of Proffit's troll army, the orcs and dwarves had settled into a stalemate—and it was one that Obould welcomed. But one that he welcomed privately, for he knew that he was working against the traditions, instincts, and conditioning of his warrior race. No voices of protest came to him directly, of course—he was too feared by those around him for that kind of insolence—but he heard the rumbles of discontent even in the grating background of praises thrown his way. The restless orcs wanted to march on, back into Mithral Hall, across the Surbrin to Silverymoon and Sundabar, and particularly Citadel Felbarr, which they had once, long ago, claimed as their own.

"The cost . . ." Obould muttered, shaking his head.

He would lose thousands in such an endeavor—even if he only tried to dislodge fierce King Bruenor. He would lose tens of thousands if he went farther, and though he would have loved nothing more than to claim the throne of Silverymoon as his own, Obould understood that if he had gathered all the orcs from all the holes in all the world, he could not likely accomplish such a thing.

Certainly he might find allies—more giants and dark elves, perhaps, or any of the other multitude of races and monsters that lived solely for the pleasure of fighting and destruction. In such an alliance, though, he could never reign, nor could his minions ever gain true freedom and self-determination.

And even if he did manage greater conquests with his orc minions, even if he widened the scope of the Kingdom of Many-Arrows, the lessons of history had taught him definitively that the center of such a kingdom could never hold. His reach was long, his grip iron strong. Long and strong enough to hold the perimeters of the Kingdom of Many-Arrows? Long and strong enough to fend off Grguch and any potential conspirators who had coaxed the fierce chieftain to the surface?

Obould clenched his fist mightily as that last question filtered through his mind, and he issued a long and low growl then licked his lips as if tasting the blood of his enemies.

Were Clan Karuck even his enemies?

The question sobered him. He was getting ahead of the facts, he realized. A ferocious and aggressive orc clan had arrived in Many-Arrows, and had taken up the fight independently, as orc clans often did, and with great and glorious effect.

Obould nodded as he considered the truth of it and realized the limits of his conjecture. In his heart, though, he knew that a rival had come, and a very dangerous one at that.

Reflexively, the orc king looked to the southwest, the direction of General Dukka and his most reliable fighting force. He would need another courier, he realized immediately. As Oktule went to summon Grguch, as Nukkels traveled to King Bruenor's Court with word of truce, so he would need a third, the fastest of the three, to go and retrieve Dukka and the warriors. For the dwarves might soon counterattack, and likely would be joined by the dangerous and outraged Moonwood elves.

Or more likely, Clan Karuck would need to be taught a lesson.

CHAPTER

ON SQUIGGLES AND EMISSARIES

20

With but one hand, for the chieftain was no minor warrior, Dnark pushed Oktule to the side and stepped past him to the edge of a mountain-view precipice overlooking King Obould's encampment. A group of riders exited that camp, moving swiftly to the south, and without the banner of Many-Arrows flying from their midst.

"War pigs, and armored," the shaman Ung-thol remarked. "Elite warriors. Obould's own."

Dnark pointed to a rider in the middle of the pack, and though they were far away and moving farther, his headdress could still be seen.

"The priest, Nukkels," Ung-thol said with a nod.

"What does this mean?" Oktule asked, his tone concurring with his body posture to relate his discomfort. Young Oktule had been chosen as a courier from the east because of his speed and stamina, but he had not the experience or the wisdom to fathom all that was going on around him.

The chieftain and his shaman turned as one to regard the orc.

"It means that you should tell Grguch to proceed with all caution," Dnark said.

"I do not understand."

"King Obould might not welcome him with the warmth promised in the invitation," Dnark explained.

"Or might greet him with more warmth than promised," Ung-thol quipped.

Oktule stared at them, his jaw hanging open. "King Obould is angry?"

That brought a laugh from the two older and more worldly orcs.

"You know Toogwik Tuk?" Ung-thol asked.

Oktule nodded. "The preacher orc. His words showed me to the glory of Grguch. He proclaimed the power of Chieftain Grguch and the call of Gruumsh to bring war to the dwarves."

Dnark chuckled and patted the air with his hand, trying to calm the fool. "Deliver your words to Chieftain Grguch as your king demanded," he said. "But seek out Toogwik Tuk first and inform him that a second courier went out from Obould's"—then he quickly corrected himself—"*King* Obould's camp, this one riding to the south."

"What does it mean?" Oktule asked again.

"It means that King Obould expects trouble," Ung-thol interrupted, stopping Dnark before he could respond. "Toogwik Tuk will know what to do."

"Trouble?" asked Oktule.

"The dwarves will likely counterattack, and more furious will they become when they learn that both King Obould and Chieftain Grguch are in the same place."

Oktule began to nod stupidly, catching on.

"Be off at once," Dnark told him, and the young orc spun on his heel and rushed away. A signal from Dnark sent a couple of guards off with him, to escort him on his important journey.

As soon as they were gone, the chieftain and the shaman turned back to the distant riders.

"Do you really believe that Obould would send an emissary to the Battlehammer dwarves?" Ung-thol asked. "Has he become so cowardly as that?"

Dnark nodded through every word, and when Ung-thol glanced over at him, he replied, "We should find out."

* * * * *

"Ye tell Emerus that we'll be lookin' for all he's to bring," Bruenor said to Jackonray Broadbelt and Nikwillig, the emissaries from Citadel Felbarr.

"The bridge'll be ready soon, I'm told," Jackonray replied.

"Forget the durned bridge!" Bruenor snapped, startling everyone in the room with his unexpected outburst. "Alustriel's wizards'll be working more on the wall for the next days. I'm wanting an army here afore the work's even begun on the bridge again. I'm wanting Alustriel to see Felbarr side-by-side with Mithral Hall, that when we're walking out that gate, she'll know the time for talkin's over and the time for fightin's come."

"Ah," Jackonray replied, nodding, a smile spreading on his hairy and toothy face. "So I'm seeing why Bruenor's the king. Ye've got me respect, good King Bruenor, and ye've got me word that I'll shove King Emerus out the durned tunnel door meself if it's needin' to be!"

"Ye're a good dwarf. Ye do yer kin proud."

Jackonray bowed so low that his beard brushed the ground, and he and Nikwillig left in a rush—or started to, until Bruenor's call turned them fast around.

"Go out through the eastern gate, under the open sky," Bruenor instructed with a wry grin.

"Quicker through the tunnels," Nikwillig dared to argue.

"Nah, ye go out and tell Alustriel that I'm wantin' the two o' ye put outside o' Felbarr in a blink," Bruenor explained, and snapped his stubby fingers in the air to accentuate his point. All around Bruenor, dwarves began to chuckle.

"Never let it be said that a Battlehammer don't know a good joke when he's seein' one," Bruenor remarked, and the chuckles turned to laughter.

Jackonray and Nikwillig left in a rush, giggling.

"Let Alustriel play a part in her own trap," Bruenor said to Cordio, Thibbledorf, and Banak Brawnanvil, who had a specially designed throne right beside Bruenor's own, a place of honor for the heroic leader who had been crippled in the orc assault.

"Suren she's to be scrunching up her pretty face," Banak said.

"When Mithral Hall and Citadel Adbar march right past her working wizards, to be sure," Bruenor agreed. "But she'll be seeing, too, that the time's past hiding from Obould's dogs. He's wantin' a fight and we're for givin' him one—one that'll take him all the way back where he came from, and beyond."

The room erupted in cheering, and Banak reached out to grab

Bruenor's offered hand, clasping tight in a shake of mutual respect and determination.

"Ye stay here and take the rest o' the audiences," Bruenor instructed Banak. "I'm for seeing Rumblebelly and the littler one. There's clues in them scrolls we brought back, or I'm a bearded gnome, and I'm wantin' all the tricks and truths we can muster afore we strike out against Obould."

He hopped down from his throne and from the dais, motioning for Cordio to follow and for Thibbledorf to stand as Banak's second.

"Nanfoodle told me that the runes on them scrolls weren't nothing he'd e'er seen," Cordio said to Bruenor as they started out of the audience chamber. "Squiggles in places squiggles shouldn't be."

"The littler one'll straighten 'em out, don't ye doubt. As clever as any I've ever seen, and a good friend o' the clan. Mirabar's lost a lot when Torgar and his boys come our way, and they lost a lot when Nanfoodle and Shoudra come looking for Torgar and his boys."

Cordio nodded his agreement and left it at that, following Bruenor down the corridors and stairwells to a small cluster of secluded rooms where Nanfoodle had set up his alchemy lab and library.

* * * * *

No one in the tribe knew if it had gotten its name through its traditional battle tactics, or if the succession of chieftains had fashioned the tactics to fit the name. Whatever the cause-effect, their peculiar battle posture had been perfected through generations. Indeed, the leaders of Wolf Jaw selected orcs at a young age based on size and speed to find the appropriate place in the formation each might best fit.

Choosing the enemy and the battleground was more important even than that, if the dangerous maneuver was to work. And no orc in the tribe's history had been better at such tasks than the present chieftain, Dnark of the Fang. He was descended from a long line of point warriors, the tip of the fangs of the wolf jaw that snapped over its enemies. For years, young Dnark had spearheaded the top line of the V formation, sliding out along the left flank of an intended target, while another orc, often a cousin of Dnark's, led the right, or bottom, jaw. When the lines stretched to their limit, Dnark would swing his assault group to a sharp right, forming a fang, and he and his counterpart would join forces, sealing the escape route at the rear of the enemy formation.

As chieftain, though, Dnark anchored the apex. His jaws of warriors went out north and south of the small encampment, and when the signals came back to the chieftain, he led the initial assault, moving forward with his main battle group.

They did not charge, and did not holler and hoot. Instead, they approached calmly, as if nothing was amiss—and indeed, why would King Obould's shaman advisor suspect anything different?

The camp did stir at the approach of so large a contingent, with calls for Nukkels to come forth from his tent.

Ung-thol put his hand on Dnark's arm, urging restraint. "We do not know his purpose," the shaman reminded.

Nukkels appeared a few moments later, moving to the eastern end of the small plateau he and his warriors had used for their pause. Beside him, Obould's powerful guards lifted heavy spears.

How Dnark wanted to call for the charge! How he wanted to lead the way up the rocky incline to smash through those fools!

But Ung-thol was there, reminding him, coaxing him to patience.

"Praise to King Obould!" Dnark called out, and he took his tribe's banner from an orc to the side and waved it around. "We have word from Chieftain Grguch," he lied.

Nukkels held up his hand, palm out at Dnark, warning him to hold back.

"We have no business with you," he called down.

"King Obould does not share that belief," Dnark replied, and he began his march again, slowly. "He has sent us to accompany you, as more assurance that Clan Karuck will not interfere."

"Interfere with what?" Nukkels shouted back.

Dnark glanced at Ung-thol, then back up the rise. "We know where you are going," he bluffed.

It was Nukkels's turn to look around at his entourage. "Come in alone, Chieftain Dnark," he called. "That we might plot our next move."

Dnark kept moving up the slope, calm and unthreatening, and he did not bid his force to lag behind.

"Alone!" Nukkels called more urgently.

Dnark smiled, but otherwise changed not a thing. The orcs beside Nukkels lifted their spears.

It didn't matter. The bluff had played its part, allowing Dnark's core force to close nearly half the incline to Nukkels. Dnark held up his hands to Nukkels and the guards then turned to address his group—ostensibly to instruct them to wait there.

"Kill them all—except for Nukkels and the closest guards," he instructed instead, and when he turned back, he had his sword in hand, and he raised it high.

The warriors of Clan Wolf Jaw swept past him on either side, those nearest swerving to obstruct their enemies' view of their beloved chieftain. More than one of those shield orcs died in the next moments, as spears flew down upon them.

But the jaws of the wolf closed.

By the time Dnark got up to the plateau, the fighting was heavy all around him and Nukkels was nowhere to be found. Angered by that, Dnark threw himself into the nearest battle, where a pair of his orcs attacked a single guard, wildly and ineffectively.

Obould had chosen his inner circle of warriors well.

One of the Wolf Jaw orcs stabbed in awkwardly with his spear, but the guard's sword swept across and shattered the hilt, launching it out to confuse the attacker's companion. With the opening clear, the guard retracted and stepped forward for the easy kill.

Except that Dnark came in fast from the side and hacked the fool's sword arm off at the elbow.

The guard howled and half-turned, falling to its knees and clutching its stump. Dnark stepped in and grabbed it by the hair, tugging its head back, opening its neck for a killing strike.

And always before, the chieftain of Clan Wolf Jaw would have taken that strike, would have claimed that kill. But he held back his sword and kicked the guard in the throat instead, and as it fell away, he instructed his two warriors to make sure that the fallen enemy didn't die.

Then he went on to the next fight in a long line of battles.

When the skirmish on the plateau ended, though, Shaman Nukkels was not to be found, either among the seven prisoners or the score of dead. He had gone off the back end at the first sign of trouble, so said witnesses.

Before Dnark could begin to curse that news, however, he found that his selections for the fangs of the formation had done his own legacy proud, for in they marched, Nukkels and a battered guard prodded before them with spears.

"Obould will kill you for this," Nukkels said when presented before Dnark.

Dnark's left hook left the shaman squirming on the ground.

* * * * *

"The symbol is correct," Nanfoodle proudly announced. "The pattern is unmistakable."

Regis stared at the large copy of the parchment, its runes separated and magnified. On Nanfoodle's instruction, the halfling had spent the better part of a day transcribing each mark to that larger version then the pair had spent several days cutting out wooden stencils for each—even for those that seemed to hold an obvious correlation to the current Dwarvish writing.

Mistaking that tempting lure, accepting the obvious runes for what they supposed them to be, Dethek runes of an archaic orc tongue called Hulgorkyn, had been their downfall through all of their early translation attempts, and it wasn't until Nanfoodle had insisted that they treat the writing from the lost city as something wholly unrecognizable that the pair had begun to make any progress at all.

If that was indeed what they were making.

Many other stencils had been crafted, multiple representations of every Dwarvish symbol. Then had come the trial and error—and error, and error, and error—for more than a day of painstaking rearranging and reevaluation. Nanfoodle, no minor illusionist, had cast many spells, and priests had been brought in to offer various auguries and inspired insights.

Thirty-two separate symbols appeared on the parchment, and while a thorough statistical analysis had offered hints of potential correlations to the traditional twenty-six runes of Dethek, the fact that none of those promising hints added up to anything substantial made much of that analysis no more than guesswork.

Gradually, though, patterns had taken shape, and spells seemed to confirm the best guesses time and time again.

More than a tenday into the work, an insight from Nanfoodle—after hearing all of Regis's stories of the strange city—proved to be the tipping point. Instead of using Dwarvish as his basis for the analysis, he decided upon a double-basis and began incorporating the Orcish tongue—in which, of course, he was fluent. More stencils were cut, more combinations explored.

Early one morning, Nanfoodle presented Regis with his completed conclusion for translation, a correlative identifying every symbol on the parchment, some that mirrored current Dwarvish or Orcish lettering.

The halfling went to work over the transcribed, larger-lettered parchment, diligently placing above each symbol the stencil Nanfoodle believed correlative. Regis didn't pause at all to consider familiar patterns, but simply placed them all as fast as he could.

Then he stepped back and stood up on the high bench Nanfoodle had placed beside the work table. The gnome was already there, staring back incredulously, his mouth hanging open, and when he took his place beside Nanfoodle, Regis understood.

For the gnome's guesses had been correct, obviously, and the translation of the text was clear to see, and to read. It wasn't unknown for orcs to steal and incorporate Dethek runes, of course, as was most evident with Hulgorkyn. But there was something more than that, a willful blending of related but disparate languages in a balanced manner, one that indicated compromise and coordination between dwarf and orc linguists.

The translation was laid bare for them to see. Digesting the words, however, proved more difficult.

"Bruenor won't like this," Regis remarked, and he glanced around as if expecting the dwarf king to crash into the room in a tirade at any moment.

"It is what it is," Nanfoodle replied. "He will not like it, but he must accept it."

Regis looked back at the translated paragraph and read again the words of the orc philosopher Duugee.

"You place too much value in reason," the halfling muttered.

PART

4

STEPPING BACK

FROM ANGER

STEPPING BACK

FROM ANGER

The questions continue to haunt me. Are we watching the birth of a civilization? Are the orcs, instead of wanting us dead, wishing to become more like us, with our ways, our hopes, our aspirations? Or was that wish always present in the hearts of the primitive and fierce race, only they saw not how to get to it? And if this is the case, if the orcs are redeemable, tamable, how then are we best to facilitate the rise of their more civilized culture? For that would be an act of great self-defense for Mithral Hall and all of the Silver Marches.

Accepting the premise of a universal desire among rational beings, a commonality of wishes, I wonder, then, what might occur should one kingdom stand paramount, should one city-state somehow attain unquestioned superiority over all the rest. What responsibilities might such predominance entail? If Bruenor has his way, and the Silver Marches rise up and drive Obould's orcs from the land and back to their individual tribes, what will be our role, then, in our resulting, unquestioned dominance?

Would the moral road be the extermination of the orcs, one tribe at a time? If my suspicions regarding Obould are correct, then that I cannot reconcile. Are the dwarves to become neighbors or oppressors?

It is all premised on a caveat, of course, on a hunch—or is it a deep-rooted prayer in the renegade soul of Drizzt Do'Urden? I desperately want to be right about Obould—as much as my personal desires might urge me to kill him!—because if I am, if there is in him a glint of rational and acceptable aspirations, then surely the world will benefit.

These are the questions for kings and queens, the principal building blocks of the guiding philosophies for those who gain power over others. In the best of these kingdoms—and I name Bruenor's among that lot—the community moves constantly to better itself, the parts of the whole turn in harmony to the betterment of the whole. Freedom and community live side-by-side, a tandem of the self and the bigger tapestry. As those communities evolve and ally with other like-minded kingdoms, as roads and trade routes are secured and cultures exchanged, what of the diminishing few left behind? It is incumbent, I believe, for the powerful to bend and grasp the hand of the weak, to pull them up, to share in the prosperity, to contribute to the whole. For that is the essence of community. It is to be based on hope and inspiration and not on fear and oppression.

But there remains the truth that if you help an orc to stand, he will likely stab your heart on the way to his feet.

Ah, but it is too much, for in my heart I see the fall of Tarathiel and want to cut the vicious orc king apart! It is too much because I know of Innovindil's fall! Oh, Innovindil, I pray you do not think less of me for my musing!

I feel the sting of paradox, the pain of the irresolvable, the stark and painful imperfections of a world of which I secretly demand perfection. Yet for all the blemishes, I remain an optimist, that in the end the ideal will prevail. And this too I also know, and it is why my weapons sit comfortably in my hands. Only from a position of unquestioned strength can true change be facilitated. For it is not in the hands of a rival to affect change. It is not in the hands of the weaker to grant peace and hope to the stronger.

I hold faith in the kingdom of common voices that Bruenor has created, that Alustriel has similarly created in Silverymoon. I believe that this is the proper order of things—though perhaps with some refining yet to be found—for theirs are kingdoms of freedom and hope, where individual aspirations are encouraged and the common good is shared by all, in both benefit and responsibility. How different are these two places from the darkness of Menzoberranzan, where the power of House presided over the common good of the community, and the aspirations of the individual overwhelmed the liberty, even the life, of others.

My belief in Mithral Hall as nearer the ideal brings with it a sense of Mithral Hall's responsibilities, however. It is not enough to field armies to thwart foes, to crush our enemies under the stamp of well-traveled dwarven boots. It is not enough to bring riches to Mithral Hall, to expand power and influence, if said power and influence is to the benefit only of the powerful and influential.

To truly fulfill the responsibilities of predominance, Mithral Hall must not only shine brightly for Clan Battlehammer, but must serve as a beacon of hope for all of those who glimpse upon it. If we truly believe our way to be the best way, then we must hold faith that all others—perhaps even the orcs!—will gravitate toward our perspectives and practices, that we will serve as the shining city on the hill, that we will influence and pacify through generosity and example instead of through the power of armies.

For if it is the latter, if dominance is attained and then maintained through strength of arm alone, then it is no victory, and it cannot be a permanent ordering. Empires cannot survive, for they lack the humility and generosity necessary to facilitate true loyalty. The wont of the slave is to throw off his shackles. The greatest aspiration of the conquered is to beat back their oppressors. There are no exceptions to this. To the victors I warn without doubt that those you conquer will never accept your dominion. All desire to emulate your better way, even if the conquered agree with the premise, will be overwhelmed by grudge and humiliation and a sense of their own community. It is a universal truth, rooted in tribalism, perhaps, and in pride and the comfort of tradition and the sameness of one's peers.

And in a perfect world, no society would aspire to dominance unless it was a dominance of ideals. We believe our way is the right way, and thus we must hold faith that others will gravitate similarly, that our way will become their way and that assimilation will sheathe the swords of sorrow. It is not a short process, and it is one that will be played out in starts and stops, with treaties forged and treaties shattered by the ring of steel on steel.

Deep inside, it is my hope that I will find the chance to slay King Obould Many-Arrows.

Deeper inside, it is my prayer that King Obould Many-Arrows sees the dwarves standing higher on the ladder in pursuit of true civilization, that he sees Mithral Hall as a shining city on the hill, and that he will have the strength to tame the orcs long enough for them to scale the rungs of that same ladder.

—Drizzt Do'Urden

CHAPTER

The wagon rocked, sometimes soothing, sometimes jarring, as it rolled along the rocky path, heading north. Sitting on the open bed and looking back the way they had come, Wulfgar watched the skyline of Luskan recede. The many points of the wizard's tower seemed like a single blur, and the gates were too far for him to make out the guards pacing the city wall.

Wulfgar smiled as he considered those guards. He and his accomplice Morik had been thrown out of Luskan with orders never to return, on pain of death, yet he had walked right into the city, and at least one of the guards had surely recognized him, even tossing him a knowing wink. No doubt Morik was in there, too.

Justice in Luskan was a sham, a scripted play for the people to make them feel secure and feel afraid and feel empowered over the specter of death itself, however the authorities decided was timely.

Wulfgar had debated whether or not to return to Luskan. He wanted to join in with a caravan heading north, for that would serve as his cover, but he feared exposing Colson to the potential dangers of entering the forbidden place. In the end, though, he found that he had no real choice. Arumn Gardpeck and Josi Puddles deserved to learn of Delly Curtie's sad end. They had been friends of the woman's for years, and far be it from Wulfgar to deny them the information.

The tears shed by all three—Arumn, Josi, and Wulfgar—had felt right to the barbarian. There was so much more to Delly Curtie than the easy, clichéd idea that many in Luskan had of her, and that Wulfgar had initially bought into himself. There was an honesty and an honor beneath the crust that circumstance had caked over Delly. She'd been a good friend to all three, a good wife to Wulfgar, and a great mother to Colson.

Wulfgar tossed off a chuckle as he considered Josi's initial reaction to the news, the small man practically launching himself at Wulfgar in a rage, blaming the barbarian for the loss of Delly. With little effort, Wulfgar had put him back in his seat, where he had melted into his folded arms, his shoulders bobbing with sobs—perhaps enhanced by too many drinks, but likely sincere, for Wulfgar had never doubted that Josi had secretly loved Delly.

The world rolled along, stamping its events into the books of history. What was, was, Wulfgar understood, and regrets were not to be long held—no longer than the lessons they imparted regarding future circumstance. He was not innocent of Josi's accusations, though not to the extent the distraught man had taken them, surely.

But what was, was.

After one particularly sharp bounce of the wagon, Wulfgar draped his arm over Colson's shoulder and glanced down at the girl, who was busying herself with some sticks Wulfgar had tied together to approximate a doll. She seemed content, or at least unbothered, which was the norm for her. Quiet and unassuming, asking for little and accepting less, Colson just seemed to go along with whatever came her way.

That road had not been fair so far in her young life, Wulfgar knew. She had lost Delly, by all measures her mother, and nearly as bad, Wulfgar realized, she had suffered the great misfortune of being saddled with him as her surrogate father. He stroked her soft, wheat-colored hair.

"Doll, Da," she said, using her moniker for Wulfgar, one that he had heard only a couple of times over the last tendays.

"Doll, yes," he said back to her, and tousled her hair.

She giggled, and if ever a sound could lift Wulfgar's heart. . . .

And he was going to leave her. A momentary wave of weakness flushed through him. How could he even think of such a thing?

"You don't remember your Ma," he said quietly, not expecting a response as Colson went back to her play. But she looked up at him, beaming a huge smile.

"Dell-y. Ma," she said.

Wulfgar felt as if her little hand had just flicked against his heart. He realized how poor a father he had been to her. Urgent business filled his every day, it seemed, and Colson was always placed behind the necessities. She had been with him for many months, and yet he hardly knew her. They had traveled hundreds of miles to the east, and then back west, and only on that return trip had he truly spent time with Colson, had he tried to listen to the child, to understand her needs, to hug her.

He gave a helpless and self-deprecating chuckle and patted her head again. She looked up at him with that unending smile, and went immediately back to her doll.

He hadn't done right by her, Wulfgar knew. As he had failed Delly as a husband, so he had failed Colson as her father. "Guardian" would be a better term to describe his role in the child's life.

So he was on that road that would pain him greatly, but in the end it would give to Colson all that she deserved and more.

"You are a princess," he said to her, and she looked up at him again, though she knew not what it meant.

Wulfgar responded with a smile and another pat, and turned his eyes back toward Luskan, wondering if he would ever travel that far south again.

* * * * *

The village of Auckney seemed to have changed not at all in the three years since Wulfgar had last seen it. Most of his last visit, of course, had been spent in the lord's dungeon, an accommodation he hoped to avoid a second time. It amused him to think of how his time with Morik had so ingratiated him to the towns of that region, where the words "on pain of death" seemed to accompany his every departure.

Unlike those guards in Luskan, though, Wulfgar suspected that Auckney's crew would follow through with the threat if they figured out who he was. So for the sake of Colson, he took great pains to disguise himself as the trading caravan wound its way along the rocky road in the westernmost reaches of the Spine of the World, toward the Auckney gate. He wore his beard much thicker, but his stature alone distinguished him from the great majority of the populace, being closer to seven feet tall than to six, and with shoulders wide and strong.

He bundled his traveling cloak tight around him and kept the cowl up over his head—not an unusual practice in the early spring in that part of the world, where the cold winds still howled from on high. When he sat, which was most of the time, he kept his legs tucked in tight so as not to emphasize the length of the limbs, and when he walked, he crouched and hunched his shoulders forward, not only disguising his true height somewhat, but also appearing older, and more importantly, less threatening.

Whether through his cleverness, or more likely sheer luck and the fact that he was accompanied by an entire parade of merchants in that first post-winter caravan, Wulfgar managed to get into the town easily enough, and once past the checkpoint, he did his best to blend in with the group at the circled wagons, where kiosks were hastily constructed and goods displayed to the delight of the winter-weary townsfolk.

Lord Feringal Auck, seeming as petulant as ever, visited on the first full day of the caravan faire. Dressed in impractical finery, including puffy pantaloons of purple and white, the foppish man strutted with a perpetual air of contempt turning up his thin, straight nose. He glanced at goods but never seemed interested enough to bother—though his attendants often returned to purchase particular pieces, obviously for the lord.

Steward Temigast and the gnome driver—and fine fighter—Liam Woodgate, stood out among those attendants. Temigast, Wulfgar trusted, but he knew that if Liam spotted him, the game was surely up.

"He casts an impressive shadow, don't he?" came a sarcastic voice from behind, and Wulfgar turned to see one of the caravan drivers looking past him to the lord and his entourage. "Feringal Auck. . . ." the man added, chuckling.

"I am told that he has a most extraordinary wife," Wulfgar replied.

"Lady Meralda," the man answered, rather lewdly. "As pretty as the moon and more dangerous than the night, with hair blacker than the darkest of 'em and eyes so green that ye're thinking yourself to be in a summer's meadow whenever she glances yer way. Aye, but every man doing business in Auckney would want to bed that one."

"Have they children together?"

"A son," the man answered. "A strong and sturdy lad, and with features favoring his mother and not the lord, thank the gods. Little lord Ferin. All in the town celebrated his first birthday just a month ago, and from what I'm hearing, they'll be buying extra stores to replenish that which they ate at the feast. Finished off their winter stores, by some accounts, and there's more truth than lie to those, judging by the coins that've been falling all the morning."

Wulfgar glanced back at Feringal and his entourage as they wound their way along the far side of the merchant caravan.

"And here we feared that the market'd be thinner with the glutton Lady Priscilla gone."

That perked up Wulfgar's ears, and he turned fast on the man. "Feringal's . . . ?"

"Sister," the man confirmed.

"Died?"

The man snorted and didn't seem the least bit bothered by that possibility, something that Wulfgar figured anyone who had ever had the misfortune of meeting Priscilla Auck would surely appreciate.

"She's in Luskan—been there for a year. She went back with this same caravan after our market here last year," the man explained. "She never much cared for Lady Meralda, for 'twas said she'd had Feringal's ear until he married that one. I'm not for knowing what happened, but that Priscilla's time in Castle Auck came to an end soon after the marriage, and when Meralda got fat with Feringal's heir, she likely knew her influence here would shrink even more. So she went to Luskan, and there she's living, with enough coin to keep her to the end of her days, may they be mercifully short."

"Mercifully for all around her, you mean?"

"That's the way they tell it, aye."

Wulfgar nodded and smiled, and that genuine grin came from more than the humor at Priscilla's expense. He looked back at Lord Feringal and narrowed his crystalline blue eyes, thinking that one major obstacle, the disagreeable Lady Priscilla, had just been removed from his path.

"If Priscilla was at Castle Auck, as much as he'd be wanting to leave, Lord Feringal wouldn't dare be out without his wife at his side. He wouldn't leave them two together!" the man said.

"I would expect that Lady Meralda would wish to visit the caravan more than would the lord," Wulfgar remarked.

"Ah, but not until her flowers bloom."

Wulfgar looked at him curiously.

"She's put in beds of rare tulips, and they're soon to bloom, I'm guessing," the man explained. " 'Twas so last year—she didn't come down to the market until our second tenday, not until the white petals were revealed. Put her in a fine, buying mood, and finer still, for by that time, we knew that Lady Priscilla would be journeying from Auckney with us."

He began to laugh, but Wulfgar didn't follow the cue. He stared across the little stone bridge to the small island that housed Castle Auck, trying to remember the layout and where those gardens might be. He took note of a railing built atop the smaller of the castle's square keeps. Wulfgar glanced back at Feringal, to see the man making his way out of the far end of the market, and with the threat removed, Wulfgar also set out, nodding appreciatively at the merchant, to find a better vantage point for scouting the castle.

Not long after, he had his answer, spotting the form of a woman moving along the flat tower's roof, behind the railing.

* * * * *

There were no threats to Auckney. The town had known peace for a long time. In that atmosphere, it was no surprise to Wulfgar to learn that the guards were typically less than alert. Even so, the big man had no idea how he might get across that little stone bridge unnoticed, and the waters roiling beneath the structure were simply too cold for him to try to swim—and besides, both the near bank and the island upon which the castle stood had sheer cliffs that rose too steeply from the pounding surf below.

He lingered long by the bridge, seeking the answer to his dilemma, and he finally came to accept that he might have to simply wait for those flowers to bloom, so he could confront Lady Meralda in the market. That thought didn't sit well with him, for in that setting he would almost surely need to face Lord Feringal and his entourage as well. It would be easier if he could speak with Meralda first, and alone.

He leaned against the wall of a nearby tavern one afternoon, staring out at the bridge and taking note of the guards' maneuvers. They weren't very disciplined, but the bridge was so narrow that they didn't have to be. Wulfgar stood up straight as a coach rambled across the structure, heading out of the castle.

Liam Woodgate wasn't driving. Steward Temigast was.

Wulfgar stroked his beard and weighed his options, and purely on instinct—for he knew that if he considered his movements, he would lose heart—he gathered up Colson and moved out to the road, to a spot where he could intercept the wagon out of sight of the guards at the bridge, and most of the townsfolk.

"Good trader, do move aside," Steward Temigast bade him, but in a kindly way. "I've some paintings to sell and I wish to see the market before the light wanes. Dark comes early to a man of my age, you know."

The old man's smile drifted to nothingness as Wulfgar pulled back the cowl of his cloak, revealing himself.

"Always full of surprises, Wulfgar is," Temigast said.

"You look well," Wulfgar offered, and he meant it. Temigast's white hair had thinned a bit, perhaps, but the last few years had not been rough on the man.

"Is that. . . . ?" Temigast asked, nodding to Colson.

"Meralda's girl."

"Are you mad?"

Wulfgar merely shrugged and said, "She should be with her mother."

"That decision was made some three years ago."

"Necessary at the time," said Wulfgar.

Temigast sat back on his seat and conceded the point with a nod.

"Lady Priscilla is gone from here, I am told," said Wulfgar, and Temigast couldn't help but smile—a reassurance to Wulfgar that his measure of the steward was correct, that the man hated Priscilla.

"To the joy of Auckney," Temigast admitted. He set the reins on the seat, and with surprising nimbleness climbed down and approached Wulfgar, his hands out for Colson.

The girl shoved her hand in her mouth and whirled away, burying her face in Wulfgar's shoulder.

"Bashful," Temigast said. Colson peeked out at him and he smiled all the wider. "And she has her mother's eyes."

"She is a wonderful girl, and sure to become a beautiful woman," said Wulfgar. "But she needs her mother. I cannot keep her with me. I am bound for a land that will not look favorably on a child, any child."

Temigast stared at him for a long time, obviously unsure of what he should do.

"I share your concern," Wulfgar said to him. "I never hurt Lady Meralda, and never wish to hurt her."

"My loyalty is to her husband, as well."

"And what a fool he would be to refuse this child."

Temigast paused again. "It is complicated."

"Because Meralda loved another before him," said Wulfgar. "And Colson is a reminder of that."

"Colson," said Temigast, and the girl peeked out at him and smiled, and the steward's whole face lit up in response. "A pretty name for a pretty girl." He grew more serious as he turned back to Wulfgar, though, and asked bluntly, "What would you have me do?"

"Get us to Meralda. Let me show her the beautiful child her daughter has become. She will not part with the girl again."

"And what of Lord Feringal?"

"Is he worthy of your loyalty and love?"

Temigast paused and considered that. "And what of Wulfgar?"

Wulfgar shrugged as if it did not matter, and indeed, regarding his obligation to Colson, it did not. "If he desires to hang me, he will have to—"

"Not that," Temigast interrupted, and looked at Colson.

Wulfgar's shoulders slumped and he heaved a deep sigh. "I know what is right. I know what I must do, though it will surely break my heart. But it will be a temporary wound, I hope, for in the passing months and years, I will rest assured that I did right by Colson, that I gave her the home and the chance she deserved, and that I could not provide."

Colson looked at Temigast and responded to his every gesture with a delighted smile.

"Are you certain?" the steward asked.

Wulfgar stood very straight.

Temigast glanced back at Castle Auck, at the short keep where Lady Meralda kept her flowers. "I will return this way before night-fall," he said. "With an empty carriage. I can get you to her, perhaps, but I disavow myself of you from that point forward. My loyalty is not to Wulfgar, not even to Colson."

"One day it will be," said Wulfgar. "To Colson, I mean."

Temigast was too charmed by the girl to disagree.

* * * * *

One hand patted the soft soil at the base of the stem, while the fingers of Meralda's other hand gently brushed the smooth petals. The tulips would bloom soon, she knew—perhaps even that very evening.

Meralda sang to them softly, an ancient rhyme of sailors and explorers lost in the waves, as her first love had been taken by the sea. She didn't know all the words, but it hardly mattered, for she hummed to fill in the holes in the verses and it sounded no less beautiful.

A slap on the stone broke her song, though, and the woman stood up suddenly and retreated a fast step when she noted the prongs of a ladder. Then a large hand clamped over the lip of the garden wall, not ten feet from her.

She brushed back her thick black hair, and her eyes widened as the intruder pulled his head up over the wall.

"Who are you?" she demanded, retreating again, and ignoring his shushing plea.

"Guards!" Meralda called, and turned to run as the intruder shifted. But as his other hand came up, she found herself frozen in place, rooted as if she was just another plant in her carefully cultivated garden. In the man's other hand was a young girl.

"Wulfgar?" Meralda mouthed, but had not the breath to say aloud.

He put the girl down inside, and Colson turned shyly away from Meralda. Wulfgar grabbed the wall with both hands and hauled himself over. The girl went to his leg and wrapped one arm around it, the thumb of her other hand going into her mouth as she continued to shy away.

"Wulfgar?" Meralda asked again.

"Da!" implored Colson, reaching up to Wulfgar with both hands. He scooped her up and set her on his hip, then pulled back his cowl, revealing himself fully.

"Lady Meralda," he replied.

"You should not be here!" Meralda said, but her eyes betrayed her words, for she stared unblinkingly at the girl, at her child.

Wulfgar shook his head. "Too long have I been away."

"My husband would not agree."

"It is not about him, nor about me," Wulfgar said, his calm and sure tone drawing her gaze back to him. "It is about her, your daughter."

Meralda swayed, and Wulfgar was certain that a slight breeze would have knocked her right over.

"I have tried to be a good father to her," Wulfgar explained. "I had even found her a woman to serve as her mother, though she is gone now, taken by foul orcs. But it is all a ruse, I know."

"I never asked—"

"Your husband's actions demanded it," Wulfgar reminded her, and she went silent, her gaze locking once more on the shy child, who had buried her face in her da's strong shoulder.

"My road is too arduous," Wulfgar explained. "Too dangerous for the likes of Colson."

"Colson?" Meralda echoed.

Wulfgar merely shrugged.

"Colson . . ." the woman said softly, and the girl looked her way only briefly and flashed a sheepish smile.

"She belongs with her mother," Wulfgar said. "With her real mother."

"I had thought her father had demanded her to raise as his princess in Icewind Dale," came a sharp retort from the side, and all three turned to regard the entrance of Lord Feringal. The man twisted his face tightly as he moved near to his wife, all the while staring hatefully at Wulfgar.

Wulfgar looked to Meralda for a clue, but found nothing on her shocked face. He struggled to figure out which way to veer the conversation, when Meralda unexpectedly took the lead.

"Colson is not his child," the Lady of Auckney said. She grabbed

Feringal by the hands and forced him to look at her directly. "Wulfgar never ravished—"

Before she could finish, Feringal pulled one of his hands free and lifted a finger over her lips to silence her, nodding his understanding.

He knew, Meralda realized and so did Wulfgar. Feringal had known all along that the child was not Wulfgar's, not the product of a rape.

"I took her to protect your wife . . . and you," Wulfgar said after allowing Feringal and Meralda a few heartbeats to stare into each other's eyes. Feringal turned a scowl his way, to which Wulfgar only shrugged. "I had to protect the child," he explained.

"I would not . . ." Feringal started to reply, but he stopped and shook his head then addressed Meralda instead. "I would not have hurt her," he said, and Meralda nodded.

"I would not have continued our marriage, would not have borne you an heir, if I had thought differently," Meralda quietly replied.

Feringal's scowl returned as he glanced back at Wulfgar. "What do you want, son of Icewind Dale?" he demanded.

Some noise to the side clued Wulfgar in to the fact that the Lord of Auckney hadn't come to the garden alone. Guards waited in the shadows to rush out and protect Feringal.

"I want only to do what is right, Lord Feringal," he replied. "As I did what I thought was right those years ago." He shrugged and looked at Colson, the thought of parting with her suddenly stabbing at his heart.

Feringal stood staring at him.

"The child, Colson, is Meralda's," Wulfgar explained. "I would not cede her to another adoptive mother without first determining Meralda's intent."

"Meralda's intent?" Feringal echoed. "Am I to have no say?"

As the lord of Auckney finished, Meralda put a hand to his cheek and turned him to face her directly. "I cannot," she whispered.

Again Feringal silenced her with a finger against her lips, and turned back to Wulfgar. "There are a dozen bows trained upon you at this moment," he assured the man. "And a dozen guards ready to rush out and cut you down, Liam Woodgate among them—and you know that he holds no love for Wulfgar of Icewind Dale. I warned you that you return to Auckney only under pain of death."

A horrified expression crossed Meralda's face, and Wulfgar squared his shoulders. His instincts told him to counter the threat, to bring Aegis-fang magically to his hand and explain to the pompous Feringal in no uncertain terms that in any ensuing fight, he, Feringal, would be the first to die.

But Wulfgar held his tongue and checked his pride. Meralda's expression guided him, and Colson, clutching his shoulder, demanded that he diffuse the situation and not escalate a threat into action.

"For the sake of the girl, I allow you to flee, straightaway," Feringal said, and both Wulfgar and Meralda widened their eyes with shock.

The lord waved his hands dismissively at Wulfgar. "Be gone, foul fool. Over the wall and away. My patience wears thin, and when it is gone, the whole of Auckney will fall over you."

Wulfgar stared at him for a moment then looked at Colson.

"Leave the girl," Feringal demanded, lifting his voice for the sake of the distant onlookers, Wulfgar realized. "She is forfeit, a princess of Icewind Dale no more. I claim her for Auckney, by Lady Meralda's blood, and do so with the ransom of Wulfgar's promise that the tribes of Icewind Dale will never descend upon my domain."

Wulfgar spent a moment digesting the words, shaking his head in disbelief all the while. When it all sorted out, he dipped a quick and respectful bow to the surprising Lord Feringal.

"Your faith in your husband and your love for him were not misplaced," he said quietly to Meralda, and he wanted to laugh out loud and cry all at the same time, for never had he expected to see such growth in the foppish lord of that isolated town.

But for all of Wulfgar's joy at the confirmation that he had been right to return there, the price of his, and Feringal's, generosity could not be denied.

Wulfgar pulled Colson out to arms' length then brought her in and hugged her close, burying his face in her soft hair. "This is your mother," he whispered, knowing that the child wouldn't begin to understand. He was reminding himself, though, for he needed to do that. "Your ma will always love you. I will always love you."

He hugged her even closer and kissed her on the cheek then stood fast and offered a curt nod to Feringal.

Before he could change his mind, before he surrendered to the tearing of his heart, Wulfgar thrust Colson out at Meralda, who gathered her up. He hadn't even let go of the girl when she began to cry out, "Da! Da!" reaching back at him plaintively and pitifully.

Wulfgar blinked away his tears, turned, and went over the wall, dropping the fifteen feet and landing on the grass below in a run that didn't stop until he had long crossed through Auckney's front gates.

A run that carried with every step the frantic cries of "Da! Da!"

"You did the right thing," he said to himself, but he hardly believed it. He glanced back at Castle Auck and felt as if he had just betrayed the one person in the world who had most trusted him and most needed him.

CHAPTER

THE PRACTICAL MORALITY

22

Certain that no orcs were about, for he could hear their revelry far over a distant hill, Tos'un Armgo settled against a natural seat of stone. Or perhaps it wasn't natural, he mused, situated as it was in the middle of a small lea, roughly circular and sheltered by ancient evergreens. Perhaps some former occupant had constructed the granite throne, for though there were other such stones scattered around the area, the placement of those two, seat and back, was perhaps a bit too convenient.

Whatever and however it had come to be, Tos'un appreciated the chair and the view it afforded him. He was a creature of the nearly lightless Underdark, where no stars shone, where no ceiling was too far above, too vast and distant, otherworldly or extraplanar, even. The canopy that floated above him every night was far beyond his experience, reaching into places that he did not know he possessed. Tos'un was a drow, and a drow male, and in that role his life remained solidly grounded in the needs of the here-and-now, in the day-to-day practicality of survival. As his goals were ever clear to him, based on simple necessity, so his limitations stayed crystalline clear as well—the boundaries of House walls and the cavern that was Menzoberranzan. For all of his life, the limits of Tos'un's aspirations hung over him as solidly as the ceiling of Menzoberranzan's stone cavern.

But those limitations were one of the reasons he had abandoned his House on their journey back to Menzoberranzan after the stunning defeat at the hands of Clan Battlehammer and Mithral Hall. Aside from the chaos that was surely to ensue following that catastrophe, when Matron Yvonnel Baenre herself had been cut down, Tos'un understood that whatever the reshuffling that chaos resolved, his place was set. Perhaps he would have died in the House warfare—as a noble, he made a fine trophy for enemy warriors, and since his mother thought little of him, he would have no doubt wound up on the front lines of any fight. But even had he survived, even had House Barrison Del'Armgo used the vulnerability of the suddenly matron-less House Baenre to ascend to the top rank in Menzoberranzan's hierarchy, Tos'un's life would be as it had always been, as he could not dare hope it would be anything but.

So he had seized the opportunity and had fled, not in search of any particular opportunity, not to follow any ambition or fleeting dream. Why had he fled, then, he wondered as he sat there under the stars?

You will be king, promised a voice in his head, startling Tos'un from his contemplations.

Without a word, with hardly a thought, the drow climbed out of the seat and took a few steps across the meadow. The snow had settled deep on that spot not long ago, but had melted, leaving spongy, muddy ground behind. A few steps from the throne, Tos'un unstrapped his sword belt and lay it upon the ground, then went back to his spot and leaned back, letting his thoughts soar up among the curious points of light.

"Why did I flee?" he asked himself quietly. "What did I desire?"

He thought of Kaer'lic, Donnia, and Ad'non, the drow trio he had joined up with after wandering aimlessly for tendays. Life with them had been good. He had found excitement and had started a war—a proxy war, which was the best kind, after all. It had been heady and clever and great fun, right up until the beastly Obould had bitten the throat out of Kaer'lic Suun Wett, sending Tos'un on the run for his life.

But even that excitement, even controlling the destiny of an army of orcs, a handful of human settlements, and a dwarven kingdom, had been nothing Tos'un had ever desired or even considered, until circumstance had dangled it before him and his three co-conspirators.

No, he realized in that moment of clarity, sitting under a canopy so foreign to his Underdark sensibilities. No tangible desire had brought him from the ranks of House Barrison Del'Armgo. It was, instead, the desire to eliminate the boundaries, the need to dare to dream, whatever dream may come to him. Tos'un and the other three drow—even Kaer'lic, despite her subservience to Lady Lolth—had run to their freedom for no reason more than to escape from the rigid structure of drow culture.

The irony of that had Tos'un blinking repeatedly as he sat there. "The rigid structure of drow culture," he said aloud, just to bask in the irony. For drow culture was premised on the tenets of Lady Lolth, the Spider Queen, the demon queen of chaos.

"Controlled chaos, then," he decided with a sharp laugh.

A laugh that was cut short as he noted movement in the trees.

Never taking his eyes from that spot, Tos'un rolled backward from the stone seat, flipping to his feet in a crouch with the stone between him and the shadowy form—a large, feline form—filtering in and out of the darker lines of the tree trunks.

The drow eased his way to the edge of the stone nearest his discarded sword belt, preparing his dash. He held still, though, not wanting to alert the creature to his presence.

But then he stood taller, blinking, for the great cat seemed to diminish, to dematerialize into a dark mist that filtered away to nothingness. For just a moment, Tos'un wondered if his imagination was playing tricks on him in that strange environment, under a sky that he had still not grown accustomed to or comfortable with.

When he realized the truth of the beast, when he recalled its origins, the drow leaped out from the stone, dived into a forward roll retrieving his belt as he went, and came up so perfectly that he had already buckled it in place before he stood once more.

Drizzt's cat! his thoughts screamed.

Pray that it is! came the unexpected and unasked for answer from his intrusive sword. *A glorious victory is at hand!*

Tos'un winced at the thought. *In Lolth's favor . . .* he imparted to the sword, recalling Kaer'lic's fears about Drizzt Do'Urden.

The priestess had been terrified at the prospect of battling the rogue from Menzoberranzan, fearing, with solid reasoning, that the trouble Drizzt had brought upon the drow city was just the sort of chaos that pleased Lady Lolth. Add to that Drizzt's uncanny luck and almost supernatural proficiency with the blade, and the idea that he was secretly in the favor of Lolth seemed not so far-fetched.

And Tos'un, for all of his irreverence, understood well that anyone who crossed Lolth's will could meet a most unpleasant end.

All of those thoughts followed his intentional telepathic message to Khazid'hea, and the sword went strangely quiet for the next few moments. Indeed, to Tos'un's sensibilities, everything seemed to go strangely quiet. He strained his eyes in the direction of the pines where he had last seen the feline shape, his hands wringing on the hilt of Khazid'hea and his other, drow-made sword. Every passing moment drew him farther into the shadows. His eyes, his ears, his sense of smell, every instinct within him honed in on that spot where the cat had disappeared as he tried desperately to discern where it had gone.

And so he nearly leaped out of his low, soft boots when a voice behind him, speaking in the drow language with perfect Menzoberranyr inflection, said, "Guenhwyvar was tired, so I sent her home to rest."

Tos'un whirled, slashing the empty air with his blades as if he believed the demon Drizzt to be right behind him.

The rogue drow was many steps away, though, standing easily, his scimitars sheathed, his forearms resting comfortably on their respective hilts.

"A fine sword you carry, son of Barrison Del'Armgo," Drizzt said, nodding toward Khazid'hea. "Not drow made, but fine."

Tos'un turned his hand over and regarded the sentient blade for a moment before turning back to Drizzt. "One I found in the valley, below . . ."

"Below where I fought King Obould," Drizzt finished, and Tos'un nodded.

"You have come for it?" Tos'un asked, and in his head, Khazid'hea simmered and imparted thoughts of battle.

Leap upon him and cut him down! I would drink the blood of Drizzt Do'Urden!

Drizzt noted Tos'un's uncomfortable wince, and suspected that Khazid'hea had been behind the grimace. Drizzt had carried the annoying sentient blade long enough to understand that its ego simply would not let it remain silent through any conversation. The way Tos'un had measured his cadence, as if he was listening to the sound of his own words coming back at him in an echo from a stone wall, revealed the continual intrusions of the ever-present Khazid'hea.

"I have come here to see this curiosity I find before me," Drizzt replied. "A son of Barrison Del'Armgo, living on the surface world, alone."

"Akin to yourself."

"Hardly," Drizzt said with a chuckle. "I carry my surname out of habit alone, and toward no familiarity or relationship with the House of Matron Malice."

"As I have abandoned my own House," Tos'un insisted, again in that stilted cadence.

Drizzt wasn't about to argue with that much of his claim, for indeed it seemed plausible enough—though of course, the events that drove Tos'un from the ranks of his formidable House might be anything but exculpatory. "To trade service to a matron mother for service to a king," Drizzt remarked. "For both of us, it seems."

Whatever Tos'un meant to reply, he bit it back and tilted his head to the side, searching the statement, no doubt.

Drizzt didn't hide his wry and knowing grin.

"I serve no king," Tos'un insisted, and with speed enough and force enough to prevent any interruptions from the intrusive blade.

"Obould names himself a king."

Tos'un shook his head, his face curling into a snarl.

"Do you deny your part in the conspiracy that prompted Obould to come south?" Drizzt asked. "I have had this conversation with two of your dead companions, of course. Or do you deny your partnering with the pair I killed? Recall that I saw you standing with the priestess when I came to battle Obould."

"Where was I, a Houseless rogue, to turn?" Tos'un replied. "I happened upon the trio of which you speak in my wandering. Alone and without hope, they offered me sanctuary, and that I could not refuse. We did not raid your dwarf friends, nor any human settlements."

"You prompted Obould and brought disaster upon the land."

"Obould was coming with his thousands with no prompt from us—from my companions, for I had no part in that."

"So you would have to say."

"So I do say. I serve no orc king. I would kill him if given the chance."

"So you would have to say."

"I watched him bite out the throat of Kaer'lic Suun Wett!" Tos'un roared at him.

"And I killed your other two friends," Drizzt was quick to reply. "By your reasoning, you would kill me if given the chance."

That gave Tos'un pause, but only for a moment. "Not so," he said.

But he winced again as Khazid'hea emphatically shot, *Do not let him strike first!* into his thoughts.

The sword continued its prompting, egging Tos'un to leap forward and dispatch Drizzt, as the drow continued, "There is no honor in Obould, no honor in the smelly orcs. They are *iblith.*"

Again his comments were broken, his cadence uneven, and Drizzt knew that Khazid'hea was imploring him. Drizzt took a slight step and shift to Tos'un's right, for in that hand he held Khazid'hea.

"You may be correct in your assessment," Drizzt replied. "But then, I found little honor in your two friends before I killed them." He half-expected his words to prompt a charge, and shifted his hands appropriately nearer his hilts, but Tos'un stayed in place.

He just stood there, trembling, waging an inner battle against the sword's murderous intent, Drizzt surmised.

"The orcs have gone on the attack once again," Drizzt remarked, and his tone changed, and his thoughts went dark, as he reminded himself of the fate of Innovindil. "In the Moonwood and against the dwarves."

"They are old enemies." Tos'un replied, as if the whole news was matter-of-fact and hardly unexpected.

"Spurred by instigators who revel in chaos—indeed, who worship a demon queen who thrives on a state of utter confusion."

"No," Tos'un answered flatly. "If you are referring to me—"

"Are there other drow about?"

"No, and no," said Tos'un.

"You would have to say that."

"I fought beside the Moonwood elves."

"Why would you not, in the service of chaos? I doubt that you care which side wins this war, as long as Tos'un realizes his gain."

The drow shook his head, unconvinced.

"And in the Moonwood, " Drizzt continued, "the orcs' attacks were cunning and coordinated—more so than one might expect from a band of the dimwitted goblinkin." As he finished, Drizzt's scimitars appeared in his hands as if they had simply materialized there, so fast and fluid was his motion. Again he sidled to his left, reminding himself that Tos'un was a drow warrior, trained at Melee-Magthere, likely under the legendary Uthegental. House Barrison Del'Armgo's warriors were known for their ferocity and straightforward attacks. Formidable, to be sure, Drizzt knew, and he could not forget for one instant that sword Tos'un carried.

Drizzt went to the right, trying to keep Tos'un using only short strokes with Khazid'hea, a weapon powerful enough to perhaps sever one of Drizzt's enchanted blades if swung with enough weight behind the blow.

"There is a new general among them, an orc most cunning and devious," Tos'un replied, his face twisting with every word—arguing against the intrusions of Khazid'hea, Drizzt clearly recognized.

That obvious truth of Tos'un's inner struggle had Drizzt somewhat hesitant, for why would this drow, if everything Drizzt presumed was true, be arguing against the murderous sword?

Before his thoughts could even go down that road, however, Drizzt thought again of Innovindil, and his face grew very dark. He turned his blades over and back again, anxious to exact revenge for his lost friend.

"More cunning than a warrior trained in Melee-Magthere?" he asked. "More devious than one raised in Menzoberranzan? More hateful of elves than a drow?"

Tos'un shook his head through all of the questions. "I was with the elves," he argued.

"And you deceived them and ran—and ran with knowledge of their tactics."

"I killed none as I left, though I surely could—"

"Because you are more cunning than that," Drizzt interrupted. "I would expect nothing less from a son of House Barrison Del'Armgo. You knew that if you struck and murdered some in your escape, the elves of the Moonwood would have understood the depths of your depravity and would have known that an attack was soon to befall them."

"I did not," Tos'un said, shaking his head helplessly. "None of . . ." He stopped and grimaced as Khazid'hea assaulted his thoughts.

He will take from you his friend's sword! Without me, your lies will not withstand the interrogations of the elf clerics. They would know your heart.

Tos'un found it hard to breathe. He was trapped in a way he never wanted, facing a foe he believed he could not defeat. He couldn't run away from Drizzt as he had Obould.

Kill him! Khazid'hea demanded. *With me in your grasp, Drizzt Do'Urden will fall. Take his head to Obould!*

"No!" Tos'un shot back audibly—and Drizzt smiled in understanding—instinctively recoiling from the orc king, an emotion that Khazid'hea surely understood.

Then take his head to Menzoberranzan, the sword offered, and again Tos'un's reasoning argued, for he hadn't the strength to return to the drow city alone along the unmerciful corridors of the Underdark.

But again the sword had the answers waiting. *Promise Dnark the friendship of Menzoberranzan. He will give you warriors to accompany you to the city, where you will betray them and assume your place as a hero of Menzoberranzan.*

Tos'un tightened his grip on both his swords and thought of Kaer'lic's warning regarding Drizzt. Before Khazid'hea could even begin to argue, though, the drow did it for himself, for Kaer'lic's warning that Drizzt might be in the graces of Lolth had been but a suspicion, and an outlandish one at that, but that mortal predicament standing before him loomed all too real.

And Drizzt watched it all, and recognized many of the fears and emotions playing through Tos'un's thoughts, and so when the son of House Barrison Del'Armgo leaped toward him, his scimitars rose in a sudden and effortless cross before him.

Tos'un executed a double-thrust wide, Khazid'hea and his other sword stabbing past the axis of Drizzt's blades. Drizzt threw his hands out wide to their respective sides, the called-for defense, each of his blades taking one of Tos'un's.

Advantage taken, Drizzt went for the greater stance offered by his curved blades. A more conventional warrior would have reversed the thrust back at his opponent, but Tos'un, expecting that, would have been too quick on the retreat for any real advantage to be realized. So Drizzt turned his scimitars over Tos'un's swords, using the curve of his blades to draw the swords in tighter, that he could send them out with more authority and perhaps even knock his foe off-balance enough that he could score a quick kill.

He rolled the scimitars over with a snap of his wrists.

But Khazid'hea. . . .

Tos'un countered by jamming the powerful sword hard into the hilt of Drizzt's scimitar—and the impossibly sharp blade cut in, catching a hold that halted Drizzt's move. Tos'un pressed forward with his right and stepped back with his left, keeping perfect balance as he disengaged his left from Drizzt's rolling blade.

Seeing disaster, Drizzt reversed suddenly, bringing Icingdeath, his right-hand blade, across hard instead of ahead, which would have left him off-balance and lunging. He drove Twinkle down hard directly away from the terrible blade of Khazid'hea, for that was the only chance to disengage before the mighty sword cut half of Twinkle's crosspiece away. Tos'un followed until the disengagement, then thrust forward at Drizzt, of course, and Icingdeath came across in the last instant, scraping along Khazid'hea's blade, shearing a line of sparks into the air.

Drizzt was half-turned, though, and Tos'un stabbed forward with his left for the ranger's exposed side.

But Twinkle came up from under Drizzt's other arm, neatly picking off the attack, and Drizzt uncrossed his arms suddenly, Icingdeath slashing back across to knock Tos'un's sword aside. Twinkle slapped back against Khazid'hea with equal fury. Tos'un leaped back, as did Drizzt, the two again circling, taking a measure of each other.

He was good, Drizzt realized. Better than he had anticipated. He managed a glance at Twinkle to note the clear tear where Khazid'hea had struck, and noted, too, a nick on Icingdeath's previously unblemished blade.

Tos'un came ahead with a lazy thrust, a feint and a sudden flurry, leading with his left then rattling off several quick blows with Khazid'hea. He moved forward with every strike, forcing Drizzt to block and not dodge. Every time Khazid'hea slapped against one of his blades, Drizzt winced, fearing that the awful sword would cut right through.

He couldn't play it Tos'un's way, he realized. Not with Khazid'hea in the mix. He couldn't use a defensive posture, as he normally would against a warrior who had trained under Uthegental, an overly aggressive sort that would allow him to simply let Tos'un's rage wear him out.

As soon as the attacks of Khazid'hea played out, Drizzt sprang forward, putting his blades up high and rolling his hands in a sudden blur. Over and over went his scimitars, as he rolled his hands left and right, striking rapidly at Tos'un from varying angles.

Tos'un's defense mirrored Drizzt's movements, hands rolling, blades turning in and out, rolling over each other with equal harmony.

Drizzt kept in tight and kept the strokes short, not willing to let Tos'un put any weight behind Khazid'hea. He thought that to be Tos'un's only possible advantage, the sheer viciousness and power of that sword, and without it, Drizzt, who had defeated the greatest weapons master of Menzoberranzan, would find victory.

But Tos'un matched his rolling fury, anticipated his every move, and even managed several short counterstrikes that interrupted Drizzt's rhythm, and one that nearly got past Drizzt's sudden reversal and defense and would have surely gutted him. Surprised, Drizzt pressed the attack even more, rolling his hands more widely, changing the angles of attack more dramatically.

He slashed—one, two, three—downward at Tos'un's left shoulder, spun suddenly as the last parry sounded, and turned lower as he went so that as he came around, both his swords tore for Tos'un's right side. He expected a down-stroke parry from Khazid'hea, but Tos'un turned inside the attack, bringing his drow blade across to block. As he turned, he stabbed Khazid'hea back and down over his right shoulder.

Drizzt ducked the brunt of it, but felt the bite as the sword sliced down his shoulder blade, leaving a long and painful gash. Drizzt ran straight out from the engagement and dived forward in a roll, turning as he came up to face the pursuing Tos'un.

It was Tos'un's turn, and he came on with fury, stabbing and slashing, spinning completely around and with perfect balance and measured speed.

Ignoring the pain and the warm blood running down the right side of his back, Drizzt matched that intensity, parrying left and right, up and down, the blades ringing in one long note as they clanged and scraped. With every parry of Khazid'hea, Drizzt caught the sword more softly, retreating his own blade upon contact, as he might catch a thrown egg to avoid breaking it. That was more taxing, though, more precise and time-consuming, and the necessity of such a concentrated defense prevented him from regaining the momentum and the offense.

Around and around the sheltered lea they went, Tos'un pressing, not tiring, and growing more confident with every strike.

He had a right to do so, Drizzt had to admit, for he fought brilliantly, fluidly, and only then did Drizzt begin to understand that Tos'un had done with Khazid'hea that which Drizzt had refused to allow. Tos'un was letting the sword infiltrate his thoughts, was following the instincts of Khazid'hea as if they were his own. They had found a complementary relationship, a joining of sword and wielder.

Worse, Drizzt realized, Khazid'hea knew him, knew his movements as intimately as a lover, for Drizzt had wielded the sword in a desperate fight against King Obould.

He understood then, to his horror, how Tos'un had so easily anticipated his rollover and second throw move after the initial cross and parry. He understood then, to his dilemma, his inability to set up a killing strike. Khazid'hea knew him, and though the sword couldn't read his thoughts, it had taken a good measure of the fighting techniques of Drizzt Do'Urden. Just as damaging, since Tos'un had apparently given over to Khazid'hea's every intrusion, the sword and the trained drow warrior had found a symbiosis, a joining of knowledge and instinct, of skill and understanding.

For a fleeting moment, Drizzt wished that he had not dismissed Guenhwyvar, as tired as she had been after finally leading him to Tos'un Armgo.

A fleeting moment indeed, for Tos'un and Khazid'hea came on again, hungrily, the drow stabbing high and low simultaneously then spinning his blades over in a cross, and back again with a pair of backhand slashes.

Drizzt backed as Tos'un pursued. He parried about half the strikes—mostly those of the less dangerous drow blade—and dodged the other half cleanly. He offered no counters, allowing Tos'un to press, as he tried to find the answers to the riddle of the drow warrior and his mighty sword.

Back he stepped, parrying a slash. Back he stepped again, and he knew that he was running out of room, that the stone throne was near. He began to parry more and retreat less, his steps slowing and becoming more measured, until he felt at last the thick granite of the throne behind his trailing heel.

Apparently sensing that Drizzt had run out of room, Tos'un came forward more aggressively, executing a double thrust low. Surprised by the maneuver, Drizzt launched a double-cross down, the appropriate parry, where he crossed his scimitars down over the two thrusting swords. Drizzt had long ago solved the riddle of that maneuver. Before, the defender could hope for no advantage beyond a draw.

Tos'un would know that, he realized in the instant it took him to begin the second part of his counter, kicking his foot through the upper cross of his down-held blades, and so when Tos'un reacted, Drizzt already had his improvisation ready.

He kicked for Tos'un's face, so it appeared. Tos'un leaned back and drove his swords straight up, his intent to knock the kicking Drizzt, already in an awkward maneuver, off his balance.

But Drizzt shortened his kick, which could have no more than glanced Tos'un's face anyway, and changed the angle of his momentum upward then used Tos'un's push from below to bolster that directional change. Drizzt leaped right up and tucked in a tight turn that spun him head-over-heels to land lightly atop the seat of the stone throne, and it was Tos'un who overbalanced as the counterweight disappeared in a back flip, the drow staggering back a step.

Typical of an Armgo, Tos'un growled and came right back in, slashing across, which Drizzt hopped easily. Up above, Drizzt had the advantage, but Tos'un tried to use sheer aggressiveness to dislodge him from the seat, slashing and stabbing with abandon. One swipe cut across short of Drizzt, who threw back his hips, and sent Khazid'hea hard into the back of the stone throne. With a crack and a spark, the sword slashed through, leaving a gouge in the granite.

"I will not let you win, and I will not let you flee!" Drizzt cried in that moment, when the stone, though it hadn't stopped the sword, surely broke Tos'un's rhythm.

Drizzt went on the offensive, hacking down at Tos'un with powerful and straightforward strokes, using his advantageous angle to put his weight behind every blow. Tos'un tried to not retreat as a drum roll of bashing blades landed against his upraised swords, sending shivers of numbness down his arms, but Drizzt had him defending against angles varying too greatly for him to ever get his feet fully under him. Soon he had no choice but to fall back, stumbling, and Drizzt was there, leaping from the seat and coming down with a heavy double chop of his blades that nearly took Tos'un's swords from his hands.

"I will not let you win!' Drizzt cried again, throwing out the words in a release of all his inner strength as he backhanded across with Icingdeath, smashing Tos'un's drow-made sword out to the side.

And that was the moment when Drizzt could have ended it, for Twinkle's thrust, turn, and out-roll had Khazid'hea too far to the side to stop the second movement of Icingdeath, a turn and stab that would have plunged the blade deep into Tos'un's chest.

Drizzt didn't want the kill, for all the rage inside him for Innovindil. He played his trump.

"I will again wield the magnificent Khazid'hea!" he cried, disengaging instead of pressing his advantage. He went back just a couple of steps, and only for a few heartbeats—long enough to see a sudden wave of confusion cross Tos'un's face.

"Give me the sword!" Drizzt demanded.

Tos'un cringed, and Drizzt understood. For he had just given Khazid'hea what it had long desired, had just spoken the words Khazid'hea could not ignore. Khazid'hea's loyalty was to Khazid'hea alone, and Khazid'hea wanted, above all else, to be wielded by Drizzt Do'Urden.

Tos'un stumbled, hardly able to bring his blades up in defense as Drizzt charged in. In came Twinkle, in came Icingdeath, but not the blades. The hilts smashed Tos'un's face, one after another. Both Tos'un's swords went flying, and he went with them, back and to the ground. He recovered quickly, but not quickly enough. Drizzt's boot slammed down upon his chest and Icingdeath came to rest against his neck, its diamond edge promising him a quick death if he struggled.

"You have so much to answer for," Drizzt said to him.

Tos'un fell back and gave a great exhale, his whole body relaxing with utter resignation, for he could not deny that he was truly doomed.

CHAPTER

BLACK AND WHITE

23

Nanfoodle lifted one foot and drew little circles on the floor with his toes. Standing with his hands clasped behind his back, the gnome presented an image of uncertainty and trepidation. Bruenor and Hralien, who had been sitting discussing their next moves when Nanfoodle and Regis had entered the dwarf's private quarters, looked at each other with confusion.

"Well if ye can't get it translated, then so be it," Bruenor said, guessing at the source of the gnome's consternation. "But ye're to keep working on it, don't ye doubt!"

Nanfoodle looked up, glanced at Regis, then bolstered by Regis's nod, turned back to the dwarf king and squared his shoulders. "It is an ancient language, based on the Dwarvish tongue," he explained. "It has roots in Hulgorkyn, perhaps, and Dethek runes for certain."

"Thought I'd recognized a couple o' the scribbles," Bruenor replied.

"Though it is more akin to the proper Orcish," Nanfoodle explained, and Bruenor gasped.

"Dworcish?" Regis remarked with a grin, but he was the only one who found any humor in it.

"Ye're telling me that the durned orcs took part of me Delzoun ancestors' words?" Bruenor asked.

Nanfoodle shook his head. "How this language came about is a mystery whose answer is beyond the parchments you brought to me.

From what I can tell of the proportion of linguistic influence, you've juxtaposed the source and add."

"What in the Nine Hells are ye babblin' about?" Bruenor asked, his voice beginning to take on an impatient undercurrent.

"Seems more like old Dwarvish with added pieces from old Orcish," Regis explained, drawing Bruenor's scowl his way and taking it off of Nanfoodle, who seemed to be withering before the unhappy dwarf king with still the most important news forthcoming.

"Well, they needed to talk to the dogs to tell them what's what," said Bruenor, but both Regis and Nanfoodle shook their heads with every word.

"It was deeper than that," Regis said, stepping up beside the gnome. "The dwarves didn't borrow orc phrases, they integrated the language into their own."

"Something that would have taken years, even decades, to come into being," said Nanfoodle. "Such language blending is common throughout the history of all the races, but it occurs, every time, because of familiarity and cultural bonds."

Silence came back at the pair, and Bruenor and Hralien looked to each other repeatedly. Finally, Bruenor found the courage to ask directly, "What are ye saying?"

"Dwarves and orcs lived together, side-by-side, in the city you found," said Nanfoodle.

Bruenor's eyes popped open wide, his strong hands slapped against the arms of his chair, and he came forward as if he meant to leap out and throttle both the gnome and the halfling.

"For years," Regis added as soon as Bruenor settled back.

The dwarf looked at Hralien, seeming near panic.

"There is a town called Palishchuk in the wastes of Vaasa on the other side of Anauroch," the elf said with a shrug, as if the news was not as unexpected and impossible as it seemed. "Half-orcs, one and all, and strong allies with the goodly races of the region."

"*Half-orcs?*" Bruenor roared back at him. "Half-orcs're half-humans, and that lot'd take on a porcupine if the durned spines didn't hurt so much! But we're talkin' me kin here. Me ancestors!"

Hralien shrugged again, as if it wasn't so shocking, and Bruenor stopped sputtering long enough to catch the fact that the elf might be having a bit of fun with the revelation, at the dwarf's expense.

"We don't know that these were your ancestors," Regis remarked.

"Gauntlgrym's the home o' Delzoun!" Bruenor snapped.

"This wasn't Gauntlgrym," said Nanfoodle, after clearing his throat. "It wasn't," he reiterated when Bruenor's scowl fell over him fully.

"What was it, then?"

"A town called Baffenburg," said Nanfoodle.

"Never heared of it."

"Nor had I," the gnome replied. "It probably dates from around the time of Gauntlgrym, but it was surely not the city described in your histories. Not nearly that size, or with that kind of influence."

"That which we saw of it was probably the extent of the main town," Regis added. "It wasn't Gauntlgrym."

Bruenor fell back in his seat, shaking his head and muttering under his breath. He wanted to argue, but had no facts with which to do so. As he considered things, he recognized that he'd never had any evidence that the hole in the ground led to Gauntlgrym, that he had no maps that indicated the ancient Delzoun homeland to be anywhere near that region. All that had led him to believe that it was indeed Gauntlgrym was his own fervent desire, his faith that he had been returned to Mithral Hall by the graces of Moradin for that very purpose.

Nanfoodle started to talk, but Bruenor silenced him and waved both him and Regis away.

"This does not mean that there is nothing of value . . ." Regis started to say, but again, Bruenor waved his hand, dismissing them both—then dismissing Hralien with a gesture, as well, for at that terrible moment of revelation, with orcs attacking and Alustriel balking at decisive action, the crestfallen dwarf king wanted only to be alone.

* * * * *

"Still here, elf?" Bruenor asked when he saw Hralien inside Mithral Hall the next morning. "Seeing the beauty o' dwarf ways, then?"

Hralien shared the dwarf king's resigned chuckle. "I am interested in watching the texts unmasked. And I would be re—" He stopped and studied Bruenor for a moment then added, "It is good to see you in such fine spirits this day. I had worried that the gnome's discovery from yesterday would cloak you in a dour humor."

Bruenor waved a hand dismissively. "He's just scratched the scribblings. Might be that some dwarves were stupid enough to trust the damned orcs. Might be that they paid for it with their city and their lives—and that might be a lesson for yer own folk and for Lady Alustriel and the rest of them that's hesitating in driving Obould back to his hole. Come with me, if ye're wantin', for I'm on me way to the gnome now. He and Rumblebelly have worked the night through, on me orders. I'm to take their news to Alustriel and her friends out working on the wall. Speak for the Moonwood in that discussion, elf, and let's be setting our plans together."

Hralien nodded and followed Bruenor through the winding tunnels and to the lower floors, and a small candlelit room where Regis and Nanfoodle were hard at work. Parchment had been spread over several tables, held in place by paperweights. The aroma of lavender permeated the room, a side-effect from Nanfoodle's preservation potions that had been carefully applied to each of the ancient writings, and to the tapestry, which had been hung on one wall. Most of its image remained obscured, but parts of it had been revealed. That vision made Bruenor cringe, for the orcs and dwarves visible in the drawing were not meeting in battle or even in parlay. They were together, intermingled, going about their daily business.

Regis, who sat off to the side transcribing some text, greeted the pair as they entered, but Nanfoodle didn't even turn around, hunched as he was over a parchment, his face pressed close to the cracked and faded page.

"Ye're not looking so tired, Rumblebelly," Bruenor greeted accusingly.

"I'm watching a lost world open before my eyes," he replied. "I'm sure that I will fall down soon enough, but not now."

Bruenor nodded. "Then ye're saying that the night showed ye more o' the old town," he said.

"Now that we have broken the code of the language, the pace improves greatly," said Nanfoodle, never turning from the parchment he was studying. "You retrieved some interesting texts on your journey."

Bruenor stared at him for a few heartbeats, expecting him to elaborate, but soon realized that the gnome was fully engulfed by his work once more. The dwarf turned to Regis instead.

"The town was mostly dwarves at first," Regis explained. He hopped up from his chair and moved to one of the many side tables, glanced at the parchment spread there, and moved along to the next in line. "This one," he explained, "talks about how the orcs were growing more numerous. They were coming in from all around, but most of the dwarven ties remained to places like Gauntlgrym, which was of course belowground and more appealing to a dwarf's sensibilities."

"So it was an unusual community?" Hralien asked.

Regis shrugged, for he couldn't be certain.

Bruenor looked to Hralien and nodded smugly in apparent vindication, and certainly the elf and the halfling understood that Bruenor did not want his history intertwined with that of the foul orcs!

"But it was a lasting arrangement," Nanfoodle intervened, finally looking up from the parchment. "Two centuries at least."

"Until the orcs betrayed me ancestors," Bruenor insisted.

"Until something obliterated the town, melting the permafrost and dropping the whole of it underground in a sudden and singular catastrophe," Nanfoodle corrected. "And not one of orc making. Look at the tapestry on the wall—it remained in place after the fall of Baffenburg, and certainly it would have been removed if that downfall had been precipitated by one side or the other. I don't believe that there were 'sides,' my king."

"And how're ye knowing that?" Bruenor demanded. "That scroll tellin' ye that?"

"There is no indication of treachery on the part of the orcs—at least not near the end of the arrangement," the gnome explained, hopping down from his bench and moving to yet another parchment across from the table where Regis stood. "And the tapestry . . . Early on, there were problems. A single orc chieftain held the orcs in place beside the dwarves. He was murdered."

"By the dwarves?" Hralien asked.

"By his own," said Nanfoodle, moving to another parchment. "And a time of unrest ensued."

"Seemin' to me that the whole time was a time of unrest," Bruenor said with a snort. "Ye can't be living with damned orcs!"

"Off and on unrest, from what I can discern," Nanfoodle agreed. "And it seemed to get better through the years, not worse."

"Until the orcs brought an end to it," Bruenor grumbled. "Suddenly, and with orc treachery."

"I do not believe . . ." Nanfoodle started to reply.

"But ye're guessin', and not a thing more," said Bruenor. "Ye just admitted that ye don't know what brought the end."

"Every indication—"

"Bah! But ye're guessing."

Nanfoodle conceded the point with a bow. "I would very much like to go to this city and build a workshop there, in the library. You have uncovered something fascinating, King Bru—"

"When the time's for it," Bruenor interrupted. "Right now I'm seeing the call of them words. Get rid of Obould and the orcs'll fall apart, as we were expecting from the start. This is our battle call, gnome. This is why Moradin sent me back here and told me to go to that hole, Gauntlgrym or not!"

"But that's not . . ." Nanfoodle started to argue, but his voice trailed away, for it was obvious that Bruenor paid him no heed.

His head bobbing with excitement and vigor, Bruenor had already turned to Hralien. He swatted the elf on the shoulder and swept Hralien up in his wake as he quick-stepped from the room, pausing only to berate Nanfoodle, "And I'm still thinking it's Gauntlgrym!"

Nanfoodle looked helplessly at Regis. "The possibilities. . . ." the gnome remarked.

"We've all our own way of looking at the world, it would seem," Regis answered with a shrug that seemed almost embarrassed for Bruenor.

"Is this find not an example?"

"Of what?" asked Regis. "We do not even know how it ended, or why it ended."

"Drizzt has whispered of the inevitability of Obould's kingdom," Nanfoodle reminded him.

"And Bruenor is determined that it will not be. The last time I looked, Bruenor, and not Drizzt, commanded the army of Mithral Hall and the respect of the surrounding kingdoms."

"A terrible war is about to befall us," said the gnome.

"One begun by King Obould Many-Arrows," the halfling replied.

Nanfoodle sighed and looked at the many parchment sheets spread around the room. It took all his willpower to resist the urge to rush from table to table and crumble them to dust.

* * * * *

"His name was Bowug Kr'kri," Regis explained to Bruenor, presenting more of the deciphered text to the dwarf king.

"An orc?"

"An orc philosopher and wizard," the halfling replied. "We think the statues we saw in the library were of him, and maybe his disciples."

"So he's the one who brought the orcs into the dwarf city?"

"We think."

"The two of ye do a lot o' thinking for so little answering," Bruenor growled.

"We have only a few old texts," Regis replied. "It's all a riddle, still."

"Guesses."

"Speculation," said Regis. "But we know that the orcs lived there with the dwarves, and that Bowug Kr'kri was one of the leaders of the community."

"Any better guesses on how long that town lived? Ye said centuries, but I'm not for believin' ye."

Regis shrugged and shook his head. "It had to be over generations. You saw the structures, and the language."

"And how many o' them structures were built by the dwarfs afore the orcs came in?" Bruenor asked with a sly smile.

Regis had no answer.

"Might've been a dwarf kingdom taken down by trusting the damned orcs," Bruenor said. "Fool dwarfs who took much o' the orc tongue to try to be better neighbors to the treacherous dogs."

"We don't think—"

"Ye think too much," Bruenor interrupted. "Yerself and the gnome're all excited about finding something so different than that which we're knowin' to be true. If ye're just finding more o' the same, then it's just more o' the same. But if ye're findin' something to make yer eyes go wide enough to fall out o' their holes, then that's something to dance about."

"We didn't invent that library, or the statues inside it," Regis argued, but he was talking into as smug and sure an expression as he had ever seen. And he wasn't sure, of course, that Bruenor's reasoning was wrong, for indeed, he and Nanfoodle were doing a lot of guessing. The final puzzle picture was far from complete. They hadn't even yet assembled the borders of the maze, let alone filled in the interior details.

Hralien walked into the room then, answering a summons Bruenor had sent out for him earlier.

"It's coming clear, elf," Bruenor greeted him. "That town's a warning. If we're following Alustriel's plans, we're to wind up a dead and dust-covered artifact for a future dwarf king to discover."

"My own people are as guilty as is Alustriel in wanting to find a stable division, King Bruenor," Hralien admitted. "The idea of crossing the Surbrin to do battle with Obould's thousands is daunting—it will not be attempted without great sorrow and great loss."

"And what's to be found by sitting back?" Bruenor asked.

Hralien, who had just lost a dozen friends in an orc assault on the Moonwood, and had just witnessed first-hand the attack on the dwarven wall, didn't need to use his imagination to guess the answer to that question.

"We can't be fightin' them straight up," Bruenor reasoned. "That's the way o' doom. Too many o' the stinking things." He paused and grinned, nodding his hairy head. "Unless they're attacking us, and in bits and pieces. Like the group that went into the Moonwood and the one that come over me wall. If we were ready for them, then there'd be a lot o' dead orcs."

Hralien gave a slight bow in agreement.

"So Drizzt was right," said Bruenor. "It's all about the one on top. He tried to get rid of Obould, and almost did. That'd've been the answer, and still is. If we can just get rid o' the durned Obould, we'll be tearing it all down."

"A difficult task," said Hralien.

"It's why Moradin gave me back to me boys," said Bruenor. "We're goin' to kill him, elf."

" 'We're'?" asked Hralien. "Are you to spearhead an army to strike into the heart of Obould's kingdom?"

"Nah, that's just what the dog's wantin'. We'll do it the way Drizzt tried it. A small group, better'n . . ." He paused and a cloud passed over his face.

"Me girl won't be going," Bruenor explained. "Too hurt."

"And Wulfgar has left for the west," said Hralien, catching on to the source of Bruenor's growing despair.

"They'd be helpin', don't ye doubt."

"I do not doubt at all," Hralien assured him. "Who, then?"

"Meself and yerself, if ye're up for the fight."

The elf gave a half-bow, seeming to agree but not fully committing, and Bruenor knew he'd have to be satisfied with that.

The dwarf looked over to Regis, who nodded with increased determination, his face as grim as his cherubic features would allow.

"And Rumblebelly there," the dwarf said.

Regis took a step back, shifting uncomfortably as Hralien cast a doubtful look his way.

"He's knowing how to find his place," Bruenor assured the elf. "And he's knowin' me fightin' ways, and them o' Drizzt."

"We will collect Drizzt on our road?"

"Can ye think o' anyone ye'd want beside ye more than the drow?"

"Indeed, no, unless it was Lady Alustriel herself."

"Bah!" Bruenor snorted. "Ye won't be getting that one to agree. Meself and a few o' me boys, yerself and Drizzt, and Rumblebelly."

"To kill Obould."

"Crush his thick skull," said Bruenor. "Me and some o' me best boys. We'll be cuttin' a quiet way, right to the head o' th' ugly beast, and then let it fall where it may."

"He is formidable," Hralien warned.

"Heared the same thing about Matron Baenre o' Menzoberranzan," Bruenor replied, referring to his own fateful strike that had decapitated the drow city and ended the assault on Mithral Hall. "And we got Moradin with us, don't ye doubt. It's why he sent me back."

Hralien's posture and expression didn't show him to be completely convinced by any of it, but he nodded his agreement just the same.

"Ye help me find me drow friend," Bruenor said to him, seeing that unspoken doubt. "Then ye make yer mind up."

"Of course," Hralien agreed.

Off to the side, Regis shifted nervously. He wasn't afraid of adventuring beside Bruenor and Drizzt, even if it would be behind orc lines. But he did fear that Bruenor was reading it all wrong, and that their mission would turn out badly, for them perhaps, and for the world.

* * * * *

The gathering fell quiet when Banak Brawnanvil looked Bruenor in the eye and declared, "Ye're bats!"

Bruenor, however, didn't blink. "Obould's the one," he said evenly.

"Not doubtin' that," replied the irrepressible Banak, who seemed to tower over Bruenor at that moment despite the fact that he was confined to a sitting position because of his injury in the orc war. "So send Pwent and yer boys to go and get him, like ye're wantin'."

"It's me own job."

"Only because ye're a thick-headed Battlehammer!"

A few gasps filtered about the room at that proclamation, but they were diffused by a couple of chortles, most notably from the priest Cordio. Bruenor turned on Cordio with a scowl, but it fast melted against the reality of Banak's words. Truer words regarding the density of Bruenor's skull, Cordio—and Bruenor—knew, had never been spoken.

"Was meself that went to Gauntlgrym," Bruenor said. He snapped his head to Regis's direction, as if expecting the halfling to argue that it wasn't Gauntlgrym. Regis, though, wisely stayed silent. "Was meself that anchored the retreat from Keeper's Dale. Was meself that battled Obould's first attack in the north." He was gaining speed and momentum, not to *bang drums for meself*, as the dwarven saying went, but to justify his decision that he would personally lead the mission. "Was meself that went to Calimport to bring back Rumblebelly. Was meself that cut the damned Baenre in half!"

"I drunk enough toasts to ye to appreciate the effort," said Banak.

"And now I'm seeing one more task afore me."

"The King o' Mithral Hall's plannin' to march off behind an orc army and kill the orc king," Banak remarked. "And if ye're caught on the way? Won't yer kin here be in fine straits then in trying to bargain with Obould?"

"If ye're thinkin' I'm to be caught livin', then ye're not knowing what it is to be a Battlehammer," Bruenor retorted. "Besides, ain't no different than if Drizzt got himself caught already, or any o' the rest of us. Ye're not for changing yer ways with orcs for meself any more than ye would for any of our boys."

Banak started to respond, but really had no answer for that.

"Besides, besides," Bruenor added, "once I'm walking out that gate, I'm not the king o' Mithral Hall, which is the whole point in us being here, now ain't it?"

"I'll be yer steward, but no king is Banak," the crippled Brawnanvil argued.

"Ye'll be me steward, but if I'm not returning then yerself is the Ninth King o' Mithral Hall and don't ye be doubting it. And not a dwarf here would agree with ye if ye were."

Bruenor turned and led Banak's gaze around the room with his own, taking in the solemn nods of all the gathering, from Pwent and his Gutbusters to Cordio and the other priests to Torgar and the dwarves from Mirabar.

"This is why Moradin sent me back," Bruenor insisted. "It's me against Obould, and ye're a fool betting if ye're betting on Obould!"

That elicited a cheer around the room.

"Yerself and the drow?" Banak asked.

"Me and Drizzt," Bruenor confirmed. "And Rumblebelly's up for it, though me girl's in no place for it."

"Ye telled her that, have ye?" Banak asked with a snicker that was echoed around the room.

"Bah, but she can't be running, if running we're needing, and she'd not ever put her friends in a spot o' staying behind to protect her," said Bruenor.

"Then ye ain't telled her," said Banak, and again came the snorts.

"Bah!" Bruenor said, throwing up his hands.

"So yerself, Drizzt, and Regis," said Banak. "And Thibbledorf Pwent?"

"Try to stop me," Pwent replied, and the Gutbuster brigade cheered.

"And Pwent," said Bruenor, and the Gutbusters cheered again. Nothing seemed to excite that group quite so much as the prospect of one of their own walking off on an apparent suicide mission.

"Begging yer pardon, King Bruenor," Torgar Hammerstriker said from the other side of the room. "But me thinking is that the Mirabar boys should be represented on yer team, and me thinking's that meself and Shingles here"—he reached to the side and pulled forward the scarred old warrior, Shingles McRuff—"be just the two to do Mirabar proud."

As he finished, the other five Mirabarran dwarves in the room exploded into cheers for their mighty leader and the legendary Shingles.

"Make it seven, then," Cordio Muffinhead added. "For ye can't be goin' on a march for Moradin without a priest o' Moradin, and I'm that priest."

"Eight, then," Bruenor corrected, "for I'm thinking that Hralien o' the Moonwood won't be leaving us after we find Drizzt."

"Eight for the road and eight for Obould!" came the cheer, and it grew louder as it was repeated a second then a third time.

Then it ended abruptly, as a scowling Catti-brie came in through the door, staring hard at Bruenor with a look that had even the doubting Banak Brawnanvil looking at the dwarf king with sympathy.

"Go and do what needs doin'," Bruenor instructed them all, his voice suddenly shaky, and as the others scattered through every door in the room, Catti-brie limped toward her father.

"So you're going for Obould's head, and you're to lead it?" she asked.

Bruenor nodded. "It's me destiny, girl. It's why Moradin put me back here."

"Regis brought you back, with his pendant."

"Moradin let me go from his hall," Bruenor insisted. "And it was for a reason!"

Catti-brie stared at him long and hard. "So now you're to go out, and to take my friend Regis with you, and to take my husband with you. But I'm not welcome?"

"Ye can't run!" Bruenor argued. "Ye can hardly walk more than a few dozen yards. If we're turning from orcs, then are we to wait for yerself?"

"There'll be less turning from orcs if I'm there."

"Not for doubtin' that," said Bruenor. "But ye know ye can't do it. Not now."

"Then wait for me."

Bruenor shook his head. Catti-brie's lips grew tight and she blinked her blue eyes as if fighting back tears of frustration.

"I could lose all of you," she whispered.

Bruenor caught on then that part of her difficulty at least had to do with Wulfgar. "He'll come back," the dwarf said. "He'll walk the road that's needin' walking, but don't ye doubt that Wulfgar'll be coming back to us."

Catti-brie winced at the mention of his name, and her expression showed her to be far less convinced of that than was her father.

"But will you?" she asked.

"Bah!" Bruenor snorted, throwing up a hand as if the question was ridiculous.

"And will Regis come back? And Drizzt?"

"Drizzt is out there already," Bruenor argued. "Are ye doubtin' him?"

"No."

"Then why're ye doubting me?" asked Bruenor. "I'm out for doing the same thing Drizzt set out to do afore the winter. And he went out alone! I won't be out there alone, girl, and ye'd be smarter if ye was worrying about the damned orcs."

Catti-brie continued to look at him, and had no answer.

Bruenor opened wide his arms, inviting her to a hug that she could not resist. "Ye won't be alone, girl. Ye won't ever be alone," he whispered into her ear.

He understood fully her frustration, for would his own have been any less if he was to be left out of such a mission, when all of his friends were to go?

Catti-brie pulled back from him far enough to look him in the eye and ask, "Are you sure of this?"

"Obould's got to die, and I'm the dwarf to kill him," said Bruenor.

"Drizzt tried, and failed."

"Well Drizzt'll try again, but this time he's got friends trying with him. When we come back to ye, the orc lines'll be breaking apart. Ye'll find plenty o' fighting then, to be sure, and most of it outside our own doors. But the orcs'll be scattered and easy to kill. Take me bet now, girl, that I'll kill more than yerself."

"You're going out now, and getting a head start," Catti-brie answered, her face brightening a bit.

"Bah, but I won't count the ones I'm killing on the road," said Bruenor. "When I get back here and the orcs come on, as they're sure'n to do when Obould's no more, then I'll be killing more orcs than Catti-brie's to fell."

Catti-brie wore a sly grin. "I'll have me bow back from Drizzt then," she said, assuming a Dwarvish accent as she threw out the warning. "Every arrow's taking one down. Some'll take down two, or might even be three."

"And every swipe o' me axe is cutting three in half," Bruenor countered. "And I'm not for tiring when there're orcs to cut."

The two stared at each other without blinking as each extended a hand to shake on the bet.

"The loser represents Mithral Hall at the next ceremony in Nesmé," Catti-brie said, and Bruenor feigned a grimace, as though he hadn't expected the stakes to be quite so high.

"Ye'll enjoy the journey," the dwarf said. He smiled and tried to pull back, but Catti-brie held his hand firmly and stared him in the eye, her expression solemn.

"Just get back to me, alive, and with Drizzt, Regis, and the others alive," she said.

"Plannin' on it," said Bruenor, though he didn't believe it any more than did Catti-brie. "And with Obould's ugly head.

Catti-brie agreed. "With Obould's head."

CHAPTER

TAKING CARE IN WHAT THEY WISHED FOR

24

Clan Wolf Jaw lined both sides of the trail, their formidable array of warriors stretching out for hundreds of feet, beyond the bend and out of Chieftain Grguch's line of sight. None moved to block the progress of Clan Karuck, or to threaten the hulking orcs in any way, and Grguch recognized the pair who did step out in the middle of the trail.

"Greetings again, Dnark," Grguch said. "You have heard of our assault on the ugly dwarves?"

"All the tribes of Many-Arrows have heard of the glory of Grguch's march," Dnark answered, and Grguch smiled, as did Toogwik Tuk, who stood to the side and just behind the ferocious chieftain.

"You march west," remarked Dnark, glancing back over his shoulder. "To the invitation of King Obould?"

Grguch spent a few moments looking over Dnark and his associate, the shaman Ung-thol. Then the huge orc warrior glanced back at Toogwik Tuk and beyond him, motioning to a trio of soldiers, two obviously of Clan Karuck, with wide shoulders and bulging muscles, and a third that Dnark and Ung-thol had parted company with just a few days earlier.

"Obould has sent an emissary, requesting parlay," Grguch explained. Behind him, Oktule saluted the pair and bowed repeatedly.

"We were there among King Obould's entourage when Oktule was sent forth," Dnark replied. "Know you, though, that he was not the only emissary sent out that day." He finished and met Grguch's hard stare for a few heartbeats, then motioned behind to the Wolf Jaw ranks. Several warriors stepped out, dragging a beaten and battered orc. They took him around Dnark, and on his signal closed half the distance to Grguch before dropping their living cargo unceremoniously onto the dirt.

Priest Nukkels groaned as he hit the ground, and squirmed a bit, but Ung-thol and Dnark had done their work extremely well and there was no chance of him getting up from the ground.

"An emissary sent to you?" Grguch asked. "But you said that you were with Obould."

"No," Toogwik Tuk explained, reading correctly the smug expressions worn by his co-conspirators. He stepped forward, daring to pass Grguch as he moved toward the battered priest. "No, this is Nukkels," he explained, looking back at Grguch.

Grguch shrugged, for the name meant nothing to him.

"King Obould's advisor," Toogwik Tuk explained. "He would not be sent to deliver a message to Chieftain Dnark. No, not even to Chieftain Grguch."

"What?" Grguch demanded, and though his tone was calm and even, there remained behind it a hint of warning to Toogwik Tuk to tread lightly, where he seemed on the verge of insult.

"This emissary was for no orc," Toogwik Tuk explained. He looked to Dnark and Ung-thol. "Nor was he heading north, to Gerti Orelsdottr, was he?"

"South," Dnark answered.

"Southeast, precisely," added Ung-thol.

Toogwik Tuk could barely contain his amusement—and his elation that King Obould had so perfectly played into their plans. He turned to Grguch, certain of his guess. "Priest Nukkels was sent by King Obould to parlay with King Bruenor Battlehammer."

Grguch's face went stone cold.

"We believe the same," said Dnark, and he moved forward to stand beside Toogwik Tuk—and to ensure that Toogwik Tuk did not claim an overdue amount of the credit for that revelation. "Nukkels has resisted our . . . methods," he explained, and to accentuate his point, he stepped over and kicked the groaning Nukkels hard in the ribs, sending him into a fetal curl. "He has offered many explanations for his journey, including that of going to King Bruenor."

"This pathetic dwarf-kisser in the dirt was sent by Obould to meet with Bruenor?" Grguch asked incredulously, as if he could not believe his ears.

"So we believe," Dnark answered.

"It is easy enough to discern," came a voice from behind, among Clan Karuck's ranks. All turned, Grguch with a wide, knowing smile, to see Hakuun step forward to stand beside his chieftain. "Would you like me to question the emissary?" Hakuun asked.

Grguch laughed and glanced around, motioning at last to a dark cluster of trees off to the side of the path. Dnark began signaling to his ranks for orcs to drag the prisoner over, but Grguch cut him short as Hakuun launched into a spell. Nukkels contorted as if in pain, and curled up on the ground—until he was not on the ground, but floating in the air. Hakuun walked for the trees, and Nukkels drifted behind him.

* * * * *

Away from the others, Hakuun obediently put his ear in line with that of Nukkels. The transfer took only a moment, with Jack the brain mole slipping out of Hakuun's ear and into Nukkels's.

As he realized what was happening to him, Nukkels began thrashing wildly in the air, but with nothing to orient him, with no pull of gravity to keep him upright or even on his side, he began to spin—which dizzied him, of course, and only made Jack's intrusion that much easier.

Jack came back out, and back into his more usual host a short while later, having ripped Nukkels's brain of every detail. He knew, and soon Hakuun knew, of Obould's true designs, confirming the fears of the trio who had summoned Clan Karuck from the bowels of the Spine of the World.

"Obould seeks peace with the dwarves," Hakuun remarked in disbelief. "He wants the war to be at its end."

A very un-orc orc, said the voice in his head.

"He defiles the will of Gruumsh!"

As I said.

Hakuun stalked out of the tree cluster, Jack's magic yanking the shivering, slobbering, floating Nukkels along behind him. When Hakuun got back to the others on the trail, he waved Nukkels in and let him drop hard to the ground.

"He was bound for King Bruenor," the shaman of Clan Karuck stated. "To undo the damage wrought by Chieftain Grguch and Clan Karuck."

"Damage?" Grguch asked, furrowing his thick brow. "Damage!"

"As we explained to you upon your arrival," said Ung-thol.

"It is as our friends have told us," Hakuun confirmed. "King Obould has lost his heart for war. He wishes no further battle with Clan Battlehammer."

"Cowardice," spat Toogwik Tuk.

"Has he found enough spoils to return to his home?" Grguch asked, his tone mocking and derogatory.

"He has conquered empty rocks," Dnark proclaimed. "All that is of value lies within the halls of the Battlehammer dwarves, or across the river in the realm of Silverymoon. But Obould—" he paused, turned, and kicked Nukkels hard—"Obould would parlay with Bruenor. He would seek a treaty!"

"With *dwarves?*" Grguch bellowed.

"Exactly that," said Hakuun, and Grguch nodded, having seen Hakuun at his work too many times to doubt a word he spoke.

Ung-thol and Toogwik Tuk exchanged knowing grins. It was all for show, all to rouse the rabble around the two chieftains, to garner outrage at the utter ridiculousness of the apparent designs of Obould.

"And he would parlay with Grguch," Dnark reminded the ferocious orc chieftain. "He would summon you to his side to gain your approval. Or perhaps to scold you for attacking the elves and dwarves."

Grguch's bloodshot eyes opened wide and a great snarl rumbled behind his trembling lips. He seemed as if he would leap forward and bite off Dnark's head, but the Chieftain of Wolf Jaw did not relent. "Obould intends to show Grguch who controls the Kingdom of Many-Arrows. He will coax you to join his way, so certain is he that he follows the true vision of Gruumsh."

"To parlay with dwarves?" Grguch roared.

"Cowardice!" Dnark cried.

Grguch stood there, clenching his fists, the muscles in his neck straining, his chest and shoulders bulging as if their sinewy power could not be contained by the orc's skin.

"Oktule!" he cried, wheeling to face the orc who had arrived with King Obould's invitation.

The emissary shrank back, as did every orc around him.

"Come here," Grguch demanded.

Oktule, trembling and sweating, gave a quick shake of his head and stumbled back even more—or would have, had not a pair of Clan Karuck's powerful warriors grabbed him by the arms and walked him forward. He tried to dig his feet in, but they just dragged him, depositing him before the wild gaze of Chieftain Grguch.

"King Obould would scold me?" Grguch asked.

A line of wetness ran down poor Oktule's leg, and he shook his head again—though whether in response to the question or in simple, desperate denial, no one around could tell. He focused on Dnark, pleading with the chieftain who knew that his role was unwitting.

Dnark laughed at him.

"He would scold me?" Grguch said again, louder. He leaned forward, towering over the trembling Oktule. "You did not tell me that."

"He would not . . . he . . . he . . . he told me to come to get you," Oktule stammered.

"That he might scold me?" Grguch demanded, and Oktule seemed about to faint.

"I did not know," the pathetic courier protested meekly.

Grguch whirled to regard Dnark and the others, his expression brightening as if he had just sorted everything out. "To gain the favor of Bruenor, Obould would have to offer something," Grguch realized. He spun back on Oktule and slapped him with a backhand across the face, launching him to the side and to the ground.

Grguch turned on Dnark again, his smile wry, nodding his head knowingly. "He would offer to Bruenor the head of the warrior who struck against Mithral Hall, perhaps."

Behind him, Oktule gulped.

"Is there truth in that?" Dnark asked Nukkels, and he kicked the prone orc hard again.

Nukkels grunted and groaned, but said nothing decipherable.

"It is reasonable," Ung-thol said, and Dnark quickly nodded, neither of them wishing to let Grguch calm from his self-imposed frenzy. "If Obould wishes to convince Bruenor that the attack was not of his doing, he would have to prove his claim."

"With the head of Grguch?" the chieftain of Clan Karuck asked as he turned to Hakuun, and Grguch laughed as if it was all absurd.

"The foolish priest showed me nothing of this," Hakuun admitted. "But if Obould truly wishes peace with Bruenor, and he does, then Chieftain Grguch has quickly become . . . an inconvenience."

"It is past time I meet this Obould fool, that I can show him the truth of Clan Karuck," said Grguch, and he gave a little laugh, clearly enjoying the moment. "It may be unfortunate that you interrupted the journey of the one in the dirt," he said, nodding toward the still-squirming Nukkels. "Greater would be King Bruenor's surprise and fear when he looked into that basket, I say! I would pay in women and good gold to see the face of the dwarf when he pulled out Obould's head!"

The orcs of Clan Karuck began to howl at that, but Dnark, Ungthol, and Toogwik Tuk just looked at each other solemnly and with nods of understanding. For there it was, the conspiracy spoken clearly, openly proclaimed, and there could be no turning back. They offered their nods of thanks to Hakuun, who remained impassive, the part of him that was Jack the Gnome not wishing to even acknowledge their existence, let alone allow them the illusion that they were somehow his peers.

Grguch hoisted his two-bladed axe, but paused then set it aside. Instead, he drew a long and wicked knife from his belt and glanced back to the Karuck orcs standing around Oktule. His smile was all the impetus those orcs needed to drag the poor courier forward.

Oktule's feet dug small trenches in the wet spring ground. He shook his head in denial, crying, "No, no, please no!"

Those pleas only seemed to spur Grguch on. He strode behind Oktule and grabbed a handful of the fool's hair, roughly yanking his head back, exposing his throat.

Even the orcs of Oktule's own clan joined in the cheering and chanting, and so he was doomed.

He screamed and shrieked in tones preternatural in their sheer horror. He thrashed and kicked and fought as the blade came against the soft skin of his throat.

Then his screams became watery, and Grguch bore him to the ground, face down, the chieftain's knees upon his back, pinning him, while Grguch's arm pumped furiously.

When Grguch stood up again, presenting Oktule's head to the frenzied gathering, the three conspirators shared another glance, and each took a deep and steadying breath.

Dnark, Toogwik Tuk, and Ung-thol had made a deal with as brutal a creature as any of them had ever known. And they knew, all three, that there was more than a passing chance that Chieftain Grguch would one day present their heads for the approval of the masses.

They had to be satisfied with the odds, however, because the other choice before them was obedience to Obould, and Obould alone. And that course of cowardice they could not accept.

* * * * *

"There will be nothing subtle about Grguch's challenge to Obould," Ung-thol warned his comrades when the three were alone later that same night. "Diplomacy is not his way."

"There is no time for diplomacy, nor is there any need," said Toogwik Tuk, who clearly stood as the calmest and most confident of the trio. "We know the options before us, and we chose our road long ago. Are you surprised by Grguch and Clan Karuck? They are exactly as I portrayed them to you."

"I am surprised by their . . . efficiency," said Dnark. "Grguch walks a straight line."

"Straight to Obould," Toogwik Tuk remarked with a snicker.

"Do not underestimate King Obould," warned Dnark. "That he sent Nukkels to Mithral Hall tells us that he understands the true threat of Grguch. He will not be caught unawares."

"We cannot allow this to become a wider war," Ung-thol agreed. "Grguch's name is great among the orcs in the east, along the Surbrin, but the numbers of warriors there are few compared to what Obould commands in the west and the north. If this widens in scope, we will surely be overwhelmed."

"Then it will not," Toogwik Tuk said. "We will confront Obould with his small group around him, and Clan Karuck will overwhelm him and be done with it. He does not have the favor of Gruumsh— have we any doubt of that?"

"His actions do not echo the words of Gruumsh," Ung-thol reluctantly agreed.

"If we are certain of his actions," said Dnark.

"He will not march against Mithral Hall!" Toogwik Tuk snarled at them. "You have heard the whimpers of Nukkels! Grguch's priest confirmed it."

"Did he? Truly?" Dnark asked.

"Or is it all a ruse?" Ung-thol posed. "Is Obould's pause a feint to fully unbalance our enemies?"

"Obould will not march," Toogwik Tuk protested.

"And Grguch will not be controlled," said Dnark. "And are we to believe that this half-ogre creature will hold the armies of Many-Arrows together in a unified march for wider glory?"

"The promise of conquest will hold the armies together far better than the hope of parlay with the likes of King Bruenor of the dwarves," Toogwik Tuk argued.

"And that is the truth," said Dnark, ending the debate. "And that is why we brought Clan Karuck forth. It unfolds before us now exactly as we anticipated, and Grguch meets and exceeds every expectation. Now that we are finding that which we decided we wished to find, we must hold fast to our initial beliefs that led us to this point. It is not the will of Gruumsh that his people should pause when great glory and conquest awaits. It is not the will of Gruumsh that his people should parlay with the likes of King Bruenor of the dwarves. Never that! Obould has pushed himself beyond the boundaries of decency and common sense. We knew that when we called to Clan Karuck, and we know that now." He turned his head and spat upon Nukkels, who lay unconscious and near death in the mud. "We know that with even more certainty now."

"So let us go and witness Grguch as he answers the summons of Obould," said Toogwik Tuk. "Let us lead the cheers to King Grguch, as he leads our armies against King Bruenor."

Ung-thol still wore doubts on his old and wrinkled face, but he looked to Dnark and shared in his chieftain's assenting nod.

In a tree not far away, a curious winged snake listened to it all with amusement.

CHAPTER

POLITICS AND ALLIANCES

25

Raised in Menzoberranzan, a male drow in the matriarchal city of Menzoberranzan, Tos'un Armgo didn't as much as grimace when Drizzt tugged his arms back hard and secured the rope on the other side of the large tree. He was caught, with nowhere to run or hide. He glanced to the side—or tried to, for Drizzt had expertly looped the rope under his chin to secure him against the tree trunk—where Khazid'hea rested, stabbed into a stone by Drizzt. He could feel the sword calling to him, but he couldn't reach out to it.

Drizzt studied Tos'un as if he understood the silent pleas exchanged between drow and sentient sword—and likely, he did, Tos'un realized.

"You have nothing further to gain or lose," Drizzt said. "Your day in the service of Obould is done."

"I have not been in his service for many tendays," Tos'un stubbornly argued. "Not since before the winter. Not since that day you battled him, and even before that, truth be told."

"Truth told by a son of House Barrison Del'Armgo?" Drizzt asked with a scoff.

"I have nothing to gain or lose, just as you said."

"A friend of mine, a dwarf named Bill, would speak with you about that," Drizzt said. "Or whisper at you, I should say, for his throat was expertly cut to steal the depth of his voice."

Tos'un grimaced at that inescapable truth, for he had indeed cut a dwarf's throat in preparation for Obould's first assault on Mithral Hall's eastern door.

"I have other friends who might have wished to speak with you, too," said Drizzt. "But they are dead, in no small part because of your actions."

"I was fighting a war," Tos'un blurted. "I did not understand—"

"How could you not understand the carnage to which you contributed? Is that truly your defense?"

Tos'un shook his head, though it would hardly turn to either side.

"I have learned," the captured drow added. "I have tried to make amends. I have aided the elves."

Despite himself and his intentions that he would bring no harm to his prisoner, Drizzt slapped Tos'un across the face. "You led them to the elves," he accused.

"No," said Tos'un. "No."

"I have heard the details of the raid."

"Facilitated by Chieftain Grguch of Clan Karuck, and a trio of conspirators who seek to force Obould back to the road of conquest," said Tos'un. "There is more afoot here than you understand. Never did I side with those who attacked the Moonwood, and who have marched south, I am sure, with intent to strike at Mithral Hall."

"Yet you just said that you were no ally of Obould," Drizzt reasoned.

"Not of Obould, nor of any other orc," said Tos'un. "I admit my role, though it was a passive one, in the early stages, when Donnia Soldou, Ad'non Kareese, and Kaer'lic Suun Wett decided to foster an alliance between Obould and his orcs, Gerti Orelsdottr and her giants, and the two-headed troll named Proffit. I went along because I did not care—why would I care for dwarves, humans, and elves? I am drow!"

"A point I have never forgotten, I assure you."

The threat took much of Tos'un's bluster, but he pressed on anyway. "The events surrounding me were not my concern."

"Until Obould tried to kill you."

"Until I was chased away by the murderous Obould, yes," said Tos'un. "And into the camp of Albondiel and Sinnafain of the Moonwood."

"Whom you *betrayed*," Drizzt shouted in his face.

"From whom I escaped, though I was not their captive," Tos'un yelled back.

"Then why did you run?"

"Because of you!" Tos'un cried. "Because of that sword I carried, who knew that Drizzt Do'Urden would never allow me to keep it, who knew that Drizzt Do'Urden would find me among the elves and strike me down for possessing a sword that I had found abandoned in the bottom of a ravine."

"That is not why, and you know it," said Drizzt, backing off just a step. " 'Twas I who lost the sword, recall?"

As he spoke he glanced over at Khazid'hea, and an idea came to him. He wanted to believe Tos'un, as he had wanted to believe the female, Donnia, when he had captured her those months before.

He looked back at Tos'un, smiled wryly, and said, "It is all opportunity, is it not?"

"What do you mean?"

"You ally with Obould as he gains the upper hand. But he is held at bay, and you face his wrath. So you find your way to Sinnafain and Albondiel and the others and think to create new opportunities where your old ones have ended. Or to recreate the old ones, at the expense of your new 'friends.' Once you have gained their trust and learned their ways, you again have something to offer to the orcs, something that will perhaps bring Obould back to your side."

"By helping Grguch? You do not understand."

"But I shall," Drizzt promised, moving off to the side, toward Khazid'hea. Without hesitation, he grabbed the sword by the hilt. Metal scraped and screeched as he withdrew the blade from the stone, but Drizzt didn't hear that, for Khazid'hea already invaded his thoughts.

I had thought you lost to me.

But Drizzt wasn't listening to any of that, had not the time for it. He forced his thoughts into the sword, demanding of Khazid'hea a summary of its time in the hands of Tos'un Armgo. He did not coddle the sword with promises that together they would find glory. He did not offer to the sword anything. He simply asked of it, *Were you in the Moonwood? Have you tasted the blood of elves?*

Sweet blood . . . Khazid'hea admitted, but with that thought came to Drizzt a sense of a time long past. And the sword had not been in the Moonwood. Of that much, the drow was almost immediately certain.

In light of Khazid'hea's open admission of its fondness for elf blood, Drizzt considered the unlikely scenario that Tos'un could have been an integral part of the planning for that raid and yet still have remained on the western side of the Surbrin. Would Khazid'hea have allowed that participation from afar, knowing that blood was to be spilled, and particularly since Khazid'hea had been in Tos'un's possession when he had been with the elves?

Drizzt glanced back at the captured drow and considered the relationship between Tos'un and the sword. Had Tos'un so dominated Khazid'hea?

As that very question filtered through Drizzt's thoughts, and thus was offered to the telepathic sword, Khazid'hea's mocking response chimed in.

Drizzt put the sword down for a few moments to let it all sink in. When he retrieved the blade, he directed his questioning toward the newcomer.

Grguch, he imparted.

A fine warrior. Fierce and powerful.

A worthy wielder for Khazid'hea? Drizzt asked.

The sword didn't deny it.

More worthy than Obould? Drizzt silently asked.

The feeling that came back at him seemed not so favorably impressed. And yet, Drizzt knew that King Obould was as fine a warrior as any orc he had ever encountered, as fine as Drizzt himself, whom the sword had long coveted as a wielder. Though not of that elite class, Catti-brie, too, was a fine warrior, and yet Drizzt knew from his last experience with the sword that she had fallen out of Khazid'hea's favor, as she opted to use her bow far too often for Khazid'hea's ego.

A long time passed before Drizzt set the sword down once again, and he was left with the impression that the ever-bloodthirsty Khazid'hea clearly favored Grguch over Obould, and just for the reasons that Tos'un had said. Obould was not pressing for conquest and battle.

Drizzt looked at Tos'un, who rested as comfortably as could be expected given his awkward position tied to the tree. Drizzt could not dismiss the plausibility of Tos'un's claims, all of them, and perhaps, whether through heartfelt emotion or simple opportunity, Tos'un was not now an enemy to him and his allies.

But after his experiences with Donnia Soldou—indeed, after his experiences with his own race from the earliest moments of his conscious life, Drizzt Do'Urden wasn't about to take that chance.

* * * * *

The sun had long set, the dark night made murkier by a fog that curled up from the softening snow. Into that mist disappeared Bruenor, Hralien, Regis, Thibbledorf Pwent, Torgar Hammerstriker and Shingles McRuff of Mirabar, and Cordio the priest.

On the other side of the ridgeline, behind the wall where Bruenor's dwarves and Alustriel's wizards worked vigilantly, Catti-brie watched the receding group with a heavy heart.

"I should be going with them," she said.

"You cannot," said her companion, Lady Alustriel of Silverymoon. The tall woman moved nearer to Catti-brie and put her arm around the woman's shoulders. "Your leg will heal."

Catti-brie looked up at her, for Alustriel was nearly half a foot taller than she.

"Perhaps this is a sign that you should consider my offer," Alustriel said.

"To train in wizardry? Am I not too old to begin such an endeavor?"

Alustriel laughed dismissively at the absurd question. "You will take to it naturally, even though you were raised by the magically inept dwarves."

Catti-brie considered her words for a moment, but soon turned her attention to the view beyond the wall, where the fog had swallowed her father and friends. "I had thought that you would walk beside my father, as he bade," she said, and glanced over at the Lady of Silverymoon.

"As you could not, neither could I," Alustriel replied. "My position prevented me from it as fully as did your wounded leg."

"You do not agree with Bruenor's goal? You would side with Obould?"

"Surely not," said Alustriel. "But it is not my place to interject Silverymoon in a war."

"You did exactly that when you and your Knights in Silver rescued the wandering Nesmians."

"Our treaties with Nesmé demanded no less," Alustriel explained. "They were under attack and running for their lives. Small friends we would be if we did not come to them in their time of need."

"Bruenor sees it just that way right now," said Catti-brie.

"Indeed he does," Alustriel admitted.

"So he plans to eradicate the threat. To decapitate the orc army and send them scattering."

"And I hope and pray that he succeeds. To have the orcs gone is a goal agreed upon by all the folk of the Silver Marches, of course. But it is not my place to bring Silverymoon into this provocative attack. My council has determined that our posture is to remain defensive, and I am bound to abide by their edicts."

Catti-brie shook her head and did not hide her disgusted look. "You act as if we are in a time of peace, and Bruenor is breaking that peace," she said. "Does a needed pause in the war because of the winter's snows cancel what has gone before?"

Alustriel hugged the angry woman a bit tighter. "It is not the way any of us wish it to be," she said. "But the council of Silverymoon has determined that Obould has stopped his march, and we must accept that."

"Mithral Hall was just attacked," Catti-brie reminded. "Are we to sit back and let them strike at us again and again?"

Alustriel's pause showed that she had no answer for that. "I cannot go after Obould now," she said. "In my role as leader of Silverymoon, I am bound by the decisions of the council. I wish Bruenor well. I hope with all my heart and soul that he succeeds and that the orcs are chased back to their holes."

Catti-brie calmed, more from the sincerity and regret in Alustriel's tone than from her actual words. Alustriel had helped, despite her refusal to go along, for she had given to Bruenor a locket enchanted to lead the dwarf toward Drizzt, an identical locket to the one she had given to Catti-brie many years before when she, too, had gone off to find a wandering Drizzt.

"I hope that Bruenor is correct in his guess," Alustriel went on, trepidation in her voice. "I hope that killing Obould will bring the results he desires."

Catti-brie didn't reply, but just stood there and absorbed the words. She couldn't bring herself to believe that Obould, who had started the war, might actually have become a stabilizing force, and yet she could not deny her doubts.

* * * * *

The two orcs stood under a widespread maple, the sharp, stark lines of its branches not yet softened by the onset of buds. They talked and chuckled at their own stupidity, for they were completely lost, and far separated from their kin at the small village. A wrong turn on a trail in the dark of night had put them far afield, and they had long ago abandoned the firewood they had come out to collect.

One lamented that his wife would beat him red, to warm him up so he could replace the fire that wouldn't last half the night.

The other laughed and his smile lingered long after his mirth was stolen by an elven arrow, one that neatly sliced into his companion's temple. Standing in confusion, grinning simply because he hadn't the presence of mind to remove his own smile, the orc didn't even register the sudden *thump* of heavy boots closing in fast from behind him. He was caught completely unawares as the sharp tip of a helmet spike drove into his spine, tearing through muscle and bone, and blasted out the front of his chest, covered in blood and pieces of his torn heart.

He was dead before Thibbledorf Pwent straightened, lifting the orc's flopping body atop his head. The dwarf hopped around, looking for more enemies. He saw Bruenor and Cordio scrambling in the shadows south of the maple, and noted Torgar and Shingles farther to the east. With Hralien in the northwest, and Regis following in the shadows behind Pwent, the group soon surmised that the pair had been out alone.

"Good enough, then," said Bruenor, nodding his approval. He held up the locket Alustriel had given him. "Warmer," he explained. "Drizzt is nearby."

"Still north?" Hralien asked, coming in under the maple to stand beside Pwent.

"Back from where ye just walked," Bruenor confirmed, holding forth his fist, which held the locket. "And getting warmer by the step."

A curious expression showed on Bruenor's face. "And getting warmer as we're standin' here," he explained to the curious glances that came his way.

"Drizzt!" Regis cried an instant later.

Following the halfling's pointing finger, the others spied a pair of dark elves coming toward them, with Tos'un bound and walking before their friend.

"Taked ye long enough to find him, eh?" Thibbledorf Pwent said with a snort. He bent and slapped his leg for effect, which sent the dead orc flopping weirdly.

Drizzt stared at the bloody dwarf, at the cargo he carried on his helmet spike. Realizing that there was simply nothing he might say against the absurdity of that image, he just prodded Tos'un on, moving to the main group.

"They hit the wall east of Mithral Hall," Hralien explained to Drizzt. "As you had feared."

"Aye, but know that we sent them running," Bruenor added.

Drizzt's confused expression didn't change as he scanned the group.

"And now we're out for Obould," Bruenor explained. "I'm knowing ye were right, elf. We got to kill Obould and break it all apart, as ye thought afore when ye went after him with me girl's sword."

"*We're* out for him?" Drizzt asked doubtfully, looking past the small group. "You've brought no army, my friend."

"Bah, an army'd just muddle it all," Bruenor said with a wave of his hand.

It wasn't hard for Drizzt to catch the gist of that, and in considering it for a moment, in considering Bruenor's leadership methodology, he realized that he should not be the least bit surprised.

"We wish to get to Obould, and it seems that we have a captive who might aid in exactly that," Hralien remarked, stepping up before Tos'un.

"I have no idea where he is," Tos'un said in his still-stinted command of the Elvish tongue.

"You would have to say that," said Hralien.

"I helped you . . . your people," Tos'un protested. "Grguch had them caught in the failed raid and I showed them the tunnel that took them to safety."

"True," Hralien replied. "But then, isn't that what a drow would do? To gain our trust, I mean?"

Tos'un's shoulders sagged and he lowered his eyes, for he had just fought that same battle with Drizzt, and there seemed no way for him to escape it. Everything he had done leading up to that point could be interpreted as self-serving, and for the benefit of a larger and more nefarious plot.

"Ye should've just killed him and been done with it," Bruenor said to Drizzt. "If he's not for helping us then he's just slowing us down."

"Meself'll be there for the task in a heartbeat, me king!" Pwent shouted from the side, and all eyes turned to see the dwarf, bent low with head forward, backing through the narrow opening between a pair of trees. Pwent set the back of the dead orc's thighs against one trunk, the poor creature's shoulder blades against another, and with a sudden burst, the dwarf tugged backward. Bones and gristle popped and ground as the barbed spike tore back through, freeing the dwarf of his dead-weight burden.

Pwent stumbled backward and fell to his rump, but hopped right back to his feet and bounced around to face the others, shaking his head so vigorously that his lips flapped. Then, with a smile, Pwent brought his hands up before him, palms facing out, extended thumbs touching tip-to-tip, lining up his charge.

"Turn the dark-skinned dog just a bit," he instructed.

"Not just yet, good dwarf," Drizzt said, and Pwent straightened, disappointment clear on his face.

"Ye thinkin' to take him along?" Bruenor asked, and Drizzt nodded.

"We could divert our course to the Moonwood, or back to Mithral Hall," Hralien offered. "We would lose no more than a day or so, and would be rid of our burden."

But Drizzt shook his head.

"Easier just to kill him," said Bruenor, and to the side, Pwent began scraping his feet across the ground like a bull readying for a charge.

"But not wiser," Drizzt said. "If Tos'un's claims are true, he might prove to be a valuable asset to us. If not, we have lost nothing because we have risked nothing." He looked to his fellow drow. "If you do not deceive us, on my word I will let you leave when we are done."

"You cannot do this," said Hralien, drawing all eyes his way. "If he has committed crimes against the Moonwood, his fate is not yours alone to decide."

"He has not," Drizzt assured the elf. "He was not there, for Khazid'hea was not there."

Bruenor yanked Drizzt aside, pulling him away from the others. "How much o' this is yer way o' hoping for a drow akin to yerself?" the dwarf asked bluntly.

Drizzt shook his head, with sincerity and certainty. "On my word, Bruenor, this I do because I think it best for us and our cause—whatever that cause may be."

"What's that meaning?" the dwarf demanded. "We're for killing Obould, don't ye doubt!" He raised his voice with the proclamation, and the others all looked his way.

Drizzt didn't argue. "Obould would kill Tos'un if given the chance, as Obould murdered Tos'un's companion. We will gamble nothing with Tos'un, I promise you, my friend, and the possibility of gain cannot be ignored."

Bruenor looked long and hard at Drizzt then glanced back at Tos'un, who stood calmly, as if resigned to his fate—whatever that fate may be.

"On my word," Drizzt said.

"Yer word's always been good enough, elf," said Bruenor. He turned and started back for the others, calling to Torgar and Shingles as he went. "Think yerselves are up to guardin' a drow?" he asked, or started to, for as soon as his intent became clear, Drizzt interrupted him.

"Let Tos'un remain my responsibility," he said.

Again Bruenor granted Drizzt his wish.

CHAPTER
CROSSROAD

26

Wulfgar lingered around the outskirts of Auckney for several days. He didn't dare show his face in the town for fear that connecting himself to the new arrival at Castle Auck would put undue pressure on Lord Feringal, and create dangerous ramifications for Colson. But Wulfgar was a man comfortable in the wilds, who knew how to survive through the cold nights, and who knew how to keep himself hidden.

Everything he heard about the lord and lady's new child brought him hope. One of the prevalent rumors whispered by excited townsfolk hinted that the girl was Feringal's and Meralda's own, and that she had been born in a sleep-state from which they had never expected her to awaken. And what joy now for the couple and the town that the child had recovered!

Another rumor attached Colson to barbarian nobility, and claimed that her presence with Lord Feringal ensured security for the folk of Auckney—a wonderful thing in the tough terrain of the frozen North.

Wulfgar absorbed it all with a growing sense that he had done well for Colson, for himself, and for Delly. Truly he had a hole in his heart that he never expected to fill, and truly he vowed that he would visit Auckney and Colson in the coming years. Feringal would have no reason to dismiss him or arrest him as time passed, after all, and indeed Wulfgar might find a level of bargaining power in the future, since he knew the truth of the girl's parentage. Lord Feringal wouldn't want him for an enemy, physically or politically.

That was the barbarian's hope, the one thing that kept him from breaking down and rushing back into the town to "rescue" Colson.

He continued to linger, to listen and to watch, for on more than one occasion he chanced to see Colson out with her new parents. He was truly amazed and heartened to see how quickly the young girl had adapted to her new surroundings and new parents, from afar at least. Colson smiled as often as she had in Mithral Hall, and she seemed at ease holding Meralda's hand and walking along in the woman's shadow.

Similarly, the love Meralda held for her could not be denied. The look of serenity on her face was everything Wulfgar had hoped it would be. She seemed complete and content, and in addition to those promising appearances, what gave Wulfgar more hope still was the posture of Lord Feringal whenever he was near to the girl. There could be no doubt that Feringal had grown greatly in character over the years. Perhaps it was due to the support of Meralda, a woman Wulfgar knew to be possessed of extraordinary integrity, or perhaps it was due to the absence of Feringal's shrill sister.

Whatever the cause, the result was clear for him to see and hear, and every day he lingered near to Auckney was a day in which he grew more certain of his decision to return the child to her rightful mother. It did Wulfgar's heart good, for all the pain still there, to think of Colson in Meralda's loving arms.

So many times he wanted to run into Auckney to tell Colson that he loved her, to crush her close to him in his arms and assure her that he would always love her, would always protect her. So many times he wanted to go in and simply say goodbye. Her cries of "Da!" still echoed in his mind and would haunt him for years and years, he knew.

But he could not go in, and so as the days became a tenday, Wulfgar melted away down the mountain road to the east, the way he had come. The next day, he arrived at the end of the eastern pass, where the road ran south through the foothills to Luskan, and north to the long dale that traversed the Spine of the World and opened up into Icewind Dale.

Wulfgar turned neither way at first. Instead he crossed the trail and scaled a rocky outcropping that afforded him a grand view of the rolling lands farther to the east. He perched upon the stone and let his mind's eye rove beyond the physical limitations of his vision, imagining the landscape as it neared Mithral Hall and his dearest friends. The place he had called home.

He turned suddenly back to the west, thinking of his daughter and realizing just how badly he missed her—much more so than he'd anticipated.

Then back to the east went his thoughts and his eyes, to the tomb of Delly, lying cold in Mithral Hall.

"I only ever tried to do the best I could," he whispered as if talking to his dead wife.

It was true enough. For all of his failures since his return from the Abyss, Wulfgar had tried to do the best he could manage. It had been so when he'd first rejoined his friends, when he'd failed and assaulted Catti-brie after a hallucinatory dream. It had been so during his travels with Morik, through Luskan and up to Auckney. So many times had he failed during those dark days.

Looking west then looking east, Wulfgar accepted the responsibility for all of those mistakes. He did not couch his admission of failure with self-serving whining about the trials he had suffered at the claws of Errtu. He did not make excuses for any of it, for there were none that could alter the truth of his behavior.

All he could do was do the best he could in all matters before him. That was what had led him to retrieve Delly's body. It was the right thing to do. That was what had led him not only to retrieve Colson from Cottie and the refugees, but to bring her home to Meralda. It was the right thing to do.

And now?

Wulfgar had thought he'd sorted it all out, had thought his plans and road determined. But with the stark reality of those plans before him, he was unsure. He knelt upon the stone and prayed to Delly for guidance. He called upon her ghost to show him the way.

Was Obould pounding on the doors of Mithral Hall yet again?

Bruenor might need him, he knew. His adoptive father, who had shown him nothing but love for all those years, might need his strength in the coming war. Wulfgar's absence could result in Bruenor's death!

The same could be true of Drizzt, or Regis, or Catti-brie. They might find themselves in situations in the coming days where only Wulfgar could save them.

"Might," Wulfgar said, and as he heard the word, he recognized that that would forever be the case. They might need him as he might need any of them, or all of them. Or perhaps even all of them together would one day soon be overcome by a black tide like the one of Obould.

"Might," he said again. "Always might."

Aside from the grim possibilities offered by the nearly perpetual state of war, however, Wulfgar had to remind himself of important questions. What of his own needs? What of his own desires? What of his own legacy?

He was approaching middle age.

Reflexively, Wulfgar turned from the east to face north, looking up the trail that would lead him to Icewind Dale, the land of his ancestors, the land of his people.

Before he could fully turn that way, however, he looked back to the east, toward Mithral Hall, and envisioned Obould the Awful towering over Bruenor.

CHAPTER
TRUST, AND VERIFY

27

"This Toogwik Tuk is aggressive," Grguch said to Hakuun, and to Jack, though of course Grguch didn't know that. They stood off to the side of the gathering force as it realigned itself for a march to the west. "He would have us wage war with Obould."

"He claims that Obould would wage war with us," the shaman agreed after a quick internal dialogue with Jack.

Grguch grinned as if nothing in the world would please him more. "I like this Toogwik Tuk," he said. "He speaks with Gruumsh."

"Are you not curious as to why Obould halted his march?" Hakuun asked, though the question had originated with Jack. "His reputation is for ferocity, but he builds walls instead of tearing them down."

"He fears rivals," Grguch assumed. "Or he has grown comfortable. He walks away from Gruumsh."

"You do not intend to convince him otherwise."

Grguch grinned even more wickedly. "I intend to kill him and take his armies. I speak to Gruumsh, and I will please Gruumsh."

"Your message will be blunt, or coaxed at first?"

Grguch looked at the shaman curiously then motioned with his chin toward a bag set off to the side, a sack that held Oktule's head.

A wry smile widened on Hakuun's face. "I can strengthen the message," he promised, and Grguch was pleased.

Hakuun looked back over his shoulder and spoke a few arcane words, strung together with dramatic inflection. Jack had predicted all of it, and had already worked the primary magic for it. Out of the shadows walked Oktule, headless and grotesque. The animated zombie strode stiff-legged to the sack and shifted aside the flaps. It stood straight a moment later and moved slowly toward the pair, cradling its lost head in both hands at its midsection.

Hakuun looked to Grguch and shrugged sheepishly. The chieftain laughed.

"Blunt," he said. "I only wish that I might view Obould's face when the message is delivered."

Inside Hakuun's head, Jack whispered, and Hakuun echoed to Grguch, "It can be arranged."

Grguch laughed even louder.

With a bellow of *"Kokto Gung Karuck,"* Grguch's orc force, a thousand strong and growing, began its march to the west, the clan of the Wolf Jaw taking the southern flank, Clan Karuck spearheading the main mass.

In the very front walked the zombie Oktule, holding a message for Obould.

* * * * *

They heard the resonating grumble of *"Kokto Gung Karuck,"* and from a high mountain ridge not far northeast of Mithral Hall, Drizzt, Bruenor, and the others saw the source of that sound, the march of Clan Karuck and its allies.

"It is Grguch," Tos'un told the group. "The conspirators are leading him to Obould."

"To fight him?" Bruenor asked.

"Or to convince him," said Tos'un.

Bruenor snorted at him, but Tos'un just looked at Drizzt and Hralien and shook his head, unwilling to concede the point.

"Obould has shown signs that he wishes to halt his march," Drizzt dared say.

"Tell it to the families of me boys who died at the wall a couple o' nights ago, elf," Bruenor growled.

"That was Grguch, perhaps," Drizzt offered, careful to add the equivocation.

"That was orcs," Bruenor shot back. "Orcs is orcs is orcs, and th' only thing they're good for is fertilizing the fields. Might that their rotting bodies'll help grow trees to cover the scars in yer Moonwood," he added, addressing Hralien, who blanched and rocked back on his heels.

"To cover the blood of Innovindil," Bruenor added, glaring at Drizzt.

But Drizzt didn't back from the stinging comment. "Information is both our weapon and our advantage," he said. "We would do well to learn more of this march, its purpose, and where it might turn next." He looked down and to the north, where the black swarm of Grguch's army was clear to see along the rocky hills. "Besides, our trails parallel anyway."

Bruenor waved his hand dismissively and turned away, Pwent following him back to the food spread out at the main encampment.

"We need to get closer to them," Drizzt told the remaining half a dozen. "We need to learn the truth of their march."

Regis took a deep breath as Drizzt finished, for he felt the weight of the task on his shoulders.

"The little one will be killed," Tos'un said to Drizzt, using the drow language, Low Drow, that only he and Drizzt understood.

Drizzt looked at him hard.

"They are warriors, fierce and alert," Tos'un explained.

"Regis is more than he seems," Drizzt replied in the same Underdark language.

"So is Grguch." As he finished, Tos'un glanced at Hralien, as if to invite Drizzt to speak to the elf for confirmation.

"Then I will go," said Drizzt.

"There is a better way," Tos'un replied. *"I know of one who can walk right in and speak with the conspirators."*

That gave Drizzt pause, an expression of doubt clouding his face and obvious to everyone nearby.

"Ye plannin' to tell us what ye're talking about?" Torgar said impatiently.

Drizzt looked at him then back at Tos'un. He nodded, to both.

After a brief private conversation with Cordio, Drizzt pulled Tos'un off to the side to join the priest.

"Ye sure?" Cordio asked Drizzt when they were alone. "Ye're just gonna have to kill him."

Tos'un tensed at the words, and Drizzt fought hard to keep the smile from his face.

"He might be full o' more information that we can coax out o' him," Cordio went on, playing his role perfectly. "Might be that a few tendays o' torture'll bring us answers about Obould."

"Or lies to stop the torture," Drizzt replied, but he ended the forthcoming debate with an upraised hand, for it didn't matter anyway. "I am sure," he said simply, and Cordio heaved an "oh-if-I-must" sigh, the perfect mix of disgust and resignation.

Cordio began to chant and slowly dance around the startled Tos'un. The dwarf cast a spell—a harmless dweomer that would have cured any diseases that Tos'un might have contracted, though of course, Tos'un didn't know that, and recognized only that the dwarf had sent some magical energy into his body. Another harmless spell followed, then a third, and with each casting, Cordio narrowed his eyes and sharpened his inflection just a bit more, making it all seem quite sinister.

"The arrow," the dwarf commanded, holding a hand out toward Drizzt though his intense stare never left Tos'un.

"What?" Drizzt asked, and Cordio snapped his fingers impatiently. Drizzt recovered quickly and drew an arrow from his magical quiver, handing it over as demanded.

Cordio held it up before his face and chanted. He waggled the fingers of his free hand over the missile's wicked tip. Then he moved it toward Tos'un, who shrank back but did not retreat. The dwarf lifted the arrow up to Tos'un's head then lowered it.

"The head, or the heart?" he asked, turning to Drizzt.

Drizzt looked at him curiously.

"Telled ye it was a good spell," Cordio lied. "Not that it'll much matter with that durned bow o' yers. Blast his head from his shoulders or take out half his chest? Yer choice."

"The head," said the amused drow. "No, the chest. Shoot center mass. . . ."

"Ye can't miss either way," the dwarf promised.

Tos'un stared hard at Drizzt.

"Cordio has placed an enchantment upon you," Drizzt explained as Cordio continued to chant and wave the arrow before Tos'un's slender chest. The dwarf ended by tapping the arrowhead against the drow, right over his heart.

"This arrow is now attuned to you," Drizzt said, taking the arrow from the dwarf. "If it is shot, it will find your heart, unerringly. You cannot dodge it. You cannot deflect it. You cannot block it."

Tos'un's look was skeptical.

"Show 'im, elf," Cordio said.

Drizzt hesitated for effect.

"We're shielded from the damned orcs," the priest insisted. "Show 'im."

Looking back at Tos'un, Drizzt still saw doubt, and that he could not allow. He drew Taulmaril from his shoulder, replaced the "enchanted" arrow in his quiver and took out a different one. As he set it, he turned and targeted, then let fly at a distant boulder.

The magical bolt split the air like a miniature lightning bolt, flashing fast and true. It cracked into the stone and blasted through with a sharp retort that had Regis and the other dwarves jumping with surprise. It left only a smoking hole in the stone where it had hit.

"The magic of the surface dwellers is strange and powerful, do not doubt," Drizzt warned his fellow drow.

"Ye ain't got a chest plate thick enough," Cordio added, and he tossed an exaggerated wink at Tos'un then turned with a great laugh and ambled away.

"What is this about?" Tos'un asked in the drow tongue.

"You wish to play the role of scout, so I will let you."

"But with the specter of death walking beside me."

"Of course," said Drizzt. *"Were it just me, I might trust you."*

Tos'un tilted his head, curious, trying to get a measure of Drizzt.

"Fool that I am," Drizzt added. *"But it is not just me, and if I am to entrust you with this, I need to ensure that my friends will not be harmed by my decision. You hinted that you can walk right into their camp."*

"The conspirators know that I am no friend of Obould's."

"Then I will allow you to prove your worth. Go and learn what you may. I will be near, bow in hand."

"To kill me if I deceive you."

"To ensure the safety of my friends."

Tos'un began to slowly shake his head.

"You will not go?" Drizzt asked.

"You need not do any of this, but I understand," Tos'un replied. *"I will go as I offered. You will come to know that I am not deceiving you."*

By the time the two dark elves got back to the rest of the group, Cordio had informed the others of what had transpired, and of the plan going forward. Bruenor stood with his hands on his hips, clearly unconvinced, but he merely gave a "harrumph" and turned away, letting Drizzt play out his game.

* * * * *

The two drow set off from the others after nightfall, moving through the shadows with silent ease. They picked their way toward the main orc encampment, dodging guards and smaller camps, and always with Tos'un several steps in the lead. Drizzt followed with Taulmaril in hand, the deadly "enchanted" arrow set on its string—at least, Drizzt hoped he had taken out the same arrow Cordio had played with, or that if he had not, Tos'un hadn't noticed.

As they neared the main group, crossing along the edge of a clearing that was centered by a large tree, Drizzt whispered for Tos'un to stop. Drizzt paused for a few heartbeats, hearing the rhythm of the night. He waved for Tos'un to follow out to the tree. Up Drizzt went, so gracefully that it seemed as if he had walked along a fallen log rather than up a vertical trunk. On the lowest branch, he paused and looked around then turned his attention on Tos'un below.

Drizzt dropped a sword belt, both of Tos'un's weapons sheathed.

You would trust me? the son of House Barrison Del'Armgo signaled up with his fingers, using the intricate silent language of the drow.

Drizzt's answer was simple, and reflected on his impassive expression. *I have nothing to lose. I care nothing for that sword—it destroys more than it helps. You will drop it and your other blade to the ground when you return to the tree, or I will retrieve it from the grasp of the dying orc who took it from you after I put an arrow through your heart.*

Tos'un stared at him long and hard, but had no retort against the simple and straightforward logic. He looked down at the sword belt, at the hilt of Khazid'hea, and truly he was glad to have the sword back in hand.

He disappeared into the darkness a moment later, and Drizzt could only hope that his guess regarding Tos'un's veracity had been correct. For there had been no spell, of course, Cordio's grand exhibition being no more than an elaborate ruse.

* * * * *

Tos'un was truly torn as he crossed the orc lines to the main encampment. Known by the Wolf Jaw orcs sprinkled among the Clan Karuck sentries, he had no trouble moving in, and found Dnark and Ung-thol easily enough.

"I have news," he told the pair.

Dnark and Ung-thol exchanged suspicious looks. "Then speak it," Ung-thol bade him.

"Not here." Tos'un glanced around, as if expecting to find spies behind every rock or tree. "It is too important."

Dnark studied him for a few moments. "Get Toogwik . . ." he started to say to Ung-thol, but Tos'un cut him short.

"No. For Dnark and Ung-thol alone."

"Regarding Obould."

"Perhaps," was all the drow would answer, and he turned and started away. With another look at each other, the two orcs followed him into the night, all the way back to the edge of the field where Drizzt Do'Urden waited in a tree.

"My friends are watching," Tos'un said, loudly enough for Drizzt, with his keen drow senses, to hear.

Drizzt tensed and drew back Taulmaril, wondering if he was about to be revealed.

Tos'un would die first, he decided.

"Your friends are dead," Dnark replied.

"Three are," said Tos'un.

"You have made others. I salute you."

Tos'un shook his head with disgust at the pathetic attempt at sarcasm, wondering why he had ever suffered such creatures to live.

"There is a sizable drow force beneath us," he explained, and the two orcs, predictably, blanched. "Watching us—watching you."

He let that hang there for a few heartbeats, watching the two shift uncomfortably.

"Before she died, Kaer'lic called to them, to Menzoberranzan, my home. There was glory and wealth to be found, she promised them, and that call from a priestess of Lady Lolth could not go unheeded. And so they have come, to watch and to wait, at first. You are advancing toward Obould."

"Ob—*King* Obould," Dnark corrected rather stiffly, "has summoned Chieftain Grguch to his side."

Tos'un wore a knowing grin. "The drow hold no love for Obould," he explained, and indeed, it seemed to Drizzt as if the orc chieftain relaxed a bit at that.

"You go to pay fealty? Or to wage war?"

The two orcs looked at each other again.

"King Obould summoned Clan Karuck, and so we go," Ung-thol said with clear determination.

"Grguch attacked the Moonwood," Tos'un replied. "Grguch attacked Mithral Hall. Without Obould's permission. He will not be pleased."

"Perhaps . . ." Dnark started.

"He will not be pleased at all," Tos'un interrupted. "You know this. It is why you brought Clan Karuck forth from their deep hole."

"Obould has no heart for the fight," Dnark said with a sudden sneer. "He has lost the words of Gruumsh. He would barter and . . ." He stopped and took a deep breath, and Ung-thol picked up the thought.

"Perhaps the presence of Grguch will inspire Obould and remind him of his duty to Gruumsh," the shaman said.

"It will not," said Tos'un. "And so my people watch and wait. If Obould wins, we will travel back to the lower Underdark. If Grguch prevails, perhaps there is cause for us to come forth."

"And if Obould and Grguch join together to sweep the northland?" Dnark asked.

Tos'un laughed at the preposterous statement.

Dnark laughed, too, after a moment.

"Obould has forgotten the will of Gruumsh," Dnark said bluntly. "He sent an emissary to parlay with the dwarves, to beg forgiveness for Grguch's attack."

Tos'un could not hide his surprise.

"An emissary who never arrived, of course," the orc chieftain explained.

"Of course. And so Grguch and Dnark will remind Obould?"

The orc didn't reply.

"You will kill Obould, and replace him with Grguch, for the will of Gruumsh?"

No answer again, but it was apparent from the posture and expressions of the two orcs that the last remark hit closer to the truth.

Tos'un smiled at them and nodded. "We will watch, Chieftain Dnark. And we will wait. And I will take great pleasure in witnessing the death of Obould Many-Arrows. And greater pleasure in taking the head of King Bruenor and crossing the River Surbrin to lay waste to the wider lands beyond."

The drow gave a curt bow and turned away. "We are watching," he warned as he started off. "All of it."

"Listen for the Horn of Karuck," Dnark said. "When you hear it blow, know that King Obould nears the end of his reign."

Tos'un didn't so much as offer a glance up at Drizzt as he crossed the clearing to the far side, but soon after the orcs had headed back to their encampment, the rogue drow returned to the base of the tree.

"Your belt," Drizzt whispered down, but Tos'un was already undoing it. He let it fall to the ground and stepped back.

Drizzt hopped down and retrieved it.

"You might have prepared them to say as much," Drizzt remarked.

"Ask the sword."

Drizzt looked down at Khazid'hea skeptically. "It is not to be trusted."

"Then demand of it," said Tos'un.

But Drizzt merely slung the sword belt over his shoulder, motioning for Tos'un to lead the way back to the waiting dwarves.

Whatever Tos'un's position, whether it was out of a change of heart or simple pragmatism, Drizzt had no reason to doubt what he had heard, and one statement in particular kept repeating in his thoughts, the orc's claim that Obould had "sent an emissary to parlay with the dwarves, to beg forgiveness for Grguch's attack."

Obould would not march. For the orc king, the war was at its end. But for many of his subjects, apparently, that was not so pleasing a thought.

CHAPTER

FOR THE GREATER GOOD

28

The scout pointed to a trio of rocky hills in the northwest, a few miles away. "Obould's flag flies atop the centermost," he explained to Grguch, Hakuun, and the others. "He has rallied his clan around him in a formidable defense."

Grguch nodded and stared toward his distant enemy. "How many?"

"Hundreds."

"Not thousands?" the chieftain asked.

"There are thousands south of his position, and thousands north," the scout explained. "They could close before us and shield King Obould."

"Or swing around and trap us," said Hakuun, but in a tone that showed he was not overly concerned—for Jack, answering that particular question through Hakuun's mouth, held little fear of being trapped by orcs.

"If they remain loyal to King Obould," Toogwik Tuk dared interject, and all eyes turned his way. "Many are angry at his decision to halt his march. They have come to know Grguch as a hero."

Dnark started as if to speak, but changed his mind. He had caught Grguch's attention, though, and when the fierce half-orc, half-ogre turned his gaze Dnark's way, Dnark said, "Do we even know that Obould intends to do battle? Or will he just posture and

347

paint with pretty words? Obould rules through wit and muscle. He will see the wisdom of coaxing Grguch."

"To build walls?" the chieftain of Clan Karuck said with a dismissive snicker.

"He will not march!" Toogwik Tuk insisted.

"He will speak enough words of war to create doubt," said Dnark.

"The only word I wish to hear from the coward Obould is 'mercy,' " Grguch stated. "It pleases me to hear a victim beg before he is put to my axe."

Dnark started to respond, but Grguch held up his hand, ending any further debate. With a scowl that promised only war, Grguch nodded to Hakuun, who commanded forth the grotesque zombie of Oktule, still holding its head before it.

"This is our parlay," Grguch said. He swung his gaze out to the side, where the battered Nukkels hung by his ankles from poles suspended across the broad shoulders of a pair of ogres. "And our advanced emissary," Grguch added with a wicked grin.

He took up his dragon-fashioned axe and stalked toward Nukkels, who was too beaten and dazed to even register his approach. Nukkels did see the axe, though, at the last moment, and he gave a pathetic yelp as Grguch swung it across, cleanly severing the rope and dropping Nukkels on his head to the ground.

Grguch reached down and hoisted the shaman to his feet. "Go to Obould," he ordered, turning Nukkels around and shoving him toward the northwest so ferociously that the poor orc went flying headlong to the ground. "Go and tell Obould the Coward to listen for the sound of *Kokto Gung Karuck.*"

Nukkels staggered back to his feet and stumbled along, desperate to be away from the brutal Karuck orcs.

"Tell Obould the Coward that Grguch has come and that Gruumsh is not pleased," Grguch shouted after him, and cheers began to filter through all of the onlookers. "I will accept his surrender . . . perhaps."

That sent the Karuck orcs and ogres into a frenzy, and even Toogwik Tuk beamed in anticipation. Dnark, though, looked at Ung-thol.

This conspiracy had been laid bare, to the ultimate fruition. This was real, suddenly, and this was war.

* * * * *

"Grguch comes with many tribes in his wake," Obould said to General Dukka. "To parlay?"

He and Obould's other commanders stood on the centermost of the three rocky hills. The foundations of a small keep lined the ground behind the orc leader, and three low walls of piled stones ringed the hill. The other two hills were similarly outfitted, though the defenses were hardly complete. Obould looked over his shoulder and motioned to his attendants, who brought forth the battered, nearly dead Nukkels.

"He's already spoken, it would seem," the orc king remarked.

"Then it will be war within your kingdom," the general replied, and his doubts were evident for all to hear.

Doubts offered for his benefit, Obould recognized. He didn't blink as he stared at Dukka, though others around him gasped and whispered.

"They are well-supported at their center," Dukka explained. "The battle will be fierce and long."

They are well-supported indeed, Obould thought but did not say.

He offered a slight nod of appreciation to Dukka, for he read easily enough between Dukka's words. The general had just warned him that Grguch's fame had preceded him, and that many in Obould's ranks had grown restless. There was no doubt that Obould commanded the superior forces. He could send orcs ten-to-one against the march of Clan Karuck and its allies. But with the choice laid bare before them, how many of those orcs would carry the banner of Obould, and how many would decide that Grguch was the better choice?

But there was no question among those on the three hills, Obould understood, for there stood Clan Many-Arrows, his people, his slavish disciples, who would follow him into Lady Alustriel's own bedroom if he so commanded.

"How many thousands will die?" he asked Dukka quietly.

"And will not the dwarves come forth when the opportunity is seen?" the general bluntly replied, and again Obould nodded, for he could not disagree.

A part of Obould did want to reach out and throttle Dukka for the assessment and for the lack of complete obedience and loyalty, but he knew in his heart that Dukka was right. If Dukka's force, more than two thousand strong, joined battle on the side of Clan Karuck and her allies, the fight could well shift before first blood was spilled.

Obould and his clan would be overwhelmed in short order.

"Hold my flank from the orcs who are not Karuck," Obould asked of his general. "Let Gruumsh decide which of us, Obould or Grguch, is more worthy to lead the kingdom forward."

"Grguch is strong with Gruumsh, so they say," Dukka warned, and a cloud crossed over Obould's face. But Dukka broke a smile before that cloud could become a full scowl. "You have chosen wisely, and for the good of the Kingdom of Many-Arrows. Grguch is strong with Gruumsh, it is said, but Obould protects the minions of the One-eye."

"Grguch is strong," the orc king said, and he brought his great-sword from its scabbard strapped diagonally across his back. "But Obould is stronger. You will learn."

General Dukka eyed that sword for a long while, recalling the many occasions when he had seen it put to devastating use. Gradually, he began to nod then to grin.

"Your flanks will be secure," he promised his king. "And any fodder prodded before Grguch's clan will be swept clean before they reach the hill. Clan Karuck alone will press the center."

* * * * *

"Ye lost yer wits, ye durned orc-brained, pointy-eared elf!" Bruenor bellowed and stomped the ground in frustration. "I come out here to kill the beast!"

"Tos'un speaks the truth."

"I ain't for trusting drow elfs, exceptin' yerself!"

"Then trust me, for I overheard much of his conversation with the orc conspirators. Obould dispatched an emissary to Mithral Hall to forbid the attack."

"Ye don't know what Tos'un told them orcs to say afore they got out to ye."

"True enough," Drizzt conceded, "but I suspected that which Tos'un reports long before I ever caught up to him. Obould's pause has run too long."

"He attacked me wall! And the Moonwood. Are ye so quick in forgetting Innovindil?"

The accusation rocked Drizzt back on his heels, and he winced, profoundly stung. For he had not forgotten Innovindil, not at all. He could still hear her sweet voice all around him, coaxing him to explore his innermost thoughts and feelings, coaching him on what it was to be an elf. Innovindil had given to him a great and wondrous gift, and in that gift, Drizzt Do'Urden had found himself, his heart and his course. With her lessons, offered in the purest friendship, Innovindil had solidified the sand beneath Drizzt' Do'Urden's feet, which had been shifting unsteadily for so many years.

He hadn't forgotten Innovindil. He could see her. He could smell her. He could hear her voice and the song of her spirit.

But her demise was not the work of Obould, he was certain. That terrible loss was the consequence of the *absence* of Obould, a prelude to the chaos that would ensue if that new threat, the beast Grguch, assumed command of Obould's vast and savage army.

"What are ye askin' me for, elf?" Bruenor said after the long and uncomfortable pause.

"It wasn't Gauntlgrym."

Bruenor locked his gaze, unblinking.

"But it was beautiful, was it not?" Drizzt asked. "A testament—"

"An abomination," Bruenor interrupted.

"Was it? Would Dagna and Dagnabbit think it so? Would Shoudra?"

"Ye ask me to dishonor them!"

"I ask you to honor them with the most uncommon courage, will and vision. In all the recorded and violent histories of all the races, there are few who could claim such."

Bruenor tightened his grip on his many-notched axe and lifted it before him.

"No one doubts the courage of King Bruenor Battlehammer," Drizzt assured the dwarf. "Any who witnessed your stand against the tide of orcs on the retreat into Mithral Hall places you among the legends of dwarf warriors, and rightly so. But I seek in you the courage *not* to fight."

"Ye're bats, elf, and I knowed ye'd be nothing but trouble when I first laid eyes on ye on the side o' Kelvin's Cairn."

Drizzt drew out Twinkle and Icingdeath and tapped them on either side of Bruenor's axe.

"I'll be watchin' the fight afore us," Bruenor promised. "And when I find me place in it, don't ye be blocking me axe, where'er it's aimed."

Drizzt snapped his scimitars away and bowed before Bruenor. "You are my king. My counsel has been given. My blades are ready."

Bruenor nodded and started to turn away, but stopped abruptly and swiveled his head back at Drizzt, a sly look in his eye. "And if ye send yer durned cat to pin me down, elf, I'll be cooking kitty, don't ye doubt."

Bruenor stomped away and Drizzt looked back at the probable battlefield, where the distant lines of orcs were converging. He pulled the onyx figurine from his belt pouch and summoned Guenhwyvar to his side, confident that the fight would ensue long before the panther began to tire.

Besides, he needed the surety of Guenhwyvar, the nonjudgmental companionship. For as he had asked for courage from Bruenor, so Drizzt had demanded it of himself. He thought of Tarathiel and Shoudra and all the others, dead now because of the march of Obould, dead at Obould's own hand. He thought of Innovindil, always he thought of Innovindil, and of Sunset, and he knew that he would carry that pain with him for the rest of his life. And though he could logically remove that last atrocity from the bloody hands of Obould, would any of it have happened in the Moonwood, in Mithral Hall, in Shallows and Nesmé, and all throughout the Silver Marches, had not Obould come forth with designs of conquest?

And yet, there he was, asking for uncommon courage from Bruenor, betting on Tos'un, and gambling with all the world, it seemed.

He brought his hand down to stroke Guenhwyvar's sleek black coat, and the panther sat down then collapsed onto her belly, her tongue hanging out between her formidable fangs.

"If I am wrong, Guenhwyvar, my friend, and to my ultimate loss, then I ask of you this one thing: dig your claws deep into the flesh of

King Obould of the orcs. Leave him in agony upon the ground, dying of mortal wounds."

Guenhwyvar gave a lazy growl and rolled to her side, calling for a scratching on her ribs.

But Drizzt knew that she had understood every word, and that she, above all others, would not let him down.

CHAPTER
DWARVEN KING, DWARVEN ARROW

29

Shingles and Torgar stood quietly, staring at Bruenor, letting him lead without question, while an eager Pwent hopped around them. Cordio kept his eyes closed, praying to Moradin—and to Clangeddin, for he understood that the road to battle was clear. For Hralien, there showed only grim determination, and beside him, the bound Tos'un matched that intensity. Regis shifted from foot to foot nervously. And Drizzt, who had just delivered the assessment that battle was soon to be joined, and that the time had come for them to either leave or engage, waited patiently.

All focus fell to Bruenor, and the weight of that responsibility showed clearly on the face of the agitated dwarf. He had brought them there, and on his word they would either flee to safety or leap into the jaws of a tremendous battle—a battle they could not hope to win, or likely even survive, but one that they might, if their gods blessed them, influence.

* * * * *

To the south, Obould saw Dukka's force rolling forward like a dark cloud, streaming toward a line of orcs moving west to flank the hills. The clan of the Wolf Jaw, he knew, and he nodded and growled softly, imagining all the horrors he would inflict upon Dnark when his business with Grguch was over.

Confident that General Dukka would keep Wolf Jaw at bay, Obould focused his gaze directly to the east, where rising dust showed the approach of a powerful force, and yellow banners shot with red proclaimed Clan Karuck. The orc king closed his eyes and fell within his thoughts, imagining again his great kingdom, full of walls and castles, and teeming cities of orcs living under the sun and sharing fully in the bounty of the world.

Kna's shriek brought him from his quiet meditation, and as soon as he opened his eyes, Obould understood her distress.

An orc approached, a zombie orc, holding its head plaintively in its hands before it. Before any of his warriors and guards could react, Obould leaped the low wall before him and charged down, drawing his greatsword as he went. A single swing cleaved the zombie in half and sent the head flying.

So it was, the orc king knew as he executed the swing. Grguch had stated his intent and Obould had answered. There was no more to be said.

Not so far to the east, a great horn blared.

* * * * *

From over the very next ridge came the sound of a skirmish, orc against orc.

"Obould and Grguch," Tos'un stated.

In the distance to the northeast, a great horn, *Kokto Gung Karuck*, sounded.

"Grguch," Drizzt agreed.

Bruenor snorted. "I can't be asking any o' ye to come with me," he started.

"Bah, but just ye try to stop us," said Torgar, with Shingles nodding beside him.

"I would travel to the Abyss itself for a try at Obould," Hralien added.

Beside him, Tos'un shook his head.

"Obould's to be found on them hills," Bruenor said, waving his axe in the general direction of the trio of rocky mounds they had determined to be Obould's main encampment. "And I'm meaning to get there. Right through, one charge, like an arrow shot from me girl's bow. I'm not for knowing how many I'll be leavin' in me wake. I'm not for knowin' how I'm getting back out after I kill the dog. And I'm not for caring."

Torgar slapped the long handle of his greataxe across his open palm, and Shingles banged his hammer against his shield.

"We'll get ye there," Torgar promised.

The sounds of battle grew louder, some close and some distant. The great horn blew again, its echoes vibrating the stones beneath their feet.

Bruenor nodded and turned to the next ridge, but hesitated and glanced back, focusing his gaze on Tos'un. "Me elf friend told me that ye done nothing worth killin' ye over," he said. "And Hralien's agreeing. Get ye gone, and don't ye e'er give me a reason to regret me choice."

Tos'un held his hands out wide. "I have no weapons."

"There'll be plenty for ye to find in our wake, but don't ye be following too close," Bruenor replied.

With a helpless look to Drizzt, then to all the others, Tos'un gave a bow and walked back the way they had come. *"Grguch is your nightmare, now,"* he called to Drizzt, in the drow tongue.

"What's that?" Bruenor asked, but Drizzt only smiled and walked over to Hralien.

"I'll be moving fast beside Bruenor," the drow explained, handing Tos'un's weapon belt over. "If any are to escape this, it will be you. Beware this sword. Keep it safe." He glanced over at Regis, clearly nervous. "This will not unravel the way we had intended. Our run will be frantic and furious, and had we known the lay of the land and the orc forces, Bruenor and I would have come out—"

"Alone, of course," finished the elf.

"Keep the sword safe," Drizzt said again, though he looked not at Khazid'hea, but at Regis as he spoke, a message all too clear for Hralien.

"And live to tell our tale," the drow finished, and he and Hralien clasped hands.

"Come on, then!" Bruenor called.

He scraped his boots in the dirt to clear them of mud, and adjusted his one-horned helmet and his foaming mug shield. He started off at a brisk walk, but Thibbledorf Pwent rushed up beside him, and past him, and swept Bruenor up in his eagerness.

They were in full charge before they crested the ridge.

They found the fighting to the west of them, back toward Obould's line, but there were orcs aplenty right below, running eagerly to battle—so eagerly that Pwent had already lowered his head spike before the nearest one turned to regard the intruders.

That orc's scream became a sudden gasp as the helmet spike prodded through its chest, and a lip-flapping head wag from Pwent sent the mortally wounded creature flying aside. The next two braced for the charge, ready to dive aside, but Pwent lifted his head and leaped at them, spiked gauntlets punching every which way.

* * * * *

Drizzt and Bruenor veered to the right, where orc reinforcements rushed past the trees and the stones. Torgar and Shingles ran straight ahead off their wake, following Pwent in his attempt to punch through this thin flank and toward the main engagement, which was still far to the north.

With his long strides, Drizzt moved ahead of Bruenor. He lifted Taulmaril, holding the bow horizontal before his chest, for the orcs were close enough and plentiful enough that he didn't even need to aim. His first shot took one in the chest and blasted it backward and to the ground. His second went through another orc so cleanly that the creature hardly jerked, and Drizzt thought for a moment that he had somehow missed—he even braced for a counter.

But blood poured forth, chest and back, and the creature died where it stood, too fast for it to even realize that it should fall over.

"Bend right!" Bruenor roared, and Drizzt did, sidestepping as the dwarf charged past him, barreling into the next group of orcs, shield bashing and axe flying left, right, and center.

With a single fluid movement, Drizzt shouldered the bow and drew forth his scimitars, and went in right behind Bruenor. Dwarf and drow found themselves outnumbered three to one in short order.

The orcs never had a chance.

* * * * *

Regis didn't argue as Hralien pulled him to the side, still well behind the other six and moving from cover to cover.

"Protect me," the elf bade as he put up his longbow and began streaming arrows at the plentiful orcs.

His little mace in hand, Regis was in no position to argue—though he suspected that Drizzt had arranged it for his protection. For Hralien, Regis knew, was the one Drizzt most expected to escape the insanity.

His anger at the drow for pushing him to the side of the fight lasted only the moment it took Regis to view the fury of the engagement. To the right, Pwent spun, punched, butted, kicked, kneed, and elbowed with abandon, knocking orcs aside with every twist and turn.

But they were orcs of Wolf Jaw, warriors all, and not all of the blood on the battlerager was from an orc.

Back-to-back behind him, Torgar and Shingles worked with a precision wrought of years of experience, a harmony of devastating axe-work the pair had perfected in a century of fighting together as part of Mirabar's vaunted watch. Every routine ended with a step—either left or right, it didn't seem to matter—as each dwarf behind moved in perfect complement to keep the defense complete.

"Spear, down!" Torgar yelled.

He ducked, unable to deflect the missile. It flew over his head, apparently to crack through the back of Shingles's skull, but hearing the warning, old Shingles threw his shield up behind his head at the last instant, turning the crude spear aside.

Shingles had to fall away as the orc before him seized the opening.

But of course there was no opening, as Shingles rolled out to the side and Torgar came in behind him with a two-handed slash that disemboweled the surprised creature.

Two orcs took its place and Torgar got stabbed in the upper arm—which only made him madder, of course.

Regis swallowed hard and shook his head, certain that if he'd followed the charge, he'd already have been dead. He nearly fainted as he saw an orc, stone axe high for a killing blow, close in on Shingles, an angle that neither dwarf could possibly block.

But the orc fell away, an arrow deep in its throat.

That startled Regis from his shock, and he looked up to Hralien, who had already set another arrow and swiveled back the other way.

For there Bruenor and Drizzt worked their magic, as only they could. Drizzt's scimitars spun in a blur, too quick for Regis to follow their movements, which he measured instead by the angles of the orcs falling away from the furious drow. What Bruenor couldn't match in finesse, he made up for with sheer ferocity, and it occurred to Regis that if Thibbledorf Pwent and Drizzt Do'Urden collided with enough force to meld them into a single warrior, the result would be Bruenor Battlehammer.

The dwarf sang as he cut, kicked, and bashed. Unlike the other trio, who seemed stuck in a morass and tangle of orcs, Drizzt and Bruenor kept moving across and to the north, chopping and slashing and dancing away. At one point, a group of orcs formed in their path, and it seemed as if they would be stopped.

But Hralien's arrows broke the integrity of the orc line, and a flying black panther crashed into the surprised creatures, scattering them and sending them flying.

Drizzt and Bruenor ran by, breaking clear of the conflict.

At first, that thought panicked Regis. Shouldn't the two turn back to help Pwent and the others? And shouldn't he and Hralien hurry to keep up?

He looked at the elf and realized it wasn't about them, any of them. It was about Bruenor getting to Obould, about Bruenor killing Obould.

Whatever the cost.

* * * * *

Cordio wanted to keep up with Bruenor, to protect his beloved king at all costs, but the priest could not pace the fiery dwarf and his drow companion, and once he noted the harmony of their movements, attacks and charges, he recognized that he would likely only get in their way.

He turned for the dwarf trio instead, angling to get into the melee near to Torgar, whose right arm drooped low from a nasty stab.

Still fighting fiercely, the Mirabarran dwarf nevertheless grunted his approval as Cordio reached toward him, sending waves of magical healing energy into him. When Torgar turned to note his appreciation more directly, he saw that Cordio's help hadn't come without cost, for the priest had sacrificed his own position against one particularly large and nasty orc for the opportunity to help Torgar. Cordio bent low under the weight of a rain of blows against his fine shield.

"Pwent!" Torgar roared, motioning for the priest as the battlerager turned his way.

"For Moradin!" came Pwent's roar and he disengaged from the pair he was battering and charged headlong for Cordio.

The two orcs gave close chase, but Torgar and Shingles intercepted and drove them aside.

By the time Pwent reached Cordio, the priest was back to an even stance against the orc. No novice to battle, Cordio Muffinhead had covered himself with defensive enchantments and had brought the strength of his gods into his arms, swinging his flail with powerful strokes.

That didn't slow Pwent, of course, who rushed past the startled priest and leaped at the orc.

The orc's sword screeched against Pwent's wondrous armor, but it hardly bit through before Pwent slammed against the orc and began to thrash, the ridges on his plate mail tearing apart the orc's leather jerkin and slicing into its flesh beneath. With a howl of pain, the orc tried to disengage, but a sudden left and right hook from Pwent's spiked gauntlets held it in place like harvest corn.

Cordio used the opportunity to cast some healing magic into the battlerager, though he knew that Pwent wouldn't feel any difference. Pwent didn't really seem to feel pain.

* * * * *

The back of the small clearing dipped even lower, down into a dell full of boulders and a few scraggly tree skeletons. Drizzt and Bruenor rushed through, leaving their fighting companions behind, and with his longer strides, Drizzt took the lead.

Their goal was to avoid battle while they closed the ground to the trio of rocky hills and King Obould. As they came up the far side of the dell, they saw the orc king, picking him out from the flames engulfing his magical greatsword.

An ogre tumbled away from him then he shifted back and stabbed up over his shoulder, skewering another ten-foot behemoth. With strength beyond all reason, Obould used his sword to pull that ogre right over his shoulder and send it spinning down the side of the hillock.

All around him the battle raged, as Clan Karuck and Clan Many-Arrows fought for supremacy.

And in truth, with Obould and his minions holding the high ground, it didn't seem as if it would be much of a fight.

But then a fireball exploded, intense and powerful, right behind the highest wall on the hill to Obould's left, the northernmost of the three, and all of the Many-Arrows archers concealed there flailed about, immolated by the magical flames. They shrieked and they died, curling up on the ground in blackened, smoking husks.

Clan Karuck warriors swarmed over the stones.

"What in the Nine Hells . . . ?" Bruenor asked Drizzt. "Since when are them orcs throwing fireballs?"

Drizzt had no answer, other than to reinforce his feelings about the entire situation, simply by stating, "Grguch."

"Bah!" Bruenor snorted, so predictably, and the pair ran on.

* * * * *

"Keep to the high ground," Hralien instructed Regis as he led the halfling along to the east. They pulled up amidst a boulder tumble, beside a single maple tree, Hralien sighting targets and lifting his bow.

"We have to go and join them!" Regis cried, for the four dwarves moved out of sight over the near ridge of the dell.

"No time!"

Regis wanted to argue, but the frantic hum of Hralien's bowstring, the elf firing off arrow after arrow, denied him his voice. More orcs swarmed along before them from the east, and a darker cloud had formed in the west as a vast army began its approach.

Regis cast a plaintive gaze to the north, where Drizzt and Bruenor had gone, where Cordio, Pwent, and the others had run. He believed that he would never see his friends again. Drizzt had done it, he knew. Drizzt had put him with Hralien, knowing that the elf would likely find a way out, where there could be no retreat for Drizzt and Bruenor.

Bitterness filled the back of Regis's throat. He felt betrayed and abandoned. In the end, when the circumstances had grown darkest, he had been set aside. Logically he could understand it all—he was, after all, no hero. He couldn't fight like Bruenor, Drizzt, and Pwent. And with so many orcs around, there really wasn't any way for him to hide and strike from points of opportunity.

But that did little to calm the sting.

He nearly jumped out of his boots when a form rose up beside him, an orc springing from concealment. Purely on instinct, Regis squealed and shouldered the thing, knocking it off-balance just enough so that its stab at Hralien only grazed the distracted archer.

Hralien turned fast, smashing his bow across the orc's face. The bow flew free as the orc tumbled, Hralien going for his sword.

Regis lifted his mace to finish the orc first, except that as he retracted his arm for the strike, something grabbed him and yanked that arm back viciously. He felt his shoulder pop out of joint. His hand went numb as his mace fell away. He managed to half turn then to duck, bringing his other arm up over his head defensively as he noted the descent of a stone hammer.

A blinding explosion spread over the back of his head, and he had no idea of whether his legs had buckled or simply been driven straight into the ground as he fell face-down in the stony dirt. He felt a soft boot come in tight against his ear and heard Hralien battling above him.

He tried to put his hands under him, but one arm would not move to his call, and the attempt sent waves of nauseating agony through him. He managed to lift his head, just a bit, and tasted the blood streaming down from the back of his skull as he half-turned to try to get his bearings.

He was back on the ground again, though he knew not how. Cold fingers reached up at him, as if from the ground itself. He had his eyes open, but the darkness crept in from the edges.

The last thing he heard was his own ragged breathing.

* * * * *

Orc armor proved no match for the fine elven sword as Hralien slid the blade deep into the chest of the newest attacker, who held a stone hammer wet with Regis's blood.

The elf slashed out to the side, finishing the first one, who stubbornly tried to regain its footing, then spun to meet the charge of a third creature coming in around the tree. His sword flashed across, turning the orc's spear in against the bark and knocking the creature off balance. The tree alone stopped it from falling aside, but that proved an unfortunate thing for the orc, as Hralien leaped out to the side and stabbed back in, catching the creature through the armpit.

It shrieked and went into a frenzy, spinning and stumbling away, grabbing at the vicious wound.

Hralien let it go, turning back to Regis, who lay so very still on the cold ground. More orcs had spotted him, he knew. He had no time. He grabbed the halfling as gently as he could and slid him down into a depression at the base of the maple, between two large roots. He kicked dirt and twigs and leaves, anything he could find to disguise the poor halfling. Then, for the sake of the fallen Regis, Hralien grabbed up his bow and sprang away, running again to the east.

Orcs closed on him from behind and below. More rose up before him, running at an angle to prevent him from going over the ridge to the south.

Hralien dropped his second sword belt, the one Drizzt had given him, and threw aside his bow, needing to be nimble.

He charged ahead, desperate to put as much ground between himself and Regis as possible, in the faint hope that the orcs would not find the wounded halfling. The run lasted only a few strides, though, as Hralien skidded to a stop, turning frantically to bring his sword around to deflect a flying spear. Swords came in at him from every angle, orcs closing for the kill. Hralien felt the hot blood of his elders coursing through his veins. All the lessons he had learned in two centuries of life flooded through him, driving him on. There was no thought, only instinct and reaction, his shining sword darting to block, angling to turn a spear and stabbing ahead to force an attacker into a short retreat.

Beautiful was his dance, magnificent his turns, and lightning-quick his thrusts and ripostes.

But there were too many—too many for him to even consider them separately as he tried to find some answer to the riddle of the battle.

Images of Innovindil flitted through his mind, along with those others he had lost so recently. He took hope in the fact that they had gone before him, that they would greet him in Arvandor when a single missed block let a sword or a spear slip through.

Behind him, back the way he had come, Regis sank deeper into the cold darkness. And not so far away, perhaps halfway to the tree, a black hand closed over Khazid'hea's hilt.

* * * * *

They had intended to follow in the wake of Bruenor and Drizzt, but the four dwarves found the route blocked by a wall of orcs. They came out of the dell to the east instead, and there, too, they met resistance.

"For Mirabar and Mithral Hall!" Torgar Hammerstriker called, and shoulder to shoulder with his beloved and longtime friend Shingles, the leader of the Mirabarran exodus met the orcs.

To the side of them, Thibbledorf Pwent snarled and bit and found within himself yet another frenzy. Flailing his arms and legs, and butting his head so often that his forward movements seemed the steps of a gawky, long-necked seabird, Pwent had the orcs on that side of the line in complete disarray. They threw spears at him, but so intent were they on getting out of his way that they threw as they turned, and thus with little or no effect.

It couldn't hold, though. Too many orcs stood before them, and they would have to pile the orc bodies as thick as the walls of a dwarf-built keep before they could even hope to find a way through.

Bruenor and Drizzt were lost to them, as was any route that would get them back to the south and the safety of Mithral Hall. So they did what dwarves do best, they fought to gain the highest ground.

Cordio wanted to tap some offensive magic, to stun the orcs with a blast of shocking air, perhaps, or to hold a group in place so that Torgar and Shingles could score quick kills. But blood flowed freely from all the dwarves in short order, and the priest could not keep up with the wounds, though his every spell cast was one of healing. Cordio was filled with Moradin's blessing, a priest of extraordinary power and piety. It occurred to him, though, that Moradin himself was not possessed of enough magical healing to win that fight. They were known, the clear spectacle of the most-hated enemy in the midst of the orcs, and behind the immediate fighting, the ugly creatures stalked all around them, preparing to overwhelm them.

Not a dwarf was afraid, though. They sang to Moradin and Clangeddin and Dumathoin. They sang of bar wenches and heavy mugs of ale, of killing orcs and giants, of chasing dwarf ladies.

And Cordio led a song to King Bruenor, of the fall of Shimmergloom and the reclamation of Mithral Hall.

They sang and they fought. They killed and they bled, and they looked continually to the north, where Bruenor their king had gone.

For all that mattered was that they had served him well that day, that they had given him enough time and enough of a distraction to get to the hills and to end, once and for all, the threat of Obould.

* * * * *

Hralien felt the sting of a sword across his forearm, and though the wound was not deep, it was telling. He was slowing, and the orcs had caught on to the rhythms of his dance.

He had nowhere to run.

An orc to his right came on suddenly, he thought, and he spun to meet the charge—then saw that it was no charge at all, for the tip of a sword protruded from the falling creature's chest.

Behind the orc, Tos'un Armgo retracted Khazid'hea and leaped out to the side. An orc lifted its shield to block, but the sword went right through the shield, right through the arm, and right through the side of the creature's chest.

Before it had even fallen away, another orc fell to Tos'un's second weapon, an orc-made sword.

Hralien had no time to watch the spectacle or to even consider the insanity of it all. He spun back and took down the nearest orc, who seemed dumbfounded by the arrival of the drow. On the elves pressed, light and dark, and orcs fell away, or threw their weapons and ran away, and soon the pair faced off, Hralien drawing a few much-needed deep breaths.

"Clan Wolf Jaw," Tos'un explained to Hralien. "They fear me."

"With good reason," Hralien replied.

The sound of battle to the north, and the sound of dwarf voices lifted in song, stole their conversation, and before Tos'un could begin to clarify, he found that he did not have to, for Hralien led their run down from the ridgeline.

CHAPTER

It had to come down to the two of them, for among the orcs, struggles within and among tribes were ultimately personal.

King Obould leaped atop a stone wall and plunged his sword into the belly of a Karuck ogre. He stared the behemoth in the face, grinning wickedly as he called upon his enchanted sword to burst into flame.

The ogre tried to scream. Its mouth stretched wide in silent horror.

Obould only smiled wider and held his sword perfectly still, not wanting to hurry the death of the ogre. Gradually, the dimwitted behemoth leaned back, back, then slid off the blade, tumbling down the hill, wisps of smoke coming from the already cauterized wound.

Looking past it, Obould saw one of his guards, an elite Many-Arrows warrior, go flying aside, broken and torn. Tracing its flight back to the source, he saw another of his warriors, a young orc who had shown great promise in the battles with the Battlehammer dwarves, leap back. The warrior stood still for a curiously long time, his arms out wide.

Obould stared at his back, shaking his head, not understanding, until a huge axe swept up from in front of the warrior, then cut down diagonally with tremendous, jolting force, cleaving the warrior in half, left shoulder to right hip. Half the orc fell away, but the other half stood there for a few long heartbeats before buckling to the ground.

And there stood Grguch, swinging his awful axe easily at the end of one arm.

Their eyes met, and all the other orcs and ogres nearby, Karuck and Many-Arrows alike, took their battles to the side.

Obould stretched his arms out wide, fires leaping from the blade of his greatsword as he held it aloft in his right hand. He threw back his head and bellowed.

Grguch did likewise, axe out wide, his roar echoing across the stones, the challenge accepted. Up the hill he ran, hoisting his axe in both hands and bringing it back over his left shoulder.

Obould tried for the quick kill, feigning a defensive posture, but then leaping down at the approaching chieftain and stabbing straight ahead. Across came Grguch's axe with brutal and sudden efficiency, the half-ogre chopping short to smash his dragon-winged weapon against Obould's blade. He turned it sidelong as he swiped, the winged blades perpendicular to the ground, but so strong was the beast that the resistance as he brought the axe across didn't slow his swing in the least. By doing it that way, his blade obscuring nearly three feet top-to-bottom, Grguch prevented Obould from turning his greatsword over the block.

Obould just let his sword get knocked out to his left, and instead of letting go with his right hand, as would be expected, the cunning orc let go with his left, allowing him to spin in behind the cut of Grguch's axe. He went forward as he went around, lowering his soon-leading left shoulder as he collided with Grguch.

The pair slid down the stony hill, and to Obould's amazement, Grguch did not fall. Grguch met his heavy charge with equal strength.

He was taller than Obould by several inches, but Obould had been blessed by Gruumsh, had been given the strength of the bull, a might of arm that had allowed him to bowl over Gerti Orelsdottr of the frost giants.

But not Grguch.

The two struggled, their weapon arms, Obould's right and Grguch's left, locked at one side. Obould slugged Grguch hard in the face, snapping his head back, but as he recoiled from that stinging blow, Grguch snapped his head forward, inside the next punch, and crunched his forehead into Obould's nose.

They clutched, they twisted, and they postured, and both tried to shove back at the same time, sending themselves skidding far apart.

Right back they went with identical blows, axe and sword meeting with tremendous force, so powerfully that a gout of flames flew free of Obould's sword and burst into the air.

* * * * *

"As Tos'un told us," Drizzt said to Bruenor as they slipped between fights to come in view of the great struggle.

"Think they'd forget each other and turn on us, elf?" Bruenor asked hopefully.

"Likely not—not Obould, at least," Drizzt replied dryly, stealing Bruenor's mirth, and he led the dwarf around a pile of stones that hadn't yet been set on the walls.

"Bah! Ye're bats!"

"Two futures clear before us," Drizzt remarked. "What does Moradin say to Bruenor?"

Before Bruenor could answer, as Drizzt came around the pile, a pair of orcs leaped at him. He snapped up both his blades and threw himself backward, quickstepping across Bruenor's field of vision and dragging the bloodthirsty orcs with him.

The dwarf's axe came crashing down, and then there was one.

And that orc twisted and half-turned, startled by Bruenor and never imagining that Drizzt could be nimble enough to reverse his field so quickly.

The orc got hit four times by Drizzt's scimitars, and Bruenor creased its skull for good measure, and the pair rambled along.

Before them, much closer, Obould and Grguch clutched again, and traded a series of brutal punches that splattered blood from both faces.

"Two roads before us," Drizzt said, and he looked at Bruenor earnestly.

The dwarf shrugged then tapped his axe against Drizzt's scimitars. "For the good o' the world, elf," he said. "For the kids o' me kin and me trust for me friends. And ye're still bats."

* * * * *

Every swing brought enough force to score a kill, every cut cracked through the air. They were orcs, one half ogre, but they fought as giants, titans even, gods among their respective people.

Bred for battle, trained in battle, hardened as his skin had calloused, and propped by magical spells from Hakuun, and secretly from Jack the Gnome, Grguch moved his heavy axe with the speed and precision with which a Calimport assassin might wield a dagger. None in Clan Karuck, not the largest and the strongest, questioned Grguch's leadership role, for none in that clan would dare oppose him. With good reason, Obould understood all too quickly, as the chieftain pressed him ferociously.

Blessed by Gruumsh, infused with the strength of a chosen being, and veteran of so many battles, Obould equaled his opponent, muscle for muscle. And unlike so many power-driven warriors who could smash a weapon right through an opponent's defenses, Obould combined finesse and speed with that sheer strength. He had matched blades with Drizzt Do'Urden, and overmatched Wulfgar with brawn. And so he met Grguch's heavy strikes with powerful blocks, and so he similarly pressed Grguch with mighty counterstrikes that made the chieftain's arms strain to hold back the deadly greatsword.

Grguch rushed around to Obould's left, up the hill a short expanse. He turned back from that higher ground and drove a tremendous overhand chop down at the orc king, and Obould nearly buckled under the weight of the blow, his feet sliding back dangerously beneath him.

Grguch struck again, and a third time, but Obould went out to the side suddenly, and that third chop cut nothing but air, forcing Grguch down the hill a few quick steps.

They stood even again, and with the miss, Obould gained an offensive posture. Both hands grasping his sword, he smashed it in from the right then the left then right again. Grguch moved to a solely defensive posture, axe darting left and right to block.

Obould quickened the pace, slashing with abandon, allowing Grguch no chance for a counter. He brought forth fire on his blade then winked it out with a thought—and brought it forth again, just to command more of his opponent's attention, to further occupy Grguch.

Left and right came the greatsword, then three overhead chops, battering Grguch's blocking blade, sending shivers through the chieftain's muscled arms. Obould did not tire, and more furious came his strikes, backing his opponent.

Grguch was no longer looking for an opening to counter, Obould knew. Grguch tried only to find a way to disengage, to put them back on even ground.

Obould wouldn't give it to him. The chieftain was worthy, indeed, but in the end, he was no Obould.

A blinding flash and a thunderous retort broke the orc king's momentum and rhythm, and as he recovered from the initial, stunning shock of it, he realized that he had lost more than advantage. His legs twitched and could hardly hold him upright. His greatsword trembled violently and his teeth chattered so uncontrollably that he tore strips of skin from the inside of his mouth.

A wizard's lightning bolt, he understood somewhere deep in the recesses of his dazed mind, and a mighty one.

His block of Grguch's next attack was purely coincidental, his greatsword fortunately in the way of the swing. Or maybe Grguch had aimed for the weapon, Obould realized as he staggered back from the weight of the blow, fighting to hold his balance with every stumbling, disoriented step.

He offered a better attempt to block the next sidelong swing, turning to the left and presenting his sword at a perfect angle to intercept the flying axe.

A perfect parry, except that Obould's twitching legs gave out under the weight of the blow. He skidded half-backward and half-sidelong down the hill and went down to one knee.

Grguch hit his sword again, knocking it aside, and as the chieftain stepped forward, bringing his blade back yet again, Obould realized that he had little defense.

A booted foot stomped hard on the back of Obould's neck, driving him low, and he tried to turn and lash out at what he deemed to be a new attacker.

But Bruenor Battlehammer's target was not Obould, and he had used the battered and dazed orc king merely as a springboard to launch himself at his real quarry.

Grguch twisted frantically to get his axe in line with the dwarf's

weapon, but Bruenor, too, turned as he flew, and his buckler, embla-
zoned with the foaming mug of Clan Battlehammer, crashed hard
into Grguch's face, knocking him back.

Grguch leaped up and came right back at Bruenor with a mighty
chop, but Bruenor rushed ahead under the blow, butting his one-
horned helmet into Grguch's belly and sweeping his axe up between
the orc chieftain's legs. Grguch leaped, and Bruenor grabbed and leaped
back and over with him, the pair flying away and tumbling down the
hill. As they unwound, Grguch, caught with his back to the dwarf,
rushed away and shoulder-rolled over the hill's lowest stone wall.

Bruenor pursued furiously, springing atop the wall, then leaping
from it, swooping down from on high with a mighty chop that sent
the blocking Grguch staggering backward.

The dwarf pressed, axe and shield, and it took Grguch many steps
before he could begin to attain even footing with his newest enemy.

Back on the hill, Obould stubbornly gained his feet and tried to
follow, but another crackling lightning bolt flattened him.

* * * * *

Hralien darted out in front as the pair crossed the narrow channel.
He leaped a stone, started right, then rolled back left around the trunk
of a dead tree, coming around face up against an unfortunate orc,
whose sword was still angled the other way to intercept his charge. The
elf struck hard and true, and the orc fell away, mortally wounded.

Hralien retracted the blade as he ran past the falling creature,
which left his sword arm out behind him.

As his sword pulled free, a sudden sting broke the elf's grasp on
it, and he glanced back in shock to see Tos'un flipping the blade over
between his two swords. With amazing dexterity, the drow slid his
own sword into its sheath and caught Hralien's flipping weapon by
the hilt.

"Treacherous dog!" Hralien protested as the dark elf moved in
behind him, prodding him along.

"Just shut up and run," Tos'un scolded him.

Hralien stopped, though, and the tip of Khazid'hea nicked him.
Tos'un's hand came against his back then, and shoved him roughly
forward.

"Run!" he demanded.

Hralien stumbled forward and Tos'un didn't let him dig in, keeping up and pushing him along with every stride.

* * * * *

Drizzt hated breaking away from Bruenor with both the orc leaders so close, but the magic-using orc, nestled in a mixed copse of evergreen and deciduous trees to the east of Obould's defenses, demanded his attention. Having lived and fought beside the wizards of the drow school Sorcere, who were skilled in the tactics of wizardry combined with sword-fighters, Drizzt understood the danger of those thunderous, blinding lightning bolts.

And there was something more, some nagging suspicion in Drizzt's thoughts. How had the orcs taken Innovindil and Sunset from the sky? That puzzle had nagged at Drizzt since Hralien had delivered the news of their fall. Did he have his answer?

The wizard wasn't alone, for he had set other orcs, large Karuck half-ogre orcs, around the perimeter of the copse. One of them confronted Drizzt as he reached the tree line, leaping forward with a growl and a thrusting spear.

But Drizzt had no time for such nonsense, and he shifted, throwing himself to the left, and brought both of his scimitars down and back to the right, double-striking the spear and driving it harmlessly aside. Drizzt continued right past the off-balance spear-wielder, lifting Twinkle expertly to slash a line across the orc's throat.

As that one fell away, though, two more charged at the drow, from left and right, and the commotion also drew the attention of the wizard, still some thirty feet away.

Drizzt pasted an expression of fear on his face, for the benefit of the wizard, then darted out to the right, quick-stepping to intercept the charging orc. He turned as they came together, rolling right around and to the left, tilting his shoulders out of horizontal as he turned so that his sweeping blades lifted the orc's sword up high.

Drizzt sprinted right for the trunk of a nearby tree, both orcs closing. He ran up it and leaped off, threw his head and shoulders back, and tucked into a tight somersault. He landed lightly, exploding into a barrage of whirling blades, and one orc fell away, the other running off to the side.

Drizzt came out from behind the tree as he pursued, to see the orc wizard waggling his fingers in spellcasting, aiming his way.

It was exactly as Drizzt had planned, for the surprise on the wizard orc's face was both genuine and delicious as Guenhwyvar crashed in from the side, bearing the creature to the ground.

* * * * *

"For the lives of your dwarven friends," Tos'un explained, pushing the stubborn elf forward. The surprising words diminished Hralien's resistance, and he did not fight against the shift when the flat of Tos'un's blade turned him, angling him more directly to the east.

"The Wolf Jaw standard," Tos'un explained to the elf. "Chieftain Dnark and his priest."

"But the dwarves are in trouble!" Hralien protested, for not far away, Pwent and Torgar and the others fought furiously against an orc force thrice their number.

"To the head of the serpent!" Tos'un insisted, and Hralien could not disagree.

He began to understand as they passed several orcs, who glanced at the dark elf deferentially and did not try to intercept them.

They sprinted around some boulders and broken ground, down past a cluster of thick pines and across a short expanse to the heart of Dnark's army. Tos'un spotted the chieftain immediately, Toogwik Tuk and Ung-thol at his side as expected.

"A present for Dnark," the drow called at the stunned expressions, and he pushed Hralien harder, nearly toppling the elf.

Dnark waved some guards toward Hralien to take the elf from Tos'un.

"General Dukka and his thousands approach," Dnark called to the drow. "But we will not fight until it is settled between the chieftains."

"Obould and Grguch," Tos'un agreed, and as the orc guards approached, he went past Hralien.

"Left hip," the dark elf whispered as he crossed past Hralien, and he brushed close enough for the surface elf to feel the hilt of his own belted sword.

Tos'un paused and nodded at both the orcs, drawing their attention and giving Hralien ample time to draw forth the blade. And so Hralien did, and even as the orc guards noted it and called out in protest, the flash of elven steel left them dead.

Tos'un stumbled away from Hralien, stumbled toward Dnark's group, looking back and scrambling as if fleeing the murderous elf. He turned fully as he put his feet under him, and saw that Toogwik Tuk had begun spellcasting, with Dnark directing other orcs toward Hralien.

"Back to the elf and finish him!" Dnark protested as Tos'un continued his flight. "Dukka is coming and we must prepare . . ."

But Dnark's voice trailed off as he finished, as he came to realize that Tos'un, that treacherous drow, wasn't running away from the elf, but was, in fact, charging at him.

Standing at Dnark's left, Toogwik Tuk gasped as Khazid'hea rudely interrupted his spellcasting, biting deep into his chest. To Chieftain Dnark's credit, he managed to get his shield up to block Tos'un's other blade as it came in at him. He couldn't anticipate the power of Khazid'hea, though, for instead of yanking the blade out of Toogwik Tuk's chest, Tos'un just drove it across, the impossibly fine edge of the sword known as Cutter slicing through bone and muscle as easily as if it were parting water. The blade came across just under Dnark's shoulder, and before the chieftain even realized the attack enough to spin away, his left arm was taken, falling free to the ground.

Dnark howled and dropped his weapon, reaching across to grab at the blood spurting from his stumped shoulder. He fell back and to the ground, thrashing and roaring empty threats.

But Tos'un wasn't even listening, turning to strike at the nearest orcs. Not Ung-thol, though, for the shaman ran away, taking a large portion of Dnark's elite group with him.

"The dwarves!" Hralien called to the drow, and Tos'un followed the Moonwood elf. He forced back his nearest attackers with a blinding, stabbing routine, then angled away, turning back toward Hralien, who had already swung around in full charge toward the dell in the west.

* * * * *

Bruenor rolled his shield forward, picking off a swing, then advanced, turning his shoulders and rolling his axe at the dodging Grguch. He swung his shield arm up to deflect the next attack, and swiped his axe across underneath it, forcing Grguch to suck in his gut and throw back his hips.

On came the dwarf, pounding away with his shield, slashing wildly with his axe. He had the much larger half-ogre off balance, and knew from the craftsmanship and sheer size of Grguch's axe that he would do well to keep it that way!

The song of Moradin poured from his lips. He swung across and reversed in a mighty backhand, nearly scoring a hit, then charged forward, shield leading. That is why he had been returned to his people, Bruenor knew in his heart. That was the moment when Moradin needed him, when Clan Battlehammer needed him.

He threw out the confusion of the lost city and its riddles, of Drizzt's surprising guesses. None of that mattered—it was he and that newest, fiercest foe, battling to the death, old enemies locked in mortal combat. It was the way of Moradin and the way of Gruumsh, or at least, it was the way it had always been.

Light steps propelled the dwarf, spinning, advancing and retreating out of every swing and every block with perfect balance, using his speed to keep his larger, stronger foe slightly off balance.

Every time Grguch tried to wind up for a mighty stroke of that magnificent axe, Bruenor moved out of range, or came in too close, or too far to the same side as the retracted weapon, shortening Grguch's strike and stealing much of its power.

And always Bruenor's axe slashed at the orc. Always, the dwarf had Grguch twisting and dodging, and cursing.

Like sweet music to Bruenor's ears did those orc curses sound.

In utter frustration, Grguch leaped back and roared in protest, bringing his axe up high. Bruenor knew better than to pursue, dropping one foot back instead, then rushing back and to the side, under the branch of a leafless maple.

Grguch, too outraged by the frustrating dwarf to hold back, rushed forward and swung with all his might anyway—and the dragon-axe crashed right through that thick limb, splintering its base and driving it back at the dwarf. Bruenor threw up his shield at the last second, but the weight of the limb sent him staggering backward.

By the time he recovered, Grguch was there, roaring still, his axe cutting a line for Bruenor's skull.

Bruenor ducked and threw up his shield, and the axe hit it solidly—too solidly! The foaming mug shield, that most recognizable of Mithral Hall's artifacts, split in half, and below it, the bone in Bruenor's arm cracked, the weight of the blow driving the dwarf to his knees.

Agony burned through Bruenor's body, and white flashes filled his vision.

But Moradin was on his lips, and Moradin was in his heart, and he scrambled forward, slashing his axe with all his might, forcing Grguch before him in his frenzy.

* * * * *

Pwent, Torgar, and Shingles formed a triangle around Cordio. The priest directed their movements, mostly coordinating Shingles and Torgar with the wild leaps and surges of the unbridled fury that was Thibbledorf Pwent. Pwent had never viewed battle in terms of defensive formations. To his credit, though, the wild-eyed battlerager did not completely compromise the integrity of their defensive stand, and the bodies of dead orcs began to pile up around them.

But more took the places of the fallen—many more, an endless stream. As weapon arms drooped from simple weariness, the three frontline dwarves took more and more hits, and Cordio's spells of healing came nearly constant from his lips, depleting his magical energies.

They couldn't keep it up for much longer, all three knew, and even Pwent suspected that it would be their last, glorious stand.

The orc immediately before Torgar rushed forward suddenly. The Mirabarran dwarf turned the long handle of his axe at the last moment to deflect the creature aside, and only when it started to fall away did Torgar recognize that it was already mortally wounded, blood pouring from a deep wound in its back.

As the dwarf turned to face any other nearby orcs, he saw the way before him cleared of enemies, saw Hralien and Tos'un fighting side by side. They backed as Torgar shifted to his right, moving beside Shingles, and the defensive triangle became two, two and one, and with an apparent escape route open to the east. Hralien and Tos'un started that flight, Cordio bringing the others in behind.

But they became bogged down before they had ever really started, as more and more orcs joined the fray—orcs thirsty for vengeance for their fallen chieftain, and orcs simply thirsty for the taste of dwarf and elf blood.

* * * * *

The panther's claws raked the fallen orc's body, but Jack's wards held strong and Guenhwyvar did little real damage. Even as Guenhwyvar thrashed, Hakuun began to mouth the words of a spell as Jack took control.

Guenhwyvar understood well the power of wizards and priests, though, and the panther clamped her jaws over the orc's face, pressing and twisting. Still the wizard's defensive wards held, diminishing the effect. But Hakuun began to feel the pain, and knowing that the magical shields were being torn asunder, the orc panicked.

That mattered little to Jack, safe within Hakuun's head. Wise old Jack was worldly enough to recognize Guenhwyvar for what she was. In the shelter of Hakuun's thick skull, Jack calmly went about his task. He reached into the Weave of magical energy, found the nearby loose ends of enchanting emanations, and tied them together, filling the area with countering magical force.

Hakuun screamed as panther claws tore through his leather tunic and raked lines of blood along his shoulder. The cat retracted her huge maw, opened wide and snapped back at his face, and Hakuun screamed louder, certain that the wards were gone and that the panther would crush his skull to dust.

But that head dissipated as the panther bit down, and gray mist replaced the dispelled Guenhwyvar.

Hakuun lay there, trembling. He felt some of the magical wards being renewed about his disheveled frame.

Get up, you idiot! Jack screamed in his thoughts.

The orc shaman rolled to his side and up to one knee. He struggled to stand then stumbled away and back to the ground as a shower of sparks exploded beside him, a heavy punch knocking him backward.

He collected his wits and looked back in surprise to see the drow lifting a bow his way.

A second lightning-arrow streaked in, exploding, throwing him backward. But inside of Hakuun, Jack was already casting, and while the shaman struggled, one of his hands reached out, answering the drow's third shot with a bolt of white-hot lightning.

When his blindness cleared, Hakuun saw that his enemy was gone. Destroyed to a smoking husk, he hoped, but only briefly, as another arrow came in at him from a different angle.

Again Jack answered with a blast of his own, followed by a series of stinging magical missiles that weaved through the trees to strike at the drow.

Dual voices invaded Hakuun's head, as Jack prepared another evocation and Hakuun cast a spell of healing upon himself. He had just finished mending the panther's fleshy tear when the stubborn drow hit him with another arrow.

He felt the magical wards flicker dangerously.

"Kill him!" Hakuun begged Jack, for he understood that one of those deadly arrows, maybe the very next one, was going to get through.

* * * * *

They had fought minor skirmishes, as anticipated, but nothing more, as word arrived along the line that Grguch and Obould had met in battle. Never one to play his hand fully, General Dukka moved his forces deliberately and with minimal risk. However things turned out, he intended to remain in power.

The Wolf Jaw orcs gave ground to Dukka's thousands, rolling down the channel on Obould's southern flank like floodwaters.

Always ready for a fight, Dukka stayed near the front, and so he was not far away when he heard a cry from the south, along the higher ridge, and when he heard the sound of battle to the north-east, and to the north, where he knew Obould to be. Lightning flashes filled the air up there, and Dukka could only imagine the carnage.

* * * * *

His arm ached and hung practically useless, and Bruenor understood that if he lost his momentum, he would meet a quick and unpleasant end. So he didn't relent. He drove on and on, slashing away with his many-notched axe, driving the oversized orc before him.

The orc could hardly keep up, and Bruenor scored minor hits, clipping him across one hand and nicking his thigh as he spun away.

The dwarf could win. He knew he could.

But the orc began calling out, and Bruenor understood enough Orcish to understand that he called for help. Not just orc help, either, the dwarf saw, as a pair of ogres moved over at the side of his vision, lifting heavy weapons.

Bruenor couldn't hope to win against all three. He thought to drive the orc leader back before him, then break off and head back the other way—perhaps Drizzt was finished with the troublesome wizard.

But the dwarf shook his head stubbornly. He had come to win against Obould, of course, until his dark-skinned friend had shown him another way. He had never expected to return to Mithral Hall, had guessed from the start that his reprieve from Moradin's halls had been temporary, and for a single purpose.

That purpose stood before him in the form of one of the largest and ugliest orcs he had ever had the displeasure to lay eyes on.

So Bruenor ignored the ogres and pressed his attack with even more fury. He would die, and so be it, but that bestial orc would fall before him.

His axe pounded with wild abandon, cracking against the blocking weapon of his opponent. He drew a deep line in one of the heads on Grguch's axe then nearly cracked through the weapon's handle when the orc brought it up horizontally to intercept a cut.

Bruenor had intended that cut to be the coup de grace, though, and he winced at the block, expecting that his time was over, that the ogres would finish him. He heard them off to the side, stalking in, growling . . . screaming.

Before him, the orc roared in protest, and Bruenor managed to glance back as he wound up for another strike.

One of the ogres had fallen away, its leg cleaved off at the hip. The other had turned away from Bruenor, to battle King Obould.

"Bah! Haha!" Bruenor howled at the absurdity of it all, and he brought the axe in at the same chopping downward angle, but more to his right, more to his opponent's left. The orc shifted appropriately and blocked, and Bruenor did it again, and again more to his right.

The orc decided to change the dynamics, and instead of just presenting the horizontal handle to block, he angled it down to his left. Since Bruenor was already leaning that way, there was no way for him to avoid the rightward slide.

The huge orc howled, advantage gained.

* * * * *

The orc had dispelled Guenhwyvar! From its back, claws and fangs digging at it, the orc had sent Drizzt's feline companion back to the Astral Plane.

At least, that's what the stunned drow prayed had happened, for when he had finished with the pair of orcs at the trees, he had come in sight just in time to watch his friend dissolve into smoky nothingness.

And that orc, so surprising, so unusual for one of the brutish race, had taken the hits of Drizzt's arrows, and had met his barrage with lightning-bolt retorts that had left Drizzt dazed and wounded.

Drizzt continued to circle, firing as he found opportunities between the trees. Every shot hit the mark, but every arrow was stopped just short, exploding into multicolored sparks.

And every arrow was met with a magical response, lightning and insidious magic missiles, from which Drizzt could not hide.

He went into the thickness of some evergreens, only to find other orcs already within. Bow in hand instead of his scimitars, and still dazed from the magical assaults, Drizzt had no intention of joining combat at that difficult moment, and so he cut to his right, back away from the magic-using orc, and ran out of the copse.

And just in time, for without regard to its orc comrades, the wizard dropped a fireball on those trees, a tremendous blast that instantly consumed the copse and everyone within.

Drizzt continued his run farther to the side before turning back at the orc. He dropped Taulmaril and drew forth his blades, and he thought of Guenhwyvar, and called out plaintively for his lost cat.

In sight of the wizard again, Drizzt dived behind a tree.

A lightning bolt split it down the middle before him, opening the ground to the orc wizard again, stealing Drizzt's protective wall, and so he ran on, to the side again.

"I won't run out of magic, foolish drow!" the orc called—and in High Drow, with perfect inflection!

That unnerved Drizzt almost as much as the magical barrage, but Drizzt accepted his role, and suspected that Bruenor was no less hard-pressed.

He swung out away from the orc wizard then veered around, finding a direct path to his enemy that would take him under a widespread maple and right beside another cluster of evergreens.

He roared and charged. He saw a tell-tale movement beside him, and grinned as he recognized it.

Drizzt reached inside himself as the wizard began casting, and summoned a globe of absolute darkness before him, between him and the mage.

Into the darkness went Drizzt. To his right, the evergreens rustled, as if he had cut fast and leaped out that way.

* * * * *

Dull pain and cold darkness filled Regis's head. He was far from consciousness, and sliding farther with every passing heartbeat. He knew not where he was, or what had put him there, in a deep and dark hole.

Somewhere, distantly, he felt a heavy thud against his back, and the jolt sent lines of searing pain into the halfling.

He groaned then simply let it all go.

The sensation of flying filled him, as if he had broken free of his mortal coil and was floating . . . floating.

* * * * *

"Not so clever, drow," Jack said through Hakuun's mouth as they both noted the movement in the limbs of the evergreens. A slight turn had the fiery pea released from Jack's spell lofting out that way, and an instant later, those evergreens exploded into flames, with, Jack and Hakuun both presumed, the troublesome drow inside.

But Drizzt had not gone out to his right. That had been Guenhwyvar, re-summoned from the Astral Plane by his call, heeding his quiet commands to serve her role as diversion. Guenhwyvar had gone across right behind Drizzt to leap into the evergreens, while Drizzt had tumbled headlong, gaining momentum, into the darkness.

In there, he had leaped straight up, finding the maple's lowest branch.

"Be gone, Guen," he whispered as he ran along that branch, feeling the heat of the flames to his side. "Please be gone," he begged as he came out of the blackness, bearing down on the wizard, who was still looking at the evergreens, still apparently oblivious to Drizzt.

The drow came off the branch in a leaping somersault, landing lightly in a roll before the orc, who nearly jumped out of his boots and threw his hands up defensively. As Drizzt came out of that roll, he sprang and rolled again, going right past the orc, right over the orc's shoulder as he turned back upright.

Anger drove him, memories of Innovindil. He told himself that he had solved the riddle, that that creature had been the cause.

Fury driving his arms, he slashed back behind him and down with Icingdeath as he landed, and felt the blade slash hard through the orc's leather tunic and bite deeply into flesh. Drizzt skidded to an abrupt stop and pirouetted, slashing hard with Twinkle, gashing the back-bending orc across the shoulder blades. Drizzt stepped back toward him, moving around him on the other side, and cut Twinkle down hard across the creature's exposed throat, driving it to the ground on its back.

He moved for the kill, but stopped short, realizing that he needn't bother. A growl from over by the burning pines showed him that Guenhwyvar hadn't heeded his call to be gone, but neither had the panther, so swift and clever, been caught in the blast.

Relief flooded through Drizzt, but with the diversion, he didn't take notice of a small winged snake slithering out of the dead orc's ear.

* * * * *

Bruenor's axe slid down hard to the side, and Bruenor stumbled that way. He saw the huge orc's face twist in glee, in the belief of victory.

R.A. SALVATORE

But that was exactly the look he had hoped for.

For Bruenor was not stumbling, and had forced the angled block for that very reason, to disengage his axe quickly and down to the side, far to the right of his target. In his stumble, Bruenor was really just re-setting his stance, and he spun away from the orc, daring to turn his back on it for a brief moment.

In that spin, Bruenor sent his axe in a roundabout swing at the end of his arm, and the orc, readying a killing strike, could not redirect his heavy two-bladed axe in time.

Bruenor whirled around, his axe flying out wide to the right, setting himself in a widespread stance, ready to meet any attack.

None came, for his axe had torn the orc's belly as it had come around, and the creature crumbled backward, holding its heavy axe in its right hand, but clutching at its spilling entrails with its left.

Bruenor stalked forward and began battering it once more. The orc managed to block a blow, then a second, but the third slipped past and gashed its forearm, tearing its hand clear of its belly.

Guts spilled out. The orc howled and tried to back away.

But a flaming sword swept in over Bruenor's one-horned helmet and cut Grguch's misshapen head apart.

* * * * *

Guenhwyvar's roar saved him, for Drizzt glanced back at the last moment, and ducked aside just in time to avoid the brunt of the winged snake's murderous lightning strike. Still the bolt clipped the drow, and lifted him into the air, flipping him over more than a complete rotation, so that he landed hard on his side.

He bounced right back up, though, and the winged snake dropped to the ground and darted for the trees.

But the curved edge of a scimitar hooked under it and flipped it into the air, where Drizzt's other blade slashed against it.

Against it, but not through it, for a magical ward prevented the cut—though the force of the blade surely bent the serpent over it!

Undeterred, for that mystery within a mystery somehow confirmed to Drizzt his suspicions about Innovindil's fall, the drow growled and pushed on. Whether his guess was accurate or not hardly mattered, for Drizzt transformed that rage into blinding, furious action. He flipped the serpent again, then went into a frenzy, slashing left, right, left, right, over and over again, holding the serpent aloft by the sheer speed and precision of his repeated hits. He didn't slow, he didn't breathe, he simply battered away with abandon.

The creature flapped its wings, and Drizzt scored a hit at last, cutting up and nearly severing one where it met the serpent's body.

Again the drow went into a fury, slashing back and forth, and he ended by turning one blade around the torn snake. He fell into a short run and turn behind that strike and used his scimitar to fling the snake out far.

In mid-air, the snake transformed, becoming a gnome as it hit the ground in a roll, turning as it came up and slamming its back hard against a tree.

Drizzt relaxed, convinced that the tree was the only thing holding the surprising creature upright.

"You summoned . . . the panther . . . back," the gnome said, his voice weak and fading.

Drizzt didn't reply.

"Brilliant diversion," the gnome congratulated.

A curious expression came over the diminutive creature, and it held up one trembling hand. Blood poured from out of his robe's voluminous sleeve, though it did not stain the material—material that showed not a tear from the drow's assault.

"Hmm," the gnome said, and looked down, and so did Drizzt, to see more blood pouring out from under the hem of the robe, pooling on the ground between the little fellow's boots.

"Good garment," the gnome noted. "Know you a mage worthy?"

Drizzt looked at him curiously.

Jack the Gnome shrugged. His left arm fell off then, sliding out of his garment, the tiny piece of remaining skin that attached it to his shoulder tearing free under the dead weight.

Jack looked at it, Drizzt looked at it, and they looked at each other again.

And Jack shrugged. And Jack fell face down. And Jack the Gnome was dead.

CHAPTER

GARUMN`S GORGE

31

Bruenor tried to stand straight, but the pain of his broken arm had him constantly twitching and lowering his left shoulder. Directly across from him, King Obould stared hard, the fingers of his hand kneading the hilt of his gigantic sword. Gradually that blade inched down toward the ground, and Obould dismissed its magical flames.

"Well, what of it, then?" Bruenor asked, feeling the eyes of orcs boring into him from all around.

Obould let his gaze sweep across the crowd, holding them all at bay. "You came to me," he reminded the dwarf.

"I heared ye wanted to talk, so I come to talk."

Obould's expression showed him to be less than convinced. He glanced up the hill, motioning to Nukkels the priest, the emissary, who had never made it near to Bruenor's court.

Bruenor, too, looked up at the battered shaman, and the dwarf's eyes widened indeed when Nukkels was joined by another orc, dressed in decorated military garb, who carried a bundle of great interest to Bruenor. The two orcs walked down to stand beside their king, and the second, General Dukka, dropped his cargo, a bloody and limp halfling, at Obould's feet.

All around them, the orcs stirred, expecting the fight to erupt anew.

But Obould silenced them with an upraised hand, as he looked

Bruenor in the eye. Before him, Regis stirred, and Obould reached down and with surprising gentleness, lifted the halfling to his feet.

Regis could not stand on his own, though, his knees buckling. But Obould held him upright and motioned to Nukkels. Immediately, the shaman cast a spell of healing over the halfling, and though it only marginally helped, it was enough for Regis to stand at least. Obould pushed him toward Bruenor, but again, without any evident malice.

"Grguch is dead," Obould proclaimed to all around, ending as he locked stares with Bruenor. "Grguch's path is not the way."

Beside Obould, General Dukka stood firm and nodded, and Bruenor and Obould both understood that the orc king had all the support he needed, and more.

"What are you wantin', orc?" Bruenor asked, and he held his hand up as he finished, looking past Obould.

Many orcs turned, Obould, Dukka, and Nukkels included, to see Drizzt Do'Urden standing calmly, Taulmaril in hand, arrow resting at ease on its string, and with Guenhwyvar beside him.

"What are ye wanting?" Bruenor asked again as Obould turned back.

The dwarf already knew, of course, and the answer was one that filled him with both hope and dread.

Not that he was in any position to bargain.

* * * * *

"It won't make her more than a surcoat, elf," Bruenor said as Drizzt folded up the fabulous garment of Jack the Gnome, wrapping it over a few rings and other trinkets he had taken from the body.

"Give it to Rumblebelly," said Bruenor, and he propped Regis up a bit more, for the halfling leaned on him heavily.

"A wizard's . . . robe," the still-groggy Regis slurred. "Not for me."

"Not for me girl, neither," Bruenor declared.

But Drizzt only smiled and tucked the fairly won gains into his pack.

Somewhere in the east, fighting erupted again, a reminder to them all that not everything was settled quite yet, with remnants of Clan Karuck still to be rooted out. The distant battle sounds also reminded them that their friends were still out there, and though Obould, after conferring with Dukka, had assured them that four dwarves, an elf, and a drow had gone back over the southern ridge when Dukka's force had sent Wolf Jaw running, the relief of the companions showed clearly on their faces when they came in sight of the bedraggled, battered, and bloody sextet.

Cordio and Shingles ran to take Regis off of Bruenor's hands, while Pwent fell all over himself, hopping around Bruenor with unbridled glee.

"Thought ye was sure'n dead," Torgar said. "Thought we were suren dead, to boot. But them orcs held back and let us run south. I'm not for knowin' why."

Bruenor looked at Drizzt then at Torgar and the others. "Not sure that I'm knowin' why, meself," he said, and he shook his head helplessly, as if none of it made any sense to him. "Just get me home. Get us all home, and we'll figure it out."

It sounded good, of course, except that one of the group had no home to speak of, none in the area, at least. Drizzt stepped past Bruenor and the others and motioned for Tos'un and Hralien to join him off to the side.

Back with the others, Cordio tended to Bruenor's broken arm, which of course had Bruenor cursing him profusely, while Torgar and Shingles tried to figure out the best way to repair the king's broken shield, an artifact that could not be left in two pieces.

"Is it in your heart, or in your mind?" Drizzt asked his fellow drow when the three of them were far enough away.

"Your change, I mean," Drizzt explained when Tos'un did not immediately answer. "This new demeanor you wear, these possibilities you see before you—are they in your heart, or in your mind? Are they born of feelings, or is it pragmatism that guides your actions?"

"He was dismissed and running free," Hralien said. "Yet he came back to save me, perhaps to save us all."

Drizzt nodded his acceptance of that fact, but it didn't change his posture as he continued to stare at Tos'un.

"I do not know," Tos'un admitted. "I prefer the elves of the Moonwood to Obould's orcs. That much I can tell you. And I will not go against the Moonwood elves, on my word."

"The word of a drow," Drizzt remarked, and Hralien snorted at the absurdity of the statement, given the speaker.

Drizzt held his hand out, and motioned toward the sentient sword belted on Tos'un's hip. With only a moment's hesitation, Tos'un drew the blade and handed it over.

"I cannot allow him to keep it," Drizzt explained to Hralien.

"It is Catti-brie's sword," the elf agreed, but Drizzt shook his head.

"It is a corrupting, evil, sentient being," Drizzt said. "It will feed the doubts of Tos'un and play into his fears, hoping to incite him to spill blood." To Hralien's surprise, Drizzt handed it over to him. "Nor does Catti-brie wish it returned to Mithral Hall. Take it to the Moonwood, I beg, for your wizards and priests are better able to deal with such weapons."

"Tos'un will be there," Hralien warned, and he glanced at the wandering drow and nodded, and relief showed clearly on Tos'un's face.

"Perhaps your wizards and priests will be better able to discern the heart and mind of the dark elf, too," said Drizzt. "If trust is gained then return the sword to him. It is a choice beyond my judgment."

"Elf! Ye done jabberin'?" Bruenor called. "I'm wanting to go see me girl."

Drizzt looked to Hralien and Tos'un in turn. "Indeed," he offered. "Let us all go home."

* * * * *

The wind howled out its singular, mournful note, a constant blow that sounded to Wulfgar of home.

He stood on the northeastern slopes of Kelvin's Cairn, not far below the remnants of the high ridge once known as Bruenor's Climb, looking out over the vast tundra, where the snows had receded once more.

Slanting light crossed the flat ground, the last rays of day sparkling in the many puddles dotting the landscape.

Wulfgar stayed there, unmoving, as the last lights faded, as the stars began to twinkle overhead, and his heart leaped again when a distant campfire appeared out in the north.

His people.

His heart was full. This was his place, his home, the land where he would build his legacy. He would assume his rightful place among the Tribe of the Elk, would take a wife and live as his father, his grandfather, and all of his ancestors had lived. The simplicity of it, the lack of the deceitful trappings of civilization, welcomed him, heart and soul.

His heart was full.

The son of Beornegar had come home.

* * * * *

The dwarven hall in the great chamber known as Garumn's Gorge, with its gently arcing stone bridge and the new statue of Shimmergloom the shadow dragon, ridden to the bottom of the gorge to its death by heroic King Bruenor, had never looked so wondrous. Torches burned throughout the hall, lining the gorge and the bridge, their firelight changing through the spectrum of colors due to the enchantments of Lady Alustriel's wizards.

On the western side of the gorge before the bridge stood hundreds of Battlehammer dwarves, all dressed in their full, shining armor, pennants flying, spear tips gleaming in the magical light. Across from them stood a contingent of orc warriors, not nearly as well-outfitted, but standing with equal discipline and pride.

Dwarf masons had constructed a platform at the center of the long bridge, and on it had built a three-tiered fountain. Nanfoodle's alchemy and Alustriel's wizards had done their work there, as well, for the water danced to the sound of haunting music, its flowing streams glowing brightly and changing colors.

Before the fountain, on a mosaic of intricate tiles fashioned to herald that very day, stood a mithral podium, and on it rested a pile of identical parchments, pinned by weights sculpted into the form of a dwarf, an elf, a human, and an orc. The bottom paper of that pile had been sealed atop the podium, to remain there throughout the coming decades.

Bruenor stepped out from his line and walked the ten strides to the podium. He looked back to his friends and kin, to Banak in his chair, sitting impassive and unconvinced, but unwilling to argue with Bruenor's decision. He matched stares with Regis, who solemnly nodded, as did Cordio. Beside the priest, Thibbledorf Pwent was too distracted to return Bruenor's look. The battle-rager, as clean as anyone in the hall had ever seen him, swiveled his head around, sizing up any threats that might materialize from the strange gathering—or maybe, Bruenor thought with a grin, looking for Alustriel's dwarf friend, Fret, who had forced a bath upon Pwent.

To the side lay Guenhwyvar, majestic and eternal, and beside her stood Drizzt, calm and smiling, his mithral shirt, his belted weapons, and Taulmaril over his shoulder, reminding Bruenor that no dwarf had ever known a better champion. In looking at him, Bruenor was amazed yet again at how much he had come to love and trust that dark elf.

Just as much, Bruenor knew, as his gaze slipped past Drizzt to Catti-brie, his beloved daughter, Drizzt's wife. Never had she looked as beautiful to Bruenor as she did just then, never more sure of herself and comfortable in her place. She wore her auburn hair up high on one side, hanging loosely on the other, and it caught the light of the fountain, reflected off the rich, silken colors of her blouse, the garment of the gnome wizard. It had been a full robe on the gnome, of course, but it reached only to mid-thigh on Catti-brie, and while the sleeves had nearly covered the gnome's hands, they flared halfway down Catti-brie's delicate forearms. She wore a dark blue dress under the blouse, a gift from Lady Alustriel, her new tutor—working through Nanfoodle—that reached to her knees and matched exactly the blue trim of her blouse. High boots of black leather completed the outfit, and seemed so appropriate for Catti-brie, as they were both delicate and sturdy all at once.

Bruenor chuckled, recalling so many images of Catti-brie covered in dirt and in the blood of her enemies, dressed in simple breeches and tunic, and fighting in the mud. Those times were gone, he knew, and he thought of Wulfgar.

So much had changed.

Bruenor looked back to the podium and the treaty, and the extent of the change weakened his knees beneath him.

Along the southern rim of the center platform stood the other dignitaries: Lady Alustriel of Silverymoon, Galen Firth of Nesmé, King Emerus Warcrown of Citadel Felbarr—looking none too pleased, but accepting King Bruenor's decision—and Hralien of the Moonwood. More would join in, it was said, including the great human city of Sundabar and the largest of the dwarven cities in the region, Citadel Adbar.

If it held.

That thought made Bruenor look across the podium to the other principal, and he could not believe that he had allowed King Obould Many-Arrows to enter Mithral Hall. Yet there stood the orc, in all his terrible splendor, with his black armor, ridged and spiked, and his mighty greatsword strapped diagonally across his back.

Together they walked to opposite sides of the podium. Together they lifted their respective quills.

Obould leaned forward, but even though he was a foot and a half taller, his posture did not diminish the splendor and strength of King Bruenor Battlehammer.

"If ye're e'er to deceive . . ." Bruenor started to whisper, but he shook his head and let the thought drift away.

"It is no less bitter for me," Obould assured him.

And still they signed. For the good of their respective peoples, they put their names to the Treaty of Garumn's Gorge, recognizing the Kingdom of Many-Arrows and forever changing the face of the Silver Marches.

Calls went out from the gorge, and horns blew along the tunnels of Mithral Hall. And there came a greater blast, a rumble and resonance that vibrated through the stones of the hall and beyond, as the great horn once known as *Kokto Gung Karuck*, a gift from Obould to Bruenor, sounded from its new perch on the high lookout post above Mithral Hall's eastern door.

The world had changed, Bruenor knew.

EPILOGUE

"How different might the world now be if King Bruenor had not chosen such a course with the first Obould Many-Arrows," Hralien asked Drizzt. "Better, or worse?"

"Who can know?" the drow replied. "But at that time, a war between Obould's thousands and the gathered armies of the Silver Marches would have changed the region profoundly. How many of Bruenor's people would have died? How many of your own, who now flourish in the Glimmerwood in relative peace? And in the end, my friend, we do not know who would have prevailed."

"And yet here we stand, a century beyond that ceremony, and can either of us say with absolute truth that Bruenor chose correctly?"

He was right, Drizzt knew, to his ultimate frustration. He reminded himself of the roads he had walked over the last decades, of the ruins he had seen, of the devastation of the Spellplague. But in the North, instead of that, because of a brave dwarf named Bruenor Battlehammer, who threw off his baser instincts, his hatred and his hunger for revenge, in light of what he believed to be the greater good, the region had known a century and more of relative peace. More peace than ever it had known before. And that while the world around had fallen to shadow and despair.

Hralien started away, but Drizzt called after him.

"We both supported Bruenor on that day when he signed the Treaty of Garumn's Gorge," he reminded. Hralien nodded as he turned.

"As we both fought alongside Bruenor on the day he chose to stand beside Obould against Grguch and the old ways of Gruumsh," Drizzt added. "If I recall that day correctly, a younger Hralien was so taken by the moment that he chose to place his trust in a dark elf, though that same drow had marched to war against Hralien's people only months before."

Hralien laughed and held up his hands in surrender.

"And what resulted from that trust?" Drizzt asked. "How fares Tos'un Armgo, husband of Sinnafain, father of Teirflin and Doum'wielle?"

"I will ask him when I return to the Moonwood," the beaten Hralien replied, but he managed to get in the last arrow when he directed Drizzt's gaze to the prisoners they had taken that day.

Drizzt conceded the point with a polite nod. It wasn't over. It wasn't decided. The world rolled on around him, the sand shifted under his feet.

He reached down to pet Guenhwyvar, needing to feel the comfort of his panther friend, the one constant in his surprising life, the one great hope along his ever-winding road.

R.A.

SALVATORE

The New York Times Best-Selling Author!

An Excerpt

THE PIRATE KING

II

TRANSITIONS

Regis glanced around nervously. The agreement was for Obould to come out with a small contingent, but it was clear to the halfling that the orc had unilaterally changed that deal. Scores of orc warriors and shamans had been set all over main encampment, hiding behind rocks or in crevices, cunningly concealed and prepared for easy and swift egress.

As soon as Elastul's emissaries had delivered the word that the Arcane Brotherhood meant to move on the Silver Marches, and that enlisting Obould would be their first endeavor, the orc king's every move had been increasingly aggressive. Lady Alustriel and King Bruenor had reached out to Obould immediately, but so too had Obould begun to reach out to them. In the four years since the treaty of Garumn's Gorge, there hadn't been all that much contact between the various kingdoms, dwarf and orc, and indeed, most of that contact had come in the form of skirmishes along disputed boundaries.

But they had joined in their first common mission since Bruenor and his friends, Regis among them, had traveled north to help Obould stave off a coup by a vicious tribe of half-ogre orcs.

Or had they? The question nagged at Regis as he continued to glance around. Ostensibly, they had agreed to come together to meet the brotherhood's emissaries with a show of united force, but a disturbing possibility nagged at the halfling. Suppose Obould instead planned to use his overwhelming number in support of the erinyes emissary and against Regis and his friends?

"You would not have me risk the lives of King Bruenor and his princess Catti-brie, student of Alustriel, would you?" came Obould's voice from behind, shattering the halfling's train of thought. Regis sheepishly turned to regard the massive humanoid, dressed in his fabulous overlapping black armor with its abundant and imposing spikes, and with that tremendous greatsword strapped across his back.

"I—I know not what you mean," Regis stammered, feeling naked under the knowing gaze of this unusual, and unusually perceptive, orc.

Obould laughed at him and turned away, leaving the halfling less than assured.

Several of the forward sentries began calling then, announcing the arrival of the outsiders. Regis rushed forward and to the side to get a good look, and when he did spy the newcomers a few moments later, his heart leaped into his throat.

A trio of beautiful, barely-dressed women led the way up the path, one stepping proudly in front flanked left and right by her entourage. Tall, statuesque, with beautiful skin, they seemed almost angelic to Regis, for from behind their strong but delicate shoulders, they each sprouted a pair of shining white feathered wings. Everything about them spoke of otherworldliness, from their natural—or supernatural—charms, like hair too lustrous and eyes a bit too shining, to their adornments such as the fine swords and delicate rope, all magically glowing in a rainbow of hues, carried on belts twined of shining gold and silver fibers that sparkled as if enchanted.

It would have been easy to confuse these women with the goodly celestials, had it not been for their escort. For behind them came a mob of gruesome and beastly warriors, the barbazu. Each carried a saw-toothed glaive, great tips waving in the light as the hunched, green-skinned creatures shuffled behind their leaders. They were also known as bearded devils because of a shock of facial hair that ran ear to ear down under their jawline, beneath a toothy mouth far too wide for their otherwise emaciated faces. Scattered about their ranks were their pets, the lemure, oozing, fleshy creatures that had no more definable shape than that of a lump of molten stone, continually rolling, spreading and contracting to propel them forward.

The group, nearly two-score by Regis's count, moved steadily up the rock path toward Obould, who had climbed to the top to directly intercept them. Just a dozen paces before him the leading trio motioned for their shock troops to stay and came forward as a group, again with same one—a most striking and alluring creature with stunning too-red hair and too-red eyes and too-red lips—taking the point.

"You are Obould, I am sure," she purred, striding forward to stand right before the imposing orc, and though he was more than half a foot taller than her and twice her weight, she did not seem diminished before him.

"Nyphithys, I assume," Obould replied.

The she-devil smiled, showing teeth blindingly white and dangerously sharp.

"We are honored to speak with King Obould Many-Arrows," the devil said, her red eyes twinkling coyly. "Your reputation has spread across Faerûn. Your kingdom brings hope to all orcs."

"And hope to the Arcane Brotherhood, it would seem," Obould said, as Nyphithys's gaze drifted over to the side, where Regis remained half-hidden by a large rock. The crinyes grinned again— and Regis felt his knees go weak— before finally, mercifully, looking back to the imposing orc king.

"We make no secret of our wishes to expand our influence," she admitted. "Not to those with whom we wish to ally, at least. To others. . . ." Her voice trailed off as she again looked Regis's way.

"He is a useful infiltrator," Obould remarked. "One whose loyalty is to whoever pays him the most gold. I have much gold."

Nyphithys's accepting nod seemed less than convincing.

"Your army is mighty, by all accounts," said the devil. "Your healers capable. Where you fail is in the arcane Art, which leaves you dangerously vulnerable to mages, who are so prevalent in Silverymoon."

"And this is what the brotherhood offers," Obould reasoned.

"We can more than match Alustriel's power."

"And so with you behind me, the Kingdom of Many-Arrows will overrun the Silver Marches."

Regis's knees went weak again at Obould's proclamation. The halfling's thoughts screamed of double-cross, and with his friends so dangerously exposed—and with himself so obviously doomed!

"It would be a beautiful coupling," the erinyes said, and ran her delicate hand across Obould's massive chest.

"A coupling is a temporary arrangement."

"A marriage, then," said Nyphithys.

"Or an enslavement."

The erinyes stepped back and looked at him curiously.

"I would provide you the fodder to absorb the spears and spells of your enemies," Obould explained. "My orcs would become to you as those barbezu."

"You misunderstand."

"Do I, Nyphithys?" Obould said, and it was his turn to offer a toothy grin.

"The brotherhood seeks to enhance trade and cooperation."

"Then why do you approach me under the cloak of secrecy? All the kingdoms of the Silver Marches value trade."

"Surely you do not consider yourself kin and kind with the dwarves of Mithral Hall, or with Alustriel and her delicate creatures. You are a god among orcs. Gruumsh adores you—I know this, as I have spoken with him."

Regis, who was growing confident again at Obould's strong rebuke, winced as surely as did Obould himself when Nyphithys made that particular reference.

"Gruumsh has guided the vision that is Many-Arrows," Obould replied after a moment of collecting himself. "I know his will."

Nyphithys beamed. "My master will be pleased. We will send—"

Obould's mocking laughter stopped her, and she looked at him both curiously and skeptically.

"War brought us to this, our home," Obould explained. "But peace sustains us."

"Peace with dwarves?" the devil asked incredulously.

Obould stood firm and did not bother to reply.

"My master will not be pleased."

"He will exact punishment upon me?"

"Be careful what you wish for, king of orcs," the devil warned. "Your puny kingdom is no match for the weight of the Arcane Brotherhood."

"Who ally with devils and will send forth a horde of barbezu to entangle my armies while their overwizards rain death upon us?"

Obould asked, and it was Nyphithys's turn to stand firm. "While my own allies support my ranks with elven arrows, dwarven war machines, and Lady Alustriel's own knights and wizards," the orc said and drew out his greatsword, willing its massive blade to erupt with fire as it came free of its sheath.

To Nyphithys and her two erinyes companions, none of whom were smiling, he yelled, "Let us see how my orc fodder fares against your barbezu and flesh beasts!"

From all around, orcs leaped out of hiding. Brandishing swords and spears, axes and flails, they howled and rushed forward, and the devils, ever eager for battle, fanned out and met the charge with one of their own.

Available in Hardcover

October 2008

from

Geno Salvatore and R.A. Salvatore

**From the author of more than a dozen *New York Times*
best sellers and his son, comes the first installment
of a brand-new fantasy trilogy for young readers**

The Stowaway

Stone of Tymora Trilogy

Twelve years old and already guarding a secret that could
jeopardize his young life, Maimun has no choice but to flee
out to sea. Stowing away on the pirate hunting ship, *Sea Sprite*,
he comes across a most unlikely ally: the dark elf Drizzt Do'Urden.
With a half-demon determined to destroy him, and a crew of sailors
resentful of the trouble he's caused, Maimun must find the courage
to prove his worth, both to his friends and to himself.

For young readers seeking the next great fantasy saga
or for long-time fans who can't miss any installment
in the Drizzt saga, this book delivers all the action, intrigue,
and magic you've come to expect from the Salvatore name.

September 2008

MIRROR
STONE

The ANCIENT

Read the *New York Times* bestseller

Saga of the First King

R. A. SALVATORE

Part One of the Saga of the First King, an all-new series set in the early days of Corona, the land of Salvatore's popular DemonWars saga.

★ "With each book, Salvatore continues to hone his storytelling talent. Fans of martial fantasy should enjoy his vivid depictions of combat."
—*Library Journal*, starred review on *The Ancient*

978-0-7653-1789-6 • 0-7653-1789-3
Hardcover

www.sagaofthefirstking.com • www.tor-forge.com/theancient

FORGOTTEN REALMS

A Reader's Guide to
R.A. Salvatore's
The Legend of Drizzt™

THE LEGEND
When TSR published *The Crystal Shard* in 1988, a drow ranger
first drew his enchanted scimitars, and a legend was born.

THE LEGACY
Twenty years and twenty books later, readers have
brought his story to the world.

DRIZZT
Celebrate twenty years of the greatest fantasy hero
of a generation.

This fully illustrated, full color, encyclopedic book celebrates the
whole world of The Legend of Drizzt, from the dark elf's steadfast
companions, to his most dangerous enemies, from the gods and
monsters of a world rich in magic, to the exotic lands he's visited.

Mixing classic renditions of characters, locales, and monsters
from the last twenty years with artwork by Todd Lockwood and
other cutting-edge illustrators, this is a must-have
book for every Drizzt fan.

THOMAS M. REID

The author of *Insurrection* and The Scions of Arrabar Trilogy
rescues Aliisza and Kaanyr Vhok from the tattered remnants
of their assault on Menzoberranzan, and sends them off on
a quest across the multiverse that will leave
FORGOTTEN REALMS® fans reeling!

THE EMPYREAN ODYSSEY

BOOK I
THE GOSSAMER PLAIN

Kaanyr Vhok, fresh from his defeat against the drow, turns to hated Sundabar for the
victory his demonic forces demand, but there's more to his ambitions than just one
human city. In his quest for arcane power, he sends the alu-fiend Aliisza on a mission
that will challenge her in ways she never dreamed of.

BOOK II
THE FRACTURED SKY

A demon surrounded by angels in a universe of righteousness, Aliisza makes what
decisions she must to survive. So how did an angel make
such simple choices so complicated?

(*November 2008*)

BOOK III
THE CRYSTAL MOUNTAIN

What Aliisza has witnessed has changed her forever, but that's nothing compared
to what has happened to the multiverse itself. The startling climax will change the
nature of the cosmos forever.

Mid-2009

*"Reid is proving himself to be one of the best up and coming authors
in the FORGOTTEN REALMS universe."*
—fantasy-fan.org

RICHARD A. KNAAK

THE OGRE TITANS

The Grand Lord Golgren has been savagely crushing
all opposition to his control of the harsh ogre lands of
Kern and Blöde, first sweeping away rival chieftains, then
rebuilding the capital in his image. For this he has had to
deal with the ogre titans, dark, sorcerous giants who have
contempt for his leadership.

VOLUME ONE
THE BLACK TALON

Among the ogres, where every ritual demands blood and every ally can
become a deadly foe, Golgren seeks whatever advantage he can obtain,
even if it means a possible alliance with the Knights of Solamnia, a
questionable pact with a mysterious wizard, and trusting an elven slave
who might wish him dead.

VOLUME TWO
THE FIRE ROSE

Attacked by enemies on all sides, Golgren must abandon his throne
to undertake the quest for the Fire Rose before Safrag, master
of the Ogre Titans can locate it and claim supremacy
over all ogres—and perhaps all of Krynn.

December 2008

VOLUME THREE
THE GARGOYLE KING

Forced from the throne he has so long coveted, Golgren makes a final
stand for control of the ogre lands against the Titans . . . against an
enemy as ancient and powerful as a god.

December 2009